Fei Wang

About the Author

ANNIE WANG grew up in Beijing, China. Her first short story was published when she was fourteen years old. She studied at the University of California, Berkeley, and worked for the *Washington Post* Beijing Bureau before becoming a contract interpreter for the U.S. State Department. She has written eight books in Chinese. Her first novel written in English, *Lili,* was published internationally to extraordinary reviews. Her writing appears in numerous publications, including *Fortune, Time,* USAToday.com, *Harper's* (China), *Elle* (China), and on National Public Radio. Wang lives in the Bay Area and in Shanghai.

www.anniewang.com

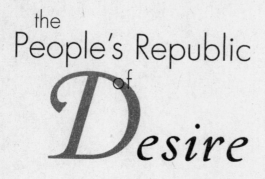

the
People's Republic
of
Desire

ALSO BY ANNIE WANG

Lili: A Novel

the
People's Republic
of
Desire

ANNIE WANG

Harper

An Imprint of HarperCollins*Publishers*

HarperCollins books may be purchased for educational, business, or sales promotional use. For information please write: Special Markets Department, HarperCollins Publishers, 10 East 53rd Street, New York, NY 10022.

FIRST EDITION

Designed by Jaime Putorti

Library of Congress Cataloging-in-Publication Data is available upon request.

ISBN-10: 0-06-078277-3
ISBN-13: 978-0-06-078277-1

06 07 08 09 10 ❖/RRD 10 9 8 7 6 5 4 3 2

TO MY GRANDMA

PREFACE

I first thought of writing this book in 2000 while I was staying at a hotel in Hong Kong overlooking Victoria Harbor. It was March then. When I left my home in California, the tulips and roses in the garden were blooming: blue, yellow, and white. The peaches and pear trees were in bloom as well. When the wind blew, it scattered peach and plum blossoms onto the stone path in my garden, reminding me of the poetry of my favorite Song Dynasty female poet, Li Qingzhao.

I love ancient China, but I live in modern China. And, at least in the case of this paradox, time is the eternal victor.

I have chosen to lead this life—going back and forth between East and West, China and the United States. I feel like a migratory bird traveling across the globe with the changing seasons.

For what? Stories, perhaps. In 2000, I gave up my job in Silicon Valley when "information technology," "Internet," "initial public offering," and "venture capital" were the hottest concepts in the world. I went back to China looking for interesting stories for the *Washington Post.* I told myself that I am a story collector of the poor, not the rich.

Looking out onto Victoria Harbor and at the skyscrapers standing out against the sky, I felt a battery of complex feelings well up in my heart. And I realized that I was thinking in Chinese again.

After years of living in the Bay Area, I had grown accustomed to talking about multiculturalism, spiritual paths, faith, identity, and the notion of belonging. Back in China, I hear people discuss at length the experience of their first taste of Starbucks coffee, the first time they drove a Buick, chatting on the Internet, experiencing a one-night stand or watching an adult movie. Divorce, oral sex, affairs, boob jobs, abortion, homosexuality, overcharged libidos, impotence—these once-taboo subjects have become daily conversations among urban women who take great pride in owning a bottle of Chanel No. 5. It's cool to be a sex dissident as long as you are not a political dissident. Conservativeness is a dirty word.

At the same time, Cuban cigars, Giorgio Armani, BMWs, and golf clubs are introduced to successful Chinese men as the symbol of their yuppie lifestyle. They hire young poor peasant boys as their bodyguards and take young poor peasant girls as their playmates.

No one remembers what happened at Tiananmen Square in 1989. Nor are they concerned with China's political future. Money and status rule the day. It seems only two types of people exist: those who admire power and wealth, and those who are being admired for their power and wealth.

China, this ancient civilization that was once suffocated under the weight of its own history, has changed so drastically, so swiftly, it is far beyond the comprehension of the Chinese themselves, let alone outsiders and the go-betweens, such as me, who are known as American Chinese or Chinese Americans.

These are unspeakably crazy and illogical times. Dynamic. Impulsive. Pragmatic. Chaotic. Brimming with desire. Cheeky. Declining. Contradictory. A time when it's more shameful to be poor than to be a whore. And, at the same time, it's an era full of glory, dreams, and primitive passions. In China, everything is laid bare. There are no secrets.

I thought to myself, forget about identifying and belonging. It has never been that important, anyway. The word "home" needs to be redefined.

What the Chinese need is a solution to the problems of modernization, for themselves as individuals, and for Chinese civilization as a whole.

The Chinese once carried so much cultural baggage. We used to laugh with teary eyes, obsessed with the memories of humiliation and sorrow, wrenched to the gut with love and hate. We acted with impulsive nationalism and with the shame of defeat. We waited with painful anxiety, overcome by uncontrollable fervor.

Perhaps a little fast food frivolity, a little Starbucks shallowness, a little Hong Kong–style materialism, a little ignorance and indifference of history simply are necessary for the new market economy. Kick back, relax, and, only then, amid the void, will China and the Chinese be able to find a way out.

That night, my thoughts slipped out of American and back into Chinese. I drank too much at Lan Kwai Fong Hong Kong with my girlfriends. In a postcolonial bar, we, a group of self-professed intelligent female graduates of distinguished American and British universities, found we were unable to define the notions of home and roots. Imported liquor, cigars, and loud music were for us a kind of comfort. Even though we shed tears that night, we still felt a temporary sense of security.

The next day, I went to a quaint, poor fishing village, stood on the dilapidated pier, and filled my nostrils with the smell of drying fish. The live sea animals in fish tanks, the skillful killing of these animals, the poor housing . . . these are the images of China that are being broadcast familiar in the West. With a shirt tied round my waist and waving my expensive digital camera, I wandered around with the other foreign tourists, gazing left and right with curiosity. I even faced the sea, stretched out my arms, and said, "This is life!"—like a character from a typical Chinese melodrama. Am I like a foreign tourist who is searching for exoticism in my home country or is the whole world becoming Westernized?

When I was fourteen, I fell in love with the Indian author Tagore and a line from one of his meditative poems: "Wisdom reaches the peak of perfection in drunkenness." So many years have passed, and I still have not found an aphorism better than that damn line. I haven't learned anything.

There was a time when I was heavy-hearted, all for the sake of writing, metaphysics, and the future of Chinese civilization. Who did I think I was? Only later did I understand how foolish I was. Now, I'm drunk with reality. No more a serious, obstinate, foolish intellectual. I want to be free-falling, free-falling with a China that is no longer homely.

I am casting off my burdens—no more will I play the role of a Confucian intellectual.

After all, aren't we the new breed? Aren't we young? Aren't we lonely modern souls? Don't we deserve to be happy and carefree? Don't we need a little fun? So let's play. After all, we have always been good at games.

ACKNOWLEDGMENTS

I would like to thank my former editor at the *South China Morning Post*, Susan Sams, who decided to publish my unconventional column "People's Republic of Desire" on page one of the "Life and City" section of the paper—which ran two years and ten months, and turned out to be more successful than we'd all expected. During the running period of the column, I received letters from readers of all nationalities, age groups, and professions. It amazed me that a Hong Kong–based paper could actually reach out to so many people around the globe. Thank you, Charlotte Harper, for showing the column samples to Susan Sams.

My gratitude also goes to four diehard supporters of this book: my best friend, Antony Dapiran, an international lawyer whose Chinese is perfect, who gave me so much help in the early stages from language, translation, to reading my contract pro bono. Without his friendship and encouragement, this book would have been impossible. Michael Davis, who started as a reader of my column in Manhattan, but has become a good friend, who wrote me feedback on almost every column and continued our conversation on the characters of this book face-to-face in New York, Fredericksburg, San Francisco, Hong Kong, and Shanghai. Also, Michael Rice and Ben Paul, both of you are wonderful! Gracias!

Finally, I thank my editor, Claire Wachtel, who has a great sense of humor; everyone at Harper, and my agent, Liza Dawson, who has helped make this book possible.

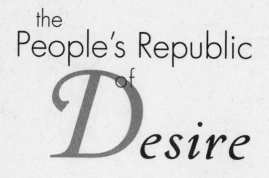

the
People's Republic
of
Desire

1

A Fake Foreign Devil

"Returnee" is a popular word nowadays in China, especially since the Chinese government called on all "patriotic overseas Chinese" to return to their homeland to build a "modern, strong China."

These returnees have a number of common traits.

First, they don't normally wear miniskirts or makeup, like so many local girls do. They often don't look very fashionable and seem to care little about such frippery.

Second, they have usually obtained advanced degrees somewhere in the West and often like to say, as casually as possible, "I went to school in Boston." (But they never forget to wear their Harvard or Yale rings on their fingers.)

Third, they are timid pedestrians. It takes them forever to cross an average Chinese road.

Fourth, they don't smoke. In fact, they get dizzy around smokers.

Fifth, they don't like people to ask where they come from, especially someone who has just met them. If they are prodded for an answer, they tend to pause for several seconds as if faced with a multiple-choice question. If they were to give the traditional response, they would tell the inquirer the birthplace of their fathers' ancestors. Knowing your ancestors' birthplace and tomb sites demonstrates that you haven't forgotten your roots. Anyone who forgets his roots is despised and accused of being a sellout. In China the phrase, "He doesn't know his last name anymore," is hurled to mock those who try to forget their roots.

But in the last twenty years, some Chinese scholars have claimed that China's long history and cultural roots have impeded its modernization. For the modern Chinerse, history is just so much cultural baggage. So the new Chinese way to answer is to name the birthplace, not of your father's ancestors but of your father. The American answer goes one step further: you simply point to your own birthplace.

So this is what is going through minds of the returnees when you ask them where they come from: Should returnees follow the traditional Chinese, the modern Chinese, or the American model? Or should they go one step further, and say that they come from California or London? Well, in China, smart people leave things vague. It's called *nandehutu.*

Twenty-something Niuniu is one such returnee. If you've been to Beijing, you might have seen her. She's no different from all the other members of the trendy young *xin xin renlei*— the "new" new generation. Her hair is short, like a boy's, and spiked up with gel, sometimes dyed red, sometimes purple. Her hands are covered with all kinds of unusual white-gold rings, with little feet, apples, skeletons, snakes, and so on. Black nails, dark brown lipstick, baggy trousers, a colorful Swiss Army watch, yellow Nokia mobile phone, palm pilot, IBM notebook, JanSport backpack, and a Louis Vuitton purse, which always holds two condoms—not for herself, but in case one of her girlfriends needs one urgently.

Everybody in China has a *dangan,* or personal file, which is kept by the government and details their political, family, educational, and employment background. I have one, too.

Let's take a look at my *dangan.* Top secret.

Height: 5'2"

Age: Twenty-something

Weight: 110 pounds

Marital Status: Single and fully detached

Birthplace: United States

Mother: Wei Mei, daughter of revolutionary opera performers. Born in Beijing, half Han and half Manchurian, granddaughter of a Manchu minister. Married three times. Moved to the United States during first marriage in mid-1970s. Currently the wife of the chief representative of an American oil company. Mother of Niuniu and a pair of Eurasian twins, Dong Dong and Bing Bing. A former Hooligan girl and shop clerk during the Cultural Revolution. Currently a social butterfly in Beijing's expatriate circle, involved in some high-level diplomatic exchanges and movie projects. No higher education, speaks fluent English.

Father: Chen Siyuan, orphan from Taiwan. Arguably Chinese, adopted by an American missionary and converted to Christianity. Ph.D. in electronic engineering from MIT. Former employee of Hewlett-Packard. Currently CEO of the Chen Computer Company. Twice married, currently to his former secretary, Jean Fang, who is eight years older than Niuniu and soon to have a baby.

Twin Sisters: Dong Dong, age nine, and Bing Bing, age nine. Students of Beijing Lido International School.

Education: B.A. in journalism from the University of Missouri at Columbia. GPA 3.8. M.A. in journalism from the University of California at Berkeley.

Profession: Reporter for the World News Agency in Beijing.

Religion: Buddhism, light.

Smoker: Nonsmoker.

Drinker: Started at fourteen. Now occasional drinker.

Sexual History: Lost virginity at sixteen. Had sex with twenty-two partners. Currently sexually inactive.

Psychological Background: Suffered from depression while in the United States after being dumped by her boyfriend, the moderately successful eye doctor Len, a third-generation Chinese American who holds an M.D. from Johns Hopkins. Six sessions with a shrink, who taught her about the eye movement treatment, about which she remained highly skeptical. Eventually she left United States for a makeover in China as an alternative strategy.

Probably, you've guessed by now that Niuniu is me. From my *dangan,* you can see why people call me a cosmopolitan woman. I love the word "cosmopolitan" as much as the drink. "Cosmopolitan" is a trendy word to toss around in China at the moment: China is building cosmopolitan megacities and luring people with a cosmopolitan background.

In a country where background and history are so important, it's increasingly popular in China to fake one's identity, origin, and accent. For one hundred yuan, you can get a fake ID, a *dangan,* or a diploma from any school in the world as easily as you can pick up a fake Rolex in Shenzhen nowadays.

Last week, I was in Shanghai, at a bar called CJW, owned by

a friend's friend, where several native Shanghainese were complaining about "some peasants claiming to be native Shanghainese after being here less than three months."

Two weeks earlier, I was in a Hong Kong teahouse where the waitresses bad-mouthed a chic patron carrying a black Prada bag, who had just walked out the door.

"She can't be a local as she claims. Her Cantonese is far from perfect!"

"She must be a *beigu*—a northern auntie!"

"Northern aunties are so bold nowadays. They'll do anything, even steal other women's husbands. Shameless."

Upon hearing the exchange, I came to the conclusion that where you come from is a political question. In China during the Cultural Revolution, one's background could determine one's fate. Many of those who were unfortunate enough to be from educated families associated with the old guard were systematically purged by the state. The leaders of the Cultural Revolution wanted to start the country over from a blank slate, and that required the elimination of intellectuals and families with backgrounds that were deemed "undesirable."

Today, family background is no longer that important, but place of origin means status. The success of years of class struggle in China has made the Chinese particularly class-conscious. Faking one's birthplace is the quickest way to diminish the discrepancy between classes, between men and women, between city and countryside. It serves its purpose as conveniently as a fake Chanel bag.

Being a returnee, I am sometimes called a fake too. Local Chinese call me a *jia yangguizi*—a fake foreign devil.

POPULAR PHRASES

DANGAN: Personal files, containing details of their political, family, educational, and employment background. Everyone in China is required to have one.

BEIGU: Northern auntie, a derogatory expression for mainland girls.

NANDEHUTU: An ancient Chinese saying meaning, Leaving things ill-defined is better. The closest English equivalent is, Ignorance is bliss.

JIA YANGGUIZ: Fake foreign devil. A word used by ultra-patriots to refer to westernized Chinese.

XIN XIN RENLEI: The "new" new generation: Gen Xers and Gen Yers whose lifestyle includes bar culture, multiple sex partners, and the Internet. A far cry from the simpler and traditional lives of their earlier generations.

2

Fashion and Abortion

The Chinese media often complain that the Western media don't give a full picture of China. Some Chinese scholars have used the popular word *yaomohua,* or "demonizing," as in: "The Western media try to demonize China because they fear the rise of a strong modern China."

Whether the Western media have painted an accurate picture of China or not, China has its own faults. It has moved forward too damned fast, beyond the average person's normal comprehension. Even Chinese returnees like me, who left the country for only seven years to earn one or two advanced degrees, cannot recognize Beijing after they get back.

Chinese TV is full of languid, pouting skinny models and small-time actors with Taiwanese accents, dressed up like Japanese cartoon characters and playing the fool. These opium-addict-looking models would be deemed totally unhealthy by the Old Revolutionary beauty standard. After all, China suffered two humiliating opium wars. And despite winning the civil war that drove the Nationalists off the Chinese mainland and onto bucolic Taiwan over fifty years ago, mainlanders now consider a Taiwanese accent a fashion asset. You can't think of China with logic.

When I walk along Beijing Street, I run into one Starbucks after another. It seems there are more Starbucks in Beijing than in Berkeley. There is even one in the Forbidden Palace! I see fashionable women in miniskirts talking into mobile phones as they ride their bicycles. Miniskirts and bicycles: socialism with Chinese characteristics. And there are more and more people who look overweight, even by American standards. Young people wear jeans and cotton T-shirts. They consider this the new fashion, although their parents still think cotton is too cheap a fabric for clothes. Boys are growing their hair long and girls are cutting their hair short. Shop signs are in English, with laughable mistakes throughout. Everyone uses Windows 2000 on their computers. Even my retired grandfather knows how to search for fortune-tellers on Yahoo. China's changes have taken me by surprise.

Luckily I have my childhood friends Lulu and Beibei to reacclimate me to the Chinese way. Lulu and Beibei were my old schoolmates from Beijing's Jingshan School. Beibei is seven years older than me, and Lulu is four years older. Jingshan included grades one to twelve all on the same school grounds. The three of us met fighting with the boys over the Ping-Pong table.

At that time Beibei was in senior high, Lulu was in junior high, and I was in primary school. I was mature for my age and liked to mix with friends older than me. The three of us got up to all sorts of mischief together, and we've been inseparable ever since.

At the time, China didn't have private schools, but Jingshan was very exclusive. Most of my classmates came from distinguished families. I was born in the United States and returned to China at age five. My family was categorized as "patriotic overseas Chinese," so I was fine. Beibei's grandfather was a high-ranking Old Revolutionary who the government assigned a big courtyard house in the best part of the town, a chauffeur, a nanny, and two assistants. She was fine. Lulu came from an ordinary family in southern China, but she was not only the cutest girl in school but also a child star who knew how to sing well.

Twelve years ago, we three girls made Beibei's grandfather's chauffeur drive us to every five-star hotel in Beijing in the Mercedes 600. At that time, Chinese people were not allowed into five-star hotels, and the doormen, not knowing what to do when they saw three scruffy girls climb out of the Mercedes 600, greeted us in Japanese. At a time when most Chinese households did not have a telephone, at my house, we used our household phone to call up male celebrities, pretending to be the hottest actresses of the time and professing our love for them. We didn't know we were privileged until much later.

Now, Beibei is president of Chichi Entertainment Company, which she founded five years ago; she currently employs five hundred people and represents one-quarter of the top actors and singers in China. Chinese singers make real bucks nowadays. Through Beibei I've learned that they can charge $100,000 for singing four songs in a concert. And this is after-tax money. Beibei keeps telling me that with such a cute face, I went into the wrong business as a reporter.

Lulu is the executive editor of the fashion magazine *Women's Friends*. After she graduated from Beijing University, she was offered many high-paying jobs, but instead she decided to be an editorial assistant at a fashion magazine. At that time, fashion magazines were so new in China that few people could afford to buy them and the pay for working there was low. So many friends told her to try something else. But Lulu has a natural passion for the beauty industry, and she stayed on the job. Now she is the second most important person at her magazine. Although her pay is so-so, she receives perks such as free memberships to gyms, spas, free gifts from Chanel, free trips to Paris, Tokyo, Milan, and New York. She is slim, graceful, and stylish. She has long flowing dark hair that always seems to rest perfectly on her shoulders, no matter what she is doing, and big, deep eyes like a Caucasian, Lulu's lover, Ximu, once described them as "pools of sex." Lulu enjoys wearing expensive high-fashion numbers from designers like Gucci and Versace. These Italian designs make her look powerful, and even a bit intimidating when she is surrounded by her Chinese colleagues and competitors. It's her moment to outshine others and find confidence.

Lulu is the most gentle and feminine of our trio, but she can also be extremely nervy. When she curses someone out, no one can be more rude. She also smokes. She looks at people from behind a cloud of smoke, giving her a vague, misty appearance. Beibei jokingly says she is a *Huli Jing* walking among men. Lulu is a total sex goddess of the fashion world.

When I returned to China, Lulu immediately realized that my Californian style was too casual: I don't use makeup, and I wear big baggy shirts and pants.

"You're too Americanized, and too ahead of the time in China," Lulu tells me.

"What do you mean?" I'm proud of my blue Ralph Lauren shirt.

"You've got a thin waist and nice skin that men love. But you need perfume, lip gloss, and polished nails, which will make you more feminine. You see people are superficial when you look expensive, they treat you with respect." She critiques my style.

The fashionable Lulu starts to teach me how to make a face mask out of pearl powder and milk, pluck my eyebrows down to only a few hairs, wear Chinese-style lined jackets and pants.

When I first arrived in the United States, I became a slave of American cosmetics. The clerk at the Estée Lauder counter of every Macy's store adored me because I bought whatever was new on the market. The reason was simple: I had never seen these things in China. By the time I left the States for China, I had been too influenced by Berkeley's feminism and lost my desire to look like a model. Now, in China, I have to go back to my old obsession with makeup and my desire to be a cover girl. It's like time travel.

Lulu loves educating me. "To survive as a girl in big cities such as Beijing, Shanghai, and Hong Kong, a thin waist and perfume are must-haves." She takes me out with her friends from the fashion crowd who are designers, models, and photographers. They are either gay or bisexual. Straight people are not cool in that circle.

Lulu has learned many tricks from me as well. Once she went to a party without wearing a bra. "This is the Berkeley style that I've learned from Niuniu," she said proudly, as everybody stares at her nipples through her silk blouse.

Lulu is stunning, svelte, elegant, with glowing skin and delicate features that every girl is dying for, but she is ill-fated in love. When she was a college girl, she met Ximu, a married man who brought her nothing but bad luck.

Ximu is a talented graduate from Tsinghua University, who went to study in France in 1989. He abandoned his electrical engineering major to take up an art major there. Five years ago, he returned to China, and has since managed to become a well-known performance artist. His wife is French, and lives in France. Ximu and his wife have lived apart for many years, but he has not divorced and does not want to remarry.

He says, "I am very French. I'm a free spirit."

Lulu has fallen for him, and willingly becomes his "little secret." She e-mailed me when I was in the States. She said, "I'd like to be Ximu's Simone de Beauvoir." In those days, she sent me her long reading notes of de Beauvoir and Marguerite Duras, who were must-reads among Chinese city girls. Lulu firmly believes that one cannot judge a genius according to ordinary standards. And Ximu, obviously, is a genius.

Lulu has undergone three abortions because of Ximu. The first was very painful: she felt that she was taking a life. With the second, she was helpless and felt that the heavens were punishing her. The third was a kind of self-destruction, like she was murdering herself.

But the physical and mental pain have not weakened Lulu's love for Ximu at all. On the contrary, she worships him without complaint or regret. No wonder some male returnees feel like kids in a candy store when they return to China. All of a sudden, they find they are as hot as Apollo!

While I was still studying in the States, Lulu e-mailed me, begging for help. At that time, Lulu had discovered that Ximu was living in Beijing with a Japanese woman who had grown up in China. Ximu said he was just that kind of guy. He needed different women: French, American, Japanese, Chinese—their different cultures stimulated him. He wasn't a one-woman man. Lulu could either accept him or leave him. Lulu was deeply hurt.

I don't understand why Ximu, who claims to be so French, always got Lulu pregnant. Why doesn't he wear a condom? Lulu says Ximu says that love must know no barriers, and they must give of each other fully.

I think Ximu is full of shit. But Lulu says, "Well, I thought every girl in love has had abortions, at least in China!" I almost faint—how can my fashionable friend Lulu be so out of touch with the world?

POPULAR PHRASES

YAOMOHUA: To demonize.

SONGGAO XIE: Platform shoes. Popular among young women in Japan, Korea, and China, where women especially want to look taller. The shoes cause accidents and broken ankles because of their fantastic but impractical platform.

XINGBAKE: Starbucks, considered one of the most "in" places for urban youth. Quite the opposite of its status in the States, where it is considered a somewhat soulless and uninteresting corporate creation.

HULI JING: The fox spirit comes in the guise of a beautiful maiden to seduce men and slowly devour them. Refers to attractive young women who make men crazy for them.

3

The Chinese Feminist
and the Little Duck

*I*f Lulu is considered a white-collar woman, women like Beibei are called gold-collar. As president of Chichi Entertainment Company, Beibei is a member of China's nouveaux riches. With an income twice that of her husband and one hundred times that of the average Chinese, Beibei drives a BMW 750. Even though it is used, it cost her more than $100,000. Imported luxury goods like cars and cosmetics are taxed almost 40 percent in China, but it doesn't stop Beibei from carrying Fendi handbags and wearing Estée Lauder makeup. Even her maids get Estée Lauder gift bags. Beibei buys her clothes only at the Scitec and World Trade malls in China. Still she complains often that the luxury brands sold in China aren't most up-to-date so she has to fly to Paris or New York to shop.

Her career success doesn't surprise me. As a matter of fact, I anticipated my friend's achievement. Among the three of us, thirty-five-year-old Beibei, granddaughter of a Chinese general, is the oldest, tallest, and most self-assured. She has always been a smart, aggressive, business-oriented go-getter, whom I admire and am disgusted by at the same time.

Beibei invites me to have dinner in the stylish and pricey Courtyard Restaurant owned by a Chinese-American lawyer near the Forbidden City. She is wearing a red *dudou*—baby doll clothing that shows off her belly button like Britney Spears and exposes her shoulders like Nicole Kidman. Beibei has a narrow face. She wears dark bangs that make her look much younger than she actually is. Youthfulness is worshipped in China to a ridiculous degree, and Beibei can't risk being thought of as old or out of date. Beibei's heels are dangerously high, but she never seems to have trouble navigating even the most difficult terrain. As she walks to the table, the lace of her Victoria's Secret underwear peaks out from above her waistline.

Lulu isn't with us. She is dashing off to Tibet with her lover Ximu, whose art show will include a hundred people taking a shower in front of the Potala Palace. But she calls us long distance, "Guess what? As I'm standing right in front of the Potala Palace, I see many Tibetan protesters! They say that Ximu tries to make fun of them and perpetuate the stereotypes that Tibetans don't like to wash themselves! But come on, this is fucking art!" Her voice reveals her deep admiration for Ximu.

"I guess being controversial is what Ximu wants. We wish him good luck!" Beibei quickly hangs up the phone.

"I *hate* Ximu. I can't stand Lulu's obsession with him. Why is she so stupid when it comes to Ximu?" Beibei complains to me.

"Everybody has her blind spot, I guess," I say.

"Have you found out that Lulu loves to mimic George Sand?" Beibei asks me.

"You mean the feminist writer who was Chopin's lover?"

"Yes."

"But I thought Lulu was more a fan of Simone de Beauvoir and Marguerite Duras!" Lulu's love life can get confusing.

"Marguerite Duras, the author of *The Lover*. The woman who had a twenty-something lover when she was in her sixties? Did she smoke too?" asks Beibei.

"I can't remember, but it's very likely."

"I think Lulu picks up smoking and swearing from George Sand. But it's all on the surface. George Sand was so ahead of her time. Lulu isn't a feminist. She is still a slave of men, but I," Beibei blows a smoke ring proudly, "am the master of men."

Beibei has a tendency to put down others in order to elevate herself. She even does this to her best friends, like Lulu and me, but without evil intentions. Sometimes, she just needs to feel like a queen. Her fortune-teller says that she was a queen in her previous life, and she genuinely believes it.

Beibei has been married for seven years and has had four lovers during that time, all young guys in their twenties. They call her Big Sis. Her latest lover is called Iron Egg, a twenty-one-year-old journalist for a local tabloid. As the owner of an entertainment company, Beibei is following the new fashion of dating young studs. Hong Kong singer Faye Wong and American actress Demi Moore are her relationship role models.

"Men had legitimate lovers for thousands of years in China. They were called concubines. Why can't we women have our male concubines?" Beibei reveals a seductive smile.

Before I can say anything, she continues, "You know Western feminists have gone too far. They are men haters. I agree with them that men are jerks. You can't give up everything for them. But I don't hate men. I love being their master. It's fun!"

"How can a woman become a master of men?" I ask while sipping fresh apple juice.

"Don't believe any of that love bullshit. You have to realize that the stupidest investment in the world is an investment in love," says Beibei. "Only when you are immune from love will you have the chance to be a master." The lesson continues.

Of course, I know Beibei has no faith in love because her husband—the one they call Chairman Hua—betrayed her.

When Beibei was studying at the Central Minority Nationalities Institute, she met Hua Dabin. Because he was chairman of the students association, everybody called him Chairman Hua—after Hua Guofeng, Mao Zedong's designated successor. Hua Dabin came from Xinjiang, was tall and striking and very popular with the girls.

Beibei fell in love with Chairman Hua, and was soon living with him off-campus. This was major news that year at school—because at the time it was forbidden for college students to marry or live together. The institute almost expelled them, and only because of Beibei's family connections were they allowed to stay.

Hua majored in literary and historical archives, and after graduation it was difficult for him to find a job. The school was going to send him back to Xinjiang. It was nearly impossible for people from the outer provinces to remain in Beijing.

Beibei decided to marry him immediately. That way, he could obtain Beijing residency and stay in Beijing. Beibei also did not hesitate to use her old revolutionary grandfather to pull some strings and find Hua a job. Her grandfather had been incorruptible all his life, but he couldn't remain so in his final years, all for the sake of his much-loved granddaughter.

Hua and Beibei joined the propaganda team at a factory. Their job was to write down socialist slogans on the blackboard of the factory every day. Their salaries were low, and they had no place to live, so they had to live with Beibei's parents.

Hua was a fiercely ambitious young man, not content to live under somebody else's roof. He recognized China's need for English-speaking businessmen and began to spend all his time studying English. He applied for the United Nations' postgraduate program held at Beijing Foreign Languages Institute and was admitted. He slaved there for three years, and during those years, Beibei worked to support them both.

After Hua graduated, he found a marketing job at Motorola China. Motorola has done well in China in the beeper and cell phone business. By 1997, Hua's monthly salary was 20,000 RMB—about $2,400—twenty times the average salary. He bought a condo for Beibei and him. They moved out of his father-in-law's house.

As the popular Beijing saying goes, "When women turn bad, they get money; when men get money, they turn bad." The word that Chairman Hua had a lover eventually reached Beibei. She refused to believe it. She was completely loyal to Hua, and couldn't imagine that he'd betray her.

But one day she returned home early from a business trip and found the door of her apartment locked. As she stood there, perplexed, the door opened a crack, and there was Hua's startled face and stark naked body. Before either of them could say anything, a woman's voice came from the room. "Is that the food delivery? You've tired me out—I'm starving."

Beibei burst into the room, kicking over a vase and toppling a fish tank. With an explosive crash, the living room floor was covered with tropical fish, flipping all over in desperation.

Hua's lover was so scared that she started to leave the apartment, still not properly dressed. Hua held his lover by the waist. "Don't go. What can she do to us, anyway?"

With Hua's support, the naked woman sat down on the sofa, crossed her legs, produced a cigarette from somewhere, and started to smoke.

After that incident, Beibei thought of divorce. But if she divorced Hua, what would she do then? At that time, her factory was about to go bankrupt, and she needed money to be independent. She didn't want to beg her grandfather again to find her a more profitable job.

Beibei did not get divorced. Instead, the girl who had always behaved like a princess swallowed her pride. She started spending her time tracking down old contacts, and soon she was representing singers who came to Beijing to break into the big time. She founded the Chichi Entertainment Company. Nowadays, the company is one of the most powerful agencies in town. It represents the hottest bands, like Made in China, Peasants, and Central Leadership. It also brought hot international singers such as Whitney Houston and Sarah Brightman to China, which allowed Beibei to make bundles of money.

And every time there is a concert, Beibei gives Lulu and me the most expensive tickets. It's not just because we are her buddies—both Lulu and I work in the media. Beibei knows the importance of promotion and publicity.

Straightforward and outspoken, Beibei is a real sharp-tongued Beijinger. She likes to be the center of attention. This, together with her extraordinary family background, means that she has been overbearing ever since she was young.

Compared to the soft-spoken feminine Lulu, Beibei is tough and even bossy. When Lulu had her abortion after being made pregnant for the third time by the despicable Ximu, and Ximu did not once go to visit her, Beibei wanted to hire a thug to castrate him. She had even taken an exquisitely carved Tibetan knife she had brought back from Lhasa, its blade shining, and given it to the thug, hidden in an envelope. Had it not been for Lulu's repeated pleading, Ximu would have been a eunuch.

Chairman Hua has confessed to Beibei that the reason that he sought a lover in the first place was because of Beibei's temper and arrogance. Although Hua's excuse is ridiculous and self-serving, he has managed to win a lot of sympathy from other Chinese men.

"Most Chinese men don't like strong women," Beibei tells me. "They like servile women who suck up to them. But a servile woman who relies on her man financially can be miserable. No matter how much she has done for him, he will still underestimate her. If he abandons her, he'd say it's because she is too needy or not smart enough. But if she makes good money, he can't ever look down on her."

Hua treats Beibei with more respect now that she has become the breadwinner at home. "But once bitten by a snake, you don't want to even come close to a rope," says Beibei. She feels things can never be the same between them, and she no longer trusts emotions. She takes her own lovers. The couple has an open marriage.

I have met Chairman Hua a few times. His eyes are always darting back and forth, his gaze fierce. This man is too ambitious and calculating. Beibei tends to like this type of man. Her lovers are all younger versions of Hua. But I don't think ambition is a terribly attractive characteristic in a man. I'm always more attracted to gentle, laid-back men. I can't explain why. Perhaps it has to do with my Buddhist background. Or perhaps because I am short-tempered, I need a relaxed person to balance my life.

Since I returned, Beibei hangs out with Lulu and me every day, working out, having makeovers, and eating out, just as if she was as single and unattached as we are. Sometimes she brings along her sleek lover, Iron Egg. We all know that Iron Egg is a gold digger. Once Beibei complained to me, "Five thousand yuan pocket money a month is not enough for Iron Egg. He asks me to buy this and that for him all the time. He won't let me sleep with Chairman Hua. Tell me, is that Iron Egg a bastard or what!? He thinks because I'm older than him, he's getting a raw deal sleeping with me. I'm like his customer. I may as well go and find a *xiao yazi*—a little duck, a real gigolo. At least he would be honest about the fact that he loves my money."

Sometimes I wish Beibei would divorce Chairman Hua and marry someone she really loves. But Beibei doesn't have much confidence in men. On the surface, Beibei is cynical, but I know that she desires true love just like everybody else.

POPULAR PHRASES

DUDOU: Sexy baby doll clothing that exposes the shoulders.

XIAO YAZI: Little duck, a gigolo or male prostitute. Because female prostitutes are called "chickens," male prostitutes become "ducks."

4

Tonics and Perfume

*I*n the last ten to fifteen years, *Shengdan,* or Christmas, and *Qingren Jie,* Lovers' Day or Valentine's Day, have probably become the two most popular Western holidays in China. Card-making companies like Hallmark were thrilled with this for many years until recently, when e-cards on Yahoo.com largely replaced the real cards. And the Chinese people are happy, too! Isn't it wonderful to have one or two more occasions for *chihe-wanle,* to eat, drink, play, and be merry?

Among Chinese yuppies, there are four popular ways to celebrate Christmas: First, go to a cathedral to observe "patriotic Catholics" perform their religious service—or just to *kan renao,* enjoy the crowd. Often on Christmas Eve the famous cathedral in Beijing's Xidan district is packed like a morning market. There aren't many opportunities to sing hymns or hear the sound of an organ in China, and Christmas is a great time to have such an experience.

Since religion is not a part of daily conversation among the Chinese, Christmas is also the perfect time to discuss religious philosophy. It's an excellent opportunity for men to impress women with their intellectual depth, tossing around words like "original sin" and "redemption." Of course, there are some English-speaking church services that are open only to foreigners, who must show their passport to attend. The government thinks it is okay for foreigners to practice religion freely as long as they don't have a bad influence on the Chinese.

My father, Dr. Chen, is a devout Christian. He became a naturalized American citizen thirty years ago. After moving back to China, he takes part in the unofficial church service held by foreign nationals every year. He never fails to attend the service, and diligently sings all the Christmas hymns too.

A second way Chinese yuppies celebrate the Yuletide is to attend some Christmas parties in a foreign hotel, preferably five-star. If you manage to show up at such a party, it means that you have connections. These parties are often sponsored by big multinational corporations or prestigious international organizations. An invitation proves you travel in the elite circle. Beibei and her husband, Chairman Hua, are invited to such parties every year. Because they sleep in separate beds, it is no surprise that they go to these parties separately as well.

A third way: *Cuo yidun,* have a feast. The most desirable places for such feasts are the revolving restaurants atop the Great Wall Sheraton and the Citic building, at T.G.I. Friday's in Sanlitun, or at the Hard Rock Cafe. Taking your family or your friends to those places means you have a sense of fashion as well as some money.

Fourth: Exchange gifts that are beautifully wrapped.

Gifts are a big deal for the Chinese. They can be very picky about gifts. Often you try to please, but you end up insulting them. I know this very well. Six months before I headed back to China from the United States, I got nervous. I was going to celebrate my first Christmas holiday in Beijing as an adult. Everybody I knew in China expected me to bring nice gifts from the States. What gifts could please my parents and grandparents and demonstrate my filial piety? I called my friend Lulu from Berkeley for advice. After all, Lulu knows everything about new fads in China.

"Chinese nowadays are obsessed with tonics. Kids want to outsmart other kids. Twenty-somethings are trying to beat stress. Middle-aged women want to postpone their menopause; middle-aged men want to be as vigorous as they were when they were eighteen. Seniors want to stop aging. It's all about *yangsheng*, cultivating your body. So I would recommend American ginseng. Korean gingseng's nature is hot and American gingseng's nature is cool. Chinese prefer the American one. Also, Deep Ocean fish oil is a surefire winner." Lulu gave me the complete rundown.

Before I could find out where to buy Deep Ocean fish oil, Lulu e-mailed me again, "The new fashionable tonic is lecithin. It's good for high blood pressure. Forget about fish oil—it's totally passé now."

Four weeks later, I got another e-mail from her. "Apparently, even people like me can be outdated in this fast-changing world. Lecithin is not cool anymore. People are talking about the powder of crab shells, and ginkgo biloba. They are good for the brain. Everybody tries to get this stuff from the United States. I'm told the prices here are triple the prices in the States."

I had waited for a month. Receiving no new updates from

Lulu, I bought these tonics made in the U.S.A., though Americans don't seem to care about them as much as the Chinese.

I'm not a fan of tonics—they are for older people. I wish to buy cooler stuff for friends. So I e-mailed Lulu again. "What about CDs, DVDs?"

"Don't mention CDs or DVDs. We have everything here on the streets. Remember, don't buy anything that says 'Made in China.' Find things saying 'Made in the U.S.A.' or 'Made in France.'" Lulu would have gone on for much longer if I had the time to listen. . . .

I drove to shopping malls. From shoes, bags, and toys to jackets and blouses, almost everything I saw is made in China. No wonder people say that China has become the workshop of the world. I was frustrated. Lulu hinted in her e-mail: "Owning foreign perfume or having a small collection of foreign perfume is fashionable nowadays. But remember, brand names are important."

I eventually decided to buy cosmetics from Gucci, Yves Saint Laurent, and Estée Lauder, and returned to Beijing with a suitcase of tonics and perfumes.

My mother Mei is thrilled to see me. On Christmas Eve, she holds a big dinner party at her million-dollar house in Riviera Villa near the Airport Road to celebrate Christmas as well as my homecoming. My whole family comes: my stepfather Big John and his children, my half-sisters, Dad and my stepmother Jean Fang, my grandparents, Nanny Momo, Nanny Momo's family, and my friends Lulu and Beibei.

Mom has prepared Chinese dumplings and American turkey. I'm so lucky to have a great cook as my mother. With her cooking skill she won my father's heart many years ago when they first met in California. I distribute my gifts after the gourmet meal, as everybody picks their teeth or burps. Old relatives get tonics; young friends get a bottle of perfume. Everybody is happy.

I have learned that Nanny Momo has become a rock 'n' roll granny ever since she reached sixty. She likes to listen to disco music, learn English, go to pop concerts, go bowling with her grandkids. To please an old lady with a young heart, I give Nanny Momo both tonics and a big bottle of Estée Lauder eau de toilette.

Momo shows much more interest in Estée Lauder than the tonics. She wears her reading glasses and reads the English on the bottle of natural spray carefully. She points her finger at the words "eau de toilette," "This word, 'toilet,' means bathroom. I learned it last week from my English teacher." She says excitedly, "See, Americans are so rich. They put such beautiful bottles and nice-smelling water in their bathroom, I wonder what their living rooms and bedrooms smell like!"

POPULAR PHRASES

CHIHEWANLE: Eat, drink, play, and be merry.

SHENGDAN: Christmas. More of an excuse to eat and spend time with family than anything having to do with Christianity or Jesus.

QINGREN JIE: Lovers' Day—Valentine's Day.

KAN RENAO: Enjoy the scene.

CUO YIDUN: Have a feast.

YANGSHENG: Cultivate one's body to keep its balance and health.

SANLITUN: A neighborhood in Beijing that offers many entertainment places like café shops, restaurants, and bars; a place where young people love to hang out.

5

Royal Desire

Since settling in Beijing, I've found that making friends is effortless here. With a cell phone in my pocket, I receive phone calls and invitations to parties and dinners almost every day. But the friends I've made are mainly single girls like me. Meeting men of quality is so much more difficult than meeting women of quality in Beijing. But after getting out of a messy relationship back in the States, I am in no hurry to enter another one.

My new best friend besides Lulu and Beibei is CC. Like me, CC is also a returnee who has lived quite a long time overseas. Many Chinese think of her as a Chinese royal-to-be.

It's true that communism is supposed to advocate egalitarianism. It's true that the last emperor of the Manchu dynasty was driven out of the Forbidden City at the beginning of the twentieth century and ever since China has been a republic. It's also true that the Chinese desire for royalty has never died out. A privileged minority can always enjoy royal treatment. Some political scholars describe Mao as a royal peasant. If you turn on Chinese TV, any channel, you will be bombarded by endless soap operas that depict life inside the imperial palace, mainly stories about the Manchu royal families. Princess Pearl (Huanzhu Gege), Emperor Kangxi, Emperor Qianlong Going South Uncovered, the Empire of Kangxi, and so on. Books about ancient emperors sell millions of copies. An author named The River of February who specializes in royal families is now the richest author in China. It seems that people just can't get enough emperor stories.

As Deng Xiaoping said, "It doesn't matter whether the cat is black or white; as long as it catches rats." Some Chinese have recently got the first taste of being rich. They are China's *xingui,* the new aristocrats, who not only want to live like royalty, but also want to *be* royalty—or at least as close to royalty as possible. They wear Rolex watches and Jimmy Choo shoes. They send their kids to private schools and hire private tutors for them, hoping the children will become little emperors and princesses.

CC is such a Chinese princess.

CC's parents are originally from a Guangdong village. During the Cultural Revolution, when class struggle was so much more important than growing crops, many of the villagers died in a famine. CC's parents, young and full of dreams and the yearning to make something of their lives, planned to sneak into Hong Kong, which was not far from their village, though the island city was a wholly different world back then. Although they knew how to swim, it was dangerous to swim across the Hong Kong border. The young peasant couple bought an enamel basin and immersed their faces in the water every day for a year to practice holding their breath. Eventually, they were ready. In those days, the government religiously patrolled the waters along Hong Kong to prevent this sort of treachery. CC's parents were dressed all in black, and even painted their faces with makeup to prevent themselves from being seen. Because they chose a night without a moon, and they were completely camouflaged, it was impossible for them to even see each other from a few feet away as they swam across. To make sure they didn't get separated in the choppy waters, they tied themselves together with a length of rope around their waists. They crossed the South China Sea successfully. The two began as a waiter and a waitress at one of Hong Kong's fast-food restaurants. Not long after, they started their own fast-food restaurant. With hard work and ambition, the pair became rich in ten years.

By the time CC was born, her parents were full-time golfers and drove around in chauffeured Mercedes. However, Hong Kong followed the English closely. Because of their humble background, her parents were still looked down upon by Hong Kong society. Their biggest dream was to upgrade their own status by making their daughter the equivalent of royalty—if not by blood, at least by marriage.

At the age of two, CC was sent to study at a private school in London. Now this Oxford-educated Hong Kong girl could speak English with a perfect Oxford accent. She also spoke fluent French, some Spanish, and some Chinese and played both the piano and chess with skill. She was also at times a ballet dancer, a violin player, and an opera singer.

Because of CC's Western upbringing, and because she is more internationally educated than my other friends, she has her own style, which is distinctively un-Chinese. In this day and age, the "fashionable" Chinese women try to be as Western as they can. Stiletto heels, low-rise jeans, dyed hair, and name-brand jackets are all a must. While this look may be considered high status and tasteful by many of China's elite, to CC it is boring and uncreative. CC has a petite body and delicate bones. Although the Chinese think whiter skin is the more beautiful, she tries to get a suntan. Her style is something of a mixture of East and West, just like she is. Her clothes are much less flashy and in-your-face than what is normally seen on the streets of Beijing or Shanghai. It is not uncommon for CC to be seen in tight American jeans, with a Shanghai Tang silk Chinese jacket. CC's mixture of fashion is an unconscious metaphor for her confusion over her own place in Chinese society.

We met at Starbucks. Immersed in European culture, CC is into bars and cafés, not necessarily Starbucks. And as for me, from my days in the States, Starbucks was another word for "breakfast." The two of us often ran into each other in the Starbucks near Beijing's Friendship Store. We would often sit facing each other, one with a cappuccino and the *Financial Times,* the other behind a mocha and the *Wall Street Journal.*

CC is a business manager at an international public relations company called Ed Consulting. She is the organizer of many events and parties Lulu and I have attended. CC is a loyal fan of the singer CoCo Lee, who sang the theme song of the movie *Crouching Tiger, Hidden Dragon.* She also worships that Singapore-born, scantily clad violinist Vanessa Mae. CC wants to emulate any Chinese woman who becomes successful overseas.

Unlike Beibei and Lulu, who have never studied abroad, CC is more Western than Chinese. For me, it's a good balance. I can cling to my roots by befriending Beibei and Lulu and keep my Western connection by being with CC. Another reason I like CC is that she is funny. She thinks of herself as a serious intellectual. Talking to her makes me feel like I'm in a salon of eighteenth-century Paris. She likes to discuss issues such as colonialism and drop high-brow names such as Tolstoy, Plato, Leonardo da Vinci, and Mozart during everyday conversations.

This little princess has an acute identity crisis: she doesn't know whether she is Chinese or English. When CC is with Chinese people, she feels she is English and could never identify with the Chinese. When she is with English people, she criticizes them for their racism in not accepting her as one of them.

Finally, CC decided that she would alternate months, being completely Chinese one month and completely English the next. When she is being English, she pretends not to understand if you speak to her in Chinese. On the other hand, when she is being Chinese and speaking her crummy Mandarin, no one dares to practice English with her.

CC's parents racked their brains to raise CC as a quasi-royal, to fulfill their dream of her someday becoming China's own Jackie Kennedy. They never expected CC to have a problem with her identity. They always hoped she would marry "a Chinese aristocrat," in keeping with her social standing. But CC is not attracted to Asian men. Sometimes, she says that she simply prefers the vanilla flavor. Sometimes, she says dating an Asian man is like dating a brother, which is quite boring.

CC's current boyfriend is a poor Welshman named Nick. After CC graduated from Oxford, she took Nick back to Asia with her. He doesn't have a full-time job. He helps a couple of Chinese Internet sites as a part-time English editor, but his salary remains a fraction of CC's. Nick works for only two or three hours each day, so he has a lot of free time, which he spends learning Chinese from Chinese people in bars, Starbucks, parties, and sometimes at his home.

Now CC's biggest headache is that Nick, her ever-faithful boyfriend from England, has discovered that in China his average Welshman looks are surprisingly well received by Asian girls. Nick often spends time with Chinese girls, in the name of studying Chinese culture. Once he even went swimming with three Chinese girls, and CC was furious at the photo of Nick hugging three hot young chicks in bikinis. Knowing that I had a failed relationship that prompted me to return to China, CC comforts me, "It's wonderful that you don't have a boyfriend right now. You don't have to worry that local girls will steal him from you. You have a fresh start." CC worries that Nick will turn into another Frank.

Who is Frank? A real character. We will get to him later.

POPULAR PHRASES

XINGUI: The new aristocrats, or nouveaux riches. During the Cultural Revolution, educated people were purged by the government and everyone was equal (equally poor that is). The new market economy has made it possible for people to have money and a strong education. This group of people constitute the "new aristocrats."

NIUJIN: An Ox and a ford—Oxford.

CHA CANTING: Popular Cantonese fast-food restaurant that offers quick meals and milk tea

6

The Postmodernist
and the Womanizer

$\mathcal{M}$y favorite necklace is Native American. It is a piece of turquoise on an ox-tendon string, which I bought in Sante Fe, New Mexico.

Sante Fe is one of my favorite American cities, a melting pot of Indian, Hispanic, Mexican, and Anglo cultures, with the distinctive little red-earth adobes set off against the cacti on the plains. It has such a raw and primitive feel. And it's a prosperous art community that attracts artists from many different cultures.

It was in Sante Fe that one of my favorite American artists, Georgia O'Keeffe, was inspired to do much of her work. O'Keeffe was an independent and well-educated woman whose artwork was original and sensual. I especially love her Sante Fe–inspired flower paintings, which resemble female sexual organs. They remind me that the female form is both beautiful and delicate and strong and resolute. O'Keeffe also had a romantic love affair with her sponsor, Alfred Stieglitz, who was the only art dealer who would show her work in his gallery. The two eventually married, even though Stieglitz was thirty-one years older than O'Keeffe. Stieglitz loved to tell people that Georgia was his muse. By visiting New Mexico I hope to feed off the same energy that inspired O'Keeffe to create some of her best work.

I remember how I sat on the second floor of the Coyote Café in the city center, gazing out at the sapphire sky above the plain and sipping a margarita. At ten o'clock at night, the arcades in the street were still open, and I could smell the enchanting scent of incense drifting up from the gallery shop. Colorfully dressed people strolled along the street. Like me, they were there on holiday. Other people were in couples, but I had come alone. I stayed at the Saint Francis Hotel, next to the Coyote Café, an old hotel where you had to use a real key, and not a magnetic card, to open the door.

I liked the feeling of the old hotel. The old walnut furniture, books whose pages had been turned countless times, and the creaking wooden staircase, all made me think of dead authors like Mark Twain and Charles Dickens. In the States, old is precious because the country is young, the exact opposite of China, where old things are seen as roadblocks to the future.

At the time, I had just been dumped by Len, the eye doctor who is twelve years older than me. This was after I had dumped my previous boyfriend for Len. I was depressed. At night the sky above the plains reminded me of my school trip to Tibet. It was the same sapphire blue, whether in the East or the West, always lucid, distant, mesmerizing. That night, I bade farewell to my failed love and decided that I'd stop seeing a psychologist and return to China.

Before coming to the United States, I had been forewarned about racism against "yellow people," so it really surprised me when I found boys liked me in school. Actually, I was a popular girl. I had several boyfriends ranging from football players to lawyers to African immigrants.

The gentle Len was the only man whom I fell passionately in love with. My body used to tremble just thinking of him, and I felt like my life couldn't get any better. I met him after I finished my bachelor's at Missouri and moved to Berkeley for graduate school. There I was, a young foreign girl living in the States, and dating an older, handsome Chinese American man. As a third-generation Chinese American, Len was more American than most American friends I knew. He never tired of introducing me to the country. We went to baseball games and operas in San Francisco, took road trips down the Pacific Coast highway, and went camping in Oregon. He even taught me how to ski and dive. He enjoyed telling me the names of cartoon characters and music bands that I hadn't heard of, and explaining psychosocial or literary terms I had not known. He was knowledgeable and fun to be with, and at the same time he retained the humbleness of a Chinese man. As a doctor, Len is patient and caring. Knowing my love for Picasso and Matisse, he bought prints of their paintings to help me decorate my dormitory. Once when I was sick, he took a day off to take care of me.

The most romantic time we ever spent together was a two-week vacation in Yucatán, Mexico. I knew that Len didn't have much of an interest in this area, but I had always wanted to know about the Maya and Native American cultures. Len had often heard me talking about wanting to go there someday, so he had secretly planned out a whole vacation without my knowing. Being surrounded by the lush rain forest and warm gulf waters was like a dream come true for me. Even more than the beautiful natural surroundings, I loved visiting the ancient pyramids and sculptures. Seeing these incredible works of a culture that has long since vanished from the world filled me with awe as well as sadness. The best night of the trip came when Len took me to the top of one of the ancient stone pyramids as the sun was setting over the forest. It was not safe to be this deep in the jungle late at night and Len had had to hire a guide as well as a guard to make sure we made it back to our hotel safely. This was the first time I seriously considered that Len might be my true soul mate. After that trip I never would have guessed that things would end the way they did.

A year has passed since Len left me, and I have been a celibate for the whole year. I can't explain why I don't have sex anymore. I haven't tried to abstain. It seems that I used up all my sexual energy with Len. Now, I'm done.

People say that I have a baby face. With a round face and a pair of sparkling almond eyes that look slightly distant, I've achieved a naïve and innocent look. Many people think of me as an inexperienced schoolgirl. Few people I know in Beijing, including my own mother, could imagine that Niuniu was quite a wild girl back in the States. Beijing isn't like the United States. All my family and friends keep me busy drinking and eating. My first priority is not to find a date but to rediscover what it means to be Chinese.

This is my new life: I race around the old city of Beijing in my red four-wheel-drive Land Cruiser, showing up at various events—art exhibitions, fashion shows, cocktail parties, masquerade balls, political conventions, press reception, and charity events. I meet people and go anywhere that is fun and newsworthy. This is the life of a journalist and a single metropolitan woman. Because the China of today is an ever-changing one, I have no shortage of stories to keep me busy. I cover everything from politics to business to social issues.

When I was first hired by the Beijing bureau of the English news agency World News, I was assigned to an apartment in the diplomatic compound. Now, I am more than ready to move out of the compound to live in a *hutong*, with their narrow alleyways and simple courtyards. I didn't return to China to live in a fishbowl, but to mingle with the people that make this country unique. The many *hutong* that dot the landscape of Beijing remind me of a different time in Chinese history—a time that I yearn for but, sadly, may soon be gone.

Living in the diplomatic compound makes me feel like a foreigner in Beijing. Whenever my Chinese friends come to visit me, they are always stopped by the guards, and I have to personally come down to let them in. If my friends drive local cars with blue license plates, they are not allowed in at all—only cars with black license plates, registered to foreigners, are allowed. As time passes, my friends stop coming by to play tennis or eat the dumplings that I cook.

"You want to move? Are you crazy? The diplomatic apartments are in downtown Beijing, next to Chang'an Avenue, a few steps away from your office." Mother disapproves of my idea on the phone. "It has the broadband you need. It's safe. You don't want to live somewhere without guards. You know many migrant workers come to Beijing to rob or kill people for a few dollars."

I talk back. "Mom, I want to live in a *hutong*. I grew up in Beijing. I want to be an ordinary Beijing person."

"Niuniu, I was an ordinary Beijing person, I lived in a *hutong* for many years. Never again in my life do I want to queue up at the public toilets to empty the shit and piss from the night pans. How will you get used to it, child? There isn't even a place to park your car!"

"I don't want special privileges; I don't want people to think of me as a fake foreign devil," I complain.

Mother points out, "You *are* a fake foreign devil. You're an American citizen, your mother is an American citizen, your father is, your stepfather is, and your half-sisters are, and your stepmother Jean Fang is dreaming of becoming a fake foreign devil right now. But what's wrong with being an American devil? The whole world is working for America!" Mother, accustomed to living at the million-dollar Riviera Villa, cannot comprehend why I want to live in a *hutong*.

I know that special privileges are exactly what Mother likes—her life has been a roller coaster. In her early days, when China was poor and closed to the outside world, she had nothing and worked as a kitchen hand in a jail, and now she lives an affluent life and is the regular guest of foreign ambassadors. Since she suffered enough during the Cultural Revolution, Mother sees being an ordinary Chinese person as shameful. An ordinary Chinese person, to her, is the synonym of poverty, backwardness, and squat toilet. To those lucky enough not to know what a squat toilet is, it is just that: a simple hole that you squat over to relieve yourself.

Growing up in China in the 1980s and 1990s, I have the idyllic memory of China. For my generation who grew up in the city, poverty can be a prank and backwardness can be a postmodern experiment. The diplomatic apartments may be considered high-end by older generations. For me, they are a bunch of ugly concrete matchboxes, neither cool nor postmodern. They simply have no character. I don't tell this to Mother, who has no clue what *hou xiandai* is. With Beibei and Lulu's help, I find a traditional courtyard house in a *hutong* near the well-preserved section of town: Drum Tower. It is convenient and close to the subway. My yard is two hundred square meters, with two large japonica trees, a grapevine pergola, and a flower garden. I can stand on the earth. As I look up, I can see trees and the sky. It's quaint.

I paint doors and roofs in blue, and the outer walls ivory. My house looks Mediterranean from the outside. I decorate the bedroom with bright pink-and-green gauze drapery and hang brocade from minority tribes in the living room. I have gone to an antique market called Panjiayuan and brought back a round sandalwood eight-seater dining table, old-fashioned wooden armchairs, and some Ming- and Qing-style vases. My grandparents give me a birdcage, snuff bottles, and incense burners as homewarming gifts. My house is a fusion of old and new.

With my encouragement, CC also moves out of her foreigner's community and shares the courtyard house with me. Not to be outdone by my efforts, CC installs a heavy opium bed in her own bedroom. Both of our jobs require us to stay connected to this new China: to follow and document and immerse ourselves in its culture. The new China can be a bland, frivolous, and even scary place, with its endless cinderblock-shaped skyscrapers and immense shopping malls. Our new home allows us to create an escape from the busy, modern world. It takes us back to an ancient place, when my Chinese ancestors still possessed the confidence and nobility that seems to have been lost in the Chinese people of today. I love my new house tremendously.

After we settle in, CC and I hear the story of the house's previous occupant, Frank, who was not only a postmodernist but also a womanizer.

Frank graduated from a small college in Indiana and was a foreign teacher at a Beijing technology university. When he was in the States, Frank was a pure and honest midwestern lad. He was modest and down-to-earth. At university he was shy, a bit of a nerd, and couldn't find a girlfriend. After graduation, Frank came to Asia, wandering around Thailand and Vietnam, teaching English to get by. Finally Frank came to Beijing to work as a foreign teacher.

Asia completely changed him. Back in the States, no one said Frank was good-looking, but Asian girls loved his Western nose and blond hair. Frank was treated like some kind of *baima wangzi,* a veritable Prince Charming. Women would take him out for meals, open doors for him, and give him candy. Sometimes, when he was walking along the street, people asked to take their photos with him. Chinese TV stations fought one another to get Frank as their special guest. Frank's confidence blossomed.

Within a year of his stay in Beijing, Frank nailed down nine girls. Living in the school's foreign expert dorm was no longer convenient for him since the guards looked suspiciously at every girl he brought back to his dorm. So he moved to a *hutong.*

He met his tenth girlfriend that year near the City Hotel area. Her name was Grace. She was a tour guide. Frank and

Grace were together for two months, Frank's record. But unlike Frank's previous Chinese girlfriends, Grace was no sucker. After Frank dumped her, she mustered a bunch of punks to beat him up. Grace even threatened to kill "this heartless bastard" for "messing with Chinese girls." Although it was Frank who had been beaten up, he felt he had brought it upon himself. He had nowhere to report it, so he just had to suffer in silence. After that, there was no way he could stay in Beijing, so he slunk back to Indiana.

Whenever anybody mentions Frank's story, everyone laughs. Wives of foreign expatriates hear about the Grace incident, and they pay much more attention to their husbands' whereabouts.

POPULAR PHRASES

HUTONG: Old-style Chinese homes that create narrow alleyways and little courtyards.

HOU XIANDAI: Postmodern.

BAIMA WANGZI: A Prince Charming on a white horse.

7

Harvard Inc.

Guess what the hottest foreign brand in China is at the moment. McDonald's? No, too cheap. Nike? Wrong again, you can't tell the real ones from the fakes. Marlboro? No, no, no. Yuppies are quitting smoking and becoming trendy environmentalists. Yves Saint Laurent? Much too hard to pronounce! Sony? Unthinkable! Many Chinese still hold a grudge against the Japanese. Motorola? Uh, uh, Nokia is more popular. Microsoft? Not everybody likes Bill Gates. Microsoft has just lost a big deal with the Chinese government and China has vowed to develop its own software to compete with Windows. What is it? I say that it is Harvard.

Status, prestige, and education are what people care about most in a Confucian society. Perhaps that explains why Harvard is the most desired brand name in China.

My girlfriend wrote a novel called *My Lover from Harvard,*

about a love affair between a Chinese girl and a Harvard-educated man. It's popular in China. Following its example, a recent Chinese graduate from Harvard wrote his own memoir, *Being a Lover from Harvard.* Every book that has Harvard in its title becomes a bestseller.

A girl from Sichuan Province was accepted into Harvard University and her parents wrote a book called *The Harvard Girl.* It has sold two million copies so far. Her parents have made enough money for her four-year tuition. Walk into any bookstore in China and you will see titles such as *How to Get into Harvard, The Harvard Genius, The Harvard Boy.* Parents buy these books to educate their kids. Kids buy these books to learn about the road to Harvard.

Travel agencies, English workshops, and bookstores are named after Harvard. Harvard professors have been invited to give talks all over China. A girl who took a couple of summer open-university courses in Harvard gave lectures to college students about "My Days at Harvard." The fact that she didn't actually go to Harvard didn't matter at all.

When Chinese people ask me which school I went to, I tell them it's Berkeley. Not many people have heard of it. Even Yale can't compete with Harvard when it comes to fame in China. Harvard is the only school that matters. Mother suggested I apply for Harvard graduate school after I received my degree in Missouri, but I didn't listen. The Mamas and the Papas' "California Dreamin'" and the Eagles' "Hotel California" brought me to Berkeley.

"You think what you did is called romanticism? No, it's called stupidity," Mother said. "How can you make such a big decision of your lifetime based on some pop songs?" Like many Chinese parents, Mother is obsessed with her kids being number one, not number two. There is only one number one.

My friend Lily came back to China after getting her M.B.A. from HBS (Harvard Business School). In this era of Harvard worship, she expects to find herself a good job and a good husband in China. Apparently, a husband is more important to Lily than a job. Instead of posting job ads, she posts a personal ad on the Internet. At Matchmakers.com, she says: "Lily, female, in her late twenties, master's degree, five feet three, average body type, long black hair, and a thin waist, not model type but kind of cute, introverted but easygoing, kindhearted, enjoys hiking, walking in the moonlight, quiet dinners, and reading on the beach. My favorite book is *Jane Eyre*, my favorite food is fish, my favorite actor is Tom Cruise, my favorite color is lilac. I'm proud to say I can make a good wife, a good mother, and a good career woman.

"You: love children, family-oriented, well-mannered, speak fluent English, well-educated, kind, honest. You don't have to have a car or a house, but you should have a nice job. You don't have to be Tom Cruise, but you should look sexy. Please no: party animals, playboys, one-night standers, male chauvinists, perverts, mama's boys, liars, or bald, overweight, divorcés."

Lily purposely makes her ad a bit dull because she doesn't fully trust cyberdating, but she still gets sixty replies in one day. Despite all her stipulations, many replies are unexpected.

Four married men are seeking trysts and sexual adventures during the day, one respondent wants to exchange nude pictures, another guy offers to clean her house naked, two claim that they like to please women in bed in creative ways, three invite her to have threesomes with them and their wives. Lily is surprised at the level of sexual liberation in her own country thanks to development and modernization. She deletes all the unsavory ones, which leaves thirty-eight replies. Among those, she finds that each starts with a similar sentence: "I'm a graduate from Tsinghua." "I have a master's degree too, but not from China, from Australia."

Lily picks an IT guy named Jason who started his own online auction site in the high-tech zone in Zhongguan Cun. He doesn't mention his education in his reply. Instead, he talks about his hobbies and the books he loves. From the pictures he has sent Lily, he is also good-looking.

They meet in a bar called 1952. Lily carries a newspaper under her arm as a sign. Jason wears a baseball cap. He is not as handsome as his pictures, but he's still cute. They nod, sit down, and order gin and rum. Then, the famous drag show at 1952 begins. As they watch the transvestites in miniskirts miming to Teresa Teng's songs, Jason complains about how he was harassed in Thailand by a girl whom he later found out was a boy. "I wanted to throw up after finding out they were men. It's like the movie," Jason says, scratching his head, trying to think of its title.

"*The Crying Game?*" Lily suggests.

"Yes, exactly. That's the movie I am talking about."

Instead of asking personal questions, such as Where do you live? and What do you do? they start to talk about their trips around the world. Lily gathers that Jason is also a returnee who got a degree from overseas; local Chinese would not have the freedom or the financial ability to travel so often.

One hour passes.

"Where did you go to school?" Jason asks Lily. His first personal question.

"A school in Boston." She tries to avoid going into details.

Jason continues his travel talk, on the cuisine and customs of other cultures. Lily listens attentively and enjoys Jason's humor. She likes men who have a sense of humor.

Another hour passes.

"So what's the name of the school you went to?" Jason asks Lily again.

"Harvard," Lili finally says reluctantly.

Jason nods. Quickly, he pays the bill and says to Lily, "I have to run, but keep in touch. It was great to meet you."

Lily never hears from Jason again. She has the same experience with Frank, Brian, and Tony. Each time, men leave when they hear the name of her school.

Why? Lily asks me for help.

To solve Lily's puzzle, I invite my girlfriends to a teahouse named Purple Wind as her consultants and focus group. We ordered fifteen-year-old Puer tea and some sunflower seeds and dry prunes. One of the women, Dr. Bi, a psychology professor, says, "Chinese men like their women to admire them, not the other way around. They can't stand their women to be better than they are, especially in the education field. The more educated women are, the more difficult it is for us to find husbands nowadays." Lulu comments, "Harvard is almost divine in the minds of many Chinese. But who wants to marry someone who's divine?"

Harvard may make some people rich and famous in China, but it keeps Lily single. Maybe it wasn't so bad that I chose Berkeley instead of Harvard after all.

8

The Tragic Love
of Jeremy Irons

Who is your favorite male actor?

This is the question my girlfriends love to ask one another.

Among our group, 30 percent are Ricky Martin fans, including me—by far the largest group. Richard Gere and the Irish-born Pierce Brosnan have the second and third biggest following. Tom Cruise and Leonardo Di Caprio arguably rank fourth and fifth. The fans often meet in online chat rooms, gossiping about their idols: whether Ricky Martin had seven children with different women, how Tom Cruise likes women that are taller than he, how the color of Pierce Brosnan's eyes changes in different James Bond movies.

Fans of different actors form their own factions to fight against other factions. Ricky Martin haters circulate e-mail rumors regarding Ricky's sexual orientation. Tom Cruise haters call him a big-butted dwarf. Richard Gere haters post his anti-China comments and mock his narrow eyes. It's ironic to imagine a group of Chinese sitting around mocking Richard Gere for having narrow eyes. They expect their idols to look European, not like them. It's part of the inferiority complex the Chinese nation suffers from.

However, one fan club does not bother to attack others. Instead, they totally indulge in themselves. It's the fan club of Jeremy Irons, the English actor with the fatal elegance of an aristocrat and a voice that comes from heaven and hell. The group, which was formed over the Internet by me, is small but exclusive. It does not take a detective to realize that the women in my club share many of the same characteristics: city girls (40 percent from Shanghai, 40 percent from Beijing, and 20 percent from Guangzhou); educated (all have B.A. or M.A. degrees); like to wear straight black long hair or short gelled hair; prefer to wear black or white outfits in cotton or linen fabric. They look mild, favor dark lipstick, but are sometimes neurotic, arrogant, and narcissistic. They are also romantic. They read Marguerite Duras, listen to Irish music, buy prints of Van Gogh's paintings, drink cappuccino, shave their legs (most Chinese girls don't), have several cyber names, own a bottle of imported perfume (the size of the bottle depends on how much money they make), and are open about sex, though they may fake orgasms during intercourse.

Jeremy Irons! He is not particularly handsome, but tall, pensive, cultured, and complex—the complete opposite of the cowboy-styled George W. Bush. He's not an actor who is well known in China since he doesn't play in films that are popular here, except *Chinese Box*. The girls know about him through pirated DVDs.

In *Damage,* he is a middle-aged man infatuated with his son's fiancée, whose damaging love destroys his son's life, his family, and his promising job. He shifts from being a successful politician with a happy family to being a hermit who relives the passionate moment in his memories.

In *Chinese Box,* he is a dying English journalist, who falls in love with a Chinese woman, the manager of a bar. He uses his camera to record his own death.

In *Lolita,* he is the notorious middle-aged French-language professor who marries an American woman, but secretly falls for her twelve-year-old daughter, Lolita. His love and desire for the girl destroys both him and Lolita's innocence.

In *Waterland,* he is a history teacher who lives in the traumatic memory of his past.

In *M. Butterfly,* he portrays a French diplomat who falls in love with a male Beijing opera performer. The diplomat lives with the performer for eighteen years and believes for the whole time that his lover is a woman. When he finally realizes that his lover is a man and a spy, he commits hara-kiri.

In all of his movies—from *Damage* to *Lolita,* from *The French Lieutenant's Woman* to *Chinese Box*—he brings to life men whose love is insane and perverse. These men often combine the evilness of a serpent and the purity of an angel.

Lulu, Beibei, CC, and I are all fans of Jeremy Irons. Lulu claims that Jeremy Irons "is the secret signal of thinking women and women of taste."

After CC and I settle into our courtyard house, we invite our fellow Jeremy Irons fans around for dinner. Mimi, a lawyer and an alumna from Cal Berkeley, and Harvard M.B.A. graduate Lily are two die-hard fans who show up at the get-together.

I make cold appetizers, sliced cucumber, tiger salad, cold

tomatoes, and deep-fried peanuts and cook some three-delicacy dumplings. After growing up with a maid in my house, I was forced to learn how to cook during my seven years living in the United States, a country that advocates an independent spirit. In the States I lived alone, and I had to learn how to cook and clean. Now I am self-sufficient. I don't need a cook or a maid, and I certainly don't want to be a cut above others.

Beibei thinks differently. She teases me: "Niuniu, why do you have to cook? I'd order catering service if I were you. There are so many Chinese people who'd work for very little money. You've got to give them job opportunities. You can't just think of entertaining yourself by cooking." She has brought Starbucks coffee and a pound of caviar.

CC has bought beer and Chinese corn liquor called Erguotou.

Lulu has brought some candied chestnuts.

Lily has brought all the DVDs of Jeremy Irons's movies.

Mimi has brought a cheesecake.

We sit under the pergola in the courtyard, eating dumplings, drinking beer, watching DVDs, and talking about Jeremy Irons.

CC, who grew up in London, comments, "I love his madness, his passion, his English accent, his pain, and his heartbreaking gaze. His English gloominess reminds me of the rainy days in England."

I remember CC had said before that modern Chinese men lack any poetic quality. Perhaps that's why she always prefers English men.

Mimi analyzes Jeremy: "He is a mature and successful man, but becomes obsessive-compulsive when it comes to love. His lack of control leads him to despair and damage. I knew a man like this once, too."

Lulu cuts in: "Nowadays, men are all cowards. Before they

fall in love, they ask if they will be hurt. If there is a chance of getting hurt, they won't fall in love in the first place. But what type of love doesn't hurt? I've had three abortions for love!"

"We love the Romeo and Juliet story because modern people are not that romantic anymore," says Lily. "Especially men. They always want to know what they can get from their women. They are takers, not givers." She frowns.

"Jeremy Irons can be cruel, even sinister," Beibei says, "but when it comes to love, he gives his all. I dream of this kind of passionate lover and dramatic soul-stirring love! But I don't have any. The men I've met are not romantic. They want to use either my connections or my money." Even though she complains, everyone knows Beibei likes to mention her connections and her money.

"The reality is that such men don't exist," adds Lulu. "Perhaps that's why there are more and more single women like us now."

"That's why we need Jeremy," I say with a dreamy smile. "He can make us fantasize we would fall madly in love at least once in our lives."

I think of Len again. Len had Jeremy's introspection, gloominess, and fervent hope. When the movie *Lolita* was showing in the States, everyone talked about it. Many people disliked the film because they thought it was immoral. But Len liked it. He said that he was fascinated with destruction and perversity. Perhaps this was a sign of how things would turn out between us. I was falling into my own morbid love with Len back then.

It snowed a lot that day, in the little town called Jackson Hole, by the Rocky Mountains. I was in a cowboy bar with country music playing in the background and Budweiser on tap. I called Len on my mobile phone. We were talking about *Lolita*. He said to me, "Perhaps because I'm a doctor, I pay particular attention to pathology. Often, I think illness is the principal part of life. *Lolita* allows us to see the abnormality beneath normal people."

Len has the pensive look of the cellist Yo-Yo Ma. He never spoke much, and had an air of elegant despair about him. Although he may have seemed stone-faced and emotionless, his eyes betrayed the passion and intensity with which he lived his life. When he did speak, the whole world listened.

Perhaps I never truly understood Len. He told me that he wasn't a healthy person. He wasn't a man who could give women happiness. "If you are smart, you'll keep your distance from me."

In the States, I had taken advantage of being far away from my parents and my rigid culture. I was like a free bird until I met Len, the man who taught me about pain, cruelty, madness, and suffering.

When I was a child, a Buddhist master who passed through my house told my mother that I had some affinity for Buddhism. They call it *huigen,* wisdom roots. He could see the halo behind my head. Because I had a round, smiling face, all of the adults called me Little Buddha. It's strange that the little me could sometimes see many things. I had premonitions about my primary school language teacher's suicide, my math teacher's lung cancer, and the disappearance of the retarded boy from down the street. I even predicted my parents' separation. They divorced when I was eleven years old—I was so calm people found it incomprehensible. I wonder when I lost the ability to see things as a child. The Little Buddha with wisdom roots couldn't resist the intensity of Len's ardent but melancholy gaze.

There is this Buddhist asceticism: "Free from human desires and passions; physical existence is vanity." I discover that as I grow older, I'm further and further away from being "free from human desires and passions." Why did I succumb to obsession, violating the greatest taboo in Buddhist doctrine? Why did love so confuse my heart and mind? Beibei says I'm a *qingzhong*, the seed of emotions. I don't object to it. After all, my parents pursued their forbidden love out of their mutual irresistible attraction. I'm a product of passion.

Here, in this entertaining, ever-changing China, all those memories of Len and the times we shared seem so far away—as far away as America itself. I sometimes find myself going days, or even weeks, without thinking about Len at all. When I do think about him, it is as if he is a burglar who has somehow snuck past the security of my busy mind and is robbing me of the peace I came to China to find.

I, the young female journalist, seem to have it all here: good pay, a nice job, a busy social life. But I still get bored easily, and I constantly look for excitement. Seek pleasure, avoid pain: perhaps I'm becoming a hedonist like Beibei. Even if a hedonist's life has no meaning, at least it is comfortable. Comfort, home, for me are vital.

POPULAR PHRASES

ERGUOTOU: Fiery Chinese corn liquor.

QINGZHONG: The seed of emotions; refers to awful romantic partners.

HUIGEN: Wisdom roots, affinity with Buddhism.

9

Taking Revenge
on Chinese Women

*A*s my friends and I are talking about Jeremy Irons, the doorbell rings. Here comes a Chinese man, a stranger.

"Is this where the Jeremy Irons fan club is meeting?" he asks, hesitating.

"Yes. Are you a fan as well?" I ask.

"Yes. My name is John," the man says. He is a bit nervous.

"Yes. Come on in. Let's watch *Damage* together." I let him in.

John has reasons to be nervous. All the other fan members at my house are women.

After watching the movie, everybody wants to know about him. He tells his story.

Like me, John is also a *haigui*, an overseas returnee. With a master's degree in sociology, he was selling life insurance in Silicon Valley for three years, making fifty grand per year—not very impressive by Silicon Valley standards.

Although he is a good-looking Chinese man, John couldn't find a girlfriend in the States. The fact is, two-thirds of the Chinese girls in the States prefer to date locals, mainly white Americans. The ones who do stick around the Chinese community become hot property, with endless streams of highly educated male admirers queuing up for their attention. Even those who are not very attractive can still afford to be choosy.

Seeing John in his mid-thirties and living a celibate life, his friend Mike set him up on a blind date in San Francisco. The lucky lady was a Chinese woman from China named Jane. She was studying nursing in a local community college. She was recently divorced and average-looking.

They met in the Borders bookstore near Union Square. As agreed, Jane carried a Gucci shopping bag as her sign. In the Borders coffee shop, they greeted each other briefly and John went to buy two cups of mocha for them. As soon as they sat down, the girl said, "Hi. I have to say I don't have much time. Your friend didn't tell me your annual income. Can you tell me now?"

It seemed Jane had certainly adapted to the fast-paced American way of life. To her surprising opening question, John replied, "I make fifty thousand dollars per year. But it does not include the bonus . . ."

She cut him off with her next question: "Do you have a house?"

"I'm renting an apartment in San Mateo at the moment. I'm saving money for . . ."

"Sorry, John. I only go out with men who have the three Ps," Jane said impatiently. She stood up and left without even touching the mocha John had bought for her.

John felt humiliated. He tried to find out what the three Ps stood for, but got different answers from different friends. Some told him they were Ph.D., permanent residency, and property. Others said they were passport (American), Porsche, and Ph.D. His best friend, Mike, comforted him: "Who cares what three Ps stand for? If Jane thinks she is so great, why doesn't she go for the Prince, the President, and the Prime Minister?!"

Just like my experience, John's heartbreaking meeting with the inhuman and arrogant Jane prompted his final decision to go back to China.

After returning, he got job offers in Shanghai, Beijing, and Shenzhen. He accepted a job in Beijing as sales manager in an electronics company. Although he makes only a third of the money he did in the United States, he is suddenly a member of society's upper class. The entire world welcomes him. He joins a dating club and becomes the most popular bachelor.

The dating club's owner approaches John one day to offer him a deal. "Please promise me you won't get yourself a girl-friend for the moment. As long as you are available and your document is with us, girls will register and come to us."

"What do I get out of it?"

"You can have half of our profit," says the owner.

John agrees. His job is to interview these single women and turn them down. As long as he is doing it, the money arrives in his bank account every month. The women he has turned down are all better-looking than the Plain Jane that spurned him in Silicon Valley. He turns down each of the women with the same excuse: "I only like a girl that has the three Ps."

Many of the women are intellectual. They all discuss with their friends what the three Ps are and come up with all kinds of ideas. There are two popular theories, one in Chinese and one in English. The Chinese one goes *pigu, pifu, piqi*—nice butt, soft skin, and sweet temperament. The English one goes: pretty, pure, and pleasing. Only John himself knows that the three P's have no meaning. In a way, he is punishing all women for what Plain Jane did to his self-esteem.

When women become too easy to obtain, they become less attractive. Plus, John has an agreement with the dating club that he will not date a girl. His interest in women fades as he interviews more and more eager, available single women. Finally, he starts to get involved with men, most of whom are foreign expatriates in Beijing. "Chinese women mean nothing to me now. Like them, I prefer the imports," he claims.

After hearing his story, I ask John, "What about Jeremy Irons? What makes you a fan of his?"

"I love making men fall madly in love with me like Jeremy Irons does for his Beijing lover in the movie *M. Butterfly*." John cracks a devious smile.

POPULAR PHRASES

HAIGUI: Sea turtles; refers to overseas returnees who come back with advanced degrees, Westernized lifestyle, and nice jobs. Unlike the endangered sea turtle, their numbers are growing every year.

PIGU: Butt.

PIFU: Skin.

PIQI: Temperament.

10

Sean and Hugh

Our company, World News, has nine people in the Beijing office. It's quite international. Sean, an Englishman, is the bureau chief and Hugh, an American, is the vice bureau chief. We also have Linda, our Oceanian reporter, who specializes in environmental issues; Mr. Chun, our financial specialist from Hong Kong; and Mr. Lai, from Singapore, our accountant. Two assistants and one driver from Beijing make up the rest of the team.

Sean and Hugh have different focuses. Sean is interested in politics, such as human rights violations and China's undeveloped interior. Hugh prefers to write about economic growth in the prosperous coastal areas. Hugh has assigned me to write on Chinese dot-coms, luxury goods users, and General Motors in Shanghai. Sean has asked me to do stories on China's think tanks, Taiwan relations, and religious issues.

I remember when I first started the job, Sean had a talk with me in his office. "Niuniu, you have many advantages as a reporter. Your Chinese and English are flawless. You've got friends and connections here. You have a strong sense of newsworthiness. You have 'unlimited potential.' But what I value most is that your views are balanced. The influences of Chinese and American culture mean you are not overly politicized. Too many Western journalists reporting on China are influenced by their own personal values. In other words, they have a tainted view of China. And I hope you are an exception."

I was so flattered by his words that ever since I have worked hard to demonstrate the diligence of a Chinese and the defiance of an American.

My two bosses' jobs are dream jobs and the competition is fierce. Normally, to become a bureau chief in a foreign country, one has to work at home for many years to pay one's dues before being posted abroad. Being a correspondent posted to a large city like Beijing, Moscow, or Paris is a sign of status and success.

Sean and Hugh both earn over $150,000 per year. They each have a company-subsidized apartment, a maid, a driver, a travel allowance, and a generous expense account. And they get both Chinese and English public holidays. Compared to the middle classes in most developed countries, they live like kings.

Sean, age thirty-seven, studied politics at Oxford University. He speaks fluent Mandarin, and whether he is speaking English or Mandarin, he likes to swear. In his Oxford accent, his speech is peppered with references to sex, genitalia, and mothers.

Sean is a workaholic. He is short-tempered and quick-thinking, and few people can keep up with him. Every day Sean arrives at the office at eight o'clock, and often works late into the night. He wants every article to leave people struck with admiration. But he is extremely circumspect and serious. Compared to the other foreigners in China, who enjoy chasing women, the handsome Sean never has any interesting sidelights. It seems that, apart from work, there is nothing else in his life. Even when he is eating out with friends, all he ever speaks about are current affairs and Sino-U.S. relations.

As his subordinate, I have never spoken with him about anything other than work. Except once. I went out at lunchtime to buy ice cream at the Häagen-Dazs next to the International Club Hotel, and I saw Sean sitting by himself on a bright yellow bench, eating a coffee-flavored Häagen-Dazs ice cream with gusto. A grown man, totally absorbed in his sickly sweet ice cream, sitting in front of the purple Häagen-Dazs sign. As I watched, I thought it was funny. I greeted Sean. He smiled at me for the first time, showing a mouthful of white teeth. "I love sweets. The sweeter the better. Especially ice cream."

My other boss, Hugh, tends to speak more outside work. Hugh studied history at Stanford and is a Fulbright Scholar. Because we both lived in the Bay Area for a while, we have more in common. Hugh and Sean are both tall and handsome but have different styles. Sean is domineering and enjoys the limelight, whereas Hugh is relaxed and refined. He once said that he was a dreamer and came to China in order to find meaning in life. He meditates and practices yoga every day. He's what people call "an egg," white on the outside, yellow on the inside.

11

A Sweet Note of Passion

One of the things I like about my journalist job is not having to spend all day in my office. This has allowed me to stay out of office politics and maintain a good relationship with most of my colleagues. But I have never imagined those relations are as good as they seem today.

I walk into my office building and board the elevator. The three people already in the elevator all greet me with exceptional warmth. There is a chorus of enthusiastic good mornings. I am a little surprised, but I try to respond in a similar manner.

"How was your weekend, Niuniu," says Mr. Lai.

"Fine, thanks," I say.

Then Mr. Lai winks at me.

The wink seems forced. Not insincere, but practiced. Almost as though Mr. Lai had been holding that wink in his pocket all morning just waiting to spring it on me. Was this a

"How do you do?" wink? No, I didn't think so. This was almost certainly a "Thanks for last night" wink.

I smile awkwardly and face the front of the elevator. When the door opens, I step out and head toward my office, Mr. Lai's eyes burning into my back.

I walk to my desk, put down my belongings, and pick up my cup. I walk to the kitchen to get some hot water when in walks Linda, a New Zealander. I have gone to lunch with Linda on several occasions and am rather fond of her.

"I, I can't believe this!" Linda says, walking up closely behind me. "You had me totally fooled. I'm so glad you had the courage to tell me. I don't think I would have felt comfortable approaching you."

"Oh, um . . . Linda, I'm sorry. I'm a bit confused."

"Oh, please don't worry about it," says Linda. "I totally understand. I was the same way. Listen, this isn't the time or place to talk, but let's have lunch, okay?"

And then Linda is gone.

On the way back to my desk, I encounter Mr. Chun, who on several occasions has asked inappropriate questions about my personal life. I have learned to steer away from him at all cost. This time, he stands in my path holding a pile of color-coded files and a box of paper clips. But he doesn't say anything to me. He just stands there smiling, bobbing his head up and down with all the apparent satisfaction of a man who can finally say, "I told you so."

"What was happening?" I think. If ever there was a day I ought to go out in the field to gather a story, this was it. I suddenly feel extremely self-conscious. Just thinking of this sequence of events causes me to shudder.

Whisking by Mr. Chun, I return to my desk hoping to quickly check my e-mail before heading out.

I see that I've got sixty-seven new messages: a surprisingly high number for a late Friday morning. But even more strange is that most of them are titled "Re: I Love You."

"Another chain letter?" I wonder.

I haven't received so many e-mails on one topic since I responded to the Internet hoax about the little girl who needed a liver transplant and had been promised a donation of $1 for every person I contacted by e-mail from the McDonald's Corporation.

I open the first e-mail, the one from Sean. It reads: "I appreciate your candor, but I am involved with someone else. I have a great deal of respect for you. Please, let's not mix business with pleasure."

Then comes one from Mr. Chun: "My wife is visiting her parents this week. Please meet me after work in the parking lot. I know a place where we can be discreet. P.S. Have you ever fantasized about us doing it on your desk at work? I have!"

Then one from my cousin: "I think you know that I love you, too. We have always had something special between us. But this kind of love is forbidden, and I think it is best we do not pursue it. It burns me that we will never be able to be together. I don't think our families would accept it."

The last e-mail is from Hugh: "Hi, Niuniu, I have to say I was quite surprised by your e-mail, it didn't seem like you at all. I'm flattered to hear that you are interested in me, but I don't think this is the right time for either of us."

Below this message, I read the text of the e-mail to which he responded. In a very convincing and eloquent manner, the message makes a brief plea for love at my request.

I have become the most recent victim of the I Love You computer virus. The virus affects Microsoft Outlook users and sends out a sweet note of passion to everyone listed in its victim's address book.

Several hours later the news of this virus becomes widespread throughout the media, at which point countless e-mails fill my mailbox from people begging me to disregard their previous correspondence.

All except one, from Mr. Chun, which reads: "Well, I'm still game if you are."

12

Have You Divorced Yet?

*I*s *Chile ma?*—Have you eaten yet?—the most popular greeting in China? It used to be.

Recently, *Lile ma*—have you divorced yet?—has taken its place among young and middle-aged Chinese, especially in big cities where the divorce rate has risen to double digits.

In the yoga class that Lulu and I go to every week, we meet quite a few professional women in their late twenties, thirties, and early forties. From talking to them, I've learned that 50 percent of the women are divorced, including our teacher Gigi.

On her fortieth birthday, the class takes the health-conscious Gigi to a Häagen Dazs shop to celebrate. Some order ice cream and some order cakes. I order both tiramisu and a green tea sundae. Gigi, although we insist that she eat something fat-rich just once, orders Perrier.

As we eat our high-calorie and high-fat ice creams and ice cream cake, we sing Happy Birthday to Gigi.

Gigi looks gloomy and she twirls her spoon in the ice cream we've given her, "Gee, I'm not happy at all. For a woman, reaching forty is pathetic. Have you heard the popular saying? Twenty-something are like basketballs. Thirty-something are like volleyballs. Forty-something are like soccer balls."

"What does that mean?" I ask.

Gigi sighs. "In basketball games, players all try to chase the ball. In volleyball games, if the ball comes to you, you need to receive it. In soccer games, you kick the ball somewhere else." Gigi kicks her leg violently for extra emphasis.

"But maturity is a kind of beauty—isn't it?" I say.

"Right!" Lulu agrees. "Fashion magazines say that truly mature women are those who have children with their second or third husbands."

"Like Yoko Ono," adds another girl, trying to help.

"Like ZsaZsa Gabor," Lulu continues.

"Catherine Deneuve has two children. Neither is from her husband. Does it mean she is more mature than other women?" I ask.

"I guess I can never be that mature. Since I divorced three years ago, I haven't been able to find a man to marry. They all want younger women. I don't understand why there are so many young Chinese women out there for men to choose from. Even married men have more chances than divorced women." Gigi is very frustrated.

Lulu has told me what she heard about Gigi's husband. He was a professor who was involved with one of his students. The student landed a good job through his connections, but soon dumped him and ran off to the United States with an American man. He went back to Gigi, but it was too late.

After Gigi mentions divorce, other women start to ask each other, "Are you divorced?"

"Yes."

"How about you? Have you divorced yet?"

"Yes."

All of a sudden, all the women except Lulu and me find a common topic and share their stories with one another.

Ah Du says, "My first husband was nice, but he was a lousy lover. You see, in China, especially among the old generations, women are proud of being cold fish. Women who have sex drives are considered bad luck. I knew that. At first, I was frustrated, but I swallowed it. I meditated, practiced tai chi, tried every way to stop my natural urges. But things changed after I got into law school."

"You met another man?" Lulu asks.

"No. I learned from the textbooks that my sexual desires are protected by law. It is legitimate to divorce someone for bad sex!" says Ah Du.

"So you've become a smart woman who knows about your rights," I tease her.

"Divorce for me is like sex. Once you've done it, you want to do it repeatedly. Now I'm divorced three times. But in order to catch up with Liz Taylor, I have to quicken my pace," says Ah Du.

"Does dumping men make you feel good?" Lulu asks.

"If men can upgrade their computers, why can't we upgrade our husbands? All we want is the same thing: better and faster performance."

An art teacher can't wait to chip in with her story. "My ex and I were college sweethearts. We came from Guangxi, a poor province. He was kind but timid."

"Typical Chinese intellectual," comments Ah Du.

"Yes. After we graduated from college, he got a job as a librarian in Beijing, making only three hundred yuan per month. I was a schoolteacher, making five hundred yuan per month. He lived in his dorm with his roommates, and as a teacher, I lived with my roommates. We couldn't afford to rent an apartment."

"In those days, if you didn't work for a *waiqi,* a foreign company, or weren't a corrupt official or the relative of a corrupt official, you had no chance of buying a flat, " says Gigi, who understands the situation of the art teacher.

"Like many young, ambitious people, we managed to stay in Beijing, the city of opportunities, but we didn't have a place of our own. The only time we had together was when our roommates were not around," the art teacher said.

"So sad," says Lulu, shaking her head.

"We lived such a sad life for five years. Finally, my school assigned me a twelve-square-meter flat in an old building. There were many cockroaches, and the flat had no private bathroom or kitchen. I had to run fifty meters to use the public restroom," the art teacher exclaims.

"Life is about struggling," I add.

"As I struggled to survive, my former roommate Colorful Clouds appeared," the art teacher said.

"Colorful Clouds?" Lulu and I can't believe it when we hear the familiar name.

The art teacher nods.

"She wasn't smart enough to get into our college, but she sat in on the classes. She wrote love letters to our teacher. Our teacher thought she was shallow. Later, she seduced the father of a classmate and went to Beijing with him. We later heard that she married an old American and went to the United States."

"Sounds like a manipulative bitch!" chimes in another girl who isn't familiar with Colorful Clouds' notoriety.

"By the time I saw her, she had become the wife of a handsome American physicist and the mother of three children. She came back to Beijing and stayed at the Great Wall Sheraton." The art teacher's sob story continues.

"A posh hotel!" I say.

"She called me up and invited me to the free breakfast the hotel provided. I saw her act like a queen in front of me . . ."

"Who does she think she is? She only uses men," Lulu says.

"That is the whole point. No matter how we dislike her, through divorce and marriage, she could afford to stay in a nice hotel. What about me? I was a hard-working woman with a college degree, and a good and faithful wife, but I lived a poor hopeless life without even my own bathroom!" The art teacher cries out.

"Nowadays, the world is for bad girls. What is that saying again? Good girls go to heaven . . ." Gigi says.

"Bad girls go everywhere," I add.

The art teacher nods. "I realized it, too. After ten years of marriage, I finally felt it was so stupid to be a good girl. Love and faith are meaningless when they can't give you a place with a private bathroom. I left my ex."

"What do you feel now?"

"It feels damn good to be a bad girl. I'm going to Australia with my new boyfriend next month!"

Lan Huahua tells her story. She is a new singer at Beibei's Chichi Entertainment Company.

"There was no particular reason for my divorce. Everybody I knew divorced, but I was still married, so it made me look boring."

"You divorced your husband just because you didn't want to look boring?" asks Gigi, sounding shocked.

"As a singer, the last thing you want people to think is that you're boring," says Lan Huahua.

"A good voice is not enough?" Gigi still can't believe her audacity.

"Of course not. To become a star, a celebrity, you have to have interesting things about yourself to tell the media. Divorce is just my first plan. If necessary, I should also be prepared to become a single mother, a lesbian, or a bi."

POPULAR PHRASES

CHILE MA: Have you eaten yet? Traditional Chinese greeting, equal to "How are you?" This phrase expresses the importance that food plays in Chinese society.

LILE MA: Have you divorced yet? A new Chinese greeting, since the divorce rate in China is skyrocketing.

WAIQI: Foreign enterprise. With the market economy, those Chinese who are able to land a job with a foreign enterprise make several times more than their domestically employed countrymen. These people are both admired and resented by other Chinese.

13

A Kid in a Candy Store

Lulu, CC, and I have just finished drinks on the roof terrace of the Beijing Grand Hotel. As we come out of the elevator, we notice a forty-something American staring at us. His eyes almost pop out behind his thick glasses.

He clears his throat, as he walks toward us to make conversation, "Excuse me, ladies. I'm James, a banker from the States and new in Beijing. I haven't talked to any young Chinese people before. May I talk to you for a few minutes?" We think this curly-haired pointy-nosed guy is a geek, but nobody shows it.

Lulu speaks for the three of us, "Yes, sure. What can we do for you?"

"Where did you go to school?" James asks. None of us expects such a question.

"Are you looking for alumni?" CC asks.

James decides to introduce himself, "I went to school at

Yale. Have you heard of Yale? It's a very old school, on the East Coast. I guess it's somewhat prestigious. Rupert Murdoch's wife graduated from there. She's Chinese, like you." James pathetically attempts to be subtle.

"Who is Rupert Murdoch?" We play dumb.

James has to switch the topic. "What do you like to do in your spare time?"

"Cooking!"

"Cleaning!"

"Sewing!"

We joke around.

"I guessed as much! Being a Chinese woman is difficult, isn't it? Because the society has many expectations of you! Do you want to know what I like to do in my spare time?"

James can't wait for us to say yes and starts to volunteer his long-prepared story.

"I love cars. I have a Mercedes E-class 420, a BMW 740, a Honda CRV, and an RV, but my favorite is my red Porsche convertible."

Look at him, trying to impress us with his Yale and his cars. I wonder if he thinks that we're local bar girls who have never seen foreigners before. I do a quick study of the hotel lobby. Most of the women are accompanied by men who look much older than they. Perhaps James has been standing in the lobby, eyeing the girls that pass by and awaiting his chance. He may think we're easy targets, but his pickup lines are lousy.

CC, Lulu, and I plan to go to The Den. James offers to hail a cab for us. After we get into the Volkswagen taxi, James squeezes in before we can say no.

He stares at us with shining eyes and says, "You are all very beautiful. It's a cultured kind of beauty, different from so many of the other Chinese girls I've seen in Beijing. You," he points to me. "You have that kind of innocent beauty, with a touch of punk, an extremely mysterious combination." He points to Lulu. "You are gentle, but your eyes have fire in them." He points to CC. "You look like Gong Li."

We look at one another, giving a what-a-nerd facial expression to each other. Nobody says a word.

The Den is located in Sanlitun, Beijing's bar district. It's known as the Meat Market. Every night trendy Chinese girls with long hair and plucked eyebrows haunt The Den. They are willing to try anything, without any limits. They dance dirty and wantonly cast their eyes left and right, looking for an opportunity, looking for romance, the corners of their mouths twisted with desire and boredom. Nevertheless, we love to go to The Den once in a while because of the DJ who plays 1970s and 1980s retro Euro house music.

The decor is trendy and funky. The whole bar is decked out in red, reminiscent of the madness of the Cultural Revolution. Antique carved mahogany doors, copper door fittings, wrought-iron tables and chairs, carved lanterns, flickering candlelight, Cultural Revolution posters, Chairman Mao badges, HBO, EPSN, and MTV, Africans with braids, Japanese with small black-rimmed glasses and dyed-blond hair, Michael Jackson's androgynous wail, Ricky Martin's hot writhing Latin hips. This combination of cynicism and hysteria suits everybody's night mood perfectly.

Another reason my friends and I like The Den is because it isn't like other disco clubs, which are full of "head shakers"— teenagers who have taken too many yao tou wan pills, more commonly known as ecstasy.

As soon as we walk in, James realizes he is the only person

in the place wearing a suit. Looking at the young Chinese girls in miniskirts posing flirtatiously in the lights, he is pleasantly shocked. "Am I mistaken? Isn't this a paternalistic society based on Confucianism? Not long ago, women still had bound feet, but look at this! Girls are wearing colorful sandals, with toenails painted a rainbow of colors, sexy, liberal, and seductive."

It goes without saying that James sticks out like a sore thumb, and the reaction from the club-goers is not one of acceptance. He is completely oblivious to the funny looks that are being sent his way by everyone that sees him. I hear all the kids joking about him in Chinese as he walks around completely clueless. "I didn't realize it was senior's night tonight." "Looks like someone's father came to pick them up." "Is that guy *lost?*" It was embarrassing just being around him.

Tonight it's a typical Friday night. It's twelve o'clock. People are still streaming in, like the day is just beginning.

James keeps babbling, "Look at these guys, Nike baseball caps on their heads, wearing Ralph Lauren cotton shirts and Calvin Klein watches. Where does their money come from? Or are all these things counterfeit? What kind of work do they do, to be able to come to a place like this? This is truly an unbelievable, illogical country."

Neither CC nor Lulu bother to talk to James. They sing along with the music and start to dance. I have played the role of a listener and decide to escape. I say to James, "Enjoy yourself," then join my friends.

Half an hour later, James pushes through the crowd and comes back to us. "You girls are hyperactive. You simply don't stop. I'm an old man. I'm exhausted and have to go back to my hotel and lie down. Before I leave, I wonder if you can give me your phone numbers. Your English is good. I might need some help from you."

"Gee, he's audacious!" CC whispers to me.

I thought James might have felt like a kid in a candy store. With so many inviting, sexy girls, we thought he'd soon forget about us since we weren't impressed by his Yalie background. But to our surprise he comes back to us. Before I can say anything, Lulu has already given him our phone numbers.

"Why?" After James leaves with his sleek smile, I ask Lulu.

"If he can't get any girls here, there's no threat in him having our numbers," Lulu says. "The only reason that I gave him our numbers was I wanted him to disappear."

After The Den, Lulu, CC, and I go to a twenty-four-hour noodle shop. It's already two in the morning.

Just then Lulu's Nokia rings. "Damn, who's calling me so late! Lucky I'm not asleep!" she curses as she looks at the strange number on her mobile.

"Who is it?"

"Darling, it's me, James. Do you want to come around here for a drink? I've got red wine, white wine, whiskey, Jim Beam. I'd really like to see you."

"I'm going to sleep."

"Really, Lulu, please come! I like you. Do you know you're very beautiful? We'll have something to drink, put on some relaxing music, turn the lights down low, dance slowly, you'll find it very relaxing, and very romantic. Then we'll have a bubble bath. I'm good at massage, too. I can give you a full body massage. Then, I'll gently, patiently kiss you on the lips; kiss you all over your body . . ."

"Get out of here, you freak!" Lulu hangs up.

"Who does this guy think he is? Richard Gere or Pierce Brosnan or something? And with those fucking thick little glasses!" Lulu starts to swear again.

Before I can voice my opinion, my mobile rings to the tune of "Fur Elise."

"Niuniu, it's James. Sorry to be calling you so late. I'm leaving tomorrow, I don't know if we'll still have a chance to meet. You know, I like you. You're a sweet girl. You know that. I can't get you out of my mind. Let's have a drink, okay?"

"I only drink with Harvard men, not Yale men." I hang up.

CC's phone beeps.

"Beijing Hotel!" CC yells.

"Let's have some fun!" She picks up the phone. "Yes, I love men massaging me, and love even more a lover who can use his tongue. You sound amazing. But I can't go to your place. The twenty-four-hour security there is not very convenient. And you can never be sure they don't have hidden cameras!" CC strings James along, barely containing her laughter.

"Then what will we do? I want to hold your body right now."

"Well, why don't you come to my place? I'm home alone, my parents are away."

"Okay, I'll come over. What's your address?"

"Number Nine, Donghua Gate. The taxi driver will know it."

"Okay, see you soon."

"Okay, bye-bye, sweetie."

After CC has hung up, I ask, "What was that address?"

"Beijing Public Security Bureau."

POPULAR PHRASES

SANLITUN: A district of Beijing that houses many foreign embassies; known for its night life and bars.

YAO TOU WAN: "Head-shaking tablets," better known as Ecstasy. Drug use is becoming increasingly popular and hard to control among Chinese youth.

14

Chinese Beauty in Western Eyes

Colorful Clouds came from the Guangxi countryside.

By sleeping with a guy from the city, she managed to leave her native village.

By marrying an American man forty years her senior, she managed to leave China.

By divorcing her husband and marrying his grandson, physicist Brian, she became an upper-middle-class American suburban housewife.

Forty-two-year-old Colorful Clouds, a has-been small-time actress, thinks her men have helped her successfully upgrade her race and status. Now is the time for her to return to China to show off. In Beijing, she finds every journalist she knows, including me, whom she met back in St. Louis. "You see, I'm an actress and a self-made Chinese-American success story who drives a Jaguar. My fellow Chinese should admire me!"

Inspired by the fact that the Oscar-winning film *Crouching Tiger, Hidden Dragon* received only a lukewarm reception in China, I want to do a story on different perceptions of beauty. After I talk to my friend Yi, who is CEO at ChineseSister.com, she says to me, "Why don't we organize an online forum on East-West concepts of beauty on my Web site? You can do a story about it!"

Colorful Clouds hears the news about the forum and begs me to invite her as a special guest so that she can have her fifteen minutes of fame.

Special guests that day are Colorful Clouds; Ken, an executive at CC's firm Ed Consulting; a couple of foreign students; and a Chinese movie director. CC has told me that Ken is a Western expert at chasing Chinese women. Colorful Clouds is wearing a low-cut black velvet dress and a fake diamond necklace—and yellow high-heeled shoes that clash with the rest of her outfit.

She has brought a stack of photos of her house, her cars, her husband, and her beach house. This was the moment she had been waiting for: everybody in China would now admire her.

As soon as the forum starts, all of the questions from the people online are directed at Ken and the foreign students.

Purple Lemon: "Why is it that Westerners' Chinese wives are always considered ugly by Chinese people? Sometimes, there's a huge difference—the guy is tall, the woman is short. And why are the girls who hang out with foreigners always so wild?"

Ken and the foreign students look at each other dumbly, and finally a tall guy called Dennis replies:

"It's not that we Westerners can't tell the difference between ugly and beautiful Chinese people, but we pay more attention to personality. Some girls may not be attractive on the outside, but they are thoughtful and independent, and to me that is beautiful. As for the question of height, I don't think it's a problem. I know that you Chinese probably consider height important, because you are all generally short. But I don't care about a girl's height that much."

"Sometimes"—no one has spoken to Colorful Clouds, but she butts in anyway—"I think many Westerners like the feeling of a small woman, especially in moments of passion. They can wrap a small woman up in their arms; it's very masculine and dominating. Am I right?" Colorful Clouds glances hotly at the young foreign students and Ken.

They are a little embarrassed.

So-So: "Why do Westerners think Gong Li and Lucy Liu are so beautiful? Why don't we Chinese think so?"

Lily: "Especially Lucy Liu, she is very plain. We think Ning Jing and Zhao Wei are pretty. What do you think?"

Ken laughs. "Personally, Gong Li and Lucy Liu aren't my favorite stars. My favorite Chinese celebrity is Faye Wong. But I do think they all have some things in common: individuality, style, and they're good actresses, not just pretty to look at. I think Zhao Wei is quite cute. She's a comedy actress. I think she could be made up to look really sexy."

At that moment, Colorful Clouds interrupts again. "Let me say a few words since I used to live in Hollywood. Lucy Liu and Gong Li both have full lips. Full, large lips are very attractive to Western men, because they're very important when kissing or giving blow jobs. And what's more, their faces are very well defined, with high cheekbones. That is what Westerners like."

Colorful Clouds will not rest until she gets enough attention.

Foxy adds, "Chinese people like small, cherry mouths and homely beauty. And Westerners like a sexy, wild beauty."

"Why do Chinese like small, cherry mouths?" Dennis asks. People on the Internet immediately post replies.

Snuff Bottle: "Smiling without showing your teeth is beautiful. If your mouth is extremely small, then when you smile, it's difficult for your teeth to show."

So-So: "A small mouth means that a woman doesn't talk too much. A quiet woman is a beautiful woman."

Colorful Clouds continues in an authoritative tone: "You're all missing the most important point, and that is the Freudian perspective on this question. A woman's mouth symbolizes a woman's genitals. The smaller her mouth, the smaller her genitals, and the more stimulation for men. This is what the Chinese man is after."

Oval Face: "I'd like to ask the French foreign student, Sophie, what kind of Asian men do you like?"

Sophie: "I like Jackie Chan's sense of humor and Bruce Lee's body. But if I were looking for a husband, I would probably go for Tony Leung. He's gentle, sophisticated, and handsome. In *The Lover*, his heavenly butt was unforgettable. I also like men who can cook."

A German student called Marcus says, "Can I ask the Chinese people, what kind of Westerners you think are good-looking?"

The people online leap in:

Bitter Cauliflower: "Ricky Martin."

Shortie: "James Bond."

China Ball: "Britney Spears."

Little Thing: "Catherine Zeta-Jones."

Lovely: "Richard Gere."

Yellow Chrysanthemum: "Audrey Hepburn."

Wolf-in-Sheep's-Clothing: "Sharon Stone."

Fleet-Foot: "Al Gore."

"What? You think even a geek like Gore is good-looking?" American student Sophie cries.

Fleet-Foot: "He looks scholarly, and he's better looking than Bush."

"But Bush is affable, don't you think?" Sophie rebuts.

"Chinese people don't think Gong Li is sexy or beautiful? Is that because they're jealous?" Dennis asks.

Go-Go: "She looks too local!"

The Chinese director, who has not yet expressed an opinion, finally speaks: "Chinese people think that 'Western style' is attractive, and that 'local style' is unattractive. Why? 'Local style' is like ourselves. Why is being like ourselves considered unattractive? It shows that Chinese people do not have any self-confidence."

Last Samurai: "I agree. Ancient Chinese people had self-confidence, and their own sense of aesthetics. In the Tang dynasty, we liked full-figured women with short eyebrows. It was totally our own sense of beauty. In modern times, our aesthetics are all Western: long legs, tall, round eyes, double eyelids, high nose, white skin. Girls are having cosmetic surgery on their eyes, dying their hair blond—it's not natural at all. Why do they think their narrow eyes and short stature are ugly? We should create our own aesthetics."

The Chinese director nods. "This is exactly what I'm talking about. Our ancestors actually had a strong sense of aesthetics. But unlike in the past, modern Chinese lack confidence."

New Shoes: "I'm proud that China's ugly women can become beautiful women on the world stage! I applaud China's dogs becoming Oriental sex goddesses overseas! I am happy that those undesirable Chinese women who can't find a boyfriend in China can be in high demand in the West."

The hour-and-a-half online forum ends. ChineseSister.com thanks the special guests and then hands out mugs, bags, and T-shirts.

Colorful Clouds is extremely pleased, and tells me, "I am a sex expert. The kids all worship me. Some had me sign their T-shirts as a souvenir. I really need people to worship me—it's such a wonderful feeling. Oh yeah, that Ken, he's a real lady-killer! If I had the time, I'd take him for a spin."

15

Colorful Clouds: "I Married My Husband's Grandson!"

Colorful Clouds shows up unexpectedly as Lulu, Beibei, CC, and I are having a manicure in a beauty salon called the Rich Wife.

She greets Lulu, who she knows is a big-time editor at *Women's Friends*, a magazine with one million circulation. Today, Lulu wears low-rise jeans with a Bebe T-shirt. She is also sporting newly highlighted hair and red stilettos. Her face is both fair and full of color and energy.

"Niuniu says you can make any woman famous in China. You have to write about me in your magazine. I'm a miracle in the West," Colorful Clouds says vainly.

"Our fashion magazine mainly features models," Lulu says, hoping Colorful Clouds will take the hint.

"My husband looks like a model. Maybe you can publish his picture instead of mine. The headline can be 'How to Win the Heart of Prince Charming.' " Colorful Clouds turns to Beibei. "You should find investors to make a movie out of my story. My only request is that I will play myself and be provided with a caravan with a bathroom, the same as Gong Li gets. "

"Don't you know that nowadays in order to obtain fame, you have to make morality irrelevant?" Beibei asks Colorful Clouds.

"It has never been a problem for me," Colorful Clouds says with a wave of her hand.

"Many people use cheap ways to make up sensational stories in order to shock the audience or the readers. Can you do that?" Beibei asks again.

"My specialty." Colorful Clouds answers eagerly.

"But still, too many women come to me and tell their bad-girls stories in order to get famous. Is yours any different?" Beibei is still not impressed.

"I married my former husband's grandson. Who can compete with me?" Colorful Clouds proudly announces, welcoming all challengers.

"No one, I guess," Lulu and Beibei answer together.

Colorful Clouds was born in a small village in Guangxi province. She claims to be of Zhuang nationality, although some say that she is pure-blooded southern Chinese, and the only reason she calls herself a Zhuang is because nowadays being a minority is cooler than being a Han.

In the early 1980s, she was attending classes at the Guangxi Art Institute. Once, a director from the Guangxi Film Production Company came to see his daughter, her roommate. Colorful Clouds talked the director into getting her a small part in an avant-garde film. Then, she seduced the long-haired director, her roommate's father. They ran off to Beijing.

In Beijing, she met a local photographer and told him that she was a movie star in Thailand who had come to China to study Chinese. The man believed it and fell for her. She dumped the old director, whose Guangxi accent was considered low-class in the big city. Through her new boyfriend's connections, she started to mix with the foreign diplomatic crowd. After seeing the foreigners' lifestyle, Colorful Clouds decided she wanted to go overseas. Of course, her first choice was the United States.

But how? No diplomat wanted to marry her. To them she was nothing more than an opportunistic local, and beneath their notice.

Colorful Clouds met a seventy-year-old American man named David on the street. He happened to specialize in false marriages to foreign women. He had earned $50,000 by marrying two Guangdong women. He told Colorful Clouds she had two choices. She could have a false marriage: he wouldn't touch her, but she had to pay him $30,000 cash within three years. Or she could have a real marriage, and not refuse any of his sexual demands.

To a Chinese person, 30,000 RMB, let alone $30,000, was an astronomical figure. In those days people worshipped "multi-thousand-aires," and didn't even know that millionaires existed. Colorful Clouds agreed to a real marriage with David, and thus joined the throng of people leaving China in the 1980s.

Later, Colorful Clouds tells many people about the awful experience of sharing a bed with a man who is older than your grandfather in order to obtain an American green card.

"The old man made all kinds of demands. He used waxes, Vaseline, and other toys I don't feel like getting into details about. He was a pervert!" Apparently Colorful Clouds, despite all her bragging, still had a little bit of Chinese modesty buried somewhere deep inside her. Every night she spent in bed with David was torture, but there was nothing she could do. She willingly tended to every one of his demands with a smile on her face, although on the inside she was filled with embarrassment, disgust, and shame.

But she also managed to win the sympathy of David's grandson, Brian.

David's family came from conservative Alabama. His children thought that David was a disgrace, earning money from fake marriages in China, each wife younger than the last, this latest even younger than his own grandson. They angrily cut off all contact with him.

It was only Brian, who was studying physics at Yale in New England and had seen something of the world, who sympathized with his grandfather. Brian came to visit him and his step-grandmother Colorful Clouds. Young, handsome, active, and erudite, Brian excited Colorful Clouds. After sleeping with that shriveled old man for years, the sight of such a young man struck her dumb. While Brian was showering, Colorful Clouds heard the sound of the water and went to the bathroom to look at him. The outline of Brian's young body, especially his protruding butt, made Colorful Clouds sprout lust. She gazed at Brian's fresh, blooming silhouette and thought how wonderful it would be to lie down with him every night.

While Colorful Clouds was in the midst of her daydream, Brian turned and saw her.

Colorful Clouds knew that although she was not considered a pretty woman in China, her high forehead, slightly protruding lips, and high cheekbones were quite attractive in the States. She actually believed that Brian thought she was very sexy. Seeing his step-grandmother, this Chinese woman, spying on him, Brian instinctively covered himself with a towel and blurted out, "You're sick!"

Colorful Clouds understood. He had not said, "You're so sexy."

Colorful Clouds ran to her room, crying like a crazy woman.

And truly, she was crazy—crazy to go home again. At such a young age, she had married an old American, come to America, where she was unable to study, had no friends, and every day faced that rough, shriveled, disgusting, greedy old body.

Was this the American Dream?

In the past two years, she didn't dare see Chinese people. Some of her classmates back home had already become hot artists; others were diplomats wives, but she? Apart from looking after an old man, she was only holding simple English conversations with a bunch of Mexican and South American immigrants at the local adult school.

Colorful Clouds thought and thought, and pretended to commit suicide by tying her bathrobe sash into a noose.

As she had expected, the kindhearted Brian burst in and held her back. "Don't. Don't do something stupid like that."

"How can I disgrace myself like this? How can I humiliate myself all for the sake of coming to America?" Colorful Clouds started to perform: "I want to die. I always dreamed of being a Hollywood film star and traveling the world. But I'm a child of the third world. Even in the third world, I was in the poor position of having no relatives overseas, so I had no other choice but to sell myself. I thought that by marrying old David I could get closer to my dreams. But in America, I'm just an old man's nursemaid and sex toy.

"I wanted one day to star in a movie about my life. This

movie would introduce the world to my people, to our folk songs, our customs, and the village I grew up in, that old banyan tree and the big bell in our village, the girls with their silver bracelets. But now I have no self-confidence at all! My life is totally meaningless. Before, when I was in Beijing, I'd often discuss existentialism with artists, but now I truly understand the futility of life."

Colorful Clouds looked into Brian's eyes, and touched his youthful face. "I don't want to do anything wrong to your grandfather. But I am a *young* woman! My mistake was that I loved America too much. Ever since I was young, America was always a dream, an ideal. I am a slave to America."

Brian dried Colorful Clouds' tears. "I'm sorry. It's my fault. I shouldn't judge you. Don't say any more. It's my fault."

"No, Brian, please don't stop me. I've been in the United States for two years, but never before have I had the chance to talk about my feelings. Everything is all bottled up inside. I need to keep talking."

"All right, I'm listening to you."

"I was eighteen years old before I went to the city. At the time I had been admitted to our province's university. Our family was very poor and couldn't afford anything. When I left, my mother gave me a basket of eggs and asked me to take them to the city. The eggs were laid by our family's hen. When that hen was small, I used to carry it around like you'd carry around a small child. I caught the long-distance bus to Nanning, and then a local bus to the university. It was the first time I had seen such big roads, with so many cars—I was petrified. When I crossed the road, I was careless and dropped the basket of eggs on the ground. They all broke. Everything my family had!

"It was at university, on my city classmates' stereo, that I first heard the Beatles. Never before had I heard such beautiful music.

I could listen to 'Yesterday' and 'Let It Be' a hundred times without getting sick of them. Later I also saw them on the television, with their guitars, long hair, and big boots—they were so handsome. The Beatles were the soundtrack to my university life."

"I like the Beatles too."

"At university, I was most jealous of Yoko Ono. John Lennon loved her so much, he even changed his middle name to Ono. Their documentary film, *Imagine,* was really great. I dreamed that, just like Yoko Ono, I could be loved by a Western man. After graduation, I drifted to Beijing. I wanted to meet all sorts of Western men. But they only wanted to sleep with me; none of them wanted to marry me. Only your grandfather, David. I should be grateful to him."

Colorful Clouds gazed at Brian's clear eyes and curling eyelashes. "I'm sorry, Brian. I am a filthy woman. I shouldn't like you. But I really do like you. I like your knowledge, your wisdom, your energy, your youth. I shouldn't. I should die." Colorful Clouds already knew that her little act had worked.

"Don't speak like that. Don't."

Colorful Clouds kissed Brian.

As she had expected, Brian welcomed Colorful Clouds' warmth. Exotic background, suffering, poverty, and her hunger for freedom and Western culture—plus her thick lips and flaming gaze, a package that definitely sells!

Colorful Clouds and Brian's unlikely affair led to Colorful Clouds becoming pregnant. This was exactly as she had planned. Because of this pregnancy, she divorced David and became Brian's wife. She didn't even have to change her married name. Colorful Clouds is extremely fond of her foreign surname. She tells me smugly, "When people see my name, they can't tell whether I'm Asian or white!"

16

It's Not a Fairy Tale

After marrying a handsome husband, Colorful Clouds finally felt proud, and resumed contact with her old acquaintances.

Brian is a physicist. He did not make Colorful Clouds work, and wanted only that she realize her dreams of leading a happy life and becoming a great performer.

Colorful Clouds became a middle-class housewife and mother of three. She vowed solemnly to break into Hollywood. She believed that her skin color and appearance, while not sought after in China, would be liked by these Westerners.

She and Brian moved the family to southern California to help her make it in Hollywood. But after countless auditions, she never won a part. Even worse, her appearance, which she thought was so special, was common in Southeast Asia, especially Thailand. She was even more common in the States than she was in China. At least in China people used to admire her Zhuang ethnic features.

What made Colorful Clouds especially unhappy was that the Chinese theater groups who visited the States had not hired her. After so many years, she appeared in only one feature movie—as a waitress in a Chinese restaurant, with a total of two lines.

As time passed, Brian became disappointed that Colorful Clouds had not found work and moved back to the Midwest. He began to feel that perhaps his mysterious wife was really just mediocre after all. Colorful Clouds watched Brian rush about making a living, getting older every day. He had much less hair than before, but much more of a belly. The handsome air he had before they were married was gone. He had become a middle-aged man. The differences between them grew greater, and they even began sleeping in separate beds. But her penchant for young men remained unchanged.

To kill time, Colorful Clouds began to hang out in the coffee shops at the University of Missouri, and there she met a lot of young men. Many of them became her lovers. Colorful Clouds had several lovers, but she still felt empty and did not know what to do with her time.

Colorful Clouds often telephoned me since I was a student there back then. She needed an audience to listen to her story—to listen to her show off, and vent, and curse everyone for her situation. She sometimes went overboard, blaming everyone and everything but herself: this girlfriend stabbed her in the back, that lover slept with her cousin, and on and on. I was like a garbage dump, taking all of Colorful Clouds' rubbish.

Colorful Clouds was a gifted liar. Her real life bore no resemblance whatsoever to the life she recounted. Sometimes she said Brian had something going with another Chinese woman. This woman, who had abandoned her husband and children in China to establish herself in the United States, was a minor actress, nowhere near as good as Colorful Clouds. Colorful Clouds plotted how to catch the adulterers in the act. Sometimes she said that her husband was the most faithful man on earth, who only had eyes for her. I never pointed out the inconsistencies in Colorful Clouds' stories. I understood that she relied on intuition. If she wanted something, she would get it, whether it was in the real world or in the world of her imagination.

17

Attention Whores

When I returned to China from the United States, the huge changes that the country has gone through were immediately clear. Most people used to take pride in their humbleness and conformity. Not only was attracting attention something that didn't interest them, it was something that people were genuinely afraid of. There is an old Chinese saying: "The bird that flies ahead of the flock is the first to be shot down." Now, with the opening up of the country and the new market economy, it seems as though everyone I meet is a braggart and an attention-seeker. Being different from the crowd is actually encouraged. These ambitious birds have no fear of being shot down.

Fifteen years ago, if you were a performer, you were guaranteed to become a household name by showing your face at the annual Spring Festival gala produced by CCTV. Nowadays you have to be not only creative but also shameless to become famous because everybody realizes that attention can bring money.

In cultural circles, there are four popular ways of seeking fame.

First, create controversy. For example, claim you are gay or bisexual. Publicize your love triangle stories, your affairs with married people, or even make them up. Pay a foreign stud to write a book about your wild sex life entitled *My Sexy Chinese Doll.* The whole point is to invite criticism and create shock. If people start to bad-mouth you, ding! Your mission is accomplished: you are known and fame sells.

Second, fake your credentials and background. For example, if your mother is a shop clerk, you would tell people that she owns several chain stores. A Danish tourist says hi to you in Chinese on a bus? You tell the media that you dated the cousin of the Danish prince. You took some open university courses at Yale? Claim you got an M.B.A. degree there.

Third, beg the government to ban you. Find connections in the Ministry of Propaganda and talk them into including your movies or your books in their blacklist. It's free advertising and attracts the attention of a worldwide audience.

Fourth, insult the establishment. You're a little potato, but by insulting famous people, you can become famous. For example, sling mud at the hottest movie star, or claim Lu Xun's books and Zhang Yimo's movies are trash.

Colorful Clouds got her first fifteen minutes of fame by being a sex expert in the online beauty forum, then she got her second fifteen minutes of fame by telling the Chinese media that she married her former husband's grandson. Now she is back in Columbia, Missouri, once again just an average housewife. She feels lonely and misses her fleeting fame in China. I'm on a business trip in St. Louis, covering the talk of China's best-known wandering poet Sing. The University of Missouri literature department has invited Sing to give a reading at the university. It's his first reading since winning a major book award.

"I've got to drive to St. Louis for this event! It's a good chance to get noticed!" Colorful Clouds tells me excitedly on the phone.

As Colorful Clouds expects, the poetry reading attracts a big crowd. She comes, dragging her fair-haired Eurasian kids.

Sing has lived in exile since 1989, and his political poetry has gained him the reputation of being China's Aleksandr Solzhenitsyn. After the poetry reading, Colorful Clouds stands up and, cradling her sleeping child, let fly at the wandering poet.

"Sing, before I left China, in 1984, I heard you speak at the Guangxi Art Institute. At the time, I was a university student, just arrived in Nanning from the country. I didn't know much of the world, and I adored you. Now more than ten years have passed, and I've been in the United States for over ten years. Why is everything you say still the same old stuff? Are you that fond of the good old days? If not, why hasn't your style evolved at all? And your English isn't even as good as those of us who are just housewives here in America!"

It's clear that Colorful Clouds is trying to insult Sing at this refined poetry-reading event in order to get attention. Sing is so angry he can't speak. His American translator is also scratching his head and doesn't know how to translate Colorful Clouds' words for the American audience.

Colorful Clouds decides to go whole hog and translates her own words into English. Turning to face the audience, she relates what she has just accused Sing of. As she speaks in her sloppy English to the shocked crowd, her eyes are wide and her face is flushed with emotion. Her arms wave vigorously and violently from side to side, as if accusing the audience of the same shortcomings merely for attending the event.

Some members of the audience are unhappy with Colorful Clouds. "How can someone be so rude to our crusader for democracy?" they say. Others just enjoy the show.

Sing controls his temper and replies with a sort of calm pity in his voice. "Chinese like you who have come to the United States are just like many of the Chinese literati. You jealously attack me, a Chinese poet with international standing." Getting visibly angrier as he goes on, Sing contends, "Of course, you have an ulterior motive. You are in cahoots with the Chinese government! It's obvious you received a Communist Party education from a young age!"

"True," Colorful Clouds rebuts, as if she is a lawyer who has just found a crack in her opponent's case. "I did receive a Communist Party education from a young age. And what about you? You grew up in America, did you? Graduated from Harvard, did you? Did you receive that kind of education? From what I hear, no university in the States would take you because your English is so poor."

At this point, Sing loses all composure and yells at Colorful Clouds. "Chinese literati are just like you. When it comes down to it, you are all just jealous of my international reputation!"

"Your reputation? What reputation? I heard you moved your family to Sweden. How come you haven't won a Nobel Prize yet? I've heard that fifteen years ago, in order to stop Gao Xingjian from winning the prize, you gave him the wrong address of the Swedish Embassy in Beijing and made him miss his appointment. Oh, and by the way, you really do flatter me. Since when have I been one of the literati. I've always just been an ignorant housewife."

"You have obviously been put up to this by some jealous Chinese who wanted you to come here to make trouble!"

"No one put me up to this, and I couldn't be bothered being jealous of you. My husband makes enough money. I live in a rich neighborhood. Why would I be jealous of you? I ask a couple of questions you don't like, and suddenly I'm making trouble?"

Sing whispers something to his translator, and the translator turns to the security guards. They escort Colorful Clouds and her children out of the auditorium. Some people say to one another, "This woman is crazy. Thank God, she is leaving." Some stand up to protest: "A crusader for democracy in a democratic country who can't even tolerate different opinions. There's no point being here." They leave the auditorium.

Colorful Clouds doesn't mind being escorted out of the poetry reading. She is an opportunist. "I got the attention I need," she tells me afterward. "Maybe I should call the *People's Daily* and tell them how I defended China's pride by debating with a traitor! If they write about me, I might get a role in the TV series *From Beijing to San Francisco!*"

POPULAR PHRASES

MAREN: To criticize or insult people.

ZHENGYI: Fight and discuss; controversy.

TOUJIZHE: An opportunist. Prior to the opening of the market economy, there was no room or need for opportunists in Chinese society. Today the culture has changed, and opportunists, seeking both money and attention, have sprouted up all over the country.

18

Me, Me, Me!

After Colorful Clouds has a verbal fight with the dissident poet Sing, she makes headline news in the Chinese community as she expected. As a result of this temporary fame, she gets the small role she desperately desired on *From Beijing to San Francisco*.

She has returned to Beijing to shoot the TV series and to seek more attention.

She calls me. Once again I am at the Rich Wife on Xinyuan Street having my hair done with Lulu and Beibei when Colorful Clouds comes in.

She asks the hairdresser to dye her hair green.

"You want a head of Norwegian Woods?" I tease her.

"Isn't green the most in color of the year?" Colorful Clouds answers triumphantly, indicating that she is up-to-date about the latest fashion and trends.

"I'm not sure if that would suit someone your age," suggests the hairdresser.

When Colorful Clouds hears that, she glares at the girl, "Are you saying I'm old? How dare you? Now listen here, I've just come back from America. In America, the customer is king. If I slip and fall in your store, you have to compensate me a million dollars. You understand? So, whatever I say goes, and don't talk back to me."

The hairdresser mutters to herself quietly, "Who cares where you are from."

Colorful Clouds is wearing a white gown and enjoys the head massage from the hairdresser. She starts to spout:

"I'm nearly forty f 'ing years old. If I don't have fun now, I'll run out of time. In America, I'm f 'ing bored to death as a housewife. Nobody pays attention to me. I had to come to Beijing to hang out." Colorful Clouds is already forty-two, but she always says she is "nearly forty."

"While you're hanging out here, what about your three kids?" I ask.

"Those little bastards—in America I was like their nanny. This time, my husband is so thrilled to hear that I've got a role in *From Beijing to San Francisco,* he says he'll give me all the support I need. We've found a Mexican nanny to look after the kids for a while, and teach them some Spanish!"

"Where have you been since you came back to China this time?" I ask.

"I went to Shenzhen and Guangzhou. In Shenzhen I'm an old fart. The people and the buildings there are no more than thirty years old. In Guangzhou, I bumped into some of my old pals, Xiang the singer and Flower doing avant-garde theater. Xiang has opened a bar, loads of gays love going there. When

Xiang saw me, she said, 'Girl, I thought you'd become a living fossil.' They're f 'ing crazy down there. Bands from all over the world come and perform. All sorts of bastards hang out there. I was out till two or three in the morning every day and slept over at the houses of people I didn't even know, or at the homes of friends of friends. I haven't been wild like that for years.

"One thing made me pretty angry. I hadn't seen Flower in years; I don't know when he gave himself such a stupid girly name. As soon as he saw me, he called me Silly Cunt, saying everybody knew I slept around behind my hubby's back in the States. I slapped him, he slapped me back, others came to stop us. 'You used to be pals. You haven't seen each other for over ten years, and as soon as you see each other you start fighting—what's going on?' Then, guess what Flower said? He said he had never considered me a friend and walked away. I've got a 2,500-square-foot house in Missouri, as well as a holiday home in Key West, Florida, and kids who speak English, French, and Spanish. That bastard rents a 20-square-meter flat in a Guangzhou suburb. He is simply a sore loser!" Colorful Clouds' U.S. wealth is her answer to everyone's criticism of her. Just like so many other Chinese today, being wealthy is a justification for being rude.

"Why do people like Flower gossip about me? Isn't it just because they're jealous? We all had the same starting point, the same small-town start and no advantages. Now I have it all and they don't. How could they possibly be comfortable around me? Of course they're jealous. They think I am trashy, so what? I don't care. I am welcomed by American men."

Colorful Clouds speaks haughtily, unable to restrain her superiority complex as an American Chinese. She always dreamed of living in America, even if she is a bored housewife who spends her time dreaming of returning to China and showing off to those she left behind. Beibei deliberately coughs. She despises Colorful Clouds' vanity.

"Did you get the chance to meet younger people?" I ask Colorful Clouds, just to be polite.

"F___, aren't Beijing and Shanghai chicks all playing the games I was playing ten years ago? Sleeping with Westerners, hanging out at embassies, going out to bars, all thinking they're so 'alternative.' But it seems to me they come pretty cheap. Häagen-Dazs ice cream and T.G.I. Friday's are expensive in their eyes. Foreign men can get laid just by paying for one meal at the Hard Rock Cafe or offering ten minutes of English tutoring! In those days, I had my birthday party at the Norwegian Embassy. Imported beer was shipped in by the truckloads. The rock star Jian Jian wanted to come to my party, but even he had to queue up outside in the cold.

"I really have contempt for these local chick writers. They write about oral sex or Western boyfriends and think they're so cutting-edge, so brave, so feminist, so superior, so revolutionary, and *so* scandalous. From old Chinese books, we know that Chinese have been doing oral sex since ancient times. The girls think they are westernized, but they are just hillbillies. It really is a case of when there are no tigers on the mountain, the monkey is king. We, the tigers of China, have all either left the country or gone into business. They talk of women's liberation? I'm the original liberated Chinese woman! I'm the one young women should be worshipping! My next move will be raising money for making a film about my experiences. The movie will be called *A Chinese Woman's Sexual Adventure in North America*. We'd need white, black, brown, and Eurasian male actors!"

The hairdresser is coloring Colorful Clouds' hair, and the chemical smell makes us all a little dizzy. Lulu and Beibei, their heads hidden under the hair dryers, listlessly inspecting their fingernails, refusing to give Colorful Clouds the attention that she desperately wants. I'm also silent because I've heard these same words too many times.

Finally, the hairdresser mutters with contempt, "It sounds like the UN General Assembly. Will those actors be shipped in by the truckload or will a freight train be necessary?"

19

Acting Your Age

As I'm getting impatient with Colorful Clouds and her bragging, my boss Sean suggests that I tie her story into a feature about the moral decline and opportunism in China resulting from the rapid growth of the economy and the slow progress of democracy.

So I have to hang out with Colorful Clouds again.

"Rich and nice-looking, I can have a good time in China." Colorful Clouds starts our day by telling me this as I pick her up from her hotel. Knowing that she's my subject, she demands that I show her around and pay for everything. This time, she says, "Take me to the Red Moon. I've heard this place is famous for its good-looking waiters and male patrons."

This kind of place sounds not too bad to me. So I agree to drive her there and spend a few minutes sitting with her.

As soon as we sit down at the Red Moon, a tall, athletic young man gets Colorful Clouds' attention. She winks at the man. The man smiles back. She feels flattered. So she becomes bolder. She wiggles her finger to invite the man to come over to join us. As the man walks in our direction, she whispers, "Niuniu, I am who I am. Although I'm a mother of three children, this man cannot resist the temptation to meet me. Don't I look young!"

I have noticed that Colorful Clouds never wears her wedding ring in China.

"You'd better be careful." I warn her about the existence of xiao yazi, male prostitutes, before she takes off.

On the way home, I receive a phone call from Colorful Clouds, proudly saying that the man is not a little duck, but a college student who is intrigued by her elegance. She is going to take him out for dinner.

Half an hour later, I join my usual friends Lulu and Beibei at a teahouse. My phone rings again.

"Guess what? I can't believe Beijing people are still as rude as they were when I left here many years ago." It is Colorful Clouds on the line.

"What happened?"

"The waiter came and asked, 'Are you and your son ready to order?' How dare he?" She's angry. "I do not look that old. I use Estée Lauder every day."

I tease Colorful Clouds. "Perhaps the waiter is jealous of your friend?"

"Perhaps!" says Colorful Clouds cheerfully.

After I hang up, my friends Beibei and Lulu ask me, "Who was that?"

"Colorful Clouds," I admit.

"The woman who thinks she's a double for Gong Li, but is really only double her size?" asks Beibei.

"The peasant woman who thinks she can become a member of the aristocracy by marrying her American grandson?" asks Lulu.

They both dislike Colorful Clouds.

I don't know what to say. I don't see Colorful Clouds as a friend, but she always contacts me. I don't want to offend her, a run-around full-time gossiper, because of possible reprisals.

Around midnight, I'm awakened by Colorful Clouds' phone call.

"Niuniu, help me! I've been robbed!"

"Where are you?" I can't help but feel a little sorry for her.

"I'm in a hotel room. I took the young man here after dinner. We were going to do it, so I said I'd take a shower first. But when I walked out of the shower, he was gone! My purse and money were all gone! Please come and get me!"

I sigh, thinking to myself, "This is what I get for always saying yes to people like Colorful Clouds."

"Bring some clothes on your way. He even stole my clothes!" says Colorful Clouds.

"He probably thinks they'd fit his mother well!" I say to myself as I head out the door, cursing Colorful Clouds' massive reluctance to harness her pumped-up ego and act her age.

20

Let's Rock

A typical Saturday late morning. I'm hanging out at Lulu's apartment. We have just finished working out to Cindy Crawford's aerobics video and had taken a sauna in the new clubhouse. Lulu is teaching me how to *baotang*, make soup, Cantonese-style. Soup is the gem of Cantonese cuisine. Cantonese people believe that soup functions as a tonic and can do amazing things for the human body.

"My father is from Canton," says Lulu. "He told me that to be a good wife in Canton, a woman has to learn to *baotang*. Cantonese put everything into their soup. They believe snake soup can reduce one's fever and turtle soup acts as an aphrodisiac for men."

Baotang takes time, often over three hours. The woman who makes it has to be patient. Lulu is very patient as she makes soup. Her dream is to be a good wife for a man she loves, but such a simple dream is hard to fulfill. She keeps bumping into married men and liars.

As we are making soup, Beibei arrives, bringing a big stack of music videos and live-concert DVDs. "Girls, I need you to *cehua* how to position our company's newest band, the Young Revolutionaries."

Cehua is one of those fashionable new Chinese words that can be used as a noun or a verb. When used as a verb, it means to plan, to promote, to publicize, to create a certain image. When used as a noun, it means people who work in such fields. A *cehua* can be an advertising campaign director, a movie producer, a publicist, or a marketing director. *Cehua* and entertainers' agents are two of the new white-collar jobs created by the market economy.

Beibei uses Lulu and me as her clients' *cehua* from time to time.

"Let's follow our usual custom. Makeover first, and then *cehua*," Lulu says as she goes to the bathroom to get the materials.

All three of us make a face pack. I choose a seaweed pack. Beibei selects black mud. Lulu uses milk and almond. Our faces are each a different color, like three witches sitting together. We eat fresh peaches and lounge on the sofa watching music videos, both classic and contemporary groups.

The Beatles' classic *Yellow Submarine*, with "I Want to Hold Your Hand."

Pink Floyd's *Dark Side of the Moon.*

Nirvana's *Nevermind.*

Westlife's *Flying Without Wings.*

Backstreet Boys' *Tell Me the Meaning of Being Lonely.*

'N Sync's *Bye Bye Bye.*

Watching Sting's solitary pride in *Desert Rose*, I again think of Len. In the music video, he is sitting alone regally in the backseat of a Jaguar S—type, chauffeured over the desert sands at full speed, the wind riffling through his hair. I always wondered where he was going and who he was going to meet. The mystery and sexiness that Sting gave off in that video gave me the same feeling I always got when I was with Len. Once we were riding along the highway in Len's Jaguar, when he suddenly stopped the car by the road and started to kiss me. At that moment I felt like the woman who was missing from the video, the one who should have been there from the beginning. "This is how that video was supposed to go," I thought to myself.

For a long time, whenever I saw a Jaguar, I thought of Len—this Len, who sometimes did crazy spontaneous things. After he had made love to me so many times, suddenly one day he said, "Don't fall in love with me. If you love me, I will hate you. I can never forgive women who love me." This announcement came out of nowhere and took me completely by surprise. What was so bad about being loved, and why was Len so afraid of it in the first place? I wondered what had happened in Len's past to make him so unwilling to let someone love him.

Now I am with my girlfriends. I'm happy, I'm confident, and I'm having fun. I tell myself, you don't need his twisted passion and pain anymore.

After watching Eminem's *My Name Is*, Beibei says, "I think we've found our inspiration. With a bit of brainstorming, I've come up with an idea for the Young Revolutionaries."

"How do you plan to position them?" I ask.

"Rebel meets Slacker meets 'To Revolt Is Good,' " Beibei smugly replies.

"Not bad. Revolt you definitely want. These days, everyone is cynical; you can't not be a rebel," Lulu agrees.

"I think they should have a little of the Backstreet Boys' youthful vigor, don't go too overboard with the bad boys style. After all, this generation still needs icons," I say.

"Why does this generation need icons? I don't agree. These days, nobody gives a damn about anything or anybody. We need iconoclasts, not icons," Lulu retorts, appearing to be very deep.

"True. Nobody believes in anything anymore. Everyone can see through those shallow, fake posers!" Beibei nods.

"Don't you think that, precisely because there's nothing to believe in, people need idols even more?" I retort.

"What do you mean?" Beibei asks.

I consider my own observations on the current status of religion in China, "Everyone rebels back and forth until they've got no faith. When they've got no faith, they've got no spirit. Without spirit, everybody feels lonely and confused. When people are lonely and confused, they desperately look for something to believe in. Sometimes they turn to cults, money, the opposite sex, or a band. In a faithless time, it's easier for a band to have a cult following and become an icon."

"You're quite right that everybody revolts back and forth until they've got no faith. Nowadays, we don't lack people to encourage others to revolt. What we need is to build something new and to bring hope." Beibei sees my point.

"That's why I said the Young Revolutionaries can't just be all beating, smashing and looting, and insisting that to rebel is good. The aim of revolution is to build a fairer world. Let's take the Beatles as an example. They were antiwar and antitradition, but they wanted peace and love. Bob Dylan talked about human rights. Even today, P. Diddy ran the New York marathon to raise money for inner-city schools. Your Young Revolutionaries have got to have something," I declare.

"It would be great if they could have both ideals and edge," Lulu concurs.

"They should not be as heavy as those old fogies Black Panther and Tang Dynasty. Nowadays you don't see any angry young idealistic proletarians anymore. In a market economy, people want lighthearted entertainment." Beibei is clearly annoyed..

"What style of music do they plan to play?" I ask.

Beibei answers, "Pop, rap, hip-hop, rock, reggae, a bit of everything. A hodge-podge. I don't want us to be pure rock 'n' rollers, because the majority of the Chinese audience doesn't understand rock."

"Why don't you add a bit of revolutionary opera? It's got a Chinese flavor, as well as satirical overtones," I suggest.

"Yeah! Great idea! Why didn't I think of that? Niuniu, I think I really should hire you to do strategy for us full-time. People who come back from overseas really are different! Gosh, I can't afford you. The British pay you much more. Isn't it sad that the most talented people all work for Westerners!"

"Don't be so nationalistic. I think you should just make the Young Revolutionaries internationalists. Isn't everybody talking about globalization? Their ideal world should simply be a fusion world. Get someone to write that kind of song for them," I recommend.

"Right, that suits the Young Revolutionaries' positioning."

"But isn't their communist flavor a little too strong? In the future when they try to make it overseas, this might be a problem." Lulu holds different political views.

"We'll worry about that later. For the Young Revolutionaries to make it here in China first would be a good start. These days stars are on a merry-go-round. Almost every star's fame is ephemeral," Beibei educates us.

"What's their styling like?" Lulu, who mixes in fashion circles, asks.

"Dyed hair, pierced ears, baggy pants, Japanese samurai tattoos on their arms, and backwards baseball caps—typical Generation X– and Y–style."

I throw my comments out first. "It sounds too familiar—like a Chinese smorgasbord of every foreign band and style. Gives people the feeling that Chinese people can't do anything else but pirate. I think that to copy others is an expression of lack of self-confidence. They should be unique."

"Yes, I agree," Lulu cuts in. "Dressing up like that won't make you look fashionable. On the contrary, you're just following the herd. I think that to highlight the Young Revolutionaries, you should let them wear military hats and belts like the Red Guards. In this way, they have their own revolutionary character."

I add, "Like designer Vivienne Tam using the Chinese flag and Mao's portrait in her clothes designs—what does she call it? China chic?"

Beibei says, "Yeah, that old Cultural Revolution stuff is really popular these days. It's China's own retro chic!"

No one seems to notice or care that there is nothing unique or rebellious at all about having a marketing agency create an image for the band. Just because Beibei's company has deemed the Young Revolutionaries "unique" and "rebellious" does not actually make it so. However, that is the nature of the industry under the new market economy. To survive, you must please the crowds, even if that means selling out.

POPULAR PHRASES

BAOTANG: To make soup.

CEHUA: To plan, promote, position, and publicize. One of those flashy new words that has entered the Chinese vocabulary along with the opening up of the market economy.

21

Matters of Size

*M*y friend, Diana, is half English and half Norwegian. When she was sixteen, she saw the movie *The Lover,* about French author Marguerite Duras's affair with her Chinese lover in Indochina. Diana fell in love with the Hong Kong actor Tony Leung, who plays the gentle and passionate lover in the film.

Diana started to learn Chinese and fantasized about dating a Chinese man someday: a Chinese man with hairless, silky skin and a tight butt, who looks younger than his age, is faithful, gentle, and wealthy like Duras's lover. It would be a great way for her to practice her Chinese—and he would, hopefully, be a good cook or the son of a good Chinese cook. Diana loves Chinese food.

After graduating from college, Diana's Chinese dream is realized. She was sent to work in a nonprofit organization's Beijing office. After moving to Beijing, Diana often saw many Western men dating Chinese women, but very few Western women with Chinese men. Most of her girlfriends are not attracted to Asian men. Sure, she saw those Chinese punk artists hanging out at places like Moon House in Haidian with their Western wives. But most of the Western wives are unattractive from a Westerner's perspective. And those sorts of relationships seem to her a bit mutually masturbatory. The Western girl feels cool because she is married to a "dissident artist," and the Chinese dissident artist guy feels proud that he is good enough to score a Western girl—*and* he can get a visa!

Diana is determined to break the stereotype and find a Chinese man. To her disappointment, it is not such an easy task. At nearly six feet tall, she is taller than most men and the rare ones who are taller are often male chauvinists. Of course, many of those Chinese punk rockers and avant-garde painters chase after her, but they are not really her type. Diana tells me that she thinks they are too westernized. She prefers conservative family men.

One evening, in a bar called Schiller's, she meets Mr. Lee, who is on a business trip to Beijing. Mr. Lee is a venture capitalist in Hong Kong, more gorgeous and gentler than Tony Leung. He is half Chinese, half American, and speaks both Chinese and English perfectly. Other than his unusual height and high Western nose, he looks like a pure-blooded Chinese man with black hair, Asian eyes, and fair silky skin.

Mr. Lee tells Diana that he is not attracted to Asian women because he prefers "big breasts, blond hair, and intelligent conversation," although he doesn't specify in what order. Diana thinks she can provide him with all three. He says, "Too many Asian women are flat-chested, materialist airheads." Hanging out with other foreigners in Beijing, Diana has met so many Asian fetishists—Western men who have caught "yellow fever"—that Mr. Lee's comments make him stand out from the crowd.

Mr. Lee flies from Hong Kong to Beijing to meet with Diana every weekend. Every time, he brings her nice gifts, perfume, jewelry. They always have pleasant conversations and candlelit dinners, but he never kisses or touches her. Diana calls afterward and tells me, "Wow, Chinese men are so much more conservative than Western men. He'll make a good husband."

Four months have passed and Mr. Lee always treats Diana with respect. She decides to take the initiative.

One Saturday night after Mr. Lee takes Diana to the St. Regis Hotel for dinner, Diana invites Mr. Lee to stay overnight at her apartment in Maizidian. Mr. Lee doesn't refuse.

In Diana's apartment, Mr. Lee asks Diana politely, "Can I make love to you?"

"Yes," Diana agrees eagerly. She has been waiting so long for this night!

"Do you have a condom?"

"Yes. I do." Diana planned ahead, and earlier that day bought a box of condoms at a nearby store.

Their moment of passion is building up when the unexpected happens. The condom doesn't fit: it's too small. "Gosh, this part of my body is American, not Chinese," Mr. Lee chuckles. "The Chinese have always believed that the size of a man's nose reflects the size of his pecker. With my Western nose, it seems to make sense."

"Gee, if the size doesn't fit, I wonder what other foreign expatriates use in Beijing. Do they need to carry boxes of condoms from home every time?" Diana is frustrated. "Can we do it without a condom?" she asks.

"No, we can't. My wife says I have to wear condoms whenever I'm with other women."

"What?! You're married?" Diana is so stunned that it takes a minute for the anger to set in.

"Yes." Mr. Lee answers. Diana later tells me that he answers her question calmly without a trace of embarrassment.

Diana's fury finally emerges. "What are you doing here, then?"

"Lots of men in Hong Kong have *xiao mi*—mistresses on the mainland! What's the problem?"

"How can your wife tolerate you having affairs?"

"My wife understands. She is fine with it. If other *taitais* from Hong Kong can put up with affairs, so can she."

"But how can your wife be from Hong Kong? I thought you said you aren't attracted to Asian women because they are too materialistic."

"One good thing about materialistic women is that they care more about how much money you allow them to spend than how many affairs you have. As long as she can still buy her Prada handbags and Gucci sunglasses at Pacific Place, she is happy."

Diana can't stand it anymore. She kicks Mr. Lee out of her apartment. She calls me, telling me everything in detail. Eventually, she says, "Niuniu, I'm grateful to the Chinese condom manufacturer for saving me from becoming Mr. Lee's latest mainland mistress. "

"Do you still want a Chinese man?" I ask her on the phone.

She pauses for a second, and then says, "What is the Chinese word—*couhe?* Perhaps one of those Chinese dissident artists might be okay after all."

POPULAR PHRASES

XIAO MI: "Little secret," slang term for mistress.

TAITAI: Wife, usually one who doesn't have to work to support the family.

MAIZIDIAN: A funky artistic, counterculture district in eastern Beijing

COUHE: "To match and combine"; settling for second-best.

22

The True Color of Ximu

I come back to Beijing from a small southern village where I covered a story on how villagers made a living through drug trafficking. Before I even get inside my courtyard house, I discover that someone has torn the badge off my Jeep, which I have left parked outside in the alley. There are also a couple of scratches down the side of the car, and someone has thrown a banana peel on the front windscreen. It is obviously a deliberate act of vandalism. My mother Wei Mei was right: it's not safe to park a car in a Beijing alley. This is the first time I have encountered something like this since moving out of the diplomatic apartment compound. In a country where people used to be equally poor, it's hard not to hate the rich—I'm not rich, I simply own an automobile. What if this was not a car, but a horse, a living, breathing animal—would it suffer the same treatment? I wonder.

I drag open the door to my courtyard and go in. I'm startled to find Lulu sitting there under the grapevine. Why is she in my house? Isn't she working today?

She is wearing a Chinese-style jacket with the collar turned up, and her hair hangs down messily. There is an open bottle of rice wine on the table next to her. She is swigging from the wine bottle and tugging at her own hair.

"Lulu, what's the matter?" I rush over. I know immediately it must have something to do with Ximu.

Lulu raises her head, her eyes full of tears. She bites her lip. Her expression is flat, ruthless, and hateful.

She suddenly stands and opens up a big colorful biscuit box beside her. It is full of ashes.

Those ashes make my hair stand on end.

"I burned all of my diaries," Lulu murmurs. "All those years, what did I write? It was all about Ximu. How to love him, understand him, wait for him, tolerate him, appreciate him, adore him, be his loyal audience. When I was hurt, I healed myself at home, and when my hurt was healed, I went back to him so he could hurt me again. All those years, everyone around me was going overseas, getting married, making money, having a career. And me? Other than him, my world has nothing. I used to think my love was so great, but only now do I realize that with all that loving, all I loved was a joke. I'm just a joke."

"Lulu, tell me, what has that bastard done?" I hold Lulu's hand and look at her, worried and distressed.

"It's not worth it. This kind of man is not even worth a beating." She waves her hand and shakes her head violently.

"Tell me, what has happened?" I press her for the story.

"What happened?" Lulu laughs coldly. "Something I should have discovered long ago. I was just an idiot. I always believed him. He said his marriage with his wife was a failure, and it was enough for his lifetime. He said he was an artist. Artists must get inspiration from the bodies of different women, so he couldn't be a monogamist. The funny thing is that there was a fool like me to believe his bullshit. I listened to him so adoringly. I accepted him staying married and fooling around with other women. He lived with other women, and I even tolerated that. I said to myself, successful men need space."

"He isn't that successful! Going to study in France is nothing special! It seems like he couldn't make it there, so he had to come back home," I say.

"Sometimes he spoke about his own dreams and ambitions for hours. He said of all the women, I was the only one who understood him. I was so flattered. I listened attentively, I applauded. If Ximu is Sartre, then I can be his Simone de Beauvoir! It didn't matter if we didn't get married. Our love had long ago surpassed such a worldly thing."

"Didn't you know they were all excuses? Men will say all the romantic, sweet-talking stuff in the world to get a woman into bed," I scold Lulu.

"When people are in love, when they are madly in love, they are fools. Don't you remember Jeremy Irons in *Damage*? He was a successful politician. Was he stupid? But in the end, didn't love leave him with nothing? Some people are demons— like Anna in *Damage*. If you love them, it's like swallowing poison, because for them you would be willing to climb razor-sharp mountains and swim in a sea of fire."

Loving them is like swallowing poison. Aren't Beibei and I the same? After Chairman Hua's betrayal, Beibei has decided to never again believe in love. She seeks comfort in the arms of young men. And I? My past with Len is like a sleeping forest. I don't talk about it with anyone.

"Psychologists say that some kinds of love are a sickness, an uncontrollable obsession," I say.

"Perhaps I'm one of those women who easily become obsessed," Lulu says. "The woman in Ricky Martin's song 'Livin' la Vida Loca' is a devil woman who runs men around in circles. Beibei often blames me, saying that I'm pretty, why can't I find a man and run him around in circles? I'm always the scapegoat. I let my girlfriends do the worrying for me. But I just don't know how to be manipulative!"

Lulu continues her story, "Recently, Ximu had disappeared for over a month. I missed him so bad, missed his big beard, his fiery eyes, his passion and wildness in bed. So, I phoned his mobile. No one answered. I knew I shouldn't have phoned, because he didn't let me ring him. Later on a woman phoned my house and asked if I was looking for Ximu.

"I asked her how she got my phone number. She said her name was Liu Hong, that Ximu was not there. She was looking after his mobile phone for him, and she saw my number on his phone. I knew this woman. She was the Japanese woman who had grown up in China, who lived with Ximu. Ximu had told me that there was nothing special about her, but she had a good body and she could do accounting. His math was terrible, and Ximu needed a woman to keep his books, so he lived with her.

"Liu Hong said she was Ximu's wife. Then she asked me if I was Lulu. I said, 'How do you know my name?' She said, 'My husband often mentions you to me, praises you. Your name has long resounded in my ears.' I said, 'You two are married? Why hasn't Ximu told me? Isn't he still married to his French wife?' She said, 'They divorced two years ago. We've been married for almost a year. We were married in my hometown of Nikko. The mayor of Nikko even came to the wedding; he said our wedding was a symbol of Sino-Japanese friendship. Did Ximu really not tell you? At the moment, he's gone to Hong Kong specifically to buy me a big diamond ring for our first anniversary. Wait until he gets back, I'll be sure to ask him how he could forget his friend Lulu like that!' Then she asked me if I had any message to pass on to Ximu. I didn't say anything, just hung up the phone.

"I thought she must be lying, to try to get at me. She was angry because Ximu loved me more than her. Because Ximu loved freedom so much he didn't want to remarry. Even if he did get married, it wouldn't be to this common woman, always flaunting that Japanese thing of hers. What's more, why would Ximu be so kitschy as to buy a diamond ring? Ximu never liked to give women gifts. He has never given me any gifts. He said that was all so vulgar.

"A couple of days later, the elusive Ximu came looking for me. We made love wildly. That night, I had eight orgasms, that feeling like you are floating with the angels, like you're going to die. Later, we listened to Yo-Yo Ma's cello solos, lit candles, drank French wine, had a bubble bath. We were exhausted. Before that we were wild, we totally didn't even have the chance to talk. Then, when we were quiet and I was nestled in his arms, I asked him, 'Where did you go? I missed you so much!' He said Hong Kong. As soon as I heard that, I thought, Liu Hong wasn't lying to me about the place.

"Then I asked Ximu why he went to Hong Kong? He said he had to buy something. When I heard that, my heart jumped. Liu Hong said he had gone to buy a diamond ring—could it be true? 'Are you remarried?' I asked him, my tone very casual. I thought the answer would be no, but his face changed instantly. 'Who told you?' he asked me very seriously.

"I was dumbfounded. My head swam. Because, it was too simple, his expression and reaction had answered everything. He really was remarried. But why? Wasn't he a free spirit? Didn't he hate those common women? Why did he secretly get divorced and then remarried? Why did he have to deceive me? I raised my head, looked at him through the steam of the bathroom. I couldn't say a word. 'Listen to me,' he said. In the steam and candlelight, his face was still so impossibly vivid. This man who had just joined his spirit and flesh with mine was nothing more than a despicable cheat. I threw my glass of wine in his face, leaped dripping out of the bath, and ran to the bed crying.

"He chased after me naked, he begged me, knelt down, and made me listen to his explanation. He said even though he was remarried it wouldn't affect our relationship. He had told Liu Hong about his love for me. He said Liu Hong understood him. He also said that the three of us could live together."

"He wants to have a wife and make you his lover?" I scream. "In his dreams! Who does he think he is? He makes me sick."

Lulu snorts, "Does he think he's an emperor, that he can keep an imperial harem? Fuck! There are men on this earth who are so full of themselves."

"He became so outrageous because you spoiled him. After he thought you were his, he started to take you for granted. He didn't take you seriously. So, you *have* to leave him," I say as I slam my fist on the table.

"He finally showed me his true face. I can finally be rid of him because I have already begun to despise him. But I just don't understand, even though he always said I was the one he loved, why did he marry Liu Hong? He said that woman was common. He said he loved me. Are men's words so unreliable?"

Lulu is exhausted from anger. She closes her eyes and rests in my arms, her face tear-stained. I use a tissue to gently wipe her face.

"Niuniu, tell me, are American girls taken advantage of just as much by guys?" Lulu whispers.

I sigh. "To be honest, American girls don't spoil men like you did. They wouldn't put up with men messing around. 'If you don't treat me well, then let's get divorced. Half of your property belongs to me!' American women are like that."

"So much self-respect! I wish I had been born in America."

"But I think American women would be devastated and have a hard time facing the truth too," I add out of sympathy.

23

The Fortune-Teller

*L*ulu's five-year love affair with the self-professed free spirit Ximu finally ends. But what can be done to bring the neurotic Lulu back down to earth?

I tell Lulu about myself. After I was dumped by Len, my shrink told me to regain my self-confidence by developing my potential and focusing on my career. Probably this is also what Lulu needs the most.

Beibei and I have formulated a Saving-Our-Comrade-in-Arms-Lulu plan. First, we buy Lulu a new computer. We hope she will start writing. Everyone who knows Lulu agrees that she is a talented writer. She is sexy, works in the fashion world, knows how to pose for the camera, and relates heartbreaking love stories: she has all the makings of a *meinu zuojia*, a pretty woman author. All she lacks is the most important part, a published book. Beibei invites Lulu to write song lyrics for her singers. Five thousand yuan per song. Not bad pay in the primary stages of socialism. I contact RedSkirt.com, which agrees to let Lulu be the part-time editor of their fashion channel over the weekend. Lulu will be so busy she won't have time to dwell on Ximu.

After everything is arranged, Beibei and I invite Lulu to dinner at Shun Feng on East Third Ring Road. I wanted to bring along a shrink, Dr. B, but Beibei believes that a fortune-teller and a *feng shui* master might be more appropriate. She brings along Master Bright Moon.

Bright Moon is from the ancient capital Xi'an and specializes in Taoist metaphysics and mysticism. He left his family at a young age to become a Taoist priest. It is said that he tells the fortunes of government leaders and celebrities. The most famous story is about an Olympic gold medalist named Wendy.

Before Wendy left for the 2000 Olympic Games in Sydney, she was depressed because she suffered from back pains But Bright Moon told her that she would definitely win if she slept on her left side instead of her right side after arriving in Sydney. Wendy followed Bright Moon's advice and her back pain disappeared. She won the gold.

Just as off-beat spiritual movements such as kabbalah are popular among the Hollywood crowd, it's fashionable these days for Chinese pop stars to have fortune-tellers and monks around them. Rumor has it that the reason certain Cantonese pop singers can stay at the top of the charts for many years continually is because they always have Taoist masters following them.

Celebrities respect Bright Moon. He charges one thousand yuan per hour, more than a psychologist, yet demand still exceeds supply. One has to wait at least one month to get an appointment with him. Plus, he accepts clients only through referral. One of Beibei's pop stars, Lan Huahua, gives up her own appointment with Bright Moon to Beibei, in order to suck up to Beibei.

First, Bright Moon asks for Lulu and Ximu's *bazi*. He counts them on his fingers, and then points out that Ximu, fifteen years older than Lulu, was born under the fire element, and Lulu the metal element. Metal is burned by fire; it is inevitable. Also they don't live in the same dimensional space, so their separation is preordained.

Next, Bright Moon asks Lulu to sketch her home's position and layout for him.

Lulu draws the outline of her apartment on a napkin. Bright Moon consults the drawing through small glasses, then shakes his head. He says Lulu's bed is in the wrong position. First, her bed is oriented east-west, while the magnetic field is oriented north-south. Every day when she sleeps, she is being cut in two by the magnetic field. This is extremely unlucky. Also, her bed is in the southeast corner of the room, next to the window. First, this is not private enough; the bed should be some distance from the window. Second, Lulu's elemental space suggests that the ideal position is the southwest. The southeast is star-crossed for her. Bright Moon also suggests that Lulu, being of the metal element, should put a goldfish bowl, a water wheel, or something of that nature in her room, to give the room a little more water.

"Water resists fire. You need the help of water," Bright Moon says calmly.

Then he points to a mole on Lulu's cheek. "You need to have the black mole beneath your eye removed. That is a crying mole, it will bring you many tears. In addition, you like wearing black, but black is unlucky for you. Your yin is already very strong to begin with. In the future, you should wear more colorful clothes. And you had best use a red pillowcase."

After Lulu hears this, she is all smiles.

When they are leaving, Bright Moon finally exhorts Lulu, "You should be grateful in your heart and have some reverence for the gods. If you don't have faith, things will be even worse. I would encourage you to go to Xiang He in Hebei to pay your respects to the ascetic Taoist holy woman there who attained the true light. Eight years after she died, her body still hasn't rotted. When you see her, you will understand everything in the darkness is long ago preordained."

Lulu nods her head constantly.

"Do you also believe in Buddhism?" I ask Bright Moon.

"I do not distinguish between Buddhism and Taoism. Faiths are all interlinked." As Bright Moon is leaving, he gives me a copy of the *I Ching*. "Go home and study this. I can see you are someone who understands."

Lulu does everything according to Bright Moon's recommendations and installs the computer Beibei and I have bought for her. Lulu decides to leave behind the hurt caused by Ximu. She writes me an e-mail: "I want to be just like the phoenix, to fly out of the ashes of my own body and be reborn."

POPULAR PHRASES

CHUJI JIEDUAN: The primary stage of socialism, the Chinese Communist Party's description of the current political system in China.

MEINU ZUOJIA: Literally, a pretty female author; in actuality, one of a group of average-looking female authors who like to include flattering photos of themselves on the covers of their books. Just as so-called political analysts such as Bill O'Reilly and Ann Coulter appear on the covers of their sensationalized books in the United States.

BAZI: "Eight characters," the Taoist reference to the year, month, day, and hour of one's birth.

24

The Last Aristocrat

Thirty-five-year-old Weiwei is my family's friend. He often claims to be the last aristocrat in China. When the government and the media promote the "noble spirit," he says to everybody, "Do you know what China lacks the most? Noble people. Too many peasants and too many nouveaux riches who drape themselves in Rolexes and gold chains. Nobility is in your blood. Money can't buy it. I'm the only Chinese aristocrat left." Although I am not sure about Weiwei's claims of aristocracy, I must agree with his critique of modern Chinese society.

Like my mother, Weiwei has Manchurian blood. Weiwei's grandfather was one of China's most famous linguistics scholars. Many of the classical Chinese university textbooks were edited by his grandfather. Weiwei's father is a famous poet and translator. When the American poet Allen Ginsberg visited China in 1984, Weiwei's father was his host.

The long-haired Weiwei is a failed artist and musician. In the past, he used to sit alone in his room all day listening to classical music and conducting along with a baton, or talking to Van Gogh through his paintings. But lately he is filling in as a part-time DJ at a bar called the Loft, playing techno music. The Loft was designed by a couple of Chinese brothers, both of them performance artists. It reminds me of those bars in Manhattan that have a similar metallic, warehouse feel.

"Niuniu, you've come back to China and you haven't called me. I've heard you've been partying like crazy. Hanging out at night in bars and discos! Is that right?" Weiwei greets me at my mother's house.

"It's all rumors. I'm working hard to serve the people," I say as I put my hand over my heart.

Weiwei laughs. "You still remember the old Chinese slogans! Anyway, when it comes to partying, I, Weiwei, am indeed your elder. These days everyone has money, everyone can party. I started hanging out in bars back in the 1980s. In those days, hanging out in bars was a privilege of the rich. While I partied, you kids were still walking around in diapers!"

"It seems to me the one thing Beijing does not lack is braggarts like you who'll boast about anything!" I tease Weiwei.

"Niuniu, you were still young back then, you don't remember. Once, in the mid-1980s, I sold my first painting, to a Japanese. Three thousand yuan in foreign-exchange certificates. In those days, three thousand yuan was like one million today. I made the deal at the Shangri-La Hotel. Then the Japanese took me home in a Toyota Crown, the classiest taxi at the time. First, I bought myself a pair of Nikes. Then, wearing my new Nikes, I took all my mates to the disco at the Peace Hotel, which was all the rage then. The cover charge was 150 yuan. I remember very clearly. Later we all started going to the Kunlun Hotel disco. And then we were always hanging out at Nightman Disco!"

"Nightman? Who goes there anymore?" The banter continues.

"Don't look down on Nightman just because it's not as trendy as Rolling Stone or Hard Rock or those other discos opened by Americans. In the 1980s, Nightman was fantastic. The people going in and out of Nightman with the diplomats were all high-class people. If you don't believe me, ask your mother Mei. Of course, I must admit that now Nightman is like a former social butterfly who's reached menopause—past its prime."

"Real heroes don't brag about their past bravery. Tell me where you've been hanging out lately," I say to the loquacious Weiwei.

"Too many women are chasing me. Girls from the art institute, the music institute, the drama institute, the film academy, the medical university and big-nosed foreign students from the Beijing Language and Culture University. They're chasing me all day, telling me they want to live with me, want to marry me. Why do girls today stick to people like plaster? I tell them I'm disrespectful, will go to any lengths for sex, am irresponsible, inconsistent, change my mind the minute I see something new, and accomplish nothing, but still they don't let me go. They say they like my honesty. It seems that there are very few men with aristocratic qualities in China, so everyone wants me."

I know that Weiwei loves boasting about women chasing him. But I can never work out whether it is true or all in Weiwei's imagination. Some women like wisecracking men like Weiwei; some women like the silent type. I think of Len. He is exactly the opposite of Weiwei: quiet, unsure, extremely polite to the point of humility. But perhaps his humbleness and politeness are a better way of showing off?

"I was told that you're a computer expert now. Are you still into it?" I ask Weiwei.

"Nope. Lately I'm hooked on cars!" says Weiwei. "Audi, Shanghai Buick, and Guangzhou Honda are following the German, American, and Japanese routes, respectively. German cars have a European prestige and quality. American cars are big, because there are many fatsos in the States. Japanese cars are economical and reliable and suit someone who wants to save money. My favorite is the BMW Z8."

"That little two-seater sports car that James Bond drives?"

"That car is exciting, sexy, and passionate, a totally new concept. Pure BMW thoroughbred, not some joint-venture hybrid. The wheels are wide, the trunk is small, the driver's seat is big. The first time I saw it, I wanted to jump right in. The body is made of aluminum alloy; the rear bumper is made of impact-resistant polyurethane. The Z8 can go from zero to one hundred in under five seconds. From one hundred kilometers per hour, it can stop in less than 2.5 seconds. Damn, our Chinese cars don't even come close." Weiwei sounds like a well-versed car salesman trying to close a deal.

"When did you strike it rich, that you can drive a BMW Z8?" I ask Weiwei.

"At the moment I am still driving my old open-top, human-powered, two-wheeled vehicle."

"A bike?" I smile.

"Yes. A bike." Weiwei laughs.

"Then how do you know so much about the Z8 that you talk about it as if you were talking about your girlfriend?"

"I saw it at the International Motor Show." Weiwei is just like his other Beijing friends. If they want to play with cars, they go to the motor show. If they want to play with computers, they go to the computer exhibition. They are familiar with the newest and most expensive models of cars, computers, even airplanes, but when they get home, they don't own anything. Weiwei, this self-proclaimed nobleman, doesn't even have a proper job.

"If the CEO of BMW knew there was someone killing themselves to give them free advertising, he'd be pleased!"

"I'm just telling it like it is. Anyway, normal people can't appreciate that sort of class. Only people with aristocratic qualities like me can understand the Z8 concept. It is often said that when you are driving, your car is an extension of your body. So I wouldn't look twice at Chinese or Japanese cars. In the future, I want either a Jaguar or a BMW series 7 or better. I wouldn't lower myself to drive any other car."

"What about Mercedes?" I ask.

"Mercedes are for big bosses. They're too orthodox for me. Furthermore, these days all those nouveaux riches in China have driven them to death. Unless it was a Mercedes sports model, I wouldn't even consider it." The only thing missing from Weiwei's aristocratic lifestyle is money.

Sometimes it is hard to tell if Weiwei is taking himself seriously or merely being facetious. Either way, he is a constant source of entertainment and a great friend.

25

American Passport

$\mathcal{M}$y stepmother Jean Fang and I are friends. In the eyes of many, this is strange. In order to get my father, Dr. Chen, Jean, the Dalian girl who is only eight years older than I am, converted to Christianity.

As my father's wife, Jean has become domineering and condescending toward my father's subordinates. She loves to hold her status over the heads of the workers and secretaries and threaten them with harsh punishment for not working hard enough. It's not that Jean is really serious about it—she's just addicted to her newfound power and loves to exercise it. Many people feel uncomfortable around her, so they come to me, asking to fix her. But somehow Jean's aggressiveness doesn't bother me much because I've seen too many Chinese people just like her. It's called *xiaorendezhi*, small people finally grab their chance.

For years since the divorce, my father lived by himself. He's a man with good taste, from clothing to people. Now that Jean is his final choice, I believe he must have his reasons besides Jean's model looks. She was my father's secretary. For years she had been reliable and loyal.

Not long ago, Jean decided that she wanted to study English in the United States. She found a language school in Manhattan and has rented an apartment close to her classes for $2000 per month. She is due to leave China in one month.

"You can learn English in China by hiring a native English speaker. You don't have to go all the way to the Big Apple to do that," I tell her on the phone. "By the way, isn't it crazy to give up your home and leave your husband?"

"Niuniu, I haven't told you this before, but I'm pregnant." Jean almost whispers on the other end of the line, as if some unauthorized person might be listening in.

"It's even crazier. You should avoid too much travel for the sake of the baby." I don't see the connection between Jean's pregnancy and her New York trip.

"Niuniu, can't you see that I'm doing everything for the sake of the baby? Do I have to explain to you that my language learning is not serious; my real goal is giving birth to the baby in the States!" Jean shouts at me, completely forgetting her previous attempt at secrecy.

"Oh, I see, you want my half-brother to have a *meiguo huzhao,* a U.S. passport!" I finally get it. Many nouveaux-riches Chinese want to give birth to their children in the United States. In order to trick American Immigration, the mothers often visit the United States on a business or a student visa when they are two or three months pregnant.

Jean replies, "Yes, exactly, girl. You know, having a Chinese passport sucks. It's such a hassle every time I walk out the door, especially that time I went to Brazil with your father. Your father's

American passport met no problem; he got a visa straight away. But when it came to mine, the local guide said, 'You have a Chinese passport. You should put twenty dollars in the cover of your passport, otherwise they will give you trouble getting the visa.' I thought, both your father and I look Chinese. How can a Chinese passport and an American passport be treated so differently? I didn't put in that twenty dollars. I didn't get the visa. In the end, I had to straight-up hand the cash over to get through Immigration.

"Another time it was even more humiliating. I was on a tourist visa traveling to the States. Another Chinese person and I were the only two who were searched by customs. The customs officer opened my suitcase and went through everything in there, including two new frilly bras I'd bought for a special occasion! My suitcase was a mess, but he wasn't satisfied. He asked me if the Rolex I brought was real. I said yes. I spent ten thousand dollars on this watch. He also asked me how much cash I had brought with me. I said, 'Nine thousand dollars.' He asked me to show him the money and count it for him. I hid the money in the pocket of the special underwear I wore. You know, most Chinese carry our money this way. I didn't know what to do. I said I could do that only if he found a female officer to replace him. He left. While he was gone, I quickly took off my pants to get the money out. Just as I was putting on my pants, he came back to the room with a big woman. I was so embarrassed since I was only half-dressed. Later, I swore to myself that my baby has to be a U.S. citizen, so he will be able to travel anywhere in the world freely and never endure the humiliation I have experienced. I'm not an American, but at least I can find a way to be the mother of an American."

Jean is not the only Chinese obsessed with snagging an American passport. Good or bad, the Chinese have tried for over a hundred years to leave China. In the eyes of many Chinese, an American passport is not just a passport; it's an ideal to be held up, a status symbol, a safeguard of freedom.

"But my father is an American citizen; his baby will automatically be one," I say.

"But I was told that American-born adults can be candidates for American presidents," says Jean.

"I didn't know you were so ambitious!" I tease her.

"You never know. I just think that being American-born will be a nice thing for my child. But even if my baby does get U.S. citizenship, there are other things that bother me, too."

"What else?" I ask.

"His future education. I wanted him to get educated in the United States. But I was told that K–12 education in the United States is very lax. Some of my friends' kids can't keep up with the math classes in Beijing after studying in the States for a few years. I am also worried that if my baby is a boy, he will be beaten up by white boys and won't be able to find a girlfriend there. Plus, American English isn't authentic English." Jean sounds like a typical overprotective Chinese parent.

"Then send him to Great Britain to learn the Queen's English!" I suggest.

"England is a very conservative society that doesn't welcome immigrants. I'm afraid that my baby will lose his self-confidence there, like your friend CC," Jean whines.

"What about Australia or Canada? Both of those countries are nice to immigrants," I say.

"But the schools there are not as prestigious as American or English schools. It'll make my kid look inferior compared to the other kids who are sent to the United States." Jean, apparently, is picky.

"I can't believe you are so snobbish!"

"It's not me that is snobbish. It's Chinese society. Taiwan, Hong Kong, and the mainland, they're all the same!" Jean cries.

"What's wrong if my little brother or sister stays in China?" I ask.

"You grew up in China and you know that the competition in Chinese schools is savage. Plus, my baby has to speak English like a native speaker."

"What about kindergarten in England so that he can be immersed in the Queen's English, primary school in an international school in China so that he can have a solid foundation for math, junior high school and high school in Canada and Australia to make friends with other immigrants in those countries, higher education in the United States to gain the prestige and the vainglory you want," I suggest.

"Yes! Perfect!" Jean takes what I have said seriously, "Niuniu, you're so smart. Such an arrangement will make your brother a global citizen. I watch news on TV. The other day, President Hu Jintao was talking about cultivating global talents. See, I'm a good Chinese citizen who follows the CCP's policy closely!"

POPULAR PHRASES

XIAORENDEZHI: "Small people finally grab their chance": the triumph of the little man. Closest English translation is probably "Every dog has his day."

MEIGUO HUZHAO: Beautiful country's documents of protection; American passport.

26

A Cool Mother

I think to myself, "Gee, Jean is so demanding that she's just like my own mother. Father must like the same type of women."

"What's Mei been doing lately?" Jean calls me to pry out information about my mother.

"She's just at home."

"I heard she is organizing a Sino-American forum on women in the twenty-first century," Jean says.

"Why wasn't I told about that?" I am surprised.

"There are always a lot of rumors about her," Jean says.

"Really? So many people are concerned about her!"

"That's right. She's always working on something. I can't believe that she could stay at home and do nothing but watch the children. She is probably cooking up something big."

"Really?"

"Yes. I recently learned that when Mei was young she looked like the pop star Faye Wong," Jean announces.

"Really?"

"They are both tall, with dark eyebrows and almond-shaped eyes, and they both have a bit of Beijing ruffian about them, and a mysterious, unfathomable spirit. I guess this kind of woman is most attractive to men."

"Jean, why are you so interested in my mother?" Jean seems to have an ulterior motive for calling.

"Sometimes, I think, perhaps your father still loves her," she finally admits.

"Don't be silly, my mother now has three children. And you? Young and pretty and well educated—there's no need for you to be jealous of her."

"It's not jealousy. It's pure admiration. I know that your father will never love me the way he loved your mother. Every time he speaks of her, he has such an admiring tone. He doesn't hold any grudges against her at all. I feel just like the famous architect Liang Sicheng's second wife, always living in the shadow of his first wife, the beautiful and popular Lin Huiyin."

"How can my mother compare to Lin Huiyin? My mother was one of those schoolgirls who were sent to learn from workers and peasants; she didn't go to college in China. In the States she didn't study for a degree, she had a child, and looked after her child, me." I try to make Jean feel better.

"Don't start. She doesn't have a college degree, but she speaks English just like an American, and for that alone, I am impressed. I took the TOEFL how many times, but as soon as I speak to a foreigner, I tremble."

"So she's got a talent for languages! That's it."

"Every time I see your stepfather John, he tells us, 'Without

Mei, I don't know how I could go on living. She really is a gift from heaven,' and so on."

"Americans love to exaggerate. You know that." Being surrounded by so many insecure modern Chinese women has made me an expert at reassurance.

"Anyway, for a woman to be like her, to make so many men adore her, is amazing! Niuniu, you should learn from her!"

Yes. I should. Already in her late forties, mother of three children, Wei Mei is still popular and looks like she's in her thirties.

Everybody says that I have a cool mother. She always knows exactly what she wants. Mother is rarely confused. She is mixed Han Chinese and Manchurian. She has that kind of healthy, hard-working, hardship-enduring proletarian natural beauty that was popular in China in the 1950s.

During the Cultural Revolution, my grandparents were both revolutionary opera performers who followed the Gang of Four, and were among the intellectuals in favor with the party. When everyone else her age had been sent down to the countryside or to join the army, Mother relied on my grandparents' connections to obtain a job working as a shop assistant in a cooperative in Beijing's West City district. At the time, this was one of the most comfortable jobs. Later, she worked as a cook's assistant in the kitchen of a city jail. Still, the job was located in the city and she always had enough to eat, not bad at all for that time.

I've heard from Grandma that toward the end of the Cultural Revolution, Mother had become one of the famous Beijing "hooligan girls."

When I ask Grandma what punk girls meant at that time, she says, "Well, punk girls were just girls who had a little more guts than others, wore more colorful clothes, and dared to speak to boys. In those days that was a really big deal. Your mother was just like that.

"She was careless and uncalculating, dared to wear her hair in bangs. At that time, it was a sign of petit bourgeois sentimentality—and she liked talking to boys, so naturally she was branded a punk girl. "

My grandparents were busy "struggling with people" all day and didn't have time to take care of their only daughter.

Before the Cultural Revolution had finished, Mother managed to leave China. At that time, she had married Fan Wen, who had suffered during the Cultural Revolution. Grandma has told me that Fan Wen's father, Fan Yingchun, was a nobleman from a wealthy old Chinese family, who at the end of the 1930s went to the States to study metallurgy. There he met Fan Wen's mother, Marguerite, a Frenchwoman who was studying there. This girl was interested in Asian culture, she herself was half Chinese, and she adored Fan Yingchun. They gave birth to Fan Wen in Minnesota in 1945.

After the People's Republic of China was established, Fan Yingchun, his head full of revolution and idealism, said he wanted to return to China to serve the motherland. His wife refused, but Fan Yingchun was determined. He left his wife for his country and returned to China, taking his little son Fan Wen, who at the time could speak only English and French.

During the Cultural Revolution, Fan Yingchun, returning from overseas and with a mixed-blood child, was accused of being an American spy. He was beaten up every day by Red Guards. Having suffered too much humiliation and filled with grief, he abandoned all hope and committed suicide. He electrocuted himself.

He had given up everything to make revolution for a new China, but in the midst of the Cultural Revolution, he gave up his own life!

Without his father, timid Fan Wen was an orphan and drifted around Beijing. He was beaten and cursed, suffered cold and hunger, was dirty and decrepit, cast himself here and there, but his Chinese improved day by day. One day, he went to the cooperative to buy some tea, and there he met Mother.

Grandma says that she was surprised that Mother fell for Fan Wen. "Your mother was unrestrained and fearless. Fan Wen was timid and quiet, soft-spoken, scruffy and clumsy, and much older than your mother. I didn't approve of the marriage, but your mother was a rebel. She ran away. Now, you're just like her, a little rebel!" Grandma points at my nose.

"Tell me more." I beg her.

Deng Xiaoping came to power, policies were relaxed, and Fan Wen left, taking his new bride, Wei Mei, to find his mother in the States. At the time, Fan Wen knew only that his mother's name was Marguerite. He didn't know what she looked like.

Marguerite had remarried. Her new husband was a successful Irish psychiatrist. They had three children, two boys and a girl, all of whom were grown-up. They lived in wealthy Tiburon, in northern California near San Francisco.

Marguerite treated Fan Wen and Mei very well. She told Fan Wen without misgivings that after all those years, in her heart she still loved Fan Wen's father Fan Yingchun. She had cried for him for a long time.

In order to make up for Fan Wen's suffering in China, Marguerite rented a house for her son and his wife, Mei, who had never received a formal education and could not speak English, and enrolled them in English classes at an adult educational school. She also deposited $10,000 in their bank account for Fan Wen to attend university or start a business.

Mei and Fan Wen led a typical new-immigrant lifestyle. They studied, worked, adapted, struggled, complained, cursed, and resigned themselves to their fate.

But everything changed that Christmas.

During the 1970s, it was very rare to meet a mainland Chinese person in the United States. Marguerite's three children returned to their parents' home in Tiburon for Christmas, and met their half-brother Fan Wen for the first time. Marguerite's second son, Mark, even brought his Taiwanese colleague, Dr Chen Siyuan, a professor from the Massachusetts Institute of Technology, so that Fan Wen and Mei could meet some Chinese friends. I have never met my Uncle Mark, but there meet him and thank him someday.

Mei was always a good cook. She cooked a Chinese and American–style Christmas banquet for Marguerite's whole family, which everyone complimented profusely. Her apple pie and fried dumplings, as well as her beauty and generosity, left a deep impression on everyone.

Especially on Mark's friend Chen Siyuan, who loved gourmet food. Perhaps the Chinese saying "To win a man, you have to win his stomach" has some validity. It has never been a problem for Mei to find a man. Perhaps I should improve my cooking skills? No—Lulu enjoys making soup, but still has so much failure in love. Perhaps it's Mei's strength that Chen Siyuan fell for. Chen Siyuan is a meek man. Until this day, it is still difficult for me to imagine that he pursued Mei while risking being branded a wife-stealer. What was the force behind this? Chen Siyuan has told me that he is simply enamored of the straightforward manner of northern women. It was something he hadn't seen in those bashful southern girls. Mother was the first northern Chinese woman he had met. He said later, "Northern Chinese women are strong and they let you know what they want, not like other girls, who love to play games and keep you guessing all the time."

Mei told me that Fan Wen and she had grown apart after they had come to the United States. Fan Wen always wanted her to take charge. Whenever he ran into difficulties, he always hid behind Mei. He took driving lessons for months but never passed his driving test. But Mei, after being behind the wheel for eight hours, had obtained her license, and started working as a delivery driver for a Chinese restaurant. Much of the time, Mei was the man of the house.

Because Fan Wen progressed more slowly than Mei, he was often angry with her over small matters. Although the handsome and erudite Chen Siyuan moved Mei with his sincerity and affection, she could not bring herself to leave the pitiable Fan Wen.

Finally Marguerite's son Mark discovered their secret. He supported their love and made a special trip home from MIT to reassure his mother, Marguerite. When Marguerite saw that Mei no longer loved Fan Wen, she could only agree. Fan Wen talked with his mother for three days and three nights. He nearly went crazy, but finally he agreed to a divorce. That was how Mei became Mrs. Chen. In 1977, I was born, a child of passion. In 1983, Father was posted to Beijing as the representative for Hewlett-Packard.

We returned to China when I was five. In Beijing, Mother helped foreign companies set up in China, organized cultural events for foreign embassies, and established sister-city relationships between Chinese and American cities. TV presenters, diplomats, chief representatives of foreign businesses, and cultural attachés often came to visit our home. Mother was always busy and was considered quite a mover-and-shaker. The Chinese government even presented her with an award, naming her a cultural ambassador between the East and the West. I really admire her for her energy, yet I haven't inherited either her ambition or her social ability.

Compared to Mother, I might have had more sexual relationships with different men because my generation is more sexually liberated than the previous one. But I don't have Mother's complex life experience. Len, just one man, has already disrupted my smooth-sailing life. Mother never let men and their love control her life.

In 1989, when I was eleven years old, my parents suddenly divorced. To this day, the reason why they divorced remains a mystery. They have kept it secret. Friends who know them well guess that they separated because of political differences during 1989. This was the year that many Chinese students protested the government's actions in Beijing. You may remember the famous picture of the solitary student with a grocery bag in his hand, holding back the line of tanks by refusing to move out of their way. Even an event as volatile as the Tiananmen Square protest shouldn't have been able to tear apart two people who love each other, should it? But how can they allow politics to intrude on their personal life? It's stupid. My parents never quarreled when they were together. They separated peacefully. Neither of them has given me a satisfying explanation. They just said that they wanted different things in life. Mother looked after me alone, but there were admirers who pursued her. They bought me candies or chocolate to win me over. I used to be annoyed by so many visitors at home. I enjoyed spending private time with my father. He liked to take me out-doors, hiking in the mountains, camping in the woods.

Mother later married a white-haired American, who is the general manager of a Texas oil company in China. The old man is tall and thin, refined, and fifteen years older than Mother. I call him Big John. When Mother was forty, she gave me twin Eurasian little sisters. They study at the Beijing International School next to the Holiday Inn Lido. Mother and my stepfather, Big John, live at Riviera Villa near the airport, with celebrities and multinational company bosses as their neighbors.

Even though we are mother and daughter, we are as differ-ent as night and day. Mei is very practical. She loves a man's power and status more than the actual man. I am the opposite. I'm much more romantic and sentimental. I want to love some-one for who he is. But I can't deny that Mother is more suc-cessful in dealing with men.

My father remained single for over ten years. I always feel that he loved Mother more than Mother loved him. I used to say this to him, and he said I was being unfair to my mother. Father put his heart entirely into his work after the divorce. In 1992, he left HP. With a group of colleagues, he set up the Chen Computer Company, manufacturing computer compo-nents for the United States and Taiwan.

Now he has several factories across China. Two years ago, Father married his former secretary, Jean Fang.

27

The New Leftist

I have a male admirer in Beijing: Professor Yuan. He is the Chicago-educated hunk who is considered a flag in the camp of the new leftists.

We met at a reading at the New China Bookstore. He moved very fast—he sent me a letter the day after we met. "Good upbringing, good education, good-looking, smart and intriguing: I met my Venus today. I felt like Goethe's young Werther. My sorrow came after she disappeared."

For the next two weeks, he faxed me love letters every day, citing Plato, Hegel, and Shakespeare. I think it is nerdy, but cute. My mother Mei encourages me to see him, "People say that Yuan is a political star. Who knows? He might become China's president someday."

I agree to have dinner with him. It's not because I am interested in being China's First Lady. I just want to move on from my past with Len. It's been a year since I came back to China. Sometimes, I feel lonely when I see boys and girls walking in pairs in the streets. It's time to have a date now.

Neither Professor Yuan nor I expected that our date would turn into a heated debate between a liberal and a new leftist.

In the Chinese ideological world at the moment, the liberals and the new leftists are engaged in a vigorous battle of name-calling. Basically, the liberals are pro-U.S. and the new leftists are anti-U.S. The new leftists call the liberals "imperialist lackeys" and *hanjian,* or Chinese traitors, while the liberals denounce the new leftists as a bunch of xenophobic nuts and opportunists.

As Professor Yuan and I drink dragon-well tea at Kongyiji, a restaurant named after a character in a story by one of China's best-known authors, Lu Xun, Professor Yuan asks me, "Are you interested in politics?"

"Yes." I smile.

"Great. I love girls who are into politics and soccer!" Professor Yuan's eyes glitter with passion. In the next hour, he indulges in jargon, dropping words and phrases like new orientalism, multipolarity, postcolonialism, globalization, and the clash of civilizations.

I keep nodding, thinking, he's hot-looking. I'll go along with this political stuff for a while, then try to change the subject with a more romantic gambit.

Yuan babbles on eagerly. "Some people call me a new leftist. I don't like it, because Chinese new leftists are all following behind the asses of some loser Western leftist intellectuals. The so-called left and right are also Western concepts. If people have to define me, they should call me a member of the Middle Kingdom school." Professor Yuan likes to talk about himself.

"Oh, yeah?" Perhaps I'm outdated. Maybe in Beijing, talking about politics is nowadays more sexy than talking about anything else. After all, politics means power, the ultimate aphrodisiac.

Professor Yuan continues as if he was preaching to his students, "Western culture is aggressive, always searching to expand. The problem with Christianity is that they think their god is the only god. Colonial expansion was undertaken in the name of getting others to discard their own faith and follow the Christian faith and system."

"What about Christianity's respect for human rights, individualism, and liberty?" I ask, thinking to myself, well, although he sounds a bit ridiculous, like the Gang of Four, at least the Versace suit he wears is cool.

"Christianity has the respect you talk about for people who act in accordance with their will. But for outsiders, it doesn't. Think about how these Christians treated the American Indians, African slaves, and the indigenous people in their colonies!"

I think, Nowadays, the legendary revolutionary Che Guevara is well liked in China. Is Professor Yuan trying to tell me that he is a reincarnation of Che who also cares for the oppressed? Otherwise, why does he indulge in political clichés?

"Are other cultures perfect? Chinese or Islamic cultures are not always humanist!" I respond.

"Islam is too complicated—I'm not an expert on that. China's uncontrolled pursuit of money today is all the result of our blind worship of the West," says Professor Yuan. Apparently China is not responsible for any of its own problems, at least not in the professor's eyes.

"What about the Cultural Revolution?" I didn't expect the Versace-clad professor to be so radical. I decide not to run my toe up his leg.

Professor Yuan replies with his long-prepared answer. "It was the result of pursuing Western Marxism and Stalinism. If China followed its own path of Confucianism and Taoism, the Chinese would never have needed to go through so much pain."

"Do you think China was peaceful in ancient times? Weren't most emperors cruel and tyrannical? The legalists, over two thousand years ago, were already totalitarians!" I also want to mention foot binding, eunuchs, *emie jiuzu*—extermination of an entire family, *shougua*—the practice of forcing women to remain unmarried after their husband's death, *wenzi yu*—execution of dissident authors, but I think better of it. No sadomasochism before dinner.

"I don't deny there is cruelty in Chinese history, but which country's history is free of blemish? Look at the United States, which flaunts itself as being the world's most civilized and most humanitarian nation, yet in the 1950s racial segregation was still legal. What I'm talking about is China's collective culture, not the culture of its rulers. The Chinese mass culture is tolerant and peaceful."

"But the pitched battles fought by Chinese peasants and clashes between local clans weren't peaceful!" I wonder if Professor Yuan would get off his soapbox and begin to think about a clash between the sheets. Can a lover of the West and a hater of the West be passionate together in one bed?

Professor Yuan disagrees. "Europe had bloody fights too. Looking only at China's dark side is the liberal point of view. Liberals think that the moon is bigger in the West than in the East. When you think of ancient China, the grand Qin and Han dynasties, the golden age of the Tang and Song dynasties—the Chinese had dignity and pride! But now we're chasing after everybody else. Before, it was Big Brother the Soviet

Union. Now it's the United States. China is always following everybody else's ass."

"If you dislike the West so much, why did you stay in the States for eight years? Why didn't you leave and come home earlier?" I don't finish the rest of it: Why are you wearing a Versace suit, Ecco shoes, a Cartier watch, and driving a Volvo? I don't want Professor Yuan to lose face, even if he does have ass on his mind.

"It was all to complete my Ph.D. and get my green card. Don't the Chinese place great importance on returning home in glory? If I didn't go to Silicon Valley and come home a dot-com millionaire, at least I could return home wearing my doctorate cap."

I can't stand Professor Yuan's hypocrisy any longer and snap back at him, "You take advantage of the West by taking their scholarship and their green card, but on the other hand, you curse the West as colonialist and imperialist. You're pathetic."

"Niuniu, I think you've become a Western thinker. Westernization of a Chinese woman often leads to the corruption of the woman. Chinese men still prefer traditional women."

I light a cigarette of Yuan's, pretending to be a smoker. "I'm already corrupt."

Professor Yuan tries a new tack: "I don't spend all my time talking about this stuff. I also love soccer. How do you think the World Cup will play out?"

"I wish my idol Ricky Martin would sing again there someday!" I say.

"Ricky Martin? A Latino bro? At least not an imperialist!"

"I wish my hero David Beckham would recover soon," I say.

"That English devil is my hero, too." Professor Yuan surrenders.

POPULAR PHRASES

HANJIAN: Chinese traitors, a historical pejorative term.

EMIE JIUZU: The ancient practice of exterminating an entire family through the ninth extended relatives as punishment for wrongdoings.

SHOUGUA: The practice of forcing widows to remain single till death to keep their purity. Obviously this is not a custom that is particurly popular in today's modern China.

WENZI YU: The execution of dissident authors.

28

One Dollar

Sometimes, while driving the roads in big cities such as Shenzhen and Beijing, I see so many luxury cars pass by that I can't help but wonder how wealthy the Chinese have become compared to twenty years ago. Take a friend of mine as an example. She came to Beijing ten years ago for schooling from a town so small and isolated that most of the people living there had never even heard of BMWs, let alone seen one. Nowadays, she works for a Beijing newspaper, drives a European car, and has just bought a condominium costing 800,000 yuan. But according to her college classmates, she is considered "just so-so." As a returnee who lived in the United States for some years, I see that young urban Chinese are finally catching up with the middle-class life of the West. And the effects of this change are both positive and negative.

Today in China, to get rich is glorious. But does a higher

standard of living make people better human beings? Are the rich more generous than the poor? What about the tension between the rich and the poor? Can money buy satisfaction? These are serious questions that I think need to be thought about more by the Chinese people.

One Saturday night, I was waiting in a line of cars to exit a crowded outdoor public parking lot. There were five cars ahead of me. For ten minutes, the line didn't move. I soon discovered that the owner of a BMW SUV, a man in his thirties, was refusing to pay the one yuan parking fee because he objected to the parking lot attendant knocking on his car in a heavy-handed manner. No damage was done to his car, but the driver remained defiant. The parking lot attendant, wearing cotton-padded clothes and looking to be at least fifty years old, insisted that the driver pay the fee. He stopped the car and gathered four buddies who work in the nearby food stand to block the BMW from exiting the lot. Then, he threatened to beat the driver if he didn't pay.

I didn't know if I should get out of my car to offer my help or just stay in the car for my own safety in case a fight broke out. At a crucial moment, a man riding a bicycle approached the group on the brink of an altercation. This passerby carried a ragged bag. He pulled out one yuan from his pocket and offered to pay the fee for the driver.

"It's not about money. I have money!" The BMW driver proudly showed the cyclist a thick stack of one-hundred-dollar bills he carried in his wallet.

The cyclist waved his hand at the BMW driver and said, "Go on, then. Drive safely."

I became curious about the cyclist. Four drivers of fancy cars behind the BMW offered no help. A policeman who witnessed the entire incident did nothing. But the poor bicyclist intervened and solved the problem. I followed him until he stopped at the bicycle repair shop next to the parking lot.

"I need my bike to be aligned and my tire to be fixed," he said to the three men working at the shop.

"We all watched you!" said one of the men. "At first, we thought you worked for that guy in the BMW—but now we see that you are not with him. You're by yourself!"

"Yes," the cyclist nodded nonchalantly.

"So, you're just a man with a good heart. We can't believe we've met such a good man tonight! We will fix everything on your bike and give you a 60 percent discount. You only need to pay six yuan!" says another shop attendant.

The bicyclist searched through his wallet, and said, "I'm sorry, I only have three yuan left." I felt moved at the thought of this poor man stepping in to help a rich man in a BMW. How can poor people be so giving? I walked toward them with three one-dollar coins. "Let me pay for him."

"Oh, another stranger that turns out to be a good person!" another repairman said with a wide grin.

I walk back to my car, feeling good about myself.

"Hey, wait a minute, is that you, Niuniu?" the cyclist called.

I turned around, again looking at the bicyclist, this time recognizing him as my grandfather. Under the dim lights of the parking lot, I had not been able to see him clearly. I am at once happy to see my grandfather and embarrassed that I didn't do anything to help sooner. What's more unnerving is that my grandfather isn't even close to being poor.

"I love you, Grandpa!" I give my grandpa a big hug and a kiss, before saying good-bye. As I walked back to my car, another thought crossed my mind. Maybe getting rich is glorious, but the combination of looking poor and offering help is so much more glorious than looking rich and acting petty. The new generation of Chinese might be getting wealthier, but are we getting any wiser? We could all take a few lessons from my grandfather.

29

Three Types of Men

On Saturday afternoon, Beibei, Lulu, and I go to play tennis at the Twenty-first Century Hotel. We are missing a fourth player, but it so happens that Beibei has a sore foot, so Lulu and I play singles.

I have been worried about Lulu's mood since she broke up with Ximu, but in the end Lulu acts like there was nothing wrong. In fact, her conscience is so clear that she is beating me easily, two to nothing.

It is Beibei who speaks less than usual, as if there was something weighing on her mind. After tennis, the three of us go to Half-Acre Garden on the East Third Ring Road and have a simple meal of Taiwanese snacks. After dinner, we go to T.G.I. Friday's to have a drink. Very few places in China offer free refills of Coke and iced tea. T.G.I. Friday's does.

With Sade's song "Lover's Rock" in the background, I ask Beibei, "What's up?"

Beibei rolls her eyes, "Don't get me started. It's been a big mess."

Lulu quickly fills me in: "One of Beibei's hottest male singers, Little Bench, got himself into trouble. Ten days ago, he had a concert at Beijing Workers' Stadium the first show of his national tour. While his limo was driving along Workers Stadium Road North, many fans were chasing him, so the driver was driving slowly, and Little Bench opened the window to wave at his fans. Just then, a man suddenly threw himself in front of the limo and stopped it. Then he poured petrol on himself and shouted to everyone: 'I've loved Little Bench for ten years. Now he's famous, he's a big star, he loves someone else, and doesn't want me anymore. My life doesn't have any meaning. I want to die for him.' No one knew what was going on—then this guy lit a match and set himself on fire. The people around tried to save him and put out the flames. He was badly injured, but luckily he didn't die."

Beibei sighs again. "As soon as this happened, everybody knew that Little Bench was gay. China is not like England, where they can easily accept openly gay pop stars like George Michael and Elton John. After this happened, our office exploded. The phone didn't stop ringing, journalists were following Little Bench every day. He was in hiding, like a criminal. The most infuriating thing is that my little lover Iron Egg, he's so underhanded. To make some money, he went to the newspapers with some inside information he learned from me. He was ruthless. After this rotten business got out, the other cities all canceled Little Bench's concerts. His CD sales have plummeted. I tried calling Iron Egg, but he's switched off the mobile phone I gave him. That traitor! He betrayed me, then he abandoned me!"

Lulu joins in, cursing. "In the past, even punks had a little loyalty. Now loyalty is something that belongs in a museum. Modern kids like Iron Egg are too shrewd. They submit to whatever hand feeds them. No sense of Confucian-style loyalty and filial piety whatsoever!"

"Still, it was my own stupidity." Beibei begins to make a self-criticism. "Actually, I knew exactly what kind of a guy Iron Egg was. But I always thought, we've been to bed together so many times, there must be at least a little emotion. I never thought he would stab me in the back. But that's exactly what he did to me. He's so cruel. Really, to be betrayed by the person who makes love to you, by someone so close to you, is the cruelest thing. And this sort of cruelty falls upon me repeatedly. Why do I have such lousy luck in love?"

In fact, Beibei knows that her young lovers just love her money, but she can't go on living without lovers after her husband cheated on her. She needs to feel loved even though that love is only temporary and bought with her money. Beibei is in her midthirties, but she feels like an old woman, full of insecurity, needing the company of young men to gain confidence. "Is this the fate of women who stop believing in love?" she asks Lulu and me.

I say, "Perhaps Chairman Hua destroyed your faith in love. You lost your faith and your judgment. You searched for love from the wrong people, like Iron Egg."

"Generally, there are only three types of men we can sleep with," says Lulu. After her experience with Ximu, Lulu seems to have become an expert. "First is the husband type, like Tom

Hanks. This type loves you more than you love him. He's responsible, loyal, you can trust him, and you are willing to grow old with him. He will still love you when you become a grandma."

This sounds so much like my father, I think. I don't plan to marry a father figure.

"The second is the lover type, like Hugh Grant. This is the type of person you love to appreciate. He is charming and educated. There can be love, passion, and romance between you, but no trust, not suitable for spending a lot of time together. You can talk about literature and art with them, but don't go hoping for marriage or kids with them."

Len definitely falls into this category, I think. Before my eyes appears the scene when Len and I went to Montmarte in Paris to see the Dali sculptures of melting clocks. Len said, "Dali works are all related to the subconscious. The subconscious is liquid. Our emotions, our instincts, our desires, are all liquid, just like time, melting here before our eyes. Do you feel how time is molten, liquid and flowing?" Len silently gazed at me and didn't speak again. I held my breath and looked at Len. I had never dared to look at Len so directly, because his gaze was so sharp, it could be almost painful. But in the silence of the Dali Museum, we stared at each other, and my heart kept repeating, "Make time solidify. Make it stop right here." At the time I had left my boyfriend and deferred my studies just to follow Len. Before long, my world had only one thing in it: Len.

"And the last type?" I ask.

"The kind of playmate you don't have to talk to or communicate with at all. He is athletic and sexy," says Lulu.

"Like the exercise trainer in our health club?" Beibei chimes in with a smile.

"Like the dark-skinned hairdresser at the RichWife?" I follow.

"Yes. In any case, he doesn't need to have the brains of Woody Allen. As soon as you see each other, you want to tear your clothes off. Everything is for sex! With this type of man, you can be kinky and wild and totally uninhibited in bed," Lulu says.

"Where did you learn this stupid theory?" asks Beibei.

"From my Internet dates," says Lulu, winking and tapping her foot to Björk's "Big Time Sensuality" in the background.

30

The Brief Moment

CC and Nick have made plans for a long weekend in Shanghai. I agree to come along at CC's request since Hugh has assigned me to write a piece about the clubs and hotels in Shanghai.

CC, Nick, and I have got a great package at the swank Portman Ritz-Carlton. On the first day, we play a round of golf, which is usually reserved for the ultrarich in a crowded city like Shanghai; have dinner at a loft-like place called The Door, known for its fusion deco: and cap the day by listening to jazz at the Cotton Club. The next day, we brunch at the lobby of the new Westin Hotel, which offers unlimited drinks of champagne and cocktails. Then we go swimming, have a massage, eat dinner at the M on the Bund, and have drinks at Face, a Southeast Asian bar owned by a Westerner.

Nick thoroughly enjoys it. Shanghai is the perfect postcolonial playground for him, but not for CC. She especially dislikes the waitress in the Portman's Tea Garden Café, Nancy Lu, who shows a much friendlier attitude toward Nick than to her and me. Nancy laughs coquettishly, even flirts with Nick right in front of CC. On the second night, CC overhears Nick calling Nancy, telling her that she's cute and he'd like to meet up with her. CC confronts Nick and they get into an argument. I am in their room as they argue. I can't stop them. Nick finally walks out, saying to CC as he goes, "I didn't come to Asia to find a stuck-up Oxford ice queen. There are plenty of them back home in the UK."

"I can't believe it!" she cries, "Nick just dumped me."

"If he's smart, he'll come back and say he's sorry," I say.

CC mutters sulkily, "I came back to China to find my roots. But everywhere we go, the place is full of local women who want to marry Westerners. It really pisses me off. And it pisses me off even more that Nick seems to love it so much!"

Another thing that pisses CC off is that she is not considered beautiful in China. Back in Oxford, her delicate bones, petite features, and almond eyes were exotic and won her the nickname Beauty Queen, but in China, people worship European-looking women. She isn't tall enough, her eyes aren't big enough, her skin isn't light enough. She's considered common and unfashionable. But wherever we go, Chinese people will praise Nick for his handsome looks. "Wow, you've got a good-looking boyfriend," they say to her, which annoys her.

"Tomorrow, let's go somewhere more Chinese. Perhaps we can talk to a Shanghai man! I've heard that Shanghai men really know how to look after women," I say to comfort CC.

After a late-morning workout at the hotel's spa, we go out for brunch at a teahouse that sells milk tea with tapioca It lacks colonial style, perfect for CC's mood. Sticking to the plan of no martinis or goose liver pâté, we order fried dumplings and bubble green tea. Although the teahouse looks traditional, we can't seem to escape the Western influence. Four teenagers sit playing poker at their table, making noises and cracking sunflower seeds. Two girls are eating ice cream while reading the latest Chinese edition of *Elle*. Two boys are playing video games at the table right next to us.

A baby-faced Chinese man who sits alone gets my attention. It looks like he is reading the *Shanghai Star*, but the paper is turned upside-down. Behind the newspaper, the man is dozing off. Even in his sleep, he looks melancholy. I nudge CC. "There's probably a good story behind this. Otherwise, why would he doze off here in the morning?"

CC decides to strike up a conversation with the man. She walks over and wakes him up. "Hey, are you okay? Do you need help?"

The man rubs his eyes and looks at his watch. "Oh, almost noon. I can go home now!"

"It looks like you've been in this teahouse for a long time now." I join them.

"I have stayed at this twenty-four-hour teahouse for the entire night. Can you believe it?!" The man sounds frustrated.

"What happened?" CC asks.

"You know how it is, *jiachou buke waiyang*. Domestic scandals shouldn't be told to outsiders. I have to go." The man makes an attempt to get up and leave.

"We heard that Shanghai men are gentlemen. Are you a native?" I keep the conversation going.

"Yes," the man nods, "Where are you from?"

"I'm a Beijinger," I say.

"I'm a Hong Konger," says CC.

"You don't look like the type to spend all night in a tea-house. Why are you here?" I probe.

"To be honest, my wife locked me out last night!" The man almost bursts into tears.

"So it's true that Shanghai husbands are henpecked by their Shanghai wives!" CC murmurs to me.

"So tell us your story. Perhaps we can help you," CC says to the man.

"She works in a nice hotel nearby," the man continues. "It's not that she likes being a waitress. But she hopes to meet some rich guests there who will be willing to sponsor us to go abroad. Last night, she was on a night shift. Around midnight, she called and told me that there was an Englishman who had his eye on her. The Englishman had asked to visit her place because he was interested in seeing how ordinary Chinese lived. She told me to clean our house. She especially asked me to hide my belongings because she said that the man might not be willing to sponsor her abroad if he knew that she was married.

"It took me an hour to clean the room. I left the house around one in the morning, before she came back home with her guest. I stayed in this teahouse and waited for her to call me. A little after two o'clock, she called and commanded me not to go home until noon. I begged her, but she said I made her lose face so I had to be punished."

"How did you make her lose face?" I ask. "You weren't even there!"

"I forgot to hide my underwear hanging outside on the balcony."

"Uh . . ." CC and I manage not to laugh out loud.

The man continues. "Yesterday before going to work, I had washed some underwear and left it hanging on the balcony. I didn't think it was a big deal, but she said it made her look very bad. The Englishman went to the balcony straightaway after he came in. He never lived as high as the twenty-fourth floor. He loved the view. Then he saw a string of underwear. My wife said that foreigners don't hang their underwear outside as if it was an art exhibition. So she felt quite awkward. Then, the man spotted the man's briefs on the line. He asked my wife whose underwear it was. She told him the truth. The man laughed. He pointed at the hole in the underwear and told my wife that she had better buy me a few new pairs of undershorts. After saying that, he left, shaking his head while muttering something in English that my wife didn't understand. My wife felt humiliated. She said that it was my fault, so I had to be punished. The door would remain locked. Sleep somewhere else, she said."

"Does your wife work for the Portman?" CC asks.

"Yes, how did you know?" The man is shocked.

"If I'm not wrong, her name is Nancy," CC says.

"Yes. But who are you?" The Shanghai man looks at CC nervously.

"If you are a wronged man, then I'm the wronged woman."

POPULAR PHRASES

JIACHOU BUKE WAIYANG: Ugly or embarrassing domestic issues shouldn't be told to outsiders. Although most personal issues such as income are open topics for discussion, this one usually is not.

31

Internet Date No. 1

After Lulu ended her five-year-long relationship with her cheating boyfriend Ximu, her friend Mary, an editor for *Family*, the most popular women's magazine in China, suggested that she try checking the Internet personal ads.

At first, Lulu was skeptical. She called me and told me about Mary's idea. "A sex goddess in the fashion world, why do I need to resort to personal ads? Aren't they for the desperate and dateless?"

Then she called me again. "Mary said I've got it all wrong. I'll find men of quality there. They are tech-savvy and private. They're just too busy to be social. . . ." She edited two Internet dating stories: in one, a Karaoke girl in Shenzhen got to know a married Hong Kong movie star via the Internet and they fell in love. The man divorced his wife and married the girl. Now they live happily in Hong Kong and the man is helping the girl to become the next Zhang Ziyi.

"And there was this Sichuan girl who met an American in a chat room. Then the man came to China on a business trip and went to see her and fell in love. A year later, they got married and she moved to the United States. Only when she got there did the lucky girl realize that she had married a multimillionaire and the grandson of a former governor. She sent pictures and letters to her friends from America."

"I've heard the new Polish president candidate is married to a Chinese lady he met online. I believe these stories. Try it." I said.

Fast-forward six weeks.

At Al-Muhan, a Muslim restaurant opposite the Australian embassy in Beijing, Lulu speaks to Beibei and me in a sullen voice.

"Fairy tales come from Europe. Europe is the birthplace of knights and damsels in distress. Do you know what China is capable of producing? Tragedy. Human tragedies and liars." Even for Lulu this is an especially dark thing to say.

"Hey, do you know that you sound very *fandong*, reactionary? Do you know that you'd have been thrown into jail during the Cultural Revolution for saying things like that. You're lucky to live in this era of reform!" I tease Lulu while eating a lamb shish kebab. Lulu must have had troubles with men again.

"I'd rather be in jail than be played like a fool!" Lulu says through clenched teeth.

Beibei has been winking at a young handsome Uighur waiter until Lulu's angry voice pulls her back to the conversation, "So what was the story with your men?"

"My Internet dating experience was a complete disaster! I don't know why I keep bumping into married men who pretend to be single!" Lulu cries.

"Do you know that MBAs are popular nowadays?" I ask Lulu.

"What do you mean?" Lulu is confused.

"MBA—Married But Available," I say.

"Ha-ha!" Lulu laughs bitterly. "I've met two of these fucking

MBAs over the Internet. They both claimed they're single in their ads. The first man was a returnee who divided his time between London and Beijing. He owned a graphic design company. He was into the arts and, you know me, I'm a big fan of artists," Lulu says, as she rolls her eyes. "We talked about cubism, dadaism, fauvism, and impressionism in our e-mails. Like me, his favorite painter was also Matisse. So I decided to meet him.

"The first three dates, we met in different galleries: first, Yan Huang Art Museum at the Asian Games Village, the second time at the Melodic Gallery near the Friendship Store, and the third time, we had a rendezvous in an art gallery in Hong Kong's Mid-Levels. I attended a fashion show in Hong Kong that day. Around dinnertime, I found myself at the Yan Gallery in Lan Kwai Fong. Guess who showed up in that small gallery?"

"He must have been stalking you!" Beibei cuts in.

"He said it was fate that we ran into each other in another city because we had *yuanfen,* affinity. We looked around the gallery together and he talked about classic realism with me. Then we went to Cubana in Soho for dinner, where he told me he was in love with me.

"So you slept with him that night!" says Beibei, flashing the I-know-you expression.

"Well, yes, in my hotel room in the Renaissance Harbor View in Wanchai." Lulu bows her head.

"Was it good?" I ask.

"With the hills, the harbor, and the views, Hong Kong is a city of romance. While we were looking out of the window at Victoria Harbor, we were very passionate." Lulu lowers her voice, "Violently passionate."

"Not too bad so far. At least you had an orgasm—or two." Beibei says hopefully.

Lulu continues. "After we returned to Beijing, he sent me a note telling me how special that night in Hong Kong was to him, and how much he wants to see me again. But he had to attend a conference in London the next day and would be back in ten days!"

"And you believed him? Just like you believed Ximu?" Beibei asks, raising her eyebrow.

Lulu rolls her eyes. "Call me an idiot, but I thought I was happily in love again." She licks her lower lip. "I even enjoyed the bittersweet feeling of missing him. On the third day after he left for London, I went to the San Wei Bookstore to find something to read.

"In the bookstore, I saw him, with a woman and a child waiting in line to buy the new Harry Potter. I overheard the woman calling him *laogong* and the boy calling him Daddy. I thought of the messages he sent to me through Yahoo Instant Messenger about London's weather and the prestigious conference. I walked right up to him—boy, was he flustered. His handsome face became so ugly. Before he could stammer anything out, I said, 'I suppose we do have *yuanfen,* as you said. Once again we share an unexpected rendezvous.' I turned on my heels and left him to explain himself."

POPULAR PHRASES

FANDONG: Reactionary.
YUANFEN: The fate that brings people together.
LAOGONG: "Hubby."

32

Internet Date No. 2

*I*n Henderson Center's Irish Bar, some men are watching sports, and some are playing darts. Lulu, Beibei, and I are here to drink imported beer. Lulu updates us on her latest Internet dating fiasco. "After what happened with the 'MBA,' that married-but-available jackass, I told myself, 'You can't be so gullible anymore. Be smarter and take better control of your libido.'"

"That's exactly what I was going to suggest to you," I say.

"This Internet date was a handsome French-language interpreter in the Chinese Ministry of Foreign Affairs—a diplomat," Lulu says. "In his e-mails, he told me about his journey from a poor fishing village to Beijing. The hardship he endured was beyond understanding to those of us who were born with silver chopsticks. He walked thirty miles every day to his high school and had to work in the fields after school. He dreamed of being China's Henry Kissinger. I was so moved."

"Perhaps he tried to win your sympathy. A trick Japanese women love to use to get their men," Beibei says.

"We first met at the Boys and Girls Bar in Sanlitun. He complimented me in French—calling me *mon amour* and *ma belle* and so on. It was romantic, but I told myself, let him keep on sweet-talking, but I am going to maintain control!"

"Sounds like mission impossible," I say.

"I stayed cool till our fifth date. On the evening of the Mid-Autumn Festival, we took a boat ride in the moat around the Forbidden City. On the boat, a girl in a traditional Chinese costume was playing the pipa for us, and two other girls were serving us tea and rice wine. All three of these chicks were pretty, but his gaze always stayed with me. Then we lit paper lanterns, put them in the water, and let them float away."

"Oh, yeah, I know, that's a tradition from southern China. The lanterns are in the shapes of lilies. You make a wish every time you light one, right?" I say.

"Yes. You know that the lily is my favorite plant. Every time the diplomat lit a paper lily, he looked into my eyes, murmuring 'I love you' in French. Just close your eyes and imagine the scene: a moon-lit autumn night, ancient towers and pavilions all around, pink lily lanterns floating on the water and casting their golden glow, a handsome young diplomat telling you that he loves you in the most romantic language in the world, plaintive ancient tunes being played on the pipa in the background . . ." Lulu closes her eyes, enraptured.

"I guess that's your excuse for not being able to say no, you big hopeless romantic!" I speak matter-of-factly.

"I thought it was *amour*. I overestimated those creatures we call men once again." Lulu speaks with tears in her eyes.

"You didn't end up in his bed, did you?" Beibei asks.

"Almost. After the boat ride, he told me that he had bought a new apartment in Tongxian and would like to take me there. I said yes right away because I thought he might propose."

"We drove for an hour and a half. As the miles rolled by, I was envisioning the two of us living in the new apartment in the suburbs and sharing a car together to go downtown to work each day. But then, he took me to a scruffy old house. In front of a rough wooden door, he told me, 'Here is our nest of passion.'"

"What was the inside like?" I ask anxiously. Beibei's eyes are also wide open in disbelief.

"The first thing I noticed after entering was the faint smell of cooking. Then I saw a pink coat on the hanger, pink slippers on the carpet. I went to the bathroom and saw a woman's toothbrush—and tampons. I confronted him. 'A woman lives here." I said.

"He nodded. 'Yes, but she's not here tonight.' He responded so brashly—as if I was asking him if he owned a pet. He tried to lead me to the bedroom. There I saw the picture of him and a woman hanging on the bedroom wall. It was clear that he had brought me to the apartment where he and his wife live every day."

"He didn't even bother to hide his wedding picture?" I yell out.

"Why did he tell you that it was a new apartment that he had bought?" Beibei asks.

"I asked him the same question. Guess what he said? He had been living there for five years, but just newly owned it. He used to rent it. I feel stupid even repeating his words!" Lulu is inconsolable.

"He took you there perhaps because his wife was out of town," I say.

Lulu says, "I asked him to take me back to town right away. He said, 'It's late. Stay here and I'll drive you back tomorrow.' I said, 'Let me go now.' Guess how he answered?" Lulu looks at Beibei and me who are holding our breath, waiting for the ending. "'I'm tired. If you want to go, go ahead, but I can't give you a ride. You'll have to get a cab.'" With these words Lulu starts to laugh hysterically.

"So did he help you call a cab?" Beibei asks.

"No. I did it myself. But there is no such service in Tongxian at night. It's too remote. "

I could picture the rest of the story: cold, scared, angry, and humiliated, Lulu, in her miniskirt, standing alone in the bleak suburb of Tongxian in the middle of the night, trying to hail a cab. Forty minutes passed, or maybe an hour, before she could finally get a cab—and then of course the cabdriver overcharged her.

"What he did to you was criminal," I yell.

"We have to get that bastard!" Beibei becomes enraged too.

"This time, I refused to be a victim," Lulu says. "I wrote to his work unit, telling them that he, a diplomat and married man, tried to seduce women on the Internet. I gave them his name, described his looks, and told them everything I knew about him."

"Good. You need to be a woman warrior!" I say.

"I bet his work unit fired him the next day. He made the glorious motherland lose face. He should not be allowed to receive French guests anymore," Beibei says.

"So did you hear from them?" I ask.

Lulu says, "Yes. In their reply, they said there was never any such person working in the Ministry of Foreign Affairs."

"They didn't say that!" Beibei whines.

I am speechless. One thing is for sure, I'd rather live alone for the rest of my life than try to find a date from the Internet.

"Yes, they did. Can I sue the Internet?" asks Lulu, almost crying.

33

Internet Date No. 3

After two cyberlove debacles, Lulu tells me, "I'm still a young woman, in my prime. I can't live my life like a nun. If I can't find love, perhaps I can meet someone online for a one-night stand."

"Lulu, you have always talked about how sex should be the 'ultimate fusion of body, mind, and emotions.' I thought you didn't approve of one-night stands," I say.

"I guess I'm a bit desperate now. I simply want to find some-body to love and to marry, but I've been so unlucky in that de-partment. So what's the point of clinging to those old values? I have a girl's needs too!" Lulu exclaims.

"Anyway, you don't have to go on the Internet to get laid. Girls like you could walk into any bar any night and pick up whoever you want, " I say.

"Humph. I can't do it. I need to take revenge on men with the help of the Internet, " Lulu says, terse and firm.

Lulu's new online identity is Beijing Lover, a bored forty-something married housewife looking for a hot one-night stand. After she posts her ad, she receives 120 replies in less than a week. She screens out all replies without pictures and those less than two lines long. Out of the twenty-one "candidates" remaining, she sends replies to the top two men, along with five of her pictures.

One of them, named Wild Heart, answers her right away through Yahoo Instant Messenger.

"How do I know your picture is real?" Lulu writes.

Wild Heart turns on his webcam. He has a handsome face and a fit body.

"Your webcam is great. Why don't you do a *touyi wu,* a little striptease for me?" Lulu types. She is shocked that she has settled in so quickly to her new bad-girl Beijing Lover identity.

"???" Wild Heart is shocked too.

Perhaps he is not as wild as his name. Lulu thinks, then types:

Beijing Lover: "Sensual body movement turns me on."

Wild Heart: "I've never done it before. I'm afraid of disappointing you."

Beijing Lover: "Are you a good lover, then?"

Wild Heart: "Yes. Satisfaction guaranteed."

Beijing Lover: "Show me."

Wild Heart starts to dance naked in front of the webcam. Because of the delay of the live video transmission over the Internet, Wild Heart looks ridiculous. Lulu feels guilty, but then she reminds herself; "This is my revenge. I'm regaining power."

Soon, they agree to get together, and arrange a time and location to meet. Wild Heart suggests a room in a public bathhouse. Lulu vetoes it because she doesn't like cheap, sleazy places. Even a one-night stand ought to be romantic, according to Lulu.

Wild Heart mentions the Kunlun Hotel, a five-star hotel that is past its prime. They agree.

At three-thirty in the afternoon, standing in the lobby of the Kunlun Hotel, Lulu suddenly becomes nervous. Wild Heart strides in. His images from the webcam are mainly in the nude, so he looks just a little strange wearing a suit and tie. Even though he has a model's good looks, Lulu isn't excited. "Am I really going to do it with some guy I've just met on the Internet?" Lulu asks herself.

"Hi, Beijing Lover, is that you?" Wild Heart recognizes her and walks to her with a full smile. He looks confident, not nervous at all. She greets him as casually as possible.

"Should we get a room?" Wild Heart says.

Lulu nods, biting her lower lip. Would they be noticed and stopped by the hotel security staff? Would the police think she was a hooker? If she was questioned, she wouldn't even be able to tell them his name.

Wild Heart goes to the counter to register. Lulu stands two meters away as Wild Heart shows his ID card.

"The executive business suite is 888 RMB per night," she hears the room clerk quote the rate.

"Sure." Wild Heart nods, patting his pockets. "Sorry. I left my wallet in my car—I'll be right back," he says to the clerk and Lulu.

"I'll split half of the cost later," Lulu thinks to herself. "At least, it shows I am his equal."

Lulu waits in the lobby alone, trying to ignore the occasional searching gaze from other men and some disapproving glances from the women who walk by. Women who loiter in Beijing hotel lobbies always arouse suspicion.

Half an hour later, Wild Heart has not returned. Lulu finally realizes that he is not coming back. She's been fooled again, but somehow, this time she is happy to be fooled. It stops her from doing something that she'd regret later.

She tells the story in great detail to me immediately. I understand why she prefers the Internet. After all, it is Beijing Lover's afternoon that has evaporated, not hers.

POPULAR PHRASES

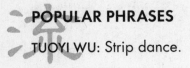

TUOYI WU: Strip dance.

34

Lining Up in China

Ask any Chinese and they'll tell you that China is undergoing sweeping changes at an incredibly fast rate. Building construction, highways, and new goods for sale in new shopping centers have changed the face of Beijing and Shanghai. But some things never change.

Take lines. For practical reasons, lines are not part of the Chinese psyche. And far be it for me to suggest that they should be. If you want to line up for something, let's say movie tickets, then be my guest. And while you're at it, feel free to politely yield to those who seem to be in a bigger hurry than you. After all, it's the civilized thing to do. But don't expect to see your movie. Not that day, anyway.

It just isn't practical to line up because you'll only be beaten out by anyone with fewer scruples, and sharper elbows than you.

When I'm with foreign guests, I refuse to engage in such tactics, so I often feel embarrassed because I am the last to be seated in the restaurant, last to get a cab, and first to be turned away at the ticket window. However, when I'm not entertaining foreign guests, I can be as rough and rowdy as anyone. I love to come away from a ticket window proudly clutching the spoils of the ticket war and leaving a wake of disappointed people.

Today, I am pushing my way toward the ticket window of the Beijing Fine Arts Museum. Tickets to the popular exhibition of European expressionism are limited. I am packed in a throng of winter-coated bodies reeking of garlic and boiled cabbage—and I am having the time of my life. But, suddenly, I am attacked from behind. I am being pushed and poked at by a squat old woman who has obviously been part of a mob before. I feel a fleeting sense of compassion: I remember the "silver seats" on public buses in California, and how people would yield a seat to a senior out of either kindness or fear of legal action. "But this is China," I think. "I must stick to my guns. If I yield, I will only be taken advantage of by every other nasty old woman in this horde."

I feel the rush of competition brewing. I face forward, ignoring the woman ramming me from behind. I have about three meters to go before I reach the window, and even then my position is not guaranteed.

I'll need to have my money out and on the counter before the others and hope the cashier chooses my offer first.

I take out some crumpled bills from my pocket and make one last surge toward the window. I push hard, and the way in front momentarily opens up when a young girl stumbles to the side—rookies! But I am not moving forward. I am being held back. I can't believe it. The old woman is holding me by the belt of my coat. That isn't in the rulebook.

Now, you might ask, isn't patience rewarded in Chinese culture? Didn't Hu Jintao wait fourteen years before becoming president? Yes—but keep in mind that Hu wasn't waiting in line for tickets to the European expressionism exhibition.

"You feisty old lady!" I scream, more out of awe than anger.

"Ay! Wait! I want to buy tickets!" the old woman is screaming along with the others in the crowd. I decide to unleash some Three Kingdoms–style war strategy, pitting two forces against each other by a third force, a tactic used after the fall of the Han dynasty, when China was divided into warring factions. I think this strategy is valid in a line for art museum tickets as well. I subtly push my opponent into a woman standing next to us, and as the two begin to quarrel, I make a triumphant rush to the ticket window.

I force my arm into the window and am now waving my bills feverishly at the cashier. I have made it. The cashier reaches for the money—but not swiftly enough. The woman is back at my side and, this time, tugs at my coat sleeve, pulling my arm—and, more important, my money—out of reach of the ticket seller.

"This is unprecedented," I think. I turn round—only to discover that the woman is my parents' neighbor, Grandma Liu. The atmosphere changes all of a sudden. In public, when we treat each other as strangers, we ignore how rude we act toward each other. But once we realize we know each other, the hostility melts away. We yield and help each other.

"Why'd you have to step on my toe, you brat," Grandma Liu says, smiling. "I ought to tell your father. Never mind. Let's go have tea first. I'm paying!"

"Let me help you get our tickets first," I say with a smile.

As I clutch the tickets just placed in my hand, I think, "Chivalry is alive and well in China. You just have to know where to look amid the rudeness."

Changes are evident everywhere. Just look at the skyline here. Indeed. I ponder that for a moment before making a note to remember Grandma Liu's patented coat-belt tug and arm pull for the next time I'm in a line.

35

City Girls and Country Girls

I go to an impoverished countryside to report on female hygiene and birth control methods. The women I interview talk to me about such exciting topics as rural abortions, improvised tampons, and child abandonment. Let's just say that, upon my return, I have a newfound appreciation for the conveniences of modern city life.

When I get back home, I invite Beibei, Lulu, and CC to my house to catch up over afternoon tea. The trip has opened my eyes to a harsh world beyond the neon lights of Beijing, Shanghai, and Hong Kong. I want to talk about everything I have seen—the poverty and the daily struggle for survival of the people in the country. With all of China's sweeping changes and economic reforms, the suffering of the poor is something that is often overlooked by the more successful city dwellers. Whether city people choose to ignore the poverty of their countrymen or whether they simply don't know about it depends on whom you ask.

Under the pagoda tree in the courtyard of my home, neither Beibei nor Lulu asks about my trip to rural China. They are too busy talking city-girl talk: men, parties, men, bars, men, celebrities, men, men, men.

"There are so many nice Chinese girls that Chinese men can choose from. But girls' choices are so limited. I'd definitely want to be born a man in my next life, or if I can't be that lucky, at least make me a lesbian," Beibei says while drinking her usual Lipton.

Lulu sips the two-thousand-yuan-per-pound oolong tea from Taiwan and sighs dramatically. "We modern girls just don't fit the traditional idea of Chinese women that Chinese men have stuck in their minds. We're too independent, too strong-willed, too well-educated."

"Perhaps China just has a shortage of men," says CC.

I see this as a good opportunity and finally speak out. "No, actually, it's the other way around. Chinese men far outnumber Chinese women—the disproportion is far greater than in most other countries."

"So where are all these men then?" Lulu asks skeptically, but she is unable to hide her enthusiasm.

Apparently, my friends are as naïve about the world outside the big cities as I was before my recent trip. I direct the conversation toward my experiences in the countryside. "Many of them are in the countryside."

"Oh, yeah." Beibei nods. "Those peasants need sons to do all the hard labor on the land, and traditionally, girls leave their family to join their husband's family when they are married anyway. Boys earn you money and girls cost you money, so of course everyone wants sons instead of daughters."

Lulu pipes up. "How could I forget about the peasants? China has eight hundred million of them! Everybody here originally came from a peasant family. I guess we city people forget about our roots from time to time. It's too bad!" Lulu speaks half-jokingly, although she senses that they are about to receive a lecture from me about the plight of rural China.

I say, "Although girls do make money for their families in one way: because women are so scarce, the groom has to pay a lot of money to the bride and her family for the wedding. The poorest ones sometimes have to save money until they are in their fifties and they still end up wifeless. Some families have to marry off their daughters in order to get the money to pay for their sons' weddings. In some extreme cases, two brothers have to share the same wife!"

"Polyandry? I read about it from Ma Jian's novella *Show the Coating on Your Tongue*. I thought it was only practiced in some Tibetan and Nepalese communities," Lulu cuts in. "So unlike us, who can't even find ourselves one man to marry, these peasant women can easily find a husband—or two! Why, it sounds almost too good to be true!"

"Don't be silly," I scold her. "Their lives aren't that easy. Many husbands in the countryside beat their wives. The wives are exploited. Unlike us—without gyms and health clubs to work out in we wouldn't be able to stay fit—they work from dawn to dark. And there are no beauty salons or foot massages to pamper them at the end of their hard day's work."

"No city girls would want to marry peasants, but city men sometimes are happy to take peasant women as their wives,"

Beibei says. "I guess they think they are caregivers and good mothers. Remember that famous Harvard-educated scholar from the May Fourth school in the 1920s, Hu Shi? He had so many intellectual female friends, including Pearl S. Buck, but his wife was an illiterate peasant."

"So perhaps China isn't lacking men, it's just short of urban men of high quality. The best ones have all gone overseas to become doctors and engineers. That's why the leftovers—even though they're second-rate—can still afford to be so choosy!" Lulu says.

"Plus, good men can become bad after being in China for too long: They become arrogant and selfish. They get used to the attention they get from women. Look at those returnees and those foreigners who live in China forever! Even the ones who are married are usually still looking," CC adds.

I go on. "One thing that has puzzled me the most about the peasant women is that they look so much older than their actual age. They don't have any kind of makeup or skin care products to help them look beautiful. They even use coarse paper made from cowshit as sanitary pads. But, despite all of that, they tell me that they are happy. The peasant women I talked to were smiling ear to ear when I saw them, even in the harsh conditions in which they were living."

"So why can't we be as happy?" Beibei asks. "We have youth, beauty, money, a good education, nice apartments, cars . . ."

"Perhaps we don't have the one thing that peasant women do," I say.

"What's that?" everyone asks in unison.

"Innocence," I say.

There is a thoughtful silence for a moment.

Finally, Beibei says, "Where are we going tonight, anyway?"

"I heard there's an MTV party going on at Vic's," says Lulu.

"I don't want to drive tonight," CC says.

All of a sudden, the countryside is put in the background. Nobody wants to talk about it.

"Great," I say, "I'll drive . . ."

36

The Gold Diggers

*H*aidian District is Beijing's college district. In Haidian, there is a popular belief that there are no beautiful female students at Tsinghua University, China's answer to MIT. In order to break this stereotype of Tsinghua girls, the student association has organized a *xuanmei,* a beauty pageant. Many girls on campus want badly to prove they are beautiful as well as intelligent.

I travel to Tsinghua to report on the beauty contest. Immediately after I enter the gates of the university, two girls who have set up an outdoor stand to sell cosmetics catch my attention. Their stand has attracted many female students. One of the sales girls is dressed in black, with heavy black eyeliner and a thick forest of hair. She gives off the scent of perfume from head to toe. She looks far more fashionable than most of the candidates who are buying her stuff. Her name is Ah-Fei.

When Ah-Fei is being interviewed, she states right away that she and her friend are not students. They are here to make money off the Tsinghua girls. Ah-Fei is a bit shy, and most of the time her friend Ding Dong answers for her.

According to Ding Dong, because of the nature of their work, Ah-Fei and Ding Dong have an opportunity to meet many foreign and rich friends. They often receive gifts, and they have more makeup and perfume than they can use, so they have decided to sell their wares to college kids who are obsessed with beauty and famous brands but who can't afford to buy Chanel or Estée Lauder in China's department stores.

I find my favorite Lancôme cosmetics in their collection. Whenever I walked into Macy's department store in the States, the first thing I would see was the Lancôme counter and the mysterious face of Juliette Binoche. Lancôme was expensive; nevertheless it was my choice. I liked Juliette Binoche's movies, *Damage*, *The Unbearable Lightness of Being*, and *The English Patient*.

Uma Thurman, from the movies *Henry and June* and *Pulp Fiction*, was later the face of Lancôme. She is also one of my idols. Uma is a tall blonde who combines Marilyn Monroe's sexiness, Audrey Hepburn's elegance, and Meryl Streep's intelligence. Uma's eyes are as mysterious as Tibet.

Through *Henry and June*'s director, Philip Kaufman, a good friend of my mother's, I got an autograph from this blond beauty when I was studying in the United States.

At that time, my American classmates all liked Julia Roberts and Mariah Carey. There weren't many people who appreciated Uma. I am not a fan of Julia Roberts, who I think is an open book. I prefer the mysterious European type. I haven't had a chance to e-mail Philip Kaufman. I'd love to tell him that reading Henry Miller and Anaïs Nin is a new fashion among young Chinese female intellectuals, and his movies *Henry and June* and *Quill* were voted among the top ten must-see erotic movies by Chinese cybermovie fans.

"I love Lancôme!" I say.

Ah-Fei shrugs. "I don't like Lancôme."

"Why?" I am curious.

"I'm not interested in anything that's imported into China and available at Chinese stores," replies Ah-Fei snobbishly.

"Oh, I see." I nod.

"If we want something, we have our friends buy it for us from New York or Paris," she adds with an upturned nose.

"I see." I take a lipstick that Ah-Fei is selling, and look at it. There is a small sticker on the lid of the lipstick that reads "Nude No. 5," and then after that quite clearly are the words "Not for Individual Sale." This is a free giveaway from Lancôme!

I also notice that there are two bottles of Christian Dior *Poison* perfume, one classic *Poison,* the other *Tendre Poison.*

"Are they your extras, or you don't like Christian Dior either?" I ask.

Ding Dong answers for Ah-Fei. "All Chinese women are using *Poison* now. Sometimes on the bus there are several women wearing it. The good brands are coming down in price! No one with any class is using *Poison* anymore!"

"Does Ah-Fei wear perfume herself?"

"What girl doesn't wear perfume? Coco Chanel in the 1920s said a woman who doesn't wear perfume has no future. Of course, our Ah-Fei has the brands she likes. But the perfume she wears is certainly not for women who go to work by bus. Oh, yeah," Ding Dong turns to Ah-Fei. "What's the name of that brand of perfume you like?"

"Miyake."

"Issey Miyake? The Japanese designer's perfume?" I ask.

"Yes. The masses don't know Issey Miyake. It's too new for them."

I notice that one of the bottles of perfume Ah-Fei is selling is only half-full, and has obviously been used. But a girl buys it nevertheless. It is only ten yuan.

I ask Ding Dong, "What jobs do the two of you have that allow you to acquire such a nice collection of expensive cosmetics?"

"We're antique appraisers," she says proudly.

"Fashionable young women like you, why are you antique appraisers?" I humor them.

"In our business, we have a high-class clientele, either foreign, Taiwanese, or Hong Kong businessmen," Ding Dong smugly replies. "They're good candidates for spouses."

"So they give you these gifts for free?"

"Yes. If they want our honest comments on the antiques they have."

"Do you like the job?"

"It's a good way to meet men of quality." Ding Dong smiles.

"Are you guys *bang dakuan,* gold diggers?" I ask bluntly, waiting for their reaction.

"What's wrong with being a gold digger? All we want is a good husband." Ding Dong doesn't mind being called *bang dakuan.*

"What is considered a good husband?" I am curious what their definition is.

"A good husband should be tall and wealthy. He should come from overseas," Ah-Fei cuts in.

"What do you mean by wealthy?" My fieldwork continues.

"If you talk about possessions, they have to have the three C's: condo, car, and credit card," says Ding Dong.

"Four C's are even better!" Ah-Fei cuts in again.

"What is the fourth C?"

"CEO! Do you understand what it means? A new word in China!"

"Yes, I guess so."

"If we talk about annual income: six digits in U.S. dollars; over one million in renminbi; and over ten million Japanese yen," Ding Dong continues, explaining their interpretation of being wealthy.

Her answer reminds me of the popular new rhyme: "First-class girls marry the Americans; second-class girls marry the Japanese; third-class girls marry the Taiwanese or Hong Kongers; fourth-class girls marry the mainlanders.

"How can you attract such wealthy men?" I ask.

"First, we study foreign languages. We are multilingual: we can speak English, German, Japanese, and some Cantonese."

"Why not French? French is the language of romance!"

"French people are generally poor by our standards!"

"But Christian Dior, L'Oréal, Lancôme, and LV are all expensive French brands. I guess *some* Frenchman must have money," I say.

"Yes, but there is an opportunity cost. We'd rather spend more time brushing up on our Japanese. The chances of meeting a well-to-do Japanese man are higher," Ding Dong says.

"Okay, then what else?"

Ding Dong continues. "We learn to cook Chinese food and some other Chinese tricks like playing the Chinese flute or doing calligraphy. Men, Chinese or foreign, like women who can be both domestic and cultural."

"What about college education?"

"No. We don't have any college education." Ding Dong shakes her head.

"Do you admire the girls in Tsinghua then?"

"No way! We don't want to become nerds with Coke-bottle glasses. Instead of studying calculus, our textbook is *How to Snare a Millionaire!*" Ding Dong says.

On the way home, I think to myself, what if I start a company, buy the copyrights of how-to-marry-rich books from the West, and sell them in China. It would be good business.

POPULAR PHRASES

BANG DAKUAN: Being gold diggers—one of the downsides of the success of the new market economy.

XUANMEI: Beauty pageant. Such practices are becoming increasingly popular in the new image-conscious China.

HAIDIAN DISTRICT: Beijing's college district. Major colleges like Beijing University, People's University, and Tsinghua University are all located in this district.

37

Cat Fights

*L*ulu and I go to the International Club to attend a press conference for the hottest TV series *From Beijing to San Francisco*. The American-sponsored TV series tells the story of three Chinese women's struggles, love affairs, successes and failures in the land of opportunity. The press conference aims at promoting three actresses—Do Little, Vivian, and J, all in their early twenties—into household names.

Now the photogenic and chic trio is sitting up at the front of the conference room in the presidential suite of Beijing's Grand Hyatt, smiling at countless cameras and basking in the limelight.

Sitting next to me in the audience is a girl called May, who plays the fourth supporting actress in the TV series. With long legs, big eyes, and a narrow European face, May is lauded by Chinese media as China's most beautiful model. The Chinese director originally wanted her to play the leading female role. But Peter, the American investor, chose Do Little over her. May's own role is boring and unimportant, and overshadowed by the three leading women. Now, she has to sit with the journalists.

"Girl, I'm a model," she complains to me. "In the fashion world, different looks come and go, but I didn't realize that the TV world could be so much worse. Look at Do Little—she looks like a peasant out of the film *Not One Less*. To be honest, Zhejiang Village, south of the city, is full of girls like that looking for nanny jobs. What's wrong with these American people? Why do they think she's so hot? She has such tiny eyes; I thought she was asleep up there when I first saw her. A big flat nose and a round face like a dried persimmon. Two windburned red cheeks, as if she's been living up on a plateau. In China, she's so ugly you couldn't marry her off, but the Americans think they've discovered a new wonder of the world. They gave her the leading role."

"Perhaps her look suits the character," I suggest. "Lucy, the woman she plays, is someone that wasn't popular in China but gains popularity and self-confidence in the United States."

"But still she would be considered ugly in China. Is this world weird or what? As soon as the Americans hired her, all these Chinese magazines started wanting her to appear on their covers, and companies have come looking for her to do advertisements. The media also praise her for being a Chinese beauty." May spits in disgust.

No sooner does May finish her complaint than Iron Egg, Beibei's former journalist lover, asks the American investor why they hired Do Little. "Any Chinese person could tell you she is just plain ugly," he says.

May confides in me. "I just gave Iron Egg a *hongbao* containing five hundred yuan. He agreed to use the word ugly to describe Do Little. We have to *cei* her in public."

Peter smiles at the question. He speaks calmly as if he was preparing for the question for a while. "Do Little is very Oriental, a little Mongolian, a little Vietnamese. Her natural style reminds me of a rural village in the morning, cool, with the faint smell of earth. She certainly makes a unique impression that I don't see in many other Chinese actresses. The success of the TV series shows that we did the right thing."

Do Little speaks for herself. "I leave whether I am beautiful or not to my audience. But I want to say that I'm natural, not plastic. Unlike some actresses, I don't need an eye job, a boob job, or a nose job to elevate my beauty. I'm no fake." Do Little looks into May's eyes as she speaks, reminding everybody that May has had several rounds of plastic surgery. As all eyes turn to May, she storms out angrily.

I find myself liking Do Little. It's her confidence that makes her beautiful. I also secretly wonder: I am judging China like another American.

After Do Little, the journalists' attention goes to Vivian. Rumor has it that Vivian got the role simply because she has married Peter's cousin, John.

Unlike first-rate stars, who often avoid family issues, Vivian enjoys talking about her private life to the media.

"I have to speak English at home. How unlucky I am compared to those girls who have Chinese husbands. But I have no choice."

It is funny to hear Vivian pretending to be unlucky when everyone knows that speaking English is a status symbol.

"Why no choice? You could divorce your American husband and marry a Chinese man. Then you could speak only Chinese. There are half a billion Chinese men out there waiting for you," a journalist says, challenging Vivian.

Iron Egg jumps in. "I've heard on the grapevine that you always wanted to marry a white man. You never dated Chinese. Do you think you're above your fellow Chinese?"

Vivian's face changes, "That's not true. I'm a traditional Chinese wife."

"I've heard that you first met your husband in the Kunlun Hotel disco five years ago—and that you chased him all over Beijing and pleaded with him until he promised to take you to America." Iron Eggs has exposed Vivian's old secrets. And the thought that Vivian frequented the Kunlun Hotel disco suggests that her interest may have been professional rather than personal. Chinese tabloids are notoriously scandalous.

It's clear to me that Iron Egg must have been bribed by Vivian's enemies.

Vivian loses her self-assurance and yells at Iron Egg. "Ridiculous! John chased me like a love-sick puppy!"

The journalists all laugh, including Iron Egg. They've got what they wanted, a perfect quote from Vivian.

Seeing Vivian tricked by the ill-willed journalists, J acts low-key and speaks cautiously.

J talks about how she came from an out-of-work family in a northeast province and managed to be accepted into Beijing Drama Academy. She was discovered by the Chinese director promoting Rémy Martin brandy in a Western-style department store, where she worked part-time while studying.

Now the producers hope she will be the "next big thing," both in China and abroad.

"What will your next project be?" one of the journalists asks her.

"You should ask my agent," she says.

At that point, a man in a white suit steps forward—he is wearing sunglasses even though everybody is inside. As soon as he opens his mouth, everyone knows he talks with a Hong Kong accent.

"Gemenr," he says—the Beijing slang sounds funny coming from this Hong Kong man, and some of the journalists in the audience laugh—"we will take J to Hong Kong, where we hope to develop her career in a number of areas."

One of the journalists pipes up: "Have you spoken to the producers of the James Bond films? They love Asian women these days."

The agent waves his hand dismissively. "In keeping with her training at the Beijing Drama Academy, J wants to stay in touch with Chinese drama projects. She is not going to totally sell herself out to foreigners. She is already considering a role in a new Hong Kong film called *No Tomorrow Anymore*. We are sure it will be a big hit."

"J has been bought by the Hong Kong triads," I hear a female voice among the journalists, loud enough to be heard, low enough to be unrecognized.

It's said that many movie stars are controlled by Hong Kong mafias. Is J one of them? Or is it just a rumor from J's enemy? In any case, it makes J more mysterious and controversial, which is not necessarily a bad thing for a rising star. Being an entertainment journalist, one needs to follow gossip and enjoy the spread of rumors. I feel lucky that I mainly cover political and social issues, which means that I don't need to write anything about today's conference. As I am thinking this, Lulu speaks. "I'm pretty. I've got so many journalist friends. Niuniu, do you think I should change my job and become an actress? It's certainly glamorous!"

"Can you act?" I ask. "Can you lie without blushing? If you can sleep your way up and still tell the public that you're a traditional Chinese woman, I suppose you can pass the test."

Lulu sighs. "Then, I'm doomed to fail."

POPULAR PHRASES

HONGBAO: A red envelope, normally containing money, used as a gift for friends and relatives on special occasions; often referred to in Hong Kong as *lai see*.

CEI: To beat and attack someone; a popular slang among the young uneducated people in Beijing.

GEMENR: Beijing slang for mate or buddy.

38

The English Patient

Y*ingyu*, or English, is big in China. After China's entry into the World Trade Organization, the whole nation was motivated to learn English. First-graders are offered English classes in school. Seniors in big cities get together every morning in their English corner to practice. Even state leaders like to drop English words into their speeches or sing songs in English to impress the public.

English workshops make millions of bucks, especially those TOEFL, GRE, LSAT, GMAT preparation classes. Every teacher there is a millionaire. The biggest English-teaching millionaire of the lot is Li Yang, whose English language course is called Crazy English. He teaches students to learn English by screaming out English phrases at the top of their voice!

What these courses are selling is not only English but also *meiguo meng*, the American dream. Everyone wants to learn

English to get a job, preferably at a *waiqi,* or foreign company, or to get the chance to study in the United States.

In this year's special gala variety program made by CCTV for the Spring Festival, people, from kindergarten kids to old grandpas, parade in front of the camera shouting "ABC," Crazy English–style, as if they were shouting old revolutionary slogans. My friend, a French journalist at AFP, is amazed at this scene: he can't figure out why an entire country is so obsessed with a foreign language—particularly if it is English!

People from different cities in China like to compete with one another over their English skills. Shanghai people think their English is better than Hong Kongers, claiming "Our education system is better than theirs!" Although I don't buy Shanghainese arrogance, my experience in Hong Kong was worse.

When I was visiting Hong Kong on business, I was in a store and I wanted to ask for help, so I decided I had better use English. When I spoke, the young shop assistant waved her hands and said, "No English!" So I said in Chinese, "Do you speak Mandarin?" The girl replied in Cantonese, "*Siu-siu*—a little . . ." It was hopeless; I had to give up and walk out of the store. So I tend to believe that people in Shanghai can speak better English than people from Hong Kong.

Beijingers believe their English is the best: "If southerners can't tell the difference between *n* and *l, s* and *sh,* even in Chinese, how can they speak better English than us?" they say. "We are especially good at American English because of our *er-hua,* We even speak Chinese with an American accent!"

Little Fang speaks perfect *putonghua.* She tutors CC's boyfriend, Nick. She offers Nick free Chinese lessons. When Nick doesn't understand Little Fang's Chinese, he asks her, in his perfect Oxford English, to explain. "It's my way to pick up the Queen's English," Little Fang says. This sort of *huxiang xuexi*, or language exchange, is common between Chinese and foreign students in China. Often more than just language is exchanged: many romances have blossomed through language exchange relationships.

But because Little Fang only teaches Nick Chinese and never goes swimming with him like his other female Chinese "tutors," CC trusts her and the two become friends. After CC's introduction, Little Fang is considered a member of our gang. We often play sports or go dancing together.

One day, at a bar called People, Little Fang introduces a girlfriend named Yu to CC and me, and begs us to speak some English to her. When Yu goes to the bathroom, Little Fang tells us Yu's story.

Yu's only dream is to speak beautiful English. At first, she tried to memorize words from her English-Chinese dictionary and tore each page out as she memorized it. Her dictionary had almost nothing left except the cover, but she still got an F in each English examination. So she started to eat the pages she had torn out. It was traditional Chinese logic: Men believe they can be more virile by eating the penises of bulls and tigers. Yu thought that she could remember all the English words by eating a dictionary.

After everything failed, Yu got desperate. She went to hotel lobbies to meet native English speakers in order to improve her oral English. Last week, she was punished by her school because she was caught by the police with a Canadian man in his hotel room alone around midnight. The man was not wearing a shirt when the two were busted. Apparently they thought she was a prostitute. There are a lot of rumors in Beijing about university students prostituting themselves to earn a little money—but doing it in order to learn English? Surely, this would be going too far!

Little Fang brings Yu to us, hoping to help Yu out.

Yu admits that her biggest dream is to speak English twenty-four hours a day. So we chat to her in English.

But she simply doesn't have a natural talent for languages. She cannot tell the difference between the sound *s* and the sound *th*.

CC and I feel awkward because we can't understand what Yu is saying when she speaks English. We don't know whether we should say, "I beg your pardon?" or "What was that?" We are afraid of hurting Yu's feelings, so we just smile and nod, and say, "Uh-huh" and, "Oh."

Little Fang notices, and says in Chinese to Yu, "Tell us about your boyfriend, Ching."

"I just dumped him!" Yu screams.

"Why?" Little Fang is surprised.

"I can't stand Ching's clumsy spoken English. When he speaks English, he sounds like an idiot!"

"How come?"

"To him, *s* and *th* sound the same!" As she says this, both sounds come out as an *s* and we try not to laugh.

"But he is a nice guy. How can you dump him just because his English isn't so good?" CC asks. "You only speak to him in Chinese!"

Yu has her theory: "It do not matter whether someone Chinese good or bad. But if he speak no good English, he have no future. Good English good job, and lots of money, but good Chinese no use!"

POPULAR PHRASES

YINGYU: English.

MEIGUO MENG: American dream.

WAIQI: Foreign enterprise; a Sino-foreign joint venture company in China.

ER-HUA: The distinctive *er* suffix added to words pronounced in the Beijing accent.

PUTONGHUA: Standard Mandarin Chinese.

HUXIANG XUEXI: Learning from each other; mutual-exchange language lessons. Many romances between foreigners and locals seem to sprout up through these relationships.

39

Beijing Pygmalion

From ancient times to the present day, purity, *chunjie*, has been the most desirable quality a Chinese man wants from his woman. One can always find those ideal "pure" girls in the romance novels written by the Taiwanese author Qiongyao: long, floating, straight black hair; long white skirt; virginal, quiet, untouchable, and selfless. In the last forty years, whether in books or TV series, Qiongyao's love stories about the stereotypical innocent Chinese girls have never failed to sell in Greater China. Men and women, young and old, all have shed tears for their sad stories.

I have never liked Qiongyao's soap operas. I think they are contrived and their heroines are prudes. My Oxford-educated friend CC feels the same way. "Why do the Chinese men love those airheads who only know how to cry and beg? Why can't they appreciate Meryl Streep and Sophia Loren?"

In order to find the answer for CC, I invite my painter friend Jia to meet us for a drink at the Red Moon bar in the new Grand Hyatt in downtown Beijing.

Jia, a fan of Qiongyao, loved the innocent type of woman so much that he always wanted to marry a minority nationality girl from the countryside.

Three years ago, Jia trekked to primitive villages in search of his ideal wife. In impoverished Guizhou Province, he walked through a forest for three days and finally arrived at a Dong tribe settlement where there was neither electricity nor automobiles. The villagers there lived as if they were still in the Stone Age. They were very hospitable and treated him, a total stranger, like a family member. Soon he met a beautiful eighteen-year-old virgin with the sweetest smile. Her name was Miya. Miya was a good dancer. When she moved, the silver anklets she wore tinkled. Jia was totally enchanted by her.

After living in the Dong tribe for a month, Jia persuaded Miya to marry him and took her to live with him back in Beijing.

His ambitious project was to train Miya to be his ideal wife. The task started with teaching Miya to speak Chinese. Previously, she spoke only the language of her tribe.

Within two years, Miya had turned into someone who had just stepped out of the pages of one of Qiongyao's novels: long straight hair, white skirt, sweet, and an avid admirer of her man. I met Miya several times. She was quiet most of the time, but when she spoke, it was always about Jia.

I asked Miya what books she loved to read; Miya said any books Jia has read. I asked Miya what food she loved to eat; Miya said any food Jia ate. I was put off. "Miya isn't one of us." My girlfriends all said that as well. But Jia enjoyed showing

Miya off to his friends. His male friends all envied him so much that they wanted to follow in his matrimonial footsteps.

Inspired by his new love, Jia held a successful painting exhibition of his rose period works in the French embassy of Beijing.

Jia felt on top of the world until two months after the exhibition. One day he came home and found that Miya had disappeared. So had his paintings and the money in his bank account. Rumor had it that Miya had met a retired French diplomat at Jia's exhibition and had run away with him to Paris, along with Jia's paintings and money.

Of course, this should not have come as a surprise to Jia. After all, Miya wasn't the first wife to betray him. He had two other tribal wives before Miya, and the beginning and the ending were always the same: he found an innocent girl from a remote village and brought her to the city till one day she left him for another man, taking all his possessions with her.

"So why are you so fixated on these tribal girls?" I inquire.

"Their sexual and emotional innocence. I believe true love can only happen once in one's life. City women have too many chances to meet men. They aren't pure anymore. My three wives were all corrupted by the city," Jia states.

"He is certainly not into the brainy type, like Meryl Streep, or the sexy type, like Sophia Loren," CC murmurs to me.

No wonder he is into tribal girls; no sophisticated urban woman would buy his nonsense. I can't help but tease him: "I guess you played a major role in the process of corrupting them."

"But I didn't get a bad deal myself. I traded my paintings and money for years of being worshipped and served like a king! It at least pumped up my ego, which helps me paint.

After all, how many people can live like a king in a people's republic?" Jia defends himself.

Here we go, I think, Jia's problem again is lack of confidence, like that of so many Chinese men.

CC, although fond of Jia's paintings, is dismayed by his male chauvinist comments. "Ha! You think you were some king," she snaps. "But this is the third time that your innocent queen ran off with your royal treasury for other men. I know what type of king you are: The King of Cuckolds."

POPULAR PHRASES

CHUNJIE: Pure and clean, meaning innocent or innocence; used both as an adjective and as a noun.

40

Eating Ants

I am on a business trip to Guangzhou. One day, I receive a phone call from a state-owned beer company called Blue Boys. "Our President Gao would like to see you." On the other line, it is the voice of a female secretary. Who is President Gao? I am confused. I don't know many people in Guangzhou.

I soon find out that President Gao is the boy once known as High Mountain. We have been out of touch for almost ten years.

High Mountain was my secret admirer in middle school. At our school, the majority of the students came from high-ranking Communist Party cadre families. High Mountain's snobbish schoolmates often teased him for his humble upbringing: his father was the secretary of the secretary of Beibei's grandfather, and a low-ranking bureaucrat. He liked me because he said I was the only girl in school that was nice to him. Before I left for the United States, he wrote me a farewell letter.

"I hope you will remain a patriotic Chinese girl and won't forget the duty of serving the Chinese people when you are in America. I hope you will not fall in love with a foreign devil, because it is not at all patriotic. An insider is an insider and an outsider should always be an outsider. I wanted to tell you how much I liked you, but I was so afraid that others will laugh at me for being a toad who wants the meat of a swan. I will demonstrate my love for you by putting my whole heart into building our country. High Mountain."

Today's High Mountain is no longer the little boy who suffered from low self-esteem. He is President Gao. He drives a Cadillac to meet me.

After I get in his car, I start to look for the seat belt.

"Americans are so gutless. I'm not afraid of death. I never wear a seat belt," brags President Gao. I didn't expect my former admirer to greet me by abusing the States, but I soon realize that making fun of overseas returnees is a new fashion among locals. I don't mind President Gao having some sour feelings. After all, he was rejected back then, not only by me but by the American universities he applied to. I smile back politely, "A Cadillac can protect you well enough, I guess."

"So what car did you drive in the States?" President Gao asks me as he swerves in and out of traffic.

"A Honda," I reply while nervously holding on to my seat.

"I guessed as much. Japanese cars are more economical. I love the luxury of American cars. Who cares about gasoline? Everything I spend from gas to parking tickets is reimbursed by my company anyway." Says President Gao.

"So you are taking advantage of both the socialist and capitalist systems," I tease.

"Of course!" President Gao says triumphantly.

He drives through a red light and brags, "I bet you had to follow all those dumb traffic laws in the States. I never have to bother here. The sheriff at the police department is my buddy."

I notice that an old pedestrian at the crosswalk stops in fear as President Gao's big Cadillac surges into the traffic. It reminds me of something my *New York Times* friend Richard Bernstein wrote in his book *The Ultimate Journey: Retracing the Path of an Ancient Buddhist Monk Who Crossed Asia in Search of Enlightenment:* "The world is divided into two kinds of countries. There are countries where the cars stop for people and countries where the people stop for cars."

"Where do you feel like eating?" President Gao asks me.

"I don't have any particular preference."

"I'm so sick of shark fins and lobsters, I want to take you to a trendy new place, very up market, where all the CEOs go. That place has a delicacy that you won't find anywhere else. Don't worry about the money—it's on me. I've heard that overseas Chinese always go dutch. We locals don't do that."

I know the money President Gao is going to spend is not really his anyway. It is all *gongkuan,* public money.

"I guess you can afford anything in China," I say, thinking, "I will not give him the chance to buy me anything."

We arrive at an unnamed restaurant in Foshan, the city adjacent to Guangzhou. The owner, a beautiful young lady, greets President Gao in a seductive voice. "Gao Zong, the usual?"

"Yes, please," President Gao says, apparently enjoying being called Gao Zong. As they walk inside, President Gao says to me, "By the way, that bitch wants to be my third wife." In the next twenty minutes, he tries to impress me by eagerly telling me how many women admire him and his money.

When the dishes arrive, I almost faint. Scrambled eggs with

ants, fried cockroaches, bat soup . . . I can't understand why these things are expensive in Guangzhou. In the United States, I saw young people eat this stuff on TV after they were paid $50 each. Apparently, it is not an exaggeration that people in Guangdong will eat anything that has legs except tables and anything that flies except airplanes.

"I can't eat this." I say.

"If you don't like Chinese food, why didn't you stay in America? I know—I bet it's because the white people treat us Asians as a second-class race! I bet you couldn't bear it any-more." President Gao sounds hurt.

I realize the most embarrassing moment for a woman is to meet a vengeful man whom she has rejected—even if she was the only one who had not teased him at school for his family background. But now I smile at President Gao. "It's not that bad, actually. Being yellow in America is at least better off than being a son of a low-ranking civil servant in Jingshan School."

POPULAR PHRASES

GONGKUAN: Public money, often refers to things that can be reimbursed or paid for by the government or work units. The Chinese are true artists when it comes to writing off expenses to the government or their companies.

41

Nick's Choice

After five years of courtship in England and two years of living together in China, Nick and CC broke up: Nick dumped her after their trip to Shanghai. Everybody in his circle of friends thought that Nick would stay in Shanghai and continue to pursue the Portman Hotel waitress with whom he was infatuated.

Instead, he is back in Beijing and has begun seeing Little Fang. CC is very upset after hearing this—especially since we have all been friends with Little Fang. CC comes to complain.

"But doesn't Xiao Fang already have someone?" I ask her as I remember Little Fang's boyfriend, an earnest young man who always seemed to have a GRE English vocabulary book in his hand.

"She's always had the hots for Nick, I guess. Otherwise, why would she have offered him free Chinese lessons?" CC says.

"I suppose you're right," I say, "But Little Fang seemed so nice. I'm sure she didn't initiate this relationship. Perhaps it was Nick."

"Whatever. If the bitch was really my friend, she wouldn't have agreed to go out with him," cries CC.

"Did Nick tell you why he wanted to break up with you?" I ask.

"He said he had decided that he liked local girls better than girls like me who grew up overseas. He said local girls aren't so snooty and stuck-up. Niuniu, do you think I'm a stuck-up, snooty princess?"

"No, CC, of course not!"

"But why did Nick dump me for Xiao Fang? Niuniu, tell me, is it because I'm not as pretty or as sexy as the local girls?" CC asks.

"You're beautiful."

"Then, I guess I'm not Chinese enough. He said I don't have the elegance of a real Chinese woman." CC sighs.

"Sounds like he has yellow fever," I say. "He really does have an Asian fetish. Time to move on, dear. Nick is just a single blade of grass on the lawn, and even as we speak, there are new seedlings blowing in the wind. And in Beijing, the grass grows quickly!"

CC looks pensive and sad, saying, "But maybe he's right, maybe I'm not Chinese enough. Whenever Westerners see me, they all think I'm Chinese, and expect me to speak perfect Chinese, to be a submissive Asian woman and drool over them just because they're foreigners. But I'm not Chinese—I'm a Westerner. I grew up in England; English is my native language. I only speak Chinese when I'm with my parents. I know far more about European culture than I do about Chinese culture. And

I'm not about to throw myself at some Western guy just because he has blue eyes and blond hair.

"When I came to China, I thought, if I study Mandarin and learn a bit about *kung fu* and *feng shui,* then I'll be Chinese. But when Westerners ask me questions about Chinese culture, I've got no idea. I've worked hard for so many years, but I'm a failure. I don't belong anywhere. Doesn't matter whether it's Nick or those men I met in Asia, so many of them want someone exotic. If they go out with a local girl, it gives them a colonial sense of victory, of conquering and taming the mysterious Orient. But me, I'm too Western, too similar to them—I see myself as one of them, as their equal. I'm not exotic enough, so these Western men don't think being with someone like me is sufficiently romantic. Am I right?"

"Why are you so worried about what Western guys think of you anyway? If they don't understand you, if they don't appreciate you, then why don't you go out with a Chinese guy instead?" I suggest. "You're pretty, smart, funny, there must be loads of Chinese guys who want to go out with you."

"I don't know—I've never been out with Chinese men before."

"Why not?" I demand.

"Somehow we just don't click. It'd be like dating one of my brothers or something. And Western guys are always so much funnier, laid-back, not so stressed about pleasing their parents. And Western guys have got much better bodies!"

"Hmph, you can blame Nick for having yellow fever, but it seems to me you're just as fixated on Western men," I say to CC.

42

The Gossip Party

$\mathcal{M}$y boss Sean and I are on assignment in Hong Kong to write about Hong Kong's crisis of confidence. On Friday evening, we receive invitations to Club Ing in Wan Chai, a farewell party for an English banker who is returning home.

Attendees include bankers, consultants, lawyers, foreign journalists, advertising agents, Chinese celebrities, and people of uncertain background who call themselves free agents or writers. Most people don't know the English banker, but it doesn't matter. Just like in the West, connections have always been important in Chinese culture, especially in Hong Kong. That's why parties are not to be missed.

White gloves, martinis, cries in English of "Hi" and "Oh yeah," hugging and kissing greetings, politely revealing teeth in a small smile, conversing in a mixture of Chinese and English. Neither Chinese nor Western—it is very Hong Kong.

I soon discover that no one actually knows anyone very well, but the warm way in which people greet one another makes it seem as if they've known each other a long time. In conversation, people constantly drop names. "Do you know So-and-So?" is a mantra. It helps people find connections but it can also rescue you when you don't know what else to say. Moreover, the more people you know, the more social you are, and the more people want to get to know you.

Among the Chinese, the names people love to drop the most are names of high-ranking officials in China, or the cousins of high-ranking officials, or the wives of the nephews of high-ranking officials, any of which automatically raises their status. Knowing even the driver of a high-ranking official can make the speaker proud and the listener stand in awe. As soon as I admit that I went to high school with the son of China's president, many show interest and come to talk to me.

Among the expats, the names dropped are often old classmates or coworkers. People who say, "So-and-So was my classmate in Boston" are Harvard or MIT people, as always. No one will say the name of the school he went to. The unspoken rule for everybody at this sort of gathering is that name-dropping is fine, but school-name-dropping is considered outré.

A woman walks past facing me. She looks me up and down and then greets me warmly. "Isn't that Niuniu? Do you still remember me—Auntie Man? I'm your old neighbor! I never would have imagined you're so grown-up. We mustn't have seen each other for many years! I never would have thought I'd bump into you at a place like this!"

I remember. This Auntie Man was my old Beijing neighbor. Auntie Man struck up a conversation with a Hong Kong businessman one day when she was walking along the street. Later, she married him and moved to Hong Kong to be a mainland wife.

"Auntie Man, how's your life in Hong Kong?" I ask.

"Hong Kong is so expensive! An apartment is several million Hong Kong dollars; a car parking space is a couple of thousand per month. Now my husband's company has set up a branch in Shanghai, and we're going to move there. Everyone's going to Shanghai, you know! Who made Shanghai so cheap? But I'll have to keep an eye on my husband. Shanghai girls are all after men!"

I introduce Auntie Man to Sean. Just as they are shaking hands, a Chinese couple walks over to Sean.

The husband has a broad face. He is wearing a polo shirt, pants with suspenders, and black-rimmed glasses, and his hair is slicked back and shining. He looks part cartoon, part tycoon.

The wife has narrow eyes that are arched slightly upward, the Asian beauty that is popular overseas now. Her lips are thick and full; they remind me of the soft-rock singer Sade. She wears high-heeled shoes with pointy toes. Her Chinese-style dress is like a giant man's hand, stroking her waiting body. She carries a small black leather handbag. The label is Prada.

They embrace Sean warmly.

Sean turns to me. "Let me introduce you. This is Kelvin Chang. I met him when I was studying Chinese in England. This is Mrs. Chang."

"Hello. I am Sean's colleague Niuniu."

"And who is this?" Mrs. Chang looks at Auntie Man.

"My old neighbor from Beijing, Auntie Man. We haven't seen each other for many years. I never would have thought we would meet at a cocktail party here. It is a small world," I say.

"It really is a small world." Auntie Man nods at the Changs and repeats my words significantly.

After the Chinese couple leave, Auntie Man pulls me to one side, looking at Mrs. Chang's swaying back, and whispers,

"That bitch sure can put on a show! Seeing me and pretending she doesn't know me."

"Do you know her?" I ask.

"Even when my bones have turned to ash I won't forget her." Auntie Man bites her lip. "We used to be in the same propaganda troupe. Her husband played the Chinese violin. Later, we went on tour overseas, and she hooked up with a local in Hawaii and stayed. She wrote to her husband back in China that she would make enough for him to join her in the United States. Eight years ago, my hubby and I spent our honeymoon in Hawaii. Guess who we saw in a strip club? This same Mrs. Chang danced on the bar stark-naked. Look at her now, she acts like she's a rose. I was her old coworker in the propaganda troupe, but she pretended not to know me. You know why? Only I know of her sordid past. But I'm still not one of those gossiping housewives. I never told anyone about her."

With these words, Auntie Man leaves me and talks to others. I don't want to hear anything. Gossip can confuse people's state-of-mind. The less I know of these sorts of things, the better. I can tell that she is repeating the story to everybody because everybody she talks to immediately glances at the Changs.

I feel a little dizzy. Tonight, I have handed out so many name cards and greeted so many people. I think of Mother. She never tires of attending these sorts of gatherings. She has not much education or even a formal job. How can she always be the center of attention in such gatherings? And I, it seems, have not inherited her social graces. A party can be nice, and knowing So-and-So is nice, but not always: there are always people at the party you wish you didn't know, just as Mrs. Chang didn't expect to meet Auntie Man.

43

Matchmaking

Since "sex goddess" editor Lulu left her abusive ex-boyfriend, Ximu, Beibei has become our matchmaker. Her plan is to find both of us fat cats who might become her business partners. Surely, Beibei has many connections with wealthy people.

Beibei has never approved of Lulu falling in love with poor artists like Ximu. She has a theory: in today's world, poor men and rich men are equally corrupt, so why not go for the rich ones? Beibei wants to arrange a party for Lulu's birthday, but she's not sure where to hold it. Not Beijing, because the Communist Party convention is about to take place, and it'll be harder to keep a low profile.

Beibei's friend in Shanghai, a banker called Dan Ke, invites Beibei, Lulu, and me to come to Shanghai where the hype is. "My company bought a colonial-style mansion in Xuhui district," he says. "We spent one million yuan just on the renovations. Let's celebrate Lulu's birthday here. I'll invite all my bachelor friends. We've got a huge living room, big enough for ballroom dancing!"

No sooner has Beibei accepted Dan's invitation than her Shenzhen friend, real-estate developer Little Wan, calls. "Why did you guys choose Shanghai?" he asks. "You'll find only middle managers and compradors, not the taipans or real bosses. I recently bought a 625-square meter villa in Shenzhen up on a mountain. Come here to party."

With two invitations, we decide to have an afternoon tea party in Shanghai at Dan's and then fly to Shenzhen for dinner at Little Wan's.

In Dan's mansion, "The Storm" by the sexy violinist Vanessa-Mae is playing in the background and the air is filled with the mingling smells of goose liver pâté, caviar, aged Irish whiskey, French wines, and Cuban cigars. The guests, all in their thirties, have names such as Vincent Yu, Johnny Chen, Michael Wu, David Lee, Peter Lam, and Eric Pan. They seem to be either directors of investment banks, CEOs of dot-coms, or chief representatives of foreign companies. Lulu's reputation for being a Chinese Marilyn Monroe, along with her enchanting eyes, grabs the attention of all the men, who are soon trying hard to impress her with their wealth—of course, without mentioning money directly.

Eric talks about his vacation at his luxury villa in the south of France, dropping words in French. Johnny tells of his gambling experiences in Las Vegas and the VIP treatment he received. Michael divulges details about his wine collection. David whines about the poor service in certain five-star hotels in different parts of the world. And Vincent compares golf courses in different countries.

"How lucky they are to have us as listeners," says Lulu with a twinkle in her eye.

I reply: "For the past twenty years, the Chinese men have been listening to the Taiwanese and Hong Kong people brag about their money. Now I guess it's their turn."

Dan, the host, suggests that Lulu and I, pick at least one potential candidate. Lulu, Beibei, and I strike up a discussion in the women's bathroom. Johnny is out of the question: a compulsive gambler is the worst choice for a husband unless he has the looks of Robert Redford (in *Indecent Proposal*). Michael is addicted to wine and spoke of a villa in southern France where he might keep a mistress. French might be his pillow language. Vincent has sexy thick lips like Tiger Woods, but when he writes down his favorite golf course in English, there is an impossible mistake: "golf" becomes "gulf."

David, chief executive of Coyote.com, is not bad. If he can complain about the service in five-star hotels, it means he travels. So we pick David to take us to the airport. But none of us expects what we find at the door. As David signals for a taxi from the waiting queue, he explains: "With the downfall of the Nasdaq, I had to sell my sedan five months ago!"

"But you still travel and stay in five-star hotels!" Beibei exclaims.

"My company pays for these trips; it doesn't cost me a thing." Without other men around, David speaks the truth.

Once he leaves, Beibei says to us: "A golfer can't spell the word golf correctly. A traveler stays in five-star hotels only when they are paid for by his company. Apparently, they misrepresented themselves."

"I thought downplaying yourself was fashionable among the rich," I say.

"It might be true in Silicon Valley , but not in Shanghai, where face is everything! They even have a bar called The Face!" Beibei says.

"Well, forget about these rich wannabes. Let's check out the men in Shenzhen!" Lulu says.

We storm to the airport and arrive in Shenzhen to attend the dinner at Little Wan's. This Little Wan is Beibei's family friend. His father, Old Wan, was Beibei's grandfather's former secretary in the early 1980s. After Old Wan retired from the army found a job in a state-owned tourist agency. Old Wan was promoted to director of the agency for the last year before his retirement. That year was 1993. Deng Xiaoping gave a talk during his trip in Shenzhen, saying that the economic reform should be faster. Inspired by the talk, his son, Little Wan, who failed to enter college that year, started his own travel agency. With his father's network and his friends' help, business has flourished.

Shenzhen turns out to be completely different from the Shanghai scene. Goose liver or caviar isn't popular among this crowd. Instead, the dinner is mainly seafood: fresh lobster flown in from Boston, Australian abalone, and shark fin soup. Here no guests bother to have English names, but they bring along secretaries who have English names. One guy even has an American as his secretary. These guys are even more blatant about their wealth than Shanghai guys.

Mr. Lam speaks Mandarin with his heavy Hong Kong accent, "Niuniu, I've been in the apparel business for twelve years. Women like you can turn your beauty into wealth. I have a proposal: There is a Western brand called Miu Miu. My company can create a Niuniu brand and use your face as our logo. I bet it will sell like hotcakes."

Mr. Leong, a real estate developer, says to Lulu, "Just tell me which style of house you like, Victorian, Spanish, or what? I can build one you like and name the development Lulu's Garden or Lulu's Verde or the Lulu Dynasty."

Mr. Lee, a Chinese media magnate says to me, "Hey, Niuniu, with your beauty and knowledge, you can be the hostess of our nightline program. You should also be the leading actress of our new TV series."

Beibei quietly says to Lulu and me, "Shanghai and Shenzhen can be different in taste and money, but they have one thing in common: they both love beauty, especially your beauty." Then she nudges Lulu. "Just think of the pain and humiliation you had to suffer with the poor designer. Doesn't it feel good now to be the focus of all these rich boys?"

"I think it's their egos that are getting all the stroking," Lulu says.

"I agree with you." I add. I say, thinking, actually, Niu Niu does sound like a nice brand for a clothing line. Surely, mother would embrace this idea. "They are using us to compete with each other."

44

Women in China

Weiwei, my family friend, is a famous Beijing slacker. With a father who is a renowned linguist and a mother who is a painter, he is witty and knowledgeable about everything from world politics and the latest model of BMW, to the most recent screening on the Discovery Channel. But Weiwei has never had a real job. Lately, he has been living off his savings.

I get him a temporary job. My friend, a Chinese American guy named Jerry, has just come to town. It's Jerry's first time in Asia and he is undecided about which city to live in. It all depends on the women. He is willing to pay 5,000 RMB—about $600—as a consulting fee to get an overview of women from different parts of China. Weiwei had so many girlfriends that he is perfect for this role, so I arrange for them to meet over dinner.

I invite my Hong Kong friend CC, who also needs an understanding of Chinese women, from a competitor's point of view. CC can't understand what makes Chinese women so good that her English boyfriend would dump her in favor of them.

Weiwei holds court. "Beijing girls tend to be direct, independent, and the most knowledgeable about arts and sports, like Niuniu," he says. "At the same time, they are arrogant and ambitious. Because many of them come from well-to-do families, they always have a bit of attitude and are not easily impressed. And don't expect them to cook well either."

"I'm not a bad cook!" I want to protest but manage to hold my tongue. After all, Weiwei is here to sell stereotypes. Why bother to disagree? Weiwei continues: "One advantage of Beijing girls is that compared to the skinny southern girls, they have breasts. Most of the girls from the northeast, Shandong Province or even Korea, all have good-sized breasts like actress Gong Li."

"What is the biggest problem with Beijing girls?" Jerry asks.

"They swear," Weiwei says.

I shrug. I can't deny this. I swear, and even worse, I enjoy it.

"Tell us about Sichuan girls," CC asks Weiwei. "The movie star, Liu Xiaoqing, who was recently put in jail, is a Sichuan woman. Bai Ling is doing well in Hollywood at the moment and she's from Sichuan. The author who wrote *Wild Swans* is pretty big in England. I heard she is from Sichuan as well."

I know CC is thinking of the Sichuan woman Little Fang, for whom Nick dumped her.

"Sichuan women are beautiful, with nice soft skin and delicate facial features," Weiwei replies. "They are hard-working and down-to-earth. You won't find Beijing girls' arrogance in them. But because they eat spicy stuff, they have a hot temper."

"Korean women are pretty hot-tempered," says Jerry. "I

dated one back in L.A.—I didn't know it had anything to do with the food they eat. What about Hunan girls? They eat spicy food too."

"Hunan girls are very much like Sichuan girls, but even more emotionally charged," says Weiwei.

"But girls in general are emotional," CC says.

"Not Shanghai girls," says Weiwei. "They are extremely clever and always keep control of their feelings in order to get what they want. They have the power to make their men wash their underwear and, at the same time, hand over their salaries."

"I was told there are a lot of materialistic girls in Shanghai," says CC, who still bears a grudge against the waitress at Shanghai's Portman Hotel that she and Nick fought over.

"Yes, there are, but they're not as expensive as Hong Kong girls, who are high-maintenance," says Weiwei, ignorant of CC's origins.

CC is offended. "I'm from Hong Kong. I chose to date a poor Englishman when my folks wanted me to marry a wealthy Hong Kong man."

Weiwei ignores the comment.

"What about Guangdong women?" I ask.

"Guangdong women are more traditional than women in other parts of China," says Weiwei. "They believe in serving their men and their kids."

"No, my mother is from Guangdong," Jerry jumps in.

"Which women are you most attracted to?" I ask.

"I want to date them all," says Jerry with relish.

"Then you have to live in Shenzhen, where the most beautiful women flock to in order to meet men." Weiwei has given his verdict, and the court is closed.

45

A Prude or a Bitch?

Our "princess," CC, really wants to know why the Sichuan girl Little Fang was able to steal Nick away from her. CC asks me to check out Little Fang's daily life and then compare it with her own.

After hanging out with Little Fang for a month, I turn my notes in to CC, "She: Shiseido makeup, Toshiba laptop, platform shoes, Sony mobile phone, drinks green bubble tea, favorite show is *Tokyo Love Stories.* You: Estée Lauder makeup, IBM think pad, Nike tennis shoes, Nokia cell phone, drinks martinis, favorite show is *Ally McBeal.*"

"Your conclusion?" CC asks me.

"She's a *ha rizu,* a fan of Japanese culture, but you're a *ha meizu,* a fan of Western culture."

"But how can she win the heart of an Englishman by being a fan of Japanese culture?" CC is puzzled. "Is it because both countries are islands? I grew up on the islands of Hong Kong and England."

"Let's find out." I say.

Since I'm involved in the Foreign Correspondent Club of Beijing, I arrange for Little Fang to discuss her favorite Japanese soap opera, *Tokyo Love Stories,* at the FCC for our members who are journalists and China-watchers. I invite CC, Beibei, Lulu, Lily, and Mimi to come.

Little Fang starts her speech. "I understand most of the members in the club are Westerners or Chinese who studied in the West. I think Chinese women are already feminists. Western influence can make us undesirable. Perhaps that explains why some of you in your thirties are still single. Your problem is that you are too strong as women. Women are meant to be water, not stone."

It's the first time CC has met Little Fang since the incident with Nick. CC wants to be friendly, but after hearing Little Fang's comments, she is upset, murmuring, "How dare she attack us! That lowlife stole my man!" CC is not the only one who is offended. No one wants to be reminded that she is still single.

Little Fang continues. "Men like gentle women, so we should learn from Japanese women. That's why I recommend that you watch *Tokyo Love Stories.*"

"Women like us only watch *Ally McBeal* and *Sex and the City,*" an audience member comments.

"American stuff is too shallow, especially Hollywood," Little Fang says.

"Neither *Ally McBeal* nor *Sex and the City* represent the Hollywood–style. They are the New York–style, which is much more sophisticated than Hollywood." I can't help but defend my two favorite shows.

"What is the sophisticated New York–style?" Little Fang asks.

"Hilarious, funny, wise, and psychological." Lily speaks for me.

"I think on American TV shows, couples go to bed far too quickly and too easily. It's quite carnal," Little Fang says.

"It's called sexy." CC retorts.

Little Fang rebuffs her. "It's sexual, but not sexy. Japanese soap operas normally don't have bed scenes. They focus on feelings and sensitivities. Women who can delay their sexual urges and who care more about love than sex are the ultimate winners."

"Those Japanese love stories are simply about mind games. The girls are all prudes. They try to be cute at first. After they get the men they want, they dump them. In their TV series, somebody either has to die or become handicapped. The ending is always sad. It's so sadistic!" Beibei speaks out. She is on CC's side and won't let Little Fang's points go unchallenged. Although Beibei hasn't studied abroad, she is a made-in-China feminist.

Little Fang defends her beloved Japanese shows ardently. "They are textbooks on how to deal with men. You learn how to be soft on the outside and firm inside, how to disguise your feelings, how to make men notice you, how to turn the passive situation around. Our Chinese mothers haven't taught us these tricks, so we have to learn it somewhere else!"

"Do these tricks really work?" another female audience member asks doubtfully, adding, "Men aren't stupid."

Little Fang says, "Yes. It is an art to know when to say no, when to say yes, when you should wait for men, when you should make them wait for you."

"We have no interest in becoming manipulative prudes!

We'd rather watch Sarah Jessica Parker!" says CC, thinking that Little Fang must have used these tricks on Nick.

"*Sex and the City* and *Ally McBeal* can't teach you anything about men. Even worse, they teach you to be bitches that men hate!" Little Fang snaps back.

Everybody is stunned.

So far, Lulu has been quiet. I say, "Lulu, you aren't as westernized as CC, Lily, Mimi, and me. Nor are you a Chinese-made feminist like Beibei. Do you prefer American TV series or Japanese ones?"

"I watch Korean soap operas," Lulu says.

"What is so good about Korean ones? All the actresses have had plastic surgery!" Little Fang shakes her head.

"I've seen several. They are all about rich kids falling in love with poor kids: the cliché Cinderella plot." CC doesn't approve of Korean soap operas either.

Lulu says, "I can dream of being a Chinese Cinderella when I watch the Korean ones."

POPULAR PHRASES

HA RIZU: Fan of Japanese culture.
HA MEIZU: Fan of American culture.

46

City Versus Country

*T*hanks to her self-made parents who fled from the mainland to Hong Kong, CC was able to study at Oxford and
learned to speak English perfectly. But most of her relatives are
still peasants living in Henan Province. CC has little idea how
poor her relatives are until she receives a letter from her Aunt
Yuxiu, whom she has never met, asking for help. The gist of
the letter is that Auntie Yuxiu, who lives in a place known as
Monkey Village, wants to come to Beijing to earn money. CC's
cousin, Auntie Yuxiu's eldest son, needs money to get married.
Auntie Yuxiu wonders whether she can work as CC's house-
keeper and CC agrees to pay her 3,000 yuan per month. Later,
Auntie Yuxiu learns, to her amazement, that this salary is equal
to that of a university professor.

Before moving to Beijing, Yuxiu cycles three hours to the
biggest supermarket in the township, searching for a gift for

her niece. She buys ten bars of Dove chocolate, the most expensive gift she can think of. But CC rejects the present politely. "Auntie Yuxiu, I don't eat chocolate. I'm afraid of gaining weight."

"My kids, my husband, and I just have enough to eat," Yuxiu once complains to me, "but she is afraid of gaining weight. I don't understand you city people."

It's the first time Yuxiu has seen her niece. She is proud of CC's success, but one thing puzzles her: in their village, people are poor, but they have enough money to buy clothes to keep themselves warm. CC wears a shirt so small it shows her belly button. Even worse, it's worn and torn. So she says to CC: "I can mend the holes and lengthen the shirt by adding a fringe. That way your stomach won't feel cold. When your stomach gets cold, you get sick easily."

"No, I don't feel cold," CC replies. "My T-shirt is designed this way. The shorter it is, the more fashionable and expensive."

Yuxiu is confused and complains to me. "Why is it more expensive? It uses less cloth, so it should cost less!"

Yuxiu has never seen cut-off T-shirts before.

In order to teach Auntie Yuxiu about city life, CC decides to take her to Starbucks. The three of us go there together. CC orders Auntie Yuxiu a coffee. Yuxiu takes a sip and almost gags. "It so bitter—like Chinese medicine!" She looks at the price and screams, "Twenty-eight yuan per cup! That's half a year's tuition for the kids in Monkey Village!"

"You might want to add some sugar and milk," CC suggests.

It amazes Yuxiu that the sugar is free, so she slips ten packets into her bag. She explains to CC that for years, her household couldn't afford to buy sugar. It was a luxury item in Monkey Village. "Do you want sugar?" she asks CC. "No. I'm afraid of getting diabetes," says CC. "What is diabetes?" Yuxiu asks. CC explains: "It means peeing sugar. . . ."

Yuxiu has only recently been able to afford sugar, yet CC is afraid of it. Yuxiu is overwhelmed. But she soon has another big discovery. The white paper napkins are also free. "They are much nicer and smoother than the coarse toilet paper we have to use at home!" She tells us as she pockets a stack.

In the next year, Yuxiu finds there are many differences between CC's life and her own, the city person and the country person, the rich and the poor. For example, she is grateful she no longer has to forage for wild herbs in the mountains and is able to eat meat every day. CC, however, is a vegetarian by choice. CC also tires herself out at a gym, which bewilders Yuxiu, who feels fortunate if she has time to rest and doesn't need to work from dawn to dusk.

Before she leaves Beijing with bundles of money for her son's wedding in Monkey Village, Auntie Yuxiu takes me aside and asks: "In the countryside, getting married late is shameful because it means you don't have enough money to pay for the wedding. Now that both you and my niece CC have enough money for a large dowry, why are you still single?"

I search for an answer and finally tell her, "Perhaps, like wearing smaller clothing, staying single is a stupid fashion followed by city people."

47

Fake Nose, Fake Breasts

Lulu asks me on the phone, "If you meet a classmate you haven't seen for ten years, what would your reaction be?"

"Thrilled." I reply.

"What if she wouldn't recognize you?"

"I was too unimportant to remember."

"What if you were her savior or benefactor."

I stop Lulu. "No more of these what-if's—just tell me what happened!"

"Have you heard of a real estate development project called GWD—Great Wall Dreamland?" Lulu asks.

"Yes. Expensive villas at the foot of the Great Wall."

"Let me tell you about an escapade at the Dreamland," Lulu says with a deep sigh.

Lulu had attended a fashion show followed by a cocktail reception at the GWD. There she ran into a stream of movie stars, TV talk-show celebrities, and high-profile singers and musical groups. Her photographers were busy photographing these people, but she was bored.

Her friend Mary, editor of *Family,* came to her. "Let me introduce you to a really cool woman—Jenny. I was told that she is going to buy one of these mansions here. She just came back to China from the United States and doesn't have many local friends. I think the two of you would hit it off."

As Lulu saw Jenny, she couldn't believe her eyes. She knew this woman! But she had known her as Yu Zhen not Jenny. Yu Zhen was Lulu's college classmate; actually, they were even closer, as they had lived in the same dorm room for four years. Yu Zhen was a bit older than the other girls. She had always been quiet. In her second year at college, she had started to skip classes and come back to the dorm late at night. Sometimes she disappeared for a few days at a time. She had become a woman of mystery. The only way to track her down was by her perfume.

At that time, most college girls couldn't afford to wear perfume. But Yu Zhen did. She came back occasionally, leaving wafts of Christian Dior's Poison or YSL's Opium in the room. Lulu's fashion education first began by guessing the brands of perfume Yu Zhen used.

Rumor had it that Yu Zhen might be dating a sugar daddy, but nobody knew exactly what had been going on with her until one night when Yu Zhen came back around midnight and all girls were sound asleep.

"Save me! Help me!" She begged the girls in the dorm, who were still only half-awake and confused.

Yu Zhen made a confession. She wanted to change her fate by going to the States. In order to earn money for application fees and tuitions to American universities, she had prostituted herself. But one time she had been stupid and greedy. She had stolen 20,000 RMB from her customer, Big Feet. He had been so angry that he hired thugs to watch her outside the campus. He sent out a message that he would have her fingers cut off if she didn't return the money.

"Give the money back to him," her roommates suggested to her.

"I've sent it to the American schools that I applied to," she said.

"Why don't you go to the police?" Lulu asked her.

"I'd be expelled for what I did."

At that time, Lulu was the richest girl in the room. Because her parents had been newly divorced, both of them sent her money to compete for her love. She gave Yu Zhen 4,000 RMB in cash. Others also donated some money. Together they collected 20,000 RMB for Yu Zhen. Yu Zhen cried and kowtowed to everybody, saying that they were her reborn parents. She would work like a dog from now on to repay their money.

Then Yu Zhen vanished totally. Of course, the money they had lent her was gone forever, like a rock thrown into a lake.

Jenny greeted Lulu gracefully in English and excused herself for her sluggish Chinese. Mary helped her explain. "Jenny was born to a Taiwanese mother and a Macau father. She spent most of her time overseas. So that's why speaking Chinese is difficult for her."

Jenny didn't recognize Lulu.

As I listen to this part of the story, I ask Lulu, "Are you sure Jenny is Yu Zhen? Maybe they just look alike! Otherwise, she'd have recognized you."

"I was wondering about that," Lulu says, her voice rising on the telephone, "because Jenny's nose looked higher than Yu Zhen's and Jenny's breasts were bigger than Yu Zhen's. But as she kept talking, she started to stutter! I realized it was the same Yu Zhen. The only difference was that back then in college she had stuttered in Chinese, and at the cocktail party, she stuttered in English."

"So she pretended she didn't know you!"

"Yes! The ungrateful bitch!"

"But how can you explain the changes to her nose and breasts?" I ask.

"If she can fake her identity, I guess it's a piece of cake for her to get a fake nose and fake breasts!" Lulu concludes.

48

The Little Empress

I decide to take a long vacation in the States. It's strange—when I was in America, I thought of China, but in China, I miss America. After living in the gray city of Beijing for more than a year, I dream of America's blue skies and green lawns. More than that, I feel part of me has never left America.

I'm not sure why I have chosen this exact moment for my visit, but I feel as though my time in China has helped to soften some of the painful memories I have of my time in the States. Through this vacation I hope to recapture the moments and things that I loved about the country. But perhaps more important, I need to find out if moving to China was really the best way to ease my pain over losing Len and having my heart broken. What better way to test if my experiment was a success than going back to the States? I must find out if I have truly exorcised those bad thoughts from my mind.

Although news on TV about the United States is not that optimistic, from terrorist threats to a bad economy, most Americans I run into still seem carefree. I feel flattered as cars come to a stop in front of me when I cross the road and as strange passersby smile at me. In China, pedestrians stop for cars and strangers don't make eye contact.

I stay at Mother Bee's. Mother Bee was my hosting mother when I first arrived in Columbia, Missouri, for college eight years ago. Returning to Missouri is refreshing. I see the trees dancing in the wind and hear birds chirping in the morning. Missouri is about as far away as you can get from Beijing. I like the idyllic, calm atmosphere. Already I can tell that this is going to be a good vacation.

Mother Bee embraces me warmly. "Welcome back! Your room is still there. Only one student stayed there briefly after you."

To my surprise, I find a voodoo doll in the room. The doll has been pierced on the chest with multiple needles. "Bee" is written on the doll's back.

I bring it to Mother Bee.

Mother Bee sighs, clasping the poor doll, "I gave it to Juju, the exchange student from China! She didn't like it because I got it from Wal-Mart and it was made in China. She said that her parents always bought her the most expensive gifts, ones that are made in either the U.S.A. or Japan!"

"So she did this to you?"

Saying neither yes nor no, Mother Bee tells me about Juju. "Unlike you, seventeen-year-old Juju was a spoiled brat who didn't know how to tie her shoelaces or boil water. Her room was always messy. Once I asked her to clean the room, and she called me a big American imperialist who was exploiting her.

She said that since her parents paid me money, I had no right to ask her to do things."

"Now that families are allowed to have only one child, children like Juju are the rulers of their families, dictating to six adults: two parents and four grandparents!" I shake my head.

Mother Bee nods. "I read about it. She might get her way in China by behaving so badly and by being so lazy, but not under my roof!"

"What else did she do?"

"Juju ordered me to wake her up every morning. I gave her an alarm clock and showed her how to use it. Juju felt ignored and threw it away."

"So how did she get up every day?"

"She made her folks call her from China every morning!" Mother Bee stresses every syllable of the sentence to drive home the point.

"Sending kids to the States is fashionable among the new rich in China!" I explain.

Mother Bee continues. "I allowed her to use my home computer. One day I tried to log on to the computer, but it had crashed. I found that she had installed the pirated version of Windows XP without consulting anybody first. I told her that we don't use pirated software in the United States. She yelled at me."

"What did she say?" I ask curiously.

"She said why should the Chinese play by American rules? The Chinese are so poor that they can't afford to buy the official version of Windows. Bill Gates is already the world's richest man—why can't he give the product to the poor for a little money or for free? It's unfair that Chinese silk clothes with hand embroideries cost so much less than shirts with a simple DKNY mark. She even started to talk about the terrorists."

"What happened next? "

"Her mother gave her three thousand dollars to buy the newest Sony laptop. The first thing Juju did after getting the new laptop was to install the pirated Windows XP to upset me. I guess everybody around her in China obeys her without question. Whoever doesn't listen to her is added to her enemies list."

Mother Bee became Juju's enemy. By studying Mao back in China, Juju had learned that an effective strategy for defeating the enemy was to set one against the other. She turned Mother Bee's son, twelve-year-old Tommy, into a defiant rebel.

Tommy washed his father's car windows twice a week to earn some extra money. But then Juju educated Tommy about Karl Marx and the capitalists versus the proletarians. She tells Tommy, "Your parents are the capitalists who have exploited you as a child laborer. It's their parental duty to buy you whatever you want. In China, my parents have never said no to me."

Naïve Tommy was successfully brainwashed and waged a war against his parents, exactly fulfilling Juju's expectations.

"This little Chinese empress Juju sounds like a troublemaker!" I say to Mother Bee.

"As the three-month exchange period was coming to an end, I thought, Thank God, it's almost time for her to return home. Since she dislikes the States so much, she will be happier back there. But . . ."

"What?"

"One day she disappeared. I called her parents, her school, and her friends. Nobody knew where she was. I reported it to the police. Three days later, they found her in Boston. I learned that she had decided to stay in the United States after the exchange was over. But because of her J-1 immigration status, she was supposed to go back. Then she came up with the idea of seeking political asylum here. She made friends with some Falun Gong people in Boston via the Internet. Guess what? I saw her on TV the other night. She was part of a Falun Gong demonstration in front of the Chinese consulate in Boston. Welcome to America!"

49

Scamming Sam?

*M*y U.S. vacation continues. One day, I have breakfast at the IHOP. One thing I missed about the States were the great breakfasts, especially pancakes. While I am enjoying my buttermilk pancakes with bacon and coffee, an old truck driver, a typical midwesterner, approaches me shyly. "Lady, excuse me, but do you speak Chinese?"

"Yes."

"Can you do me a favor?" The man is polite, yet eager. He tells me that his name is Sam. Through a matchmaking company, he has corresponded with a Chinese woman named Ying from Jiangxi Province for three months. Although they have exchanged only five letters, Ying claims that she has fallen in love with her "Uncle Sam," who is thirty years her senior. When I hear of the age difference, I think of O'Keeffe and Stieglitz, although this romance doesn't seem to have the same chance of success.

"I never expected Asian women to be so direct and open!"

Sam says to me. "Aren't we Americans ignorant about other peoples?"

"Thank you for telling me your story, but what can I do for you?" I ask.

"I've thought of calling her. Can you help me interpret on the phone?"

"Yes."

Five minutes later, we dial China from a pay phone near the restaurant.

"Hello, this is Sam. May I speak to Ying?" Sam speaks in English and I repeat it in Chinese.

"Darling, it's Ying speaking!"

"Thank you for the nice letters. I have one concern. What do you think of my age?" Sam gets to the point right away, showing his American impetuosity.

"Although you are thirty years older, you look young from your pictures. Your voice sounds young, too." Ying sounds sweet.

"Oh, I'm flattered." Sam smiles from ear to ear.

"When my heroes Anna Chan and Wendy Deng married General Claire Chennault and Rupert Murdoch, respectively, both of whom are older than the brides' fathers, age was the least of their concerns."

"But I was told that the Chinese believe in filial piety. What if your parents didn't approve of you being with an old foreigner?"

"There are prejudices and feudal thoughts in China, but I'm a woman warrior. I'll fight back!" Ying sounds determined.

"I admire you for saying this." Sam puts one hand over his heart religiously.

"Darling, I've been missing you so much that I dream of you every night. What do you think of me visiting you in America?" Ying's voice becomes more affectionate.

"Sounds like a super idea!" Sam answers cheerfully.

"Of course, you will have to pay for my trip."

"No problem. How much?" says Sam eagerly.

Ying speaks directly to me, "Hey, sister, you're also a Chinese, right?"

"Yes." I say warily.

"Then you have to help your compatriot. If this old guy is rich, I will ask more. If he isn't, I will ask less."

"Why don't you make up your own mind?" I say, thinking, she's already got her hand in his pocket. Now she is asking me how much money to take out?

"Ten grand," Ying says.

"Renminbi or U.S. dollars?" Sam asks in reply.

"Of course it's the green money I'm talking about," Ying says.

"I'd consider it, but I would like to know how you want to spend the money."

"I want to go to the United States via Hong Kong, the shopping paradise. I want to spend a week there to fully experience capitalism. Then, I would like to select a diamond ring, at least one carat. You know, the Chinese really care about face."

Sam shows hesitancy as he hears about the ring. "Darling, I'd love to buy you gifts, but I haven't even proposed yet. We're still in the process of getting to know each other. Perhaps it's too early to talk about rings, don't you think?"

Ying says, "In China, men spend money on women they are pursuing in order to show their respect to the women's parents. If I go to the United States to see you, we consider it an insult to my parents if you don't give me anything expensive."

As I repeat this part in English, I feel ashamed, but manage to translate Ying's words verbatim.

Toward the end of the conversation, Sam agrees to buy

Ying something special (but not a diamond ring), and to wire her the money right away. Ying will go to apply for a passport immediately. They air-kiss good-bye to each other.

After the phone call, I feel obligated to warn Sam. So I ask him, "What do you think of Ying?"

"She sounds full of shit! She thinks that we Americans are made of gold. I can't believe she's so provincial." His voice is no longer sweet.

I am taken aback by Sam's answer, "But you wanted to send her money!"

"Are you kidding? I'm sixty years old. No way I'd be so stupid that I'd send some stranger that much money. I've never even given my mother a thousand dollars!" Sam says, shaking his fist emphatically.

"But you said yes to her . . ." I am confused.

Sam laughs, explaining, "Did I lose anything by saying yes? If I hadn't said yes, would I have found out her real thoughts?"

"I thought you were a fool for love!" I say.

"I pretended to be," says the wily Sam with an impish grin.

"You also had me fooled. You remind me of the Chinese saying, *Jiang haishi laode la*. 'Old ginger is always spicier.'"

I decide to call Ying and tell her to forget about scamming Sam. I redial the number from the same phone.

It's a man's voice on the other line with a local accent. "How can I help you?"

I try to mimic the man's accent. "I'm looking for Ying."

"My wife has just left to apply for a passport."

POPULAR PHRASE

流行语

JIANG HAISHI LAODE LA: "Old ginger is always spicier."

50

Mental Viagra

I didn't anticipate that I would meet Yu during my trip to the United States.

Yu is the Shanghai girl that I met in Beijing a few years ago, whose biggest dream was to speak English every day. I had never met a person like Yu—she was so infatuated with English but had no language talent at all. I knew Yu's boyfriend, a kindhearted young Chinese man. Yu had dumped her boyfriend because his English was clumsy. She was determined to find a boyfriend who could speak perfect English. One time, she was caught with a Canadian man in his hotel room around midnight. Although she insisted that she was speaking English with him, her school expelled her. After the incident, the rumors of Yu prostituting herself spread around the campus and among her circle of friends. Nobody ever heard from Yu again. She disappeared. Many thought she might have ended up in a mental institution because of her obsession with speaking perfect English.

This time, I run into Yu in my friend's church, a church predominantly serving the Chinese community. Even though I am not Christian, I enjoy visiting churches and appreciate the beautiful architecture and songs. This is a luxury that people can rarely enjoy in China, where religion is watched closely by the government. Yu recognizes me first. For the first hour of our conversations, she talks passionately about her discovery of religion. "God is the Almighty. Other religions from Buddhism to Hinduism believe in deities. There can be many deities, but only one true God. Before, I was so unhappy in China. The reason was simple: I didn't find God."

"I thought you were unhappy because you weren't able to converse in English with native speakers every day," I tease her.

"Perhaps because English is the language that God loves," Yu replies in a serious tone.

"So how did you end up here? Fill me in!" I ask.

"It's a really long story." And Yu recounts . . .

After Yu was expelled by her school, she desperately wanted to leave China. Within three months, she found herself a middle-aged Chinese-American husband, Eric, who had been looking for a young wife in China.

After coming to the United States, she learned that Eric had lied to her about his job and his salary. He wasn't a computer engineer, but a warehouse janitor for a computer company. He made seven dollars instead of seventy dollars per hour. Although disappointed, Yu cheered herself up by thinking, "After all, now I'm able to speak English with a native English speaker every day."

But soon after the marriage, Eric quit his job and stayed at home. Yu had to work two shifts as a waitress in a Chinese restaurant to support them. Even worse, Eric never showed any interest in sleeping with her. Because Yu came to the States on a marriage visa, she swallowed all her pain. In order to get a green card, she had to stay in the marriage for two years.

During the interviews at the Immigration and Naturalization Service, the immigration officer asked the couple questions about their daily life. When he asked if she remembered any mark on her husband's body, she couldn't answer. Her application was rejected, and her hopes were smashed.

Desperate, Yu sought help from the church people, who showed tremendous support. One church member, a lawyer named Mark, thought it was strange that Eric didn't want to sleep with Yu. Mark had a plan for Yu. After implementing the plan, Yu discovered that Eric was impotent. Because of this, she was successful at getting a divorce and received her green card at the same time.

After telling the story, she says to me, "I realized how stupid I was, judging people only by how good their English is. We should be careful what we wish for."

"It seems God redeemed you! Do you ever think of going back to China and returning to your old boyfriend?" I ask, secretly hoping that Yu would end up back with him.

"No. My former husband is impotent. What he needs is Viagra. At least, he could buy it if he had the money. But what my former boyfriend needs is mental Viagra, which you can't buy over the counter."

"But I don't understand why you are so harsh on your boyfriend. He loves you and cares about you," I say.

"You see, not speaking perfect English is another kind of impotency."

51

Dating a Republican

On the second week of my vacation in Missouri, I meet a twenty-something boy named Tom at a party. Tom works as a guard in a federal prison, but he is very smart and talented. He writes crime stories in his spare time. He also believes in Buddhism. The best part about Tom is that he respects women. Every so often, he will cook for me; preparing his own recipes for corn bread and smoked tuna. I love spending time with Tom. We ride horses, play golf, go shooting and fishing together. The dating life is idyllic.

Tom and I often joke that if we had depended on a computer dating service, we'd never have been matched because we are completely different species. Check out our dating bios.

Tom's thumbnail sketch would read: Country boy, Southern Baptist, 6'5", 225 pounds, conservative, Republican, and an ex-army ranger. Voted for George W. Bush; very much in favor of the Iraq war; hates the United Nations and the French; loves the quiet country life, professional wrestling, boxing, and car racing; disapproves of homosexuality and abortion.

And mine: Megacity girl, Asian, 5'2", 110 pounds, liberal, Democrat, and a cosmopolitan journalist. Plans to vote for Hillary Clinton once she runs for president; very much against American invasion in Iraq: believes that the UN Security Council should be used to balance the hawks; enjoys the busy city life of Beijing, Shanghai, New York, and Hong Kong; watches *Ally McBeal* and *Oprah*; has gay friends and girl-friends who have had abortions; does not understand profes-sional wrestling in any way, shape, or form.

From political views to occupations, Tom and I share noth-ing in common. I have never dreamed that I would date a jailer who watches stupid professional wrestling. Normally, on my chart, rednecks barely beat out Neanderthals, and this is the last type of person I like to associate with. But somehow, Tom has been the best date I have ever had. He's a teddy bear— sensitive, attentive, loyal, and protective. He always teaches me things that I don't know, from how to putt to how to bait a hook. Another big plus, he is great in bed. It has been over a year since I have been intimate with anyone, and it's reassuring to find out that there is nothing wrong with me. After being with Tom I can't believe there was actually a time when I had no appetite for sex! I think perhaps I should write to Match-makers.com and tell them that opposites attract. But my girl-friends back in China are all astounded that I am dating a prison guard.

Both Beibei and Lulu call me.

"It's a big loss of face if you come back with a man who works in the prison," Beibei says.

It still saddens me that in China—the "People's Republic"—there is still such an obsession with social class. In the United States, it's so much easier to mingle and socialize with people who would be considered beneath me in the East. But what can I do? I'm a Chinese woman with Chinese parents and Chinese friends. How can I lead a great life without their approval?

Lulu says, "Fishing? Making bread? It sounds so boring. The American suburban life is not for us."

"But Tom is so nice," I say.

"But he is not one of us," Beibei comments. "He's not a yuppie, nor is he international enough for you."

"But Tom is a man of integrity and honor. I've met too many international yuppie jerks from San Francisco to Beijing." I sigh, as the thought of Len once again creeps into my head. My time in the States has made me think of him more often. That's why I have decided not to return to Berkeley this time.

"Now you know why we are still single," Lulu speaks. "We love our lifestyle better than we love love."

52

The Striptease Club

What Tom and I have shared is a short fling that doesn't have any future. I know that my friends are right. I can't change my lifestyle for Tom. I leave Missouri for Washington, D.C., to visit my friend Ann, another overeducated single gal.

Ann lives in Dupont Circle and works for the Department of State. We go to the nice restaurants and bars in the neighborhood to hang out. D.C. is a place full of young, single, and politically ambitious professional men. But I am not in the mood to date: I am leaving town soon—too soon to develop any serious relationships. Plus, I feel guilty for leaving Tom.

On the last day in D.C., I take a walk along Pennsylvania Avenue. I'm dressed in baggy clothes. In Lafayette Park behind the White House, I run into six Asian tourists who are sitting on the lawn, smoking and chattering. From the small bags under their arms, the Olympus cameras they carry, the badly fitting suits and ties they wear, and the ever-present cloud of cigarette smoke, it's easy to tell that they're from China. Of course, the fact that they are also speaking Chinese is a bit of a tipoff as well. . . .

In the past few years, Chinese delegations have been a major part of the American tourist scene. They arrive in groups and their expenses are often paid by their companies or work-units as some kind of bonus.

"Hi!" I greet the Chinese tourists warmly.

"Are you Chinese?" asks a man who wears bottle glasses.

"Yes."

"Are you American Chinese?" Another young man asks.

"Yes."

"You don't work for the CIA or the FBI, do you?" A stocky middle-aged man asks. It's difficult to tell whether he is joking or serious.

"Of course not." I laugh.

"We were told that we might be tailed by spies in the United States. We have to be careful about speaking to strangers here." The stocky man is serious.

"Who told you that? I don't believe that bullshit. Where are you from?"

"Linyi County, Shandong Province," the young man replies.

"What do you think of D.C.?" I ask them.

"At first, I thought I was in Africa. I didn't expect to see so many blacks in D.C. You know, the Hollywood movies mainly feature white actors. So I thought . . ." the young man quickly voices his opinion.

"In D.C., 62 percent of the population is African American," I tell him.

"I think the guesthouse for foreign state guests doesn't look luxurious at all, at least from the outside," the man with glasses says.

"I thought the United States was a rich country and it should be full of skyscrapers. But it is disappointing that D.C. doesn't have as many skyscrapers as Beijing or Shanghai," says the stocky man.

"Washington has a rule that no buildings can be taller than the Capitol. Since they cannot be tall, they are quite wide," I explain.

"Okay, I can understand why the buildings are so wide now, but why are the people as well?" The stocky man asks me, eying the pedestrians.

"Show some respect to the American people!" Before I can speak, a tall authoritarian-looking man who has been silent stops everyone.

The tall man seems to be the leader. He raises his arms to the sky, faces the White House, and says in a loud voice, "Long live the friendship between the American people and the Chinese people!"

"Where are you going next?" I ask the young man.

"Vegas. Of course. We are going to eat lobsters and watch strippers dance and gamble!" The young man answers with pride and excitement.

"Have fun!" I am about to leave.

"Can I talk to you in private?" The tall man stops me.

"Sure."

"You see, what Little Wang just said was just his own agenda in Vegas. I haven't approved yet. As a matter of fact, I'm worried these young people will be badly influenced by the West. Thanks to Deng Xiaoping's open-door policy and the great vision of our great Communist Party, we can eat lobsters quite often in China now. It's no longer a big deal or something corrupting. As for his second agenda, at first I disapproved of it. I wanted to protect these young officials from corrupt thoughts and behaviors. Then Little Wang and the other younger members argued with me, saying that the party encourages older officials like me to be more open-minded. So I think, in order to show some respect for the young and be open-minded, I can't be too arbitrary, which means that I need to make a decision based on facts. That is to say, only when I see how decadent the dance is and make a fair evaluation can I make the right decision."

"So why are you telling me this?" I ask.

"I'm thinking of going to a strip club tonight here to check it out by myself. It will help me make a decision for our group."

"To be honest, I'm not familiar with Washington either. If you have a local tour guide, you can ask him."

"We do have a tour guide, but if he told other group members about my inquiry, it would make me look bad. I told everybody to preserve the purity of us all, I wouldn't go to a strip club. But now I've decided to sacrifice my own purity to protect the purity of the other party members. If you take me there, I can pay your ticket and tips as well. The expenses can be reimbursed by our work-unit if it says entertainment fee."

For a second, I want to take him up on his offer and bring him to a male strip joint where I imagine myself throwing free money to hunks who strip-dance for me. But I kill the idea right away.

"It will be much more fun if you go there with your wife or girlfriend," I say to the man and wave good-bye.

As I walk back, I realize that I am going back to China tomorrow. America without Len is fine. I can have fun *and* have a relationship.

53

Shenzhen, Shenzhen

$\mathcal{M}$y returning itinerary is a flight from D.C. to Los Angeles, then from Los Angeles to Hong Kong. From Hong Kong, I will stop over in Shenzhen for a story of the factory workers there who are an important part of the global economic chain that produces the goods that Wal-Mart or Nike stores sell in the United States. Even though Nike shoes can sell for sixty to a hundred dollars a pair in the United States (and nowadays in China too!), the factory workers that produce them get paid pennies in comparison.

On the airplane from L.A. to Hong Kong, I sit next to a middle-aged American man named Steve. Steve tells me that he is an engineer manager of a well-known American high-tech company, Sun Microsystems. In recent years, more and more American companies have either moved their manufacturing sites to China or use Chinese factories as their OEM sites because of the lower costs here. This new geo-economic shift has also changed Steve's lifestyle. With his company's growing business in this part of the world, he commutes between China and California. This time, he is going to visit the company's OEM site in Shenzhen.

I have noticed that Steve's face turns red and his eyes sparkle as he mentions the city's name.

"You seem to be very excited about the trip to Shenzhen. Is it your first time?" I ask.

"No. My third time, " Steve answers, then volunteers his story. "My job is to help my company select manufacturing sites in Asia. So I have been to most of the big cities there. I think Hong Kong is a beautiful city, but too westernized and expensive. Now, it's become a transit point. I find the city of Taipei has no character; I don't find it interesting. Singapore is very boring. I love Shenzhen."

"Why?"

"Actually, my colleagues and I all know that everywhere is pretty much the same in terms of the capacity of one manufacturing site. The defining factor is always the women of that place. If we like the women there, we can manipulate the data a little bit and give a glowing recommendation so the factories can be set up there. So we can travel there later."

"Sounds like you like the women in Shenzhen," I say.

"Yes, they are beautiful and friendly. I was a former naval officer. Shenzhen reminds me of the Philippines and Hong Kong fifteen or twenty years ago. Back in the States, I have my middle-age crisis. But every time I come to Shenzhen, I feel younger and recharged. Those available, open-minded young Chinese women make me feel good about myself. After all, I can still get attention!"

"How do you meet them?" I am curious.

"I've met several girls on the Internet and I've picked girls up at bars and disco clubs. Or simply, my vendors introduce them to me. My colleagues are all doing the same thing. Often we go hunting together." Steve says.

I didn't expect that Steve would be so blatant in talking about his sexual conquests.

"Guess what I don't like about Asian women," Steve says.

"What?"

"Southerners are too skinny."

"How much does your wife back in the States weigh?"

"Two hundred pounds."

Clearly Steve likes an alternative to his heavier wife; his protestations notwithstanding, his eyes give away his desire. The conversation continues for a while as Steve orders a series of drinks. I am becoming concerned as Steve looks at me longingly, not even attempting to hide his intentions.

Steve's conversation becomes more and more personal as the hours and miles flow by.

"Those earrings are charming."

"Your sweater fits you so well."

"You should wear only short skirts or tight slacks."

Fortunately, I have the aisle seat, so I don't have to climb over him to go to the toilet. As the plane is somewhere over Japan, Steve plays his trump card. "Niuniu, do you want to become a member of the mile-high club?" he asks.

"The mile-high club? What's that?" I ask.

Steve leers at me and says, "That's a club of people who have made love at thirty-five thousand feet above sea level in an airliner's toilet."

I smile sweetly. "Sounds great. Let me get ready. I'll be in the toilet on the right in the tail section. Give me about three minutes." But I head directly to the stewardesses in the galley. The plane has plenty of available seats in business class, so I get myself a midflight upgrade, and Steve gets a bracing surprise when he finds himself facing a hulking six-foot male steward who is waiting in the toilet stall on the right in the tail section.

"You can pick your day to travel, how much you are willing to pay, and where you want to sit, but you can't pick your companion in the next seat when you fly solo. Nowadays, you have to pray it's not some horny old goat," I think as the plane taxies in at Hong Kong. Now I know why some women want to marry rich men who have private jets.

54

The Death of a Singer

Once safely off the plane and away from Steve's gaze I catch a cab back from the airport. It is four in the morning, and as the car makes its way through the quiet city that is just starting to come to life, I think back longingly on the United States and the life I had there. This has been my first time back since my relationship with Len took a nosedive into the San Francisco Bay. I had been nervous that the trip would bring back only bad memories, but it turned out to be just what I needed. Visiting so many familiar and friendly places, I sometimes wondered why I chose to leave in the first place. I think I made the right choice by not going to the Bay Area. I'm not ready to go back to Berkeley, a place I cherish and fear at the same time. I love the intellectual stimulation and the free-wheeling lifestyle there, but all my memories of sunny Berkeley are linked to Len in some way. I did regret not getting a chance to hike in Muir

Woods, or drive my car up to Big Sur, or just sit on Telegraph Avenue and watch the hippies mingle with the doomsday prophets, middle-class college students, and local street kids.

Despite what I had heard in China, everything is still going great in the United States. People are friendly and happy as usual. I realize now that when I chose to leave, there wasn't anything wrong with the United States; there *was* something wrong with my state of mind. I am able to enjoy everything that the United States has to offer. It is as if my time in China really has healed me.

I spend three days in Shenzhen on my interviews. Then I'm finally back in Beijing. Beibei is supposed to pick me up at the airport. However, Beibei doesn't show up; instead, she sends her driver, Da Chen.

"President Beibei is preoccupied," Da Chen explains to me. "Little Bench has just died of pneumonia."

Little Bench was the gay singer whose former lover tried to set himself on fire in public after being dumped. The incident exposed the secret of Little Bench's sexual orientation and initially hurt Chichi Entertainment Company's record sales tremendously. Beibei had to pour in bundles of money to hire a Chicago-based public relations firm to rebuild Little Bench's image in China.

The American PR firm was brilliant. They had reporters write articles about how Little Bench suffered from humiliation and poverty during his childhood as a peasant boy and how he was seduced by a wealthy businessman during his teenage years and eventually became his sex slave. Little Bench tried to commit suicide many times, but music saved his life. Little Bench turned into a tragic hero as his traumatic experiences were revealed, and this won both the sympathy and the understanding of his fans. His record sales climbed up the charts in the following year.

I am still in shock over Little Bench's demise when Beibei rings me. "I'm sorry that I wasn't able to pick you up at the airport myself. I need to tell you what happened when you were away. Niuniu, I'm a businesswoman, but I'm not heartless. I can't believe what the young people in my company have done. They make money out of death. Can you believe it?"

I exclaim, "What? Tell me more!"

Two hours later, I meet with Beibei in W8, a bar owned by author Wang Shuo and director Jiang Wen.

Beibei orders a martini and begins to talk. "After learning that Little Bench was close to death, I called a top-level executive meeting. Little Bench's agent Song Dynasty said that it was the time to promote his death. I vetoed the idea right away, but he argued, 'To be a legend, one has to die young and in a dramatic fashion like James Dean, Marilyn Monroe, Elvis Presley, and John Lennon. The more dramatic and mysterious the death is, the more interest one can generate.' I thought he was just ridiculous and hideous, but I didn't expect the majority to agree with his proposal. They told me I had been simply outvoted and this was how democracy worked."

I say, "I guess because Little Bench was young, and because many people suspect that he had AIDS, those people in your company thought his death would be a hot topic."

Beibei nods. "Exactly. It's a good time for them to promote his records. You see, the Chinese have quickly learned the art of marketing."

I remark, "I wonder if the MBA students in Harvard Business School or Wharton would be so 'business-savvy' to use death to promote products. I bet not. They must have a class called Work Ethics they have to take. This story reminds me of Columbia Asia's newly released movie *The Big Shot's Funeral.* Life mimics art!"

Beibei lights a cigarette, "Life is more ludicrous than art. The hospital where Little Bench stayed was a mess after the news broke. People from all walks of life flocked there. Some self-proclaimed tai chi masters came. They were making movements and giving demonstrations, claiming that they could prolong Little Bench's life for three more days. The fortune-tellers came. They tried to predict the exact time of his death. Reporters came trying to find AIDS-related information. The paparazzi came too, with their cameras and sleeping bags. They were not permitted to camp out in the hospital. Then lawyers came, hoping to find a possible lawsuit, after two reporters were pushed to the ground by a visiting celebrity's bodyguard. Coyote.com came. They set up a Web site so people off-site could get an update of the events. . . ."

I comment, "Sounds like the hospital became a circus! Everybody there was out to make a buck."

Beibei takes a sip of the martini and adds, "I haven't even told you about Little Bench's uncle yet. Right after Little Bench took his last breath, the uncle held a press conference to announce Little Bench's death and launch his newly published book *Tuesdays with Little Bench: The Story of My Nephew and His Lovers.*"

I ask, "Where was the funeral held?"

"Song Dynasty suggested holding the funeral in the Workers Stadium where Little Bench had performed. He wanted to sell tickets to the public. I objected mightily, but the majority ruled again. More tickets were sold to the funeral than to his last three concerts combined!"

55

Christmas Thoughts

Christmas grows more and more popular in China. Beibei's company Chichi Entertainment gives its employees a half-day off on December 24 and takes them bowling. Beibei has invited us to join her. Lulu can't make it because she is attending a fashion show in Hong Kong. CC and I come.

We talk about Christmas shopping. CC shows the Gucci watch she has bought for herself. I show them the iPod I have bought for my half-sisters. Beibei shows us a key. "I didn't buy anything for myself, but I bought this as a Christmas gift for my folks."

"What is it? A car? I was told people over sixty are not eligible to take driving tests. Are your parents already licensed to drive?" CC asks.

"No. It's not a car—it's a condo," Beibei says proudly.

CC exclaims, "Holy cow! Such an expensive gift!"

Beibei says, "If I didn't buy it for them, they could never afford to buy a new place. They've lived in the shitty place their factory assigned to them for twenty years."

CC is confused. "Beibei, your grandfather was a high-ranking officer in the Chinese military. Why do your parents still live so poorly?"

Beibei sighs. "During the Cultural Revolution, my grandfather was labeled a counterrevolutionary and my folks suffered as his son and daughter-in-law. It wasn't until Lin Biao's failed coup in 1971, when the fundamentalists and radicals were purged from the party, that the government finally began to depoliticize and my grandparents were rehabilitated. After the Cultural Revolution, my parents were afraid of being called members of *taizi dang,* the "Prince Party," and bringing trouble to my grandfather, so they never used my grandfather's title to do things for themselves. They fear this and fear that and they always follow the rules, and they taught me to follow the rules. But what did they really get? Some award certificates, soaps and towels as prizes, and a small apartment with a concrete floor."

I sigh. "Your father's generation suffered a lot in China. They spent their prime time in the worst years of China. They can never understand the wealth the young generation can enjoy, such as owning an apartment with two floors, taking a vacation in Europe . . ."

Beibei says, "I gave my parents money so that they can take taxis every day. But the idea of taking a cab every day will never be comfortable for them. They end up putting all the taxi money in the bank and still take buses."

I tease Beibei. "I guess your spending three thousand yuan on a shirt is simply beyond their imagination."

Beibei nods. "Yes. I've become corrupt. I used to listen to

them. I tried to be a loving and obedient girl. What did I get? My husband cheated on me and my factory tried to lay off female workers like me. Unlike my folks, I have taken advantage of my high-ranking grandfather. I've made it. Money, respect, and lovers, you name it. Have you seen an American movie called *The Emperor's Club?* The world doesn't appreciate people who follow principles and values. It's no fun at all to be a nice person. You end up a tragic hero. More fun to be a winner. I celebrate my transformation into a bad girl!"

"Beibei, you can wear Western clothes, drive a Western car, or take a Western lover," I comment, "but you can't forget your role as a dutiful Chinese daughter."

CC says, "My situation is the opposite of Beibei's. My folks took advantage of the golden time of Hong Kong's growth in the 1970s. I guess I can never be as rich as they are. They don't need any material things from me. But unlike Beibei, I hated my folks for a long time because they always tried to control my life with their money."

Beibei asks carefully so as not to ignite a touchy situation, "Are you going to see them on Christmas?"

CC sighs. "I hadn't planned to. I guess I should. I'll see if I can catch a flight to Hong Kong tonight."

Beibei says to CC, "Yes. Go now. I have to hurry off to my parents too."

After both of my friends are gone, I start to think of my own parents. Mother, Big John, and my half-sisters are in the States for the holidays. Father and Jean are with Jean's family. I would love to spend Christmas evening with my family, but now I wonder where I should go. Definitely not parties. I have been invited to three parties tonight, but I decide to spend the evening quietly in my own house.

My cell phone rings. It's CC. "All flights to Hong Kong are full for the evening. I guess I can't give my parents a nice surprise."

"You can make it up during the Spring Festival."

"I guess you're right. Besides, they are Chinese. The Chinese New Year is a bigger deal. But what about me? It will be so lonely just to be by myself. I spent the last three Christmases in Beijing with Nick."

"Come to my place! Let the two single women hang out and drink hot toddies. And if Santa Claus is late, we will still have Jeremy Irons and Brad Pitt to entertain us."

POPULAR PHRASES

TAIZI DANG: A party made of princes. It refers to those who hold high positions in government or business as a result of their families' high-ranking political background. Nepotism was once common practice in China.

56

In Search of Mr. Right

*F*inding Mr. Right always takes time. It can be a tough decision when there are so many men to choose from. Each of my girlfriends has a different personality and outlook on life. Beibei loves to dominate men, so she prefers younger men who worship her (at least on the surface). CC finds only white men attractive and doesn't click with Asian men. Lulu loves the artsy macho type of man. I always seem to pay attention to reserved, low-key men who aren't obsessed with trying to act tough or show off how much money they have.

Lulu invites us to have drinks at Buddha's Bar near Beihai Park on Saturday night. After we order bubble tea and almond cookies, Lulu takes several cards out of her purse. Each has detailed notes on men she recently met. She passes the cards to Beibei. Beibei takes a bite of almond cookie and reads the notes aloud.

"Candidate No. 1: International lawyer based in Beijing. Late thirties, handsome, intelligent, Yale-educated, witty, worldly, preppy, narcissistic, talented in bed, a womanizer with a bad temper. American.

"Candidate No. 2: Self-made billionaire from Shenzhen. Owns several real estate businesses, middle-school education, married but will divorce soon, generous, honest, tough, stubborn, swears a lot, bald, smoker, has a big belly.

"Candidate No. 3: Banker from New York. Between thirty-seven to forty-five, pale, ordinary-looking, a graduate of MIT, gentlemanly, respects women, hard-working, divorced, two children, a good listener, a wonderful cook, boring, no hobbies, can't ski or swim.

"Candidate No. 4: Scientist. Thirty-something, meek, honest, caring, loving, sensitive, balanced, into outdoor activities, introverted, not ambitious, and never gets angry.

"Candidate No. 5: Art professor. Model looks, romantic, passionate, intelligent, knowledgeable, interesting, emotionally traumatized by previous relationship, unstable, and schizophrenic."

"Give me some advice!" Lulu begs us.

Knowing Lulu's weaknesses too well, Beibei says immediately: "I vote out No. 5. Better not deal with emotional disasters. They can destroy your sanity."

I dismiss No. 2 right away. "You don't need to marry money. Without a rich guy, you can live comfortably as a professional woman. You need men of taste to match up with you."

CC vetoes No. 1. "Although the lawyer's looks and money would satisfy your vanity, he has no sense of loyalty," she says. "He is worth nothing, just like Nick." CC can't stand womanizers like her former English boyfriend Nick, who won't quit until he sleeps with every woman he meets in Asia.

"So only the banker and the scientist are left," Beibei says, turning to Lulu. "What do you think?"

Lulu pauses and then says: "The banker is too boring. I'm still young. I feel that I would miss all the excitement of life by marrying him. I'd rather have a roller-coaster life than a boring one."

CC asks: "What about the scientist?"

Lulu sighs. "He's not ambitious enough. My own problem is lack of ambition. I'd love my other half to make up for me. Plus, I studied liberal arts in school. I rather prefer my man to have a similar educational background so we can have many things to talk about."

"Can you introduce him to me then?" I cut in. "Loving, caring, and sensitive—he sounds like a million bucks to me. I always prefer men who are content and happy. Ambition can easily turn into greed. And I can learn science from him and he can learn arts and literature from me."

Before Lulu can say anything, Beibei jumps in: "I'd like to get to know the international lawyer. He sounds like a wonderful lover to have. I don't mind that he's a womanizer since I sleep with other men apart from my husband. No strings attached on either side; it makes things a lot easier for me."

CC chimes in: "The banker is good for me. I'm talkative and need to have a pair of attentive ears. As for boredom, it's bad, but better than betrayal."

Beibei takes another look at Lulu's notes. "Lulu, can I have No. 5 as well? Model looks, passionate, romantic, another great lover I need. When can you introduce them to us?"

"Anytime you like, my friends," Lulu says with a shrug.

"Great!" We chorus, then talk ecstatically among ourselves about meeting these men.

Feeling ignored, Lulu concludes, "I guess it's not too bad for me since I still get the billionaire. That will make plenty of Shanghai girls jealous."

57

Easy Money?

The economy has been bad. Wherever I go to a party, I bump into people who are out of work, from the United States to Hong Kong to Beijing. The people I meet are often hard-working white-collar people. The sad reality is that hard work and kindness are simply not enough for survival, and these noble qualities no longer gain the respect that they deserve.

Mark, a friend from Silicon Valley, tells me that every morning, many of the homeowners on the street where he lives now greet each other before they begin to mow their lawns and fix their yards. They have all lost their jobs.

"Niuniu," he says, "perhaps I should work for Home Depot. They are recession-proof. When the economy is doing well, people have the money to buy new homes. When the economy is bad, people have nothing else to do but stay at home and improve the ones they have!'"

Mark would like to find a job just to make ends meet, but other people find some creative ways to make big money. Lately, two of my former acquaintances have put their creative thinking into action. One woman named Stacy sued her employer for sexual harassment. She has just been awarded $2 million. Because the case will be appealed, it may take her a few years to collect all the money. Nevertheless, she is ready to retire. My former classmate at Berkeley, an Irish American guy named Neil, is suing his company for racial discrimination. He believes that he can get the $3 million he is asking for. If not, he'll find other ways to sue someone.

Making money out of lawsuits is creative. Win one or two cases, and you can retire financially free like Robert T. Kiyosaki and Suze Orman.

Though it sounds creative and easy, suing someone is a game plan that does not work for most people, who still have to put up with their routine drudgery and the bad temperament of their bosses.

If one can make money by suing people in the States, what about in China, a country that is not as wealthy and has fewer lawyers? How can one make easy money here?

Beibei's company Chichi Entertainment has recently signed up a twenty-one-year-old singer named Beijing Doll. She apparently has the answer: it's easier to stand out in a relatively conformist society like China. Once you stand out, you get attention. Once you get attention, you get the market. The Chinese market is a big one, which translates into big money. After all, it's all about competing for attention at a time when there is an information explosion. But how do you get attention? Simple—

by placing a few hot news items, tailored by a savvy PR rep, into selected media, for the starved-for-scandal public to read and discuss.

Beijing Doll's first CD *I Was Born in Beijing* didn't sell well. She quickly changed her appearance on the stage by sporting an artificial mole on the corner of her mouth and wearing her undergarments on the outside of her clothes. She knows that China needs a Madonna!

Not only a Madonna, but also a Monica Lewinsky. While on tour promoting her new CD, she invited a famous movie star to her hotel room, and later claimed that he tried to make sexual advances toward her. The movie star fiercely defended himself, saying "I didn't have sex with *that* woman." But Beijing Doll claimed that she had proof.

China is conducting a media reform and encourages newspapers to become more commercial. The movie star's scandal with Beijing Doll appears on page one in newspapers big and small for weeks. Beijing Doll becomes a notorious celebrity just like Monica Lewinsky. Reporters and entertainment columnists mass in hotel lobbies and concert venues in order to have the chance for a face-to-face interview with her.

Beijing Doll is aware of the notoriety of some of the media that followed her like a pack of dogs. When she is interviewed by some of the bigger newspapers and TV stations, she claims that what has happened between her and the movie star has simply been misrepresented by some irresponsible reporters, trying to make her story more mysterious. Using big journalists to attack smaller journalists, she has gained free publicity, which generates the sales of her CD rapidly.

Still, many people are annoyed by Beijing Doll's shameless manipulation of the media. But she doesn't care. She tells

Beibei, "I'm just trying to get ahead. I don't ever want to take crowded buses to work. That's all!"

Beibei asks me if sex and scandal can sell more newspapers than news of politics and social development. I tell her that I think the society is, unfortunately, really this shallow. She says she feels sad. But in a fleeting second, she probes the sensational singer, searching for an angle to keep her in the news. Fifteen minutes of fame can always be followed by another media campaign designed to recapture the audience. After all, Beijing Doll gives up her reputation in order to make money, not just for herself but for Beibei as well.

58

Reimbursements

$\mathcal{M}$y close friends seldom call me before eleven in the morning. They know that I am a night owl and keep late hours as a journalist and a writer. But one rainy morning as I am sleeping deeply beneath my down quilt, Beibei wakes me up with a phone call. It is not even nine o'clock.

Beibei says, "Tomorrow is the deadline for me to turn in my receipts from last month. I haven't spent enough on T & E. Now, I need ten-thousand yuan worth of receipts!"

I rub my sleepy eyes in a daze without the full understanding of Beibei's urgency, I tell her, "Remember the hot-looking stranger I told you about? He came back to my dream again last night. This time he really liked me, and was just about to kiss me!"

Beibei says, "I'm sorry if I just destroyed the most romantic dream you've had in the last two weeks! But did you hear what I just said?"

"You need some receipts?" I mumble.

"Right!" Beibei quickly explains, "I need ten thousand yuan worth of receipts for reimbursement purposes. Can you help me find some? Only last month's receipts are good."

I tease, "Wow! Twelve hundred dollars! This is one of the benefits of the market economy with socialist characteristics that applies only to you. Unfortunately, I work for a capitalist company. I don't really save up receipts. I can't get reimbursement for anything, even my cell phone bills. Everything I pay for is out of my earnings."

Beibei says, "No, Niuniu, I don't think there is a difference between capitalism and socialism in terms of reimbursements. Think of Worldcom or Enron. In my opinion, reimbursements are to do with one's ranking in the company. For example, general managers and chief representatives of big foreign companies' Chinese offices can get all kinds of allowances and reimbursements."

I agree with Beibei. "I guess you're right. My position is not high up yet. That's why I don't have the power to get freebies."

"I remember five years ago, the former Beijing bureau chief of your news agency, a British man who went to school with CC, was reported, by his driver, for using the newspaper's money to pay for toilet paper at his home and the paintings in his wife's office!"

"If only one day I could become the bureau chief." I sigh.

"But I thought you'd save up receipts for tax purposes," says Beibei.

I sigh. "My income is too insignificant compared to yours. I don't really bother."

Beibei says, "Even if you don't save receipts, you should have some you haven't tossed, like taxi fares, minibus fares, meals, books, gasoline, or different kinds of entertainment expenses. Anything is good except for bus tickets. They cannot be reimbursed."

"It seems to me that your company discourages people from saving money on transportation," I say.

"The rule is the rule! Have you got some receipts for last month?" Beibei asks me.

"Let me check." I rummage through my purse and pockets and find some receipts. After counting, I tell Beibei, "I found receipts for some novels I just bought, but they are only for two hundred yuan. Chinese books are too inexpensive. Next time, if you'd tell me in advance, I'd buy some big pricey art books."

"Niuniu, are you still in bed? Please get up quickly!" Beibei demands.

"Why?"

"It seems to me that the only choice we have is to spend as much money as we can today."

"You want me to go with you to spend money so that you can get reimbursed the next day?" I ask.

Beibei says, "Of course, the best choice would be getting receipts for things I didn't pay for. It would be another source of income. If I can't get that, at least we can have fun and let Chichi Entertainment pay for it!"

"Beibei," I protest, "you sound so corrupt!"

"Not nearly as corrupt as those corrupt government officials!"

Huise shouru, or gray income, is popular in China. In Beibei's case, besides her salary, she gets reimbursed for gasoline, cell phone bills, meals, and gifts. This cash is considered her gray income. Even Lulu, whose pay is one-fourth of mine, can write off the cost of her clothes, her hairdo, her membership at the gym, etc. Plus, she gets boxes of free cosmetics, shampoos, and body massages every month from her magazine. She has told me that when the advertisers can't pay them money, they use their goods in exchange for advertising pages. As for CC, who works in a public relations firm, her cell phone, palm pilot, and the Omega watch are all from clients who give her such a big discount that the items become almost freebies. I'm the only one who works for a foreign company and lives on my salary and has no gray income.

One hour later.

Beibei and I meet in front of the spa. We go to the sauna and take a hot shower. Then, each of us gets a one-hour foot massage, a two-hour back massage, pedicures, manicures, and facials. Beibei and I have spent five hours in the spa. Next on the program is dinner.

"Let's go someplace expensive!" Beibei suggests.

"I'm not into shark fins or fancy nest soups," I say. "I feel this is already sad."

"Yes, I know, you're so Americanized that you've become an animal-rights activist," Beibei teases.

We choose to have a buffet at the revolving restaurant on the top floor of the International Hotel and then hang out at an Irish bar nearby for drinks.

By eleven o'clock Beibei has spent only 5000 RMB—about $600—not nearly half her goal.

But her luck changes after I go to the lady's room where I find a handwritten ad on the wall: "Need receipts? I sell them cheaply. Page me at XXXX-XXXX."

I immediately inform Beibei. Beibei rushes into the bathroom, gets the number, and makes the call immediately.

When she comes back to join me, her face radiates joy. "Niu-

niu, you've helped me make five thousand yuan in three minutes!" Beibei says, hugging me.

"Still no guilty feelings about the easy money?" I ask Beibei.

"Not really. Everybody has to have some sort of gray income. At least, I pay for my own toilet paper."

POPULAR PHRASE

HUISE SHOURU: Gray income; income other than one's
salary, often cash under the table or reimbursements for
expenses.

59
Nick, the Star

On New Year's Eve, I invite my single girlfriends Lulu and CC to my house for a potluck dinner. After dinner, we watch the specials on TV together.

One channel features a national English competition of elementary school students. Each contestant gives a five-minute speech on his or her dreams and hopes for the New Year. There are six judges present to award points, and the final score of each contestant is the average of the points, the same as the rules of a diving match. English contests are extremely popular in China; for example, the *One-Million-Dollar Show* in Hong Kong can draw huge audiences.

"Look. It's Nick on TV!" Lulu has a margarita in one hand and is pointing at the TV screen with the other.

Nick is sitting in the middle of the judges' panel. The camera gives him several close-ups, as the TV presenter explains twice that Nick is an expert from Oxford University. Apparently, he is highly respected.

"My grades were much better than his in Oxford. Why didn't they invite me?" CC protests.

"I guess you look too Chinese. The Chinese like foreign faces better sometimes, especially when it comes to the English." I say.

"Right. I forgot that I'm a fake foreign devil here," CC comments sarcastically.

"I've heard there is a beauty pageant on another channel. Let's appreciate beautiful models instead of that heartbreaker Nick!" I suggest.

We switch the channel to the beauty pageant. Seeing these young, thin, yet beautiful women walk so gracefully on the stage clad only in bikinis, I feel uncomfortable about my own body. I will lose weight and eat less chocolate in the New Year, I silently vow to myself.

After the bikini test, it is announced that each beauty will be given a Q & A in English.

"Although I'm not as tall and thin, I speak the Queen's English perfectly." CC comforts herself, trying to find a psychological equilibrium.

But her smile soon freezes as we again see Nick on the TV. On this channel, he is acting as a guest MC. His role is to ask the questions in English to each beauty and to crack jokes. He is confident and princely.

"I didn't know that he's turned into a TV star in such a short time period," CC murmurs. "Before coming to China, Nick was so shy and timid. But now, he has gained confidence. China seems to be a paradise for men. But what about women? These young women here could easily make me, once a college queen, feel fat, plain, unfeminine, and even old. Was it a wise decision to have returned to China from England with Nick?" She wonders.

"This local channel is boring. Let's watch CCTV!" Lulu says.

"Right! Let's watch something intellectual. Like *The 59 Minutes*," I add.

CC quietly grabs the remote control and quickly switches the channel.

The 59 Minutes features a special edition about China's progress in the world community over the last year, as well as a forecast of cultural and socioeconomic changes in the New Year.

The host says, "With China's entry into the WTO, more foreign products will come to China, and vice versa. We will see more interaction between the Chinese and foreigners than ever. Romance is one kind of interaction. But fears and misunderstandings can cause problems in interracial romances due to the language and cultural barrier. How can the new generation be prepared for interracial dating? Let's hear what this couple says . . ."

Unbelievable! This time not only Nick is being interviewed but also Little Fang. They are holding hands in front of the camera, and every few moments, Nick puts his arm around Little Fang's shoulders to give her an affectionate hug.

Nick speaks. "Sometimes it is better not to understand everything the other side says. How does the Chinese saying go? *Nande hutu:* ignorance is bliss."

Little Fang says, "I'm going to publish a book called *How to Date an Englishman*. All my advice is in the book. All you need to make your relationship work is to read my book."

The studio audience applauds in admiration.

I steal a glimpse of CC.

CC seems calm. She says to us, "We should all make some New Year's resolutions and share them before midnight. I already have my three wishes for the New Year. One: I want to lose weight. Two: I will find my true love. And three: I will write a small book called *How to Dump an Englishman*.

60

Going Gaga
for Designer Labels

*M*y American girlfriend Sue is in her second year of the M.B.A. program at Purdue University. The Chinese economic changes she's seen on TV as well as the colorful Chinese life described in my e-mails have inspired her to write a China-related thesis. Her topic is foreign brand awareness in China.

After the New Year, Sue rushes to China to do research. When I tell Hugh about the subject Sue is working on, he thinks it could be a great story for Western readers to get to know the perceptions of Western brands in China.

To make the story more convincing and the research more authoritative, I have asked Lulu to conduct a national survey on Chinese women's impressions of foreign brands in Lulu's magazine *Women's Friends*. A total of 663 women, in the eighteen-to-thirty-five age bracket, mainly with office jobs, have participated and answered the survey.

After the survey results are tabulated, Sue is shocked. The brand images in China are quite different from those in the States. For example, 24 percent of women think to dine at TGI Friday's and to drink coffee at Starbucks is a symbol of wealth. And McDonald's is not deemed low-class, but rather chic. When it comes to cars, American cars are considered most prestigious: 92 percent of the participants consider a Cadillac or a Lincoln fancier than a Benz or a Lexus. Standard brands such as Lee's jeans and Ikea furniture carry no cachet in the States or Europe, but become premium here. Häagen-Dazs ice cream, which one can buy in cheap grocery stores anywhere in the States, is emblematic of fashion and money in the eyes of young Chinese women.

With the unexpected answers and data in hand, Sue believes that if she can understand the psychology behind Chinese consumers, she can land a job in any of these American companies without problems. She might even be able to select from many offers.

Lulu and I organize a talk on foreign brands in the conference room of Lulu's magazine *Women's Friends*. We've invited young women from different parts of China. On the day of the meeting, ten women come as Sue's focus group. Lulu and I also sit in on the meeting.

Sue shoots her first question. "Tell me, what does Häagen-Dazs ice cream have to do with fashion?"

A young woman named Li, with long permed hair, clad in a black miniskirt and black boots answers eagerly. "First, the Häagen-Dazs stores are very cute, always colorful and stylish, with a designer's taste. Second, it's the most expensive ice cream one can buy, the Rolls Royce of ice creams. Two coffees and one scoop of ice cream there will be more expensive than a Chinese dinner with five dishes. Because it's so expensive, most people stay away from Häagen-Dazs. The stores are lonely places. So it makes you noticeable when you walk into a Häagen-Dazs store. Sitting on the beautifully designed chairs and seeing the outside world through its glass windows, I feel on top of the world with a taste of the creamy American ice cream."

Another girl, named Ting, with gelled red hair and leather jacket, nods in agreement. "What Li said is very true. I love Häagen-Dazs so much I broke up with my boyfriend because of it."

"Why?" Sue asks, looking puzzled.

Ting says, "One day I said to my ex, citing the advertisement, 'If you love me, buy me a Häagen-Dazs ice cream.' When we walked into the store, he said he refused to spend seventy yuan on an ice cream. I decided to dump him right there."

"Why?" Sue asks.

"He simply isn't a member of the middle class yet. I want to marry somebody so that I can move up to the middle class," Ting adds dismissively .

"The middle class? What do you mean?" asks Sue.

"Someone who knows and can afford to eat Häagen-Dazs, use Ikea furniture, and wear CK's underwear."

Conspicuous consumption may be an American invention, but it has been perfected in China.

"Why Ikea?" Sue wonders, thinking Ikea isn't very upscale in the States, and is actually considered quite tacky in some quarters.

Ting continues. "I love Ikea's designs, but I can't afford it. I have to take a carpenter with me to the Ikea stores and tell him to copy their style. My dream is to own a room of Ikea furniture."

"What about cars? What is your dream car?"

"A Buick!" Another woman, Yo-Yo, jumps in.

I explain to Sue that a Buick usually costs $40,000 or more in China.

Sue is disappointed at the taste of these women, so she decides to let them know what the real fashions and tastes are.

"Do you like Versace clothes or Omega watches?" she asks the women.

"Everyone can wear Versace clothing and an Omega watch nowadays," Ting says, not impressed.

"Really?" Sue probes.

"The knockoffs, of course," I explain to Sue quietly in English.

After talking to the girls, Sue thanks Lulu and me for our help.

"So do you think it will help you land a job?" I ask Sue.

"Yes. Apparently, in order to make big bucks, I should work for GM or Häagen-Dazs Asia. Or I can go back to school to study law and become a lawyer that specializes in IPR," Sue concludes.

61

Culture, with a Bitter Aftertaste

Sue is puzzled by another phenomenon in China: a bowl of noodles costs only six yuan, whereas a cup of coffee costs thirty yuan or more. Sue asks me, "Why has coffee become so expensive in China? It's virtually a luxury item. You actually have to make a thoughtful decision before sitting down to have a cup."

My answer is simple: coffee is culture, coffee is fashion, and drinking coffee is a symbol of status. You pay thirty or forty yuan not just for the coffee but also for the background music, the candlelight on the table, and the yuppie ambience in a coffee shop.

"It sounds like coffee carries a deeper meaning here!" Sue comments.

"Yes, indeed." I nod, and tell Sue the story of my friend Fu and his coffee religion.

In the 1980s, when Nestlé's instant coffee was first introduced to China, Fu was one of the first to try it. But he didn't fall in love with the taste of coffee. It reminded him of the taste of *banlangen,* the bitter Chinese medicine his mother gave him every time he was sick.

Soon he learned that instant coffee didn't taste as good as regular coffee. He decided to buy regular coffee. At that time, the Chinese didn't have access to regular ground coffee, much less coffee beans. With the help of my mother, he got a jar of Columbia coffee at the Beijing Friendship Store.

How to make coffee? He didn't know of the existence of coffee makers. But from the TV advertisements, he learned that coffee needed to be boiled. He put the coffee into a wok that was filled with water. When it was boiled, he drank it along with the residue, thinking it was part of the coffee-drinking experience, just like drinking the tea leaves in the bottom of a cup of tea.

The taste was awful. It ended his passion for coffee until Starbucks came into China almost twenty years later.

Fu discovered that among his wide circle of fashionable friends, all of a sudden "espresso," "latte," and "cappuccino" became cool words to toss around during conversations. His coworkers always brought a cup of Starbucks coffee back to the office after lunch. In order to be fashionable, he turned the Starbucks on the corner into his classroom of culture. He gave himself a crash course on words like "mocha" and "grande," "tall" and "short."

Although the taste of coffee still didn't appeal to him, whenever he was in a restaurant with friends, he always ordered coffee, not tea.

The taste of status was much more appealing than the taste of coffee itself.

At one time, Fu dated a girl named Yao. On their second date, he chose to meet at Starbucks and ordered black coffee for himself and cappuccino for Yao.

Yao had never had a cappuccino in her life. She drank the coffee with the small spoon still in the cup. The spoon, of course, fell to the floor. Fu was displeased and attempted to educate Yao. "You should use the spoon to stir the coffee and then put it down before you drink the coffee."

Yao was humiliated by Fu's condescending tone, "It's not a big deal. I like to drink coffee any way I want."

"Culture is culture," Fu retorted. "If you don't bother to learn about culture, what do we have in common?"

Evidently, they didn't have much in common anyway, as the girl stood up and said, "Stir this," then stormed away angrily.

After hearing the story, Sue is shocked, "So your friend lost his date just like that?"

"Yes!" I say.

"What does he do now, I wonder," Sue asks.

"A few years ago, seeing that Starbucks makes so much money by charging twenty-eight yuan for a cup of coffee, he decided to get himself a share of this lucrative business. So he opened his own independent coffee shop. He charges people thirty-five yuan per cup," I say.

"But in the States, Starbucks is the one that charges more than the independent coffee shops," says Sue, a bit confused.

"I know. For luxury products, here in China, the more expensive it is, the better people think it is. I've heard he is opening his thirteenth coffee shop and is being romanced by investment bankers. He plans to go public and sell shares!"

62

Class Differences in Communist China

*B*eing called *xiaozi,* or petit bourgeois, was dangerous during the Cultural Revolution. Although not as bad as being labeled counterrevolutionary, the petit bourgeois were condemned and assaulted by Red Guards if they so much as wore high-heeled shoes, permed their hair, or committed some other "offense" against the People's Fashion.

Gone are the days when beauty and fashion are deemed counterrevolutionary. Today, *xiaozi* is one of the most glorious words in the Chinese lexicon, representing an emerging army of cool people. They read the Chinese versions of *Elle* and *Cosmopolitan* instead of the *People's Daily* and take pride in drinking coffee rather than tea. They may not be rich enough to own cars or condos, but they own taste. They don't hesitate to spend a third of their monthly salary on a Luciano Pavarotti concert.

Lulu proudly calls herself a *xiaozi*. During a break in our weight-loss class, Lulu chats with Beibei and me about the new class concepts in China. "Because China is changing so fast, the society has become more segmented than ever," Lulu lectures. "Everybody is looking for a new label. Our magazine has to constantly study demographics to get a handle on our readers. Results show that our magazine serves *xiaozi* people like me, but not people like Beibei."

"I'm not a petit bourgeois?" asks Beibei.

"Of course not," Lulu replies, as if it was obvious. "You're a *xingui*, a member of the new elite who reads *Fortune* magazine or *Business Week*."

"What makes me a member of the new elite?" asks Beibei.

I interject: "Your income and your lifestyle. You drive a BMW. You have lovers. You attend banquets every week."

"Who are we?" Beibei wonders.

Lulu explains: "You're the group that has benefited most from the open-door policy. You can be Communists or Capitalists, but often the combination of the two are the biggest winners."

I ask, "What type of people are both communists and capitalists? I read Karl Marx's *Capital*. They are certainly not in there."

Lulu explains: "They are the kids who grew up in upper-class families in Beijing or Shanghai, then received an education in the West, and later work for multinational investment banks or Fortune 500 companies. Chief executives and presidents of privatized companies that were formerly state-owned. Popular singers, actors . . ."

Beibei asks Lulu: "What about Niuniu? Which group does she belong to?"

"I'm definitely an antielitist. I'd never drive a BMW to show off," I say to Beibei.

"Niuniu, you're a bobo!" Lulu says, as if she is a scientist classifying rare animals.

"A bobo?" I laugh.

"Yes," says Lulu, "the most fashionable group, better sounding than the middle class or the petite bourgeoisie. The bobo concept, of course, comes from an American book called *Bobos in Paradise: The New Upper Class and How They Got There.*"

"What does it mean?" I ask, not having read the book.

"Bourgeois bohemians," Lulu explains. "The next issue of my magazine is a special issue about the bobos. I know everything about this group."

"Bourgeois bohemians. I love the sound of it. So what makes me a bobo?" I ask.

"You drive an SUV," says Lulu.

"Yes. I love camping." I nod.

"You read *Time* magazine. Your English is perfect. You love to travel and toss around words like Tibet, Bali, and Shangri-la. You're almost a vegetarian. You have more than fifteen years of education. You sleep under down quilts. You are often seen with a Sony or an Apple laptop at Starbucks. You have an iPod. You listen to new age music and do yoga. You're no different from those bobos in New York except that you carry the latest cell phone model and they don't really care much about cell phones. You pay less for manicures and dermabrasion and rentals than they do. The whole point is that among the Chinese, bobos are the most cosmopolitan group."

I say: "It does sound like me. But I don't like stereotypes."

"You even sound boboistic!" Lulu says, smiling at me, proud of the word she has just coined. "You believe in individualism and refuse to be categorized. But you should feel lucky to be categorized in the bobo class. You might have been born into the hobo class, like the migrant workers who live in the south of the city."

I reply: "Communism's goal is to eliminate class differences. But now Chinese people seem to enjoy classifying themselves."

Lulu continues the analysis: "I guess China is on the move. Young people will go wherever it is fashionable."

I put my arm around Lulu. "And if they aren't sure what is fashionable, they can always buy Lulu's magazine."

POPULAR PHRASES

XIAOZI: Petite bourgeois; refers to an emerging group of young people who enjoy things Western, from coffee to jazz. They are not rich, but pay attention to their lifestyle. They would fit in quite well with their counterparts in the West.

63

Returning Home

The Chinese New Year is drawing near. Thousands and even millions of people are on the move in trains, airplanes, and buses, rushing to reunite with their loved ones. It is the time to *huijia,* or return home. In increasingly cosmopolitan Beijing, home is a concept that constantly needs to be redefined. Over dinner, Beibei, Lulu, and I discuss which home we will return to.

The most common definition of home for a Chinese woman is where her husband is. In our case, both Lulu and I are single women. Although Beibei is the only one that is married, she no longer has any affection for her husband, Chairman Hua. "Impermanence and homelessness probably are evitable feelings of modern souls, even though we do have a roof over our heads," Lulu says philosophically.

"I think when the Chinese talk about returning home, we

don't mean our own homes," says Beibei. "We mean our parents' homes."

"Do you plan to spend the Chinese New Year at your parents' place?" I ask Beibei.

"Yes," Beibei says cheerfully. "They will teach me how to make dumplings and I will teach them how to taste red wine. Then we might play mahjong for a few days and nights. What about you, Niuniu?"

"I envy you for being able to spend time with your folks together," I reply. "Since my parents are divorced, I have to choose one over the other for my holiday visits. This year, my father wants to take his new wife to the States. . . . So I guess I'll go to my mother's home. What about you, Lulu?"

Lulu casts her eyes downward. Returning home is a painful issue for her. Lulu's family is in a small town in the south. Her parents divorced a long time ago. Her father was a successful businessman and sent her to Beijing for schooling. But he passed away when Lulu was in college and his secretary stole all of his money. The rest of Lulu's family still lives in the small town.

Today, she is the biggest achiever in her family, a legend in her hometown: she was the most beautiful girl in town, the only graduate from a top Beijing university, and, now, the editor of a well-known fashion magazine. At one time when she returned home with ginseng and stacks of cash, the whole town celebrated. Small kids followed her around, asking for red envelopes. But things have changed in the last few years.

As her childhood playmates become mothers of toddlers, she is still single, without a decent boyfriend. The boys who used to have a crush on her have all "jumped into the sea"—started their businesses. The last few years have been good for business owners in small towns. They have built nice houses, they drive nice cars, and some are already working on their second or third girlfriends or marriages. Lulu still can't afford to buy a house in Beijing. She doesn't own a car. The neighbors all ask her mother the same question: "Has Lulu got a steady boyfriend this year?" Seeing her come home by herself, her mother no longer happily notifies every neighbor. The pride has been replaced by worry.

Last year, the tension really escalated when Lulu went home for the New Year. Any incoming phone calls from men became a family matter. Her mother insisted on answering all her phone calls. She shamelessly asked every man, "What do you think of our Lulu? . . . If you like her, when do you plan to be my son-in-law?"

Lulu quickly ran back to Beijing. This year, she decides not to go back to her hometown to be humiliated once more.

"Where do you want to go?" Beibei asks, jerking Lulu back to the conversation.

Lulu says, "A philosopher has said that nature is our real home. I plan to celebrate the Chinese New Year in a deep forest. I want to return to our spiritual home."

Before Beibei and I can comment on Lulu's idea, her cell phone rings. She starts to talk in her local dialect. So much for returning to her spiritual home.

"Who was it?" Beibei asks after Lulu hangs up.

"It was my mother calling from home," Lulu says.

"What did she say?" I ask.

Lulu answers, "She says she will come to Beijing to visit me for the Chinese New Year! I guess I will just stay in Beijing."

"Remember, Beijing has become your home!" Beibei tells Lulu.

I add, "Home is a relative term. Anywhere your bed and pillow are becomes your real home for that night, New Year's or otherwise!"

Lulu screams, "Oh, no! Talking about bed and pillow, I just remembered that my mom said she'd like to sleep in the same bed with me so that we could have good mother-daughter conversations at night. The same bed, can you believe it? I'm already over thirty and she still wants to tuck me in. Give me a break!"

POPULAR PHRASES

HUIJIA: Return home. Family and home are extremely important in the Chinese culture. One must never forget where he or she came from, and returning home for special events is more than just a nice thing to do; it is a requirment of any self-respecting Chinese.

XIAHAI: To jump into the sea: to go into business. In China, starting a business is probably even *more* risky than jumping into the sea!

64

Country Mother
and City Daughter

*L*ulu's mother comes to visit her a week before the Chinese New Year. She plans to stay with Lulu for a month and insists that they sleep in the same bed.

For a single, independent, big-city girl, it might sound like a nightmare to share a bed with her unworldly country-bumpkin mother for a month. But it turns out to be not as unpleasant as Lulu had expected. It is actually fun . . . for a while.

Lulu's mother is an excellent cook and a clean and tidy woman. Whenever Lulu comes back home, the dinner is cooked and ready to be served, and everything from her keys to her gloves has been organized and put in good order. Moreover, having someone waiting for you at home makes Lulu feel so warm. It is this sense of family that she hasn't had for so

long. There is only one moment that turns out to be a bit embarrassing. One evening, Lulu and her mother are watching the
Discovery Channel. That day's program showcases a primitive
tribe on the Amazon, and some of the tribal members have no
clothes. "Nudity! It's so awful!" Lulu's mother screams and
hastily switches the channel. Lulu thinks her mother is making
a fuss. Other than that incident, the first week Lulu and her
mother spend together is nearly idyllic.

But mothers have their own set of priorities. And before too
long, things start to change. Lulu's mother, like most Chinese
mothers, is curious about her daughter's private life. She pep-
pers Lulu with questions about her relationships with men.
Other generational, social, and cultural differences begin to appear.

One day, Lulu comes home, takes a shower, and starts to get
dressed to meet Beibei and me. She suddenly discovers that all
of her sexy underwear is missing. Lulu is partial to thongs, brief
panties, and lace bras that reveal as well as support. She is dismayed. "Mom, did you do the laundry? Where did you put my
underwear? I can't find a single clean set."

Her mother tells her that she thought they were not only
not functional but also way too small. "I threw them away and
bought you new big, roomy underwear. Why should you
squeeze yourself into such tiny bits of fabric that don't even
cover anything?"

From there it only gets worse. Another day when Lulu
comes back from work, her mother is waiting for her at the
kitchen table. She is holding a package of condoms in her hand.

"Lulu, what is this?"

Lulu's mind begins to reel. She is embarrassed; discussing
sex with one's parents is never easy. It is just not done in Chi-

nese culture. So she tells her mother they are balloons. "Black balloons? Black is not a lucky color. Why do you have black balloons?" her mother keeps the questions coming.

Lulu cannot tell her mother that this is for girls who have fantasies of black men like her, so she has to make up an answer on the spot. "Mom, that is the most fashionable color. Don't you see that so many young women always love to wear black clothes?"

Her mother murmurs, "I also wonder why they smell like cherry."

Lulu cannot tell her mother that it actually tastes like cherry too. She dodges the question by saying, "Let's go get some red balloons for New Year's Day."

But the worst is yet to come. One day Lulu comes home. Nothing happens during dinner. They watch some TV, then they decide to go to sleep. Once they are in bed, her mother says bluntly and without warning, "Adult movies are not proper for unmarried girls like you."

This is a totally unexpected statement. "What do you mean?" But Lulu can already guess the rest.

Her mother scolds her, "I was putting away the laundry, and I opened the bottom drawer of your bureau. I found a collection of adult movies. Why do you have them? It's not right for you to watch movies like these. Only bad girls do that. You aren't married yet and you have to care about your reputation."

Lulu tells her mother that this is Beijing, not the small town she came from. People can watch anything they like, and it is not considered evil for a single woman to enjoy the privileges of married women. Lulu considers giving her mother some more detailed examples from her own love life but quickly decides against it.

Her mother shuts down and becomes quiet. Both of them toss and turn in the bed. A few hours later, Lulu, who is already half-asleep, receives a nudge from her mother. "Lulu, are you still awake?"

"What?" Lulu asks her mother in the darkness.

Her mother finally reveals the puzzle in her mind. "Lulu, I watched one of those videos. Do foreigners really do that in bed? That is so dirty!"

65

Sun-Tzu on the Art of Love

When her mother lives with her, the most awkward moment for Lulu is not that her mother throws her small sexy underwear away. Nor is it when her mother finds her adult video collection and black condoms.

"It's the moment when Chang calls from the United States and my mother picks up the phone," she tells me when we meet for a late cup of tea.

Chang is Lulu's childhood friend. At that time, Lulu was the best student in sports and academics. Moreover, she was able to speak perfect Mandarin, which was considered a symbol of status. Thus, she was deemed a princess. Chang was her quiet admirer.

By the time Lulu was admitted to the best university in Beijing, Chang had failed his college entrance examination. But he studied hard, joining Lulu in Beijing being his only motivation.

A year later, he got into the English program in the same university Lulu attended.

Since both were in Beijing, Chang thought it would be a good chance to develop their relationship. Lulu had never thought of him in a romantic way. After all, she had defeated him in virtually every arena, including height. Chang was too shy to proclaim his love and Lulu pretended that she didn't know he was enamored of her, so the two acted like normal friends.

After graduation, Lulu worked for *Women's Friends* in Beijing and Chang was hired by the Ministry of Foreign Affairs as an interpreter.

Six years pass.

Chang has become a promising diplomat working in the Chinese embassy in Washington, D.C. He was afraid of being a lonely celibate in the States, so before leaving for Washington, he selected a woman from among the many Chinese girls who dreamed of being the wife of a foreign diplomat. His wife is a traditional Chinese woman, thin, shy, quiet, worshipful of her man.

When Chang calls Lulu from overseas, there is much to catch up on. I imagine he wants to tell her about the beautiful cherry blossoms in Washington, the different ethnic foods along Embassy Row, the art galleries and museums and the charming Georgetown area . . . but Lulu isn't home. Instead, her mother answers the phone. She has seen Chang grow up. Hearing his voice from the other side of the earth, she almost burst into tears.

"Chang, I knew that you were such a good boy from the very beginning. I knew that you'd be so excellent some day. I always dreamed that you and Lulu would become a pair when you were young. But I didn't want to interfere because I thought kids should make their own choices. Before Lulu's father died, his biggest hope was to have Lulu bring him back a nice boy. Such a simple wish still hasn't come true yet. Chang, my good boy, tell me, what's wrong with our Lulu? Is it that she is not beautiful enough? Is she too independent? Is she too old?" Lulu's mother is really laying it on thick.

As her mother is talking, Lulu returns and overhears everything. She doesn't know what Chang's answers are on the other line. But it's clear that all those cold shoulders she gave Chang when they were young are now being returned. Chang finally has his revenge.

She feels a deep sense of defeat. All her previous victories over him, from grades to love, have just become history, with no current value. Henry Kissinger once said that the ultimate aphrodisiac is power. Between them, two friends and two rivals, she is the failure—and she has been betrayed by her own mother. It's a power game, reversed.

By the time she enters the room, her mother has just hung up. Lulu suppresses her rage, but her voice still trembles.

"Mother, even though I'm the lowest of the low, I thought that I still had my pride. But just now, my last shred of pride and privacy has been taken away!"

She later tells me, "Game, set, match, I just lost to Chang 40-Love."

Her mother tries to reassure her. "Totally submitting without pride is a winning strategy in Sun Tzu's *Art of War*."

Lulu is confused, not sure what an ancient general has to do with twenty-first-century love in Beijing. "What do you mean?"

Her mother smiles like a flower. "Lulu, I just used fake

weeping to test him. He still has feelings for you. Can you win him back? I want to be the mother-in-law of a diplomat and see cherry blossoms in Washington, D.C.!"

As I listen to the stories of her mother, I think, Lulu's mother isn't as conservative as she thinks after all.

66

The Delicate Art of Bribery

*L*ulu lives in company-subsidized housing. Her three-bedroom apartment in Beijing's upscale San Yuan Qiao neighborhood is worth 700,000 yuan. Recently she found out that the magazine she works for wants to sell the flat to a staffer—and she is being considered.

"I would like to buy it, but I can't afford it," Lulu tells Sukang, her boss.

"Yes you can. We are selling it for just seventy thousand yuan!" he replies.

"Really? Just one-tenth of its market price?"

"Yes," says Sukang winking. "As a perk for an employee."

Buying apartments and selling them cheaply to employees is common practice in China. Both employers and employees get a tax break. But normally it's 10 percent or 20 percent off the market value. Offering a place for one-tenth of the market value is rare indeed. Last year, ugly arguments usually erupted when there was a similar announcement. Four older, married senior editors almost went to war over one apartment offered way below market price. Now it could be her turn.

Sukang tells Lulu there are two other senior editors under consideration. "Who is chosen depends on your performance," Sukang says with a subtle smile. "This is the last time an offer like this will be made. I am your superior and you had better make me happy."

Lulu understands what Sukang means, but she has never been good at sucking up to her boss. She also knows that whoever gets the apartment will receive the equivalent of 640,000 yuan. It's a terrific deal. Later, she hears her competitors have already visited Sukang's home bearing expensive gifts.

"What should I do?" she asks Beibei and me.

"Take gifts to your boss at once," Beibei suggests.

"Isn't that bribery?" Lulu asks. "I've never given him anything. Now, all of a sudden, I go to his house bearing gifts? That is too obvious."

Beibei replies: "Bribery is an art. If you give your boss money, he must refuse, but if you put the money in a red envelope as a gift to his kid, he won't say no. Always avoid a direct and obvious bribe. Rule No. 1: Be subtle. Rule No. 2: Timing is everything. Chinese New Year is the perfect time to give gifts. The bribe is concealed within a legitimate gift. You've come to pay seasonal respects, and never mention the apartment in conversation."

"What gift should I give?" Lulu asks.

"What are his vices? If he is a drinker, give him imported liquor," I suggest.

"Brandy or scotch whiskey or cognac?" Lulu asks.

"How old is he?" Beibei asks.

"Fifty-five."

"Choose something in a nice bottle with fancy wrapping," Beibei says. "What about a bottle of VSOP? Men his age can't tell the difference in price between a VSOP and an XO. For them it's good as long as it has English letters."

Following our advice, Lulu rushes out and buys the VSOP. At the bank, she withdraws ten new one-hundred-yuan notes. She puts the money in a red envelope with a small card saying, "To Dede from Auntie Lulu." Dede is her supervisor's son. But later, she throws away the card, deciding instead to slip the envelope into the VSOP package. Everything had better be subtle.

On New Year's Eve, she visits Sukang's home. He appears gracious and friendly. He receives gifts all the time, so to him it is quite normal. For the first time, he asks her about her hobbies and her family. She feels at ease, sensing definite rapport.

A few days later Lulu gets together with Beibei and me.

Before she can start to describe the whole affair concerning the apartment, Beibei says, "I'm exhausted. Too many employees visited me. They gave me so much stuff, I don't have enough space for it so I'm giving you each a bottle of VSOP."

We say thanks and unwrap the bottle. Amazingly, Lulu sees a familiar red envelope that falls out from her bottle of VSOP. Inside the envelope are ten crisp one-hundred-yuan notes.

Beibei says, "I'll take the money back and leave you the VSOP if that's okay."

"But it's my money!" Lulu screams.

"Why yours? I just gave this to you. You're so ungrateful!" Beibei says as she snatches the money out of Lulu's hands.

"Who is it from?" asks Lulu.

"One of my employees. His wife teaches but wants to become a singer. She wants to sign with us."

"Where does she teach?"

"The Anan English Elementary School," says Beibei.

"That's an expensive gift for a teacher to give, isn't it?" I say.

"Come on, nowadays all the kids in school are from one-child families. Most parents try to curry favor with nice gifts," Beibei says. "I bet teachers get lots of liquor as gifts. That's why she didn't bother to open this package."

"Sukang's child Dede goes to that school. I gave Sukang the VSOP and the money!" Lulu says, shocked.

"What goes around, comes around," Beibei says as she reaches for the bottle. "Let's have a drink and use up this one thousand yuan."

67

A New Dating Strategy

Since Lulu's mother has come to Beijing, Lulu has told us many funny stories about her. Lately, she asks Lulu to update her about her boyfriends on a daily basis. If Lulu has a date, she wants to know everything in detail so she can make some judgmental comments. Her mother's opinions often irritate Lulu. If Lulu doesn't have a date, her mother will sigh and say things like, "Why are you so unattractive? Something must be wrong with your character. You are too strong." Her constant nagging hurts Lulu.

Lulu's mother married at twenty-five, already considered late at that time. She would like Lulu to get married so that both of them can have emotional and financial security. As she continually whines about Lulu being so picky in choosing a husband or ending up an old maid, Lulu can only joke lightly, "Mom, the later I get married, the better my man will be."

When she really falls for someone, her mother isn't happy either. She says that Lulu is being stupid. "Other girls all use their brains. Only a stupid girl like you will give her heart and her body so quickly. When I was young, I never let boys get me so easily."

When Lulu doesn't like some man she met, her mother will say things like, "You're already over thirty. You'd be undesirable in my time. You're lucky to have some man who would like to go out with you."

Lulu is distressed by her mother's interference in her love life, but she manages to contain her anger. She never loses her temper—until her mother finally goes too far.

One day, Lulu's mother is especially unhappy when Lulu makes negative comments about a man named Ching, whom her mother likes. "He's bald, with a Buddha belly," she tells her mother. "He uses a toothpick without covering his mouth at the dining table. I can't stand him."

Her mother thinks differently. Besides having a good job, Ching is honest, which will make him a good son-in-law. Plus, Ching's affection for Lulu is obvious. So when Ching calls later that day and Lulu is out, her mother answers the phone and chats with Ching.

Ching asks for Lulu's e-mail address. Her mother says that she doesn't have one—perhaps Ching could set up one for her. After Ching gets an e-mail account for Lulu, he calls. Once again, Lulu's mother picks up the phone. Ching asks her to pass on the instructions to Lulu about how to send e-mails. Her mother doesn't pass on the information to Lulu. Instead, she pretends to be Lulu, sending affectionate e-mails to Ching.

Lulu's mother, such a fast learner, even picks up things like chatting via MSN Messenger. She even learns some of the Chinese acronyms such as MM for "girl," BB for "baby," and GG for "brother."

Ching is overjoyed by the warm and emotional e-mails he's getting from Lulu. Three months later, on Lulu's birthday, he decides not to wait anymore. He tells Lulu in the e-mail that he will come and propose with a diamond ring he has bought for her and tell her mother that he is going to marry her.

After reading the e-mail, Lulu's mother realizes that she has to tell Lulu about the correspondence between Ching and her, and that she has done it for Lulu's own good. But Lulu gets very angry after hearing what her mother has done.

"I'm going out tonight! After writing to him for so long, you must know how to deal with him. You don't really need me," Lulu yells at her mother and leaves angrily.

Ching comes with his ring at six o'clock. Not seeing Lulu, he is confused. Lulu's mother has made up a story. She says to Ching that it's Lulu's friend who has been writing on Lulu's behalf, not Lulu. Her friend thought it would give a chance for Ching and Lulu to get to know each other better, but only finds out later that Lulu is too stubborn to change.

After hearing the story, Ching is not as hurt as Lulu's mother had expected. Instead, he says to Lulu's mother, "Auntie, help me find her friend. She has written to me with such beautiful words. She seems to understand me so well that I'd rather date her than Lulu!"

Lulu's mother blushes.

68

Fake Car, Fake Man

When former U.S. vice president Dan Quayle asked his Chinese daughter-in-law to name the first thing she wanted to do upon arriving in the States, her answer was simple. "Drive," she said. Quayle was shocked. Considering all the attractions the country offered, why would anyone choose to tackle traffic?

For many young Chinese, car ownership is something to aspire to. If they can't afford it, most feel they should at least have a driver's license to carry around. It's like a membership card.

Lulu had her driver's license for five years before buying her first car. It's a Chinese-made sports utility vehicle costing only 100,000 yuan—about $12,000. Still, it's a big deal for her. She owns something worth six digits, feels luckier than pedestrians and cyclists who must give right-of-way to cars, and also has an edge over the owners of the minicar Autuo, who are often bullied by bigger cars on the road. Some even have bumper stickers declaring, "My name is Au-tuo. My brother is Au-di. So don't mess with me!"

With an SUV, Lulu will never need to worry about being cut off. She feels majestic on the road. She sends her family a picture of her new car, telling them she's no longer a have-not in the automotive world. But they are not impressed. First, her SUV is Chinese-made rather than imported, so there's no prestige attached. Second, her family in the rural south thinks SUVs aren't really cars. Her brother writes: "SUVs are like pickup trucks—they are meant to carry goods, not human beings. Why didn't you get a real car, like a sedan?"

Lulu quickly responds, feeling obligated to educate her family on fashion in the city. She tells them that driving an SUV is chic among the middle class in the United States and in Beijing; it's even cooler than driving a standard Honda Accord.

"Americans pay more money for insurance and luxury taxes if they buy an SUV," she writes. "Pickups don't represent blue-collar workers. From business magazines like *Fortune* and *Forbes*, I've learned that when Silicon Valley was in its heyday, many CEOs drove their beat-up pickups to work proudly." A few days later, she gets a reply from her brother, writing on behalf of her mother. "Lulu, we are proud you have a car now, even if it is just a Chinese-made one. We hope that when you marry, you will be driven in a nice, big Lincoln town car, or a Cadillac, or your brother's dream car, a nice, blue Buick."

To many Chinese, an American car is prestigious. The Chinese share the American notion of "bigger is better."

From the tone of their letter, Lulu senses that her family isn't enthusiastic about her car. She complains to me: "Why am I always not good enough in their eyes? First, they complained that I don't make enough money. Now I finally get my own car and they think a Chinese car isn't good enough."

To cheer her up, I go on a ride with her in her new SUV. On the road, a Toyota 4Runner swerves dangerously, cutting us off. Lulu has to brake hard. She honks the horn at the Toyota and the driver gives us the one-finger salute.

Now she's furious.

Generally, Lulu is sweet and ladylike, but behind the wheel, she becomes an aggressive, bad-tempered bitch. She follows the Toyota to a gas station and hops out of the car ready to swear at the driver. When he gets out of his Toyota and fixes his eyes on her, her anger instantly fades. The man is a Chinese version of Brad Pitt.

"You getting gas too?" he says. His tone is friendly, as if the cut-off and gesture had never happened.

"Well, yes, I guess," says Lulu. I remain sitting in the passenger's seat, watching them.

"You like SUVs too?" the man asks.

"Yes, but yours is better," Lulu replies with a brush of her hair.

"Actually, mine is also Chinese-made, exactly like yours," he says.

"Really?" asks Lulu.

"I just changed the hood ornament and all the signs, and have replaced them with Toyota ones," he explains. "Now it looks exactly like a Toyota 4Runner. The switch cost me less than a thousand yuan. Guess how much a real Japanese import costs? Three times as much as our Chinese-made cars."

"What a bargain you got," Lulu says.

"Well, a Toyota is not my dream car," the man says. "My dream car is the new Cherokee SUV V6."

Lulu closes her eyes. I guess she is drifting into a daydream: the wind is in her hair as she drives off with him. But when she comes to and says, "I guess you love American cars too," he is already pulling out of the station.

And with a wave, he's gone.

"Why didn't you stop him?" Lulu scolds me.

"I thought you didn't like fake men," I murmur.

69

Cross-Cultural Romance

People don't seem to get tired of talking about women like Jackie Kennedy or Princess Diana. There is something powerful about being the woman who is able to tie down a powerful, wealthy man for herself.

Being in the right place at the right time and using beauty as a lure certainly enhances one's chance of landing a prominent man.

Little Fang befriended CC, Lulu, Beibei, and me while she tutored CC's English boyfriend, Nick, in Chinese.

She admired Lulu's beauty and glamour, CC's Western education, and Beibei's well-connected family. She once said that compared to them, she felt plain and unremarkable. "I grew up in a humble family and graduated from an unknown college. But you guys have everything." She tried hard to adopt Lulu's fashion style, and she mimicked CC's accent and Beibei's "in" expressions.

But after she stole Nick, who held a degree from Oxford, Little Fang was no longer modest. She appeared on television talk shows to discuss interracial dating or promote her book *How to Date an Englishman*.

She became a role model for many young Chinese women who dreamed of a cross-cultural romance.

Then, Little Fang disappeared from view for a while.

So when she resurfaced, we were all excited.

CC knocks on my door, rushes in, and before even taking off her coat flashes the invitation from Little Fang.

"Did you get one?" CC asks with her eyes wide open.

I immediately check a stack of unopened mail on my desk and find an invitation. As I open the envelope, a picture falls to the floor.

In the picture, Little Fang, wearing a beautiful bridal gown, stands in front of a majestic, ivy-covered Welsh castle. Beside her stands the groom, a tuxedo-clad Westerner—but it isn't Nick.

I glance at CC. It's clear she is upset. I read the invitation quickly. It says Little Fang and Sir William York have just held a church wedding in Wales. Now the newlywed couple is going to have a Chinese wedding at the Grand Hyatt Hotel in Shanghai and the groom will pay for the invited guests' hotel accommodations and plane tickets.

"I guess Nick is too poor for this woman," CC says.

"Are you going?" I ask.

"Absolutely not! She just wants to show off," CC cries, remembering her betrayal.

As they are talking, Lulu calls. "Have you received an invitation for Little Fang's wedding?" Lulu asks me.

"Yes," I reply.

"Heavenly Grandpa!" Lulu exclaims. "The expenses of every guest will be paid for. The man must be stinking rich. Did you see that he has a title? Sir William York. He's old money!"

"I wonder how she met him," I muse.

"I got all the details from Nick," Lulu says.

"You met Nick?" CC grabs the phone from me and screams into the receiver.

"Yes. His heart is broken," Lulu tells her.

"He broke my heart first," CC shouts into the phone.

"In any event, come over to our place," I say to Lulu and hang up the phone.

Soon, Lulu joins CC and me at my house. Lulu relates what Nick had told her. "When Nick proposed to Little Fang and asked her to go back to England with him, Little Fang said no. She didn't want to leave for England through marriage. She said she had been influenced by the classic book *Jane Eyre*. Like Jane Eyre, she wouldn't marry Nick until she felt she was his equal."

"How was she supposed to become his equal?" I ask.

"She wanted to study at Oxford," Lulu says.

"With her low command of English?" CC screams.

"Nick might have helped her polish her essays," I say with a shrug. "You never know. I remember when I was in the States, I helped a Chinese friend write an English essay about herself. She managed to get into Stanford."

"So Little Fang was granted admission into Oxford?" CC asks, looking stunned.

"Yes"—Lulu nods—"but we don't know if it was a regular program or some short program that anybody with money can get into. Anyway, she studied there for only one semester. She quit after falling in love with someone she met on campus."

"Sir William?" CC asks, still in disbelief. She can't believe that Little Fang was able to go to the same school as she did, even if it was just some short training program. Even worse, she quit Oxford!

"Yes," Lulu says. "But he was married at that time. Later, he divorced his wife after Little Fang's repeated and persistent requests."

"I guess the real purpose for Little Fang to get into Oxford was to nail down a rich man," I say.

"But I am still impressed by her wedding. The roses, the gown, and the castle. I wish I had her luck," Lulu says.

"Luck?" CC sneers. "Come on. When she was in China, Nick was the best man she could imagine having. After moving to England, she knew there were better men out there. Women like Little Fang spend all their time trying to get the best man in sight. Doesn't matter if he is available or not. She's a homewrecker!"

70

Walk This Way!

CC, Lulu, and I have gathered at Flamingo. Our conversation topic still centers on Little Fang, who has just sent us shocking news, the announcement of her marriage to Sir William York. We all decide not to go to her wedding in order to show emotional support and camaraderie for CC. We are debating the finer points of marrying well or becoming a self-made success.

"Do you think women tend to admire women who marry power and money or self-made women?" I ask the others.

"Self-made women like Oprah Winfrey are my role models," says CC.

"I think people seem more interested in a woman who marries well. It shows how charming she is! A woman's power over men is more important than anything else. That's why Princess Diana attracted more media coverage than any other women of her time," Lulu contends.

"Do you admire Little Fang then?" CC asks.

"No, of course not. But her Cinderella story makes my life look boring," Lulu says.

"You've got a better package. But I guess you just can't do things like that," CC states.

"Do what?" Lulu asks.

"Always try to nail the most powerful and richest man in sight. Doesn't matter if he is taken or not."

"I can't do that, that's for sure. I don't click with men of power and money. I always fall in love with poor artists or struggling writers, dreamers who wear ponytails and beards and look cool, but don't have enough money to take me out for a nice dinner." Lulu is equally frustrated with herself and proud of her immunity to money and wealth.

"That's the difference between you and Little Fang. You've chosen to follow the flow of your emotions and submit to your real feelings. But Little Fang values power and money more than love," I say as I analyze their personality types.

"I guess that's why I'm still poor and single even though my folks have given me a beautiful face! What I need is a head full of ambitious plans." Lulu sighs and hits her head as if to wake up the dormant ambition inside.

"I'm no better than you are." CC softens her tone. "My parents wanted me to marry a rich kid like myself. I dated Nick, who didn't have money. I thought I was being rebellious and independent. I wanted to send a message to my Hong Kong parents that there is something in this world called love and it is more valuable than money. But Nick dumped me, just like that. Then I had to listen to my parents say those four words that no one wants to hear: 'I told you so.'"

"Niuniu, what about you?" CC asks.

"No. I can't leave a good man for a man of power and money. Nor can I move from one man to another. If I did things like that, I would feel guilty for the rest of my life," I say.

"Too bad you have a strong sense of guilt," Lulu says.

"It's not a strong sense of guilt. Niuniu, you have a great sense of values and ideals." CC speaks for me.

"We might be failures in love, but we are still better off than Beibei. Although we don't chase after men of power and money, at least we don't have to pay our lovers like Beibei does," Lulu comments.

CC defends Beibei. "But I think it shows that she is strong. I'd rather give out money to a lover than take money from a powerful man that I don't love."

The conversation whirls around like a tornado, as each girl jumps in with a comment about another.

As soon as Beibei's name is mentioned, she shows up. As usual, she is late.

"What have you guys been talking about?" Beibei asks, ordering a martini

"Little Fang," Lulu says.

"Ha!" Beibei laughs. "Why are you wasting your time and energy talking here? Why don't you go to a golf resort or fly first-class to some exotic place to enhance your chance of meeting your Sir William York? This place is for empowered women like me." Beibei has a sip of her fruit tea, winking at the hot-looking waiter.

"Don't tease us." Lulu pleads. "You said that because you're rich yourself."

Beibei answers, "Why envy Little Fang? I think you all miss the point completely. Women really don't need to have money. With the right look at the right time, and with just the right amount of leg or cleavage showing, a woman can have any man she wants! The rich, the mighty, and even that hot-looking waiter!"

After saying this, she gets up to go to the powder room, walking as provocatively as she can, and guess what, every man in the room turns to watch her.

71

The Veterinarian
and the Poet

While Little Fang's wedding with Sir William York is taking place at Shanghai's Grand Hyatt Hotel, Lulu, Beibei, CC, and I are seeing the new Gong Li movie *Zhou Yu's Train*.

In the movie, Gong Li plays the title character, a tempestuous young painter who is torn between her two lovers. One is a poor, sensitive, quiet poet who works as a librarian to support himself and is played by Tony Leung Ka-fai. The other is an aggressive veterinarian filled with machismo.

We come away from the theater in love with the impressionistic cinema. After the movie, we go to a teahouse to play poker and talk about the movie.

As usual, Beibei, the boss in the clique, makes the first comment. "Tony Leung's performance was so brilliant! I fell in love with him ten years ago when I saw him in the French movie *The Lover*. He is as sexy as ever!"

Lulu says, "I read in the newspaper that in real life Gong Li prefers the poetic type of man to the machismo type. What about you guys? What type of men do you like better?"

I reply first. "I like the poet better. I also find this type of man attractive: gentle, sexy, a bit vulnerable, sensitive, smart, sometimes a bit melancholy. They have a tender side that, when mixed with passion, becomes quite combustible. They make you feel motherly and make your heart tremble and ache, and you feel on fire when they touch you." As I speak, I realize I'm talking about my feelings while I was with Len.

"Sounds like how I feel when I listen to Chopin," CC comments.

I nod. "Yes, exactly. I like Chopin. I've never liked men who never shut up. They're intimidating, and at the same time, they lack romance."

"But successful men are often assertive and talkative," Lulu cuts in.

"That's why I'm not up to finding men of power and money like Little Fang. I'm all for passion, like Zhou Yu, who travels on the rail of love," I say.

"I agree with Niuniu totally," CC jumps in. "I've found most men who have achieved a successful career and money are self-centered and hard to deal with. You have to put up with their bad temperament and their overwhelming characteristics. It's hard to feel like you are a partner in life with men like that. You always feel like they want you to walk behind them and not with them."

Lulu says, "Here in Asia, most of the women are docile and subservient. They don't mind if their men are selfish male chauvinists or much older than they are. As long as they bring wealth and material comfort into their lives, these women seem to be fine with the emotional alienation."

I say, "Gong Li seems to always play strong-willed women who have the courage to reveal their fervent sexual desires. Her characters are not fake. Perhaps that's why she is so well liked internationally. But in real life, I don't see many Chinese women like the Zhou Yu character, whose love is so steadfast, without material aggrandizement. For example, she didn't get any gifts from the poet except poetry. I have seen and interviewed so many girls who always enjoy men buying them Fendi bags or nice expensive jewelry."

"Yes!" CC agrees. "They even envy those young women who marry old ugly men simply because the men are rich."

"That's why strong women like us are left single." CC sighs. "I've found it is so difficult to find a good man in China. It's either that they think I'm too aggressive as a woman or vice versa."

"So that means aggressive women and men don't click? Does a man of power have to find a weak, mild woman? Can a strong woman fall in love with a strong man, like the Clinton couple?" I continue the debate.

Beibei speaks. "This American model doesn't apply here in this culture. That's why poor Zhou Yu has to die at the end of the movie. I think the director chooses such an ending because he knows that Zhou Yu is too noble for this shallow era we live in. In my humble opinion, women in Asia have three choices. First, to be cute and dumb, hoping to find a rich daddy to take care of them. Second, to be single forever or to leave China before it's too late. Third, to be like me, strong, rich, and tough. I'm just like a man who has the power to buy lovers."

"What about love and passion?" I cry out.

"You're still single because you think like that," Beibei says, not just to me, but to everyone. Her words are a proclamation of bloody honesty, but I am a hopeless romantic. I replay the love scene from the movie in my head. I feel like crying. Bravo, Zhou Yu.

72

A Woman Warrior
or a Demure Bride?

The depressed economy is making everyone at Lulu's workplace nervous. A new policy has been introduced, requiring workers to evaluate each other's performance regularly. Suddenly, the atmosphere in the office has changed from friendly to antagonistic.

Everyone pays attention to what time others start work and leave the office and who they talk to or don't talk to.

Office politics don't bother Lulu. She tries to stay above it. She is a high-calibre editor, a quick writer, and a first-class interviewer. After the magazine's editor is forced to retire at fifty-five, the rumor mill says that Lulu may be promoted as the new editor. She also feels confident that she is the best choice. But to her disappointment, it turns out that Jenny, who is junior to Lulu, is named editor-in-chief.

Everyone in the office speaks privately in support of Lulu, saying the owner's decision is unfair. The truth is, nobody likes Jenny.

She is relatively new but arrogant. She talks only to those whom she thinks are useful, and she treats her subordinates coldly.

One of the colleagues, Little Ma, tells Lulu, "Do you know how Jenny got the job? I've heard she is the owner's mistress."

"I can't believe it. I'll go and ask her!" Lulu says in anger.

"Are you out of your mind? She is your boss now. She can hire you or fire you. You can't just march into her office and ask her this type of question. If you dislike her, bide your time—a little sabotage here and there—and give her a hard time, but not so she notices," Little Ma says.

"I can't do things like that. I have to find out why and hear it from her own mouth," Lulu says.

"You got the subsidized apartment and she gets the editor-in-chief job. So why do you have to make her hate you? You should come to terms with life," Little Ma says.

Lulu ignores Little Ma, and rushes off to Jenny's big corner office with glass windows facing Beijing's Avenue of Eternal Peace.

Jenny looks at Lulu. "You come in without even knocking! What's so urgent?"

Lulu, clearly in a huff, asks directly, "Is it true that you and the owner are lovers?"

Jenny doesn't show any surprise or irritation with such a provocative question. She answers calmly: "We're good friends. I know what you are thinking. You can say I got the editor position because of our friendship, but it doesn't matter. Nowadays, corporate culture demands emphasis on end results. How you get these results is not the priority."

"But you're married. Does your husband know?" Lulu asks Jenny, who replies: "He's broad-minded and understanding."

Jenny's audacity makes Lulu think of the Chinese saying *sizhu bupa reshui tang:* dead pigs aren't afraid of boiling water.

"I'd rather you cover it up. It seems to me that you don't really care if your coworkers know about this scandal," Lulu says as she throws her arms up in frustration.

Jenny smiles again. "I can't really seal their lips, can I? Gossip is their right. After all, maybe it's not too bad for them to know, so they won't mess with me. If they don't like me or care for my work style, they can take a hike. One thing China doesn't lack is people."

Lulu listens with growing disbelief and anger. "Jenny, I guess with the owner's support, you have a free hand. In that case, I quit."

"No. I didn't mean you," Jenny immediately replies. "You can't quit. I really like you. I plan to give you a forty percent raise. Lulu, don't go sour on me. I'm your friend. Unlike others, you're a real treasure. I'll do whatever I can to keep you." Jenny softens her tone. Bossy and sympathetic at the same time, she certainly knows how to use both carrots and sticks.

Before Lulu can respond, Jenny adds: "Lulu, don't rush your decision. Take a few days to think clearly and then come back to me. I really think you'll like working with me." Jenny smiles like a boss. Lulu sees that smile, and immediately thinks of a crocodile.

Lulu nods, ready to leave.

"Wait." Jenny stops Lulu. "Now as a true friend, I want to give you some womanly advice."

"What?" Lulu almost feels like crying. This is so humiliating.

"You're smart and beautiful. You could easily win the world if you wanted to."

"Win the world? How?"

"Make use of what you have to get what you don't. Remember, you won't always be this young." Jenny sounds like a mother.

"I guess I can never be as talented as you are," Lulu says, and leaves Jenny's office, muttering "You bitch" under her breath. She is not in Jenny's league when it comes to office politics. Should she accept Jenny's condescending offer of the 40 percent raise or should she just quit? If she quits, who is going to support her and her mother? Neither of them has a husband to rely on. Luckily, she had already bought the subsidized apartment and it was a done deal.

She calls me. "Should I make husband searching my full-time job or should I get the book *How to Succeed in the Dirty Games of Office Politics*?"

"Be a woman warrior instead of a demure bride," I say firmly.

POPULAR PHRASES

SIZHU BUPA RESHUI TANG: Dead pigs aren't afraid of boiling water.

73

The Soap Opera Business

Lulu quits her job.

In the following weeks, her life has changed dramatically. She unplugs the phone, declines all invitations to parties and dinners, and hides at home. I take a few days off and spend time with her. We rent soap operas from Blockbuster. With a bowl of instant noodles and a cup of coffee on the stand next to her sofa, we watch the videos around the clock, living in a fantasy world that takes Lulu away from reality.

Yes, soap opera is Lulu's way of escaping. First of all, there is no more bombardment with news of devastating wars or terrible diseases. Second, instead of getting herself into real catfights, dirty tricks, office politics, or heartbreaking relationships with men, she watches other people suffer. Their torment makes her feel not too bad about her own situation.

Third, soap operas are silly and melodramatic, and it doesn't matter if they are Japanese, Korean, Taiwanese, Chinese, American, or Mexican. As she cries and laughs over their silliness, she feels she outsmarts them.

Lulu's favorite genre is *kung fu* soap operas such as *The Water Marshals* and *The Eagle-Shooting Heroes. Kung fu* stories always have beautiful settings in a desert or near a lake or forest that is totally different from the concrete jungle she lives in. They are always about integrity, honor, chivalrous knights, and the sacrifices of the ancient Chinese. These are the precise qualities that modern people lack. At times, the scenes and the fights are violent, but they are aesthetically violent.

One time, as we see a duel on screen, Lulu says, "I wish to have a duel with Jenny."

"It would perhaps be more honorable than behind-the-back mischievousness," I say.

Because Lulu has rented so many videos and DVDs, Blockbuster sends her a free gift. It's Robert Kiyosaki's *Rich Dad, Poor Dad* series workshop. Lulu watches it for the sake of practicing her English and as a change of pace. But soon, she is captivated. In the video, Mr. Kiyosaki talks about the cash-flow quadrant and the differences between an employee and a business owner, and he explains why most employees go from job to job while others quit their jobs and go on to build business empires. According to the legendary Robert Kiyosaki, one can get rich as a business owner, but only be a member of the middle class as an excellent employee. He encourages people to find their own business models rather than relying on big corporations for financial freedom. Lulu is totally inspired and cheered up by this god-sent video.

"I'm on the right track to financial freedom by quitting my job. I should have my own business and be my own boss," she tells me. "My next step is to find the business. That is to say, what can I do?"

I look at the piles of videos and DVDs on the carpet of her living room, and have an idea,

"What about manufacturing soap operas? Isn't our life like a soap opera? The parties, the dinners, and the dates we've had."

"Sounds wonderful! But it probably would take me ten years to finish it."

"But remember what Jenny told you? The only thing China doesn't lack is people," I say to her.

"Yes, you are so right, Niuniu. If I can hire a team of writers to work with me, we can form several production lines. Networks need content to fill in their time slots. We can even go international since we can sell the rights to other countries!" She yells happily.

Lulu is a go-getter. A week later, she asks me to accompany her to meet a producer in the lobby of the Shangri-la Hotel. The producer is a good-looking, well dressed, smooth man in his forties. Lulu tosses around her ideas for the soap opera. He says he wants to hear more, and they can meet the next day.

Lulu arrives at the hotel the next day and rings him in his room. He says, "Come upstairs." Lulu gets suspicious. It's a gorgeous room and he's got wine, soft music, and cheese and crackers. After three glasses of this marvelous California mountain chablis, the man puts his hand on her thigh and his other arm around her. Lulu moves away.

"Is this also part of your job?" she asks him.

"Yes," he answers.

"Do you feel ashamed?" she asks.

"I love women. My job allows me to meet lovely women like you. It's a privilege. Why should I feel ashamed?"

"I love your honesty. Welcome to my first reality TV show!" Lulu points at the concealed camera she just set up while he was opening the wine in the kitchen. The man stares at the small red light, dumbfounded.

74

Got Kids?

*B*eibei's sister Baobao returns to China from the United States with her Taiwanese-born husband and American-born kids. This visit is her first trip home after living in the States for sixteen years.

During the Cultural Revolution, being the oldest kid of a *heiwulei* family, one of the "five black types" of counterrevolutionaries, Baobao was humiliated and discriminated against as a student. Under Deng Xiaoping's open-door policy, Baobao's grandparents were rehabilitated and offered prominent positions in the party. Baobao enjoyed privileges as a *gaogan zidi,* or a child of high-ranking Communist Party officials.

This roller-coaster life turned young Baobao into a cynical rebel who loathed inequality and "special treatment." While most children with connections cashed in their opportunities for nice jobs, she dreamed of finding a fairer life in the United

States, the land of equal opportunity. In the mid-1980s, she received a government grant to study engineering at the University of Texas. Chinese who received this type of grant were normally required to go back after they had finished their studies to "serve the motherland." But all Chinese in the United States were granted green cards after *Liu Si,* the Tiananmen uprising in 1989. Baobao stayed in the United States and became a chemical engineer. She later married a civil engineer from Taiwan.

None of her family came to the States to attend the wedding because her husband was the son of a Nationalist general that her Communist grandfather had fought against during the Civil War. She settled down in San Antonio, living a middle-class life and had three kids. China slowly faded away from her quiet suburban life until eventually the closest she felt to China was in the video shop around the corner that carried Jackie Chan's DVDs. As her kids grew up, she realized that they needed more exposure to Chinese culture.

The first stop after arrival is Lijiang, Yunnan, where the kids' grandparents grew up. Baobao is amazed that Lijiang is so modernized and so traditional at the same time. The river around the town reminds her of the Riverwalk back in San Antonio. Unlike the Riverwalk, there aren't any clubs featuring jazz bands, but there are bands featuring eighty-year-old musicians playing the theme song from *Titanic* on their erhu. There is no Hard Rock Cafe, but you can always find bars selling margaritas under ancient roofs.

Her hometown, Beijing, is unrecognizable, not only because of the new tall buildings but also because of the looks of the people. All of a sudden, Beijing women have become fashion experts, looking both confident and beautiful. But nothing is more incredible than seeing her little sister Beibei's lifestyle. Designer clothes, a German car, beauty salon memberships, a maid, a driver, a chef, several lovers—she lives like a queen.

In a massage parlor, the two sisters are enjoying a foot massage. Beibei says, to Baobao, "My income is considered only so-so in America. It's a matter of choosing between living like a queen in the third world and living a middle-class life in the States."

"I'd choose equality and freedom over living like a queen," Baobao says, sounding very American. "What about you?"

"I've learned to enjoy privilege," Beibei admits, "but I also feel guilty about my wealth. I know part of the reason I'm able to lead a luxurious life is there are so many poor Chinese people—cheap laborers, especially those peasants who come to the big cities to *da gong*. For example, the kids here who are massaging us only make one-twentieth of what I earn. They work seven days a week, twelve hours a day, and sleep on the sofas we are sitting on. I feel bad for them. But at the same time, the contrast can also make you feel good about yourself. For example, it's nothing special owning a car in the United States, but here, it is quite something."

"Especially when you cruise around Beijing *hutongs* in your BMW 750." Baobao teases Beibei, "I guess it makes you feel like those colonials who lived in one of the old foreign concessions in Donghua Gate. I drive a Honda back in the States. Japanese cars use less gasoline.

"But one thing you don't have is freedom. For example, the freedom to have three children like me!" Baobao adds.

"Who wants kids? I don't want kids." Beibei shrugs. "Especially after seeing that your kids speak no Chinese."

"You're so patriotic, voluntarily applying the family planning policy?" Baobao snaps back.

"We are the first generation of Chinese women who have learned to love ourselves. I don't want to be called 'mother of my kids' like our mother was," Beibei states firmly.

"Not having kids might be cool now, but everyone grows old one day. Your children are the continuation of your youth. Even Hillary Clinton and Madonna have children," Baobao argues.

"You sound more like our mother now. I can't believe you've come all the way from America!" Beibei says.

Seeing that Beibei won't change her mind, Baobao asks the girl who is giving her a foot massage: "What do you say, as a woman——do you want children in the future?"

"That depends on who I marry," the girl speaks in a Henan accent. "If I got lucky, like you, and my children could be born in the United States, then I'd have five or six. One of them might even become president of the United States! If I married someone even poorer than me, then I wouldn't want children. I don't want to see my kid grow up in a place like this, full of smelly feet and smelly shoes."

Her words remind me of my stepmother Jean Fang, who has the same dream of giving birth to a candidate for American president. But I wonder to myself if Asian Americans can hold high positions in the American government? Even if they don't become president, I suppose their lives would be better than that of a foot massager.

"Both the rich and the poor have their reasons for limiting the size of their family," Baobao mutters. "I guess the one-child policy works."

Beibei doesn't hear a word that Baobao says. She is looking

at her own feet. She has them sprayed with the lemongrass foot spray she bought from the Body Shop. She sniffs her shoes, absolutely sure that her shoes don't smell. After all, she has sixty-six pairs.

POPULAR PHRASES

HEIWULEI: Five black types, jargon used in the Cultural Revolution to identify those deemed to be reactionaries.

GAOGAN ZIDI: Children of high-ranking Communist Party officials: privileged rich kids in China.

LIU SI: The Tiananmen uprising of June 4, 1989.

ERHU: Two-stringed Chinese musical instrument.

DA GONG: To work in order to make a living. It especially refers to peasants who migrate to the cities to become manual laborers. In a broader sense, it refers to all employees who work for others instead of themselves. Since entrepreneurship is encouraged by the market economy, many Chinese consider being a boss more successful than working for someone else.

75

In the Time of SARS

*S*ARS has changed my life.

Gone are the days with decadent lewd banquets with ten people eating twenty dishes. At home, I cook frozen dumplings.

Gone are the days that a gang of friends raids my house, drinking up my collection and taking away everything I store in my fridge. *Yinsi,* or privacy, once such a foreign concept, becomes a notion that everybody embraces. They don't show up unexpectedly. Instead, they talk to me by e-mails.

I am the city girl who used to crawl from one party to another. Now I have time to read, write and meditate, and do yoga! Instead of window shopping for fun, I order everything from books to noodle soups online!

As for my friends, they do the same. Lulu plans to do an exhibition called Mask Fashions after the SARS epidemic is over. But at the moment, she hides at home, writing her first soap opera *Love in the Time of SARS*. She locks herself in the bedroom and writes eighteen hours a day. Her mother is back in Beijing to take care of her and leaves food at the door for her to pick up. Beibei is thinking of holding an outdoor concert outside a big hospital. At the moment, all the concerts her company has sponsored have been canceled, including Rolling Stone's first China trip. As for her personal life, for the first time in seven years her marriage has become monogamous. Both she and her husband, Chairman Hua, have temporarily shut down their extramarital contacts. Chairman Hua is even learning to cook. From time to time, Beibei comes home to find him in the kitchen. CC has written her first will after her parents sent their own will to her from Hong Kong. She spends most of her time talking with a doctor in England via Yahoo Messenger. He is her cyberromance.

I realize that it's not just the lives of my friends and me that have changed so dramatically, but the whole society as well.

Vegetarianism is cool now. Restaurants that used to make a lucrative business by butchering wild animals have lost money and closed down. Some see SARS as the revenge of the animal kingdom on greedy human beings.

Bar girls, karaoke girls, and travel agents are out of jobs.

I feel that SARS has made China more like the States: people flush the toilet after they use it. They wash their hands more often. They don't stand as close when they speak. They tend not to flock into places anymore. Shops and restaurants close earlier than before—around seven o'clock. Doctors have gained respect. The economy has slowed down, and the country is cleaner, less crowded, more environmentally conscious—the slow, laid-back pace seems a little unnatural here.

76

SARS Wars

Are humans born good or evil? Why does it make some people feel better about themselves when they put others down? Why is a sense of superiority needed to boost these people's egos? Regional discrimination is common in China, which has become even more evident during the SARS outbreak. SARS makes us wear masks as a protective measure. At the same time, the disease helps unmask our true nature, normally hidden behind the soft veils of personalities. Now, every raw emotion is exposed.

As usual, I log on to a popular Internet chat room to gather information for my stories and discover that a heated debate is raging.

It started with a provocative message from someone called Hong Kong Babe. Hong Kong Babe posts her message on the Web site owned by a mainland company. The message reads:

"You mainlanders make the Chinese look bad in front of the world. You mainlanders are so backward! We Hong Kong people are forced to suffer with you now. We want to go back to British rule!"

As could be expected, and probably hoped for, Hong Kong Babe's message creates a stir. Northern Love responds: "You must be a skinny flat-chested babe who is not civilized enough to speak *putonghua.* Don't you understand that the whole thing started because people in your region eat anything with legs except tables, anything that flies except airplanes, and anything that swims except ships? Because of your eating habits, we northerners catch the germs from you, who catch the germs from animals!"

Before Hong Kong Babe can reply, a message from Spring Ocean appears: "Hi, anybody from Taiwan? I'm from Taipei. Our situation in Taiwan is not as bad as Hong Kong because we aren't cramped; we have more space. We aren't as bad as the mainland because Taiwan is more advanced, medically and politically."

Hong Kong Babe finally posts a reply: "FYI: I live in the Mid-Levels on Hong Kong Island. Here, life is better than on the Kowloon side. Those who live in old, dirty, inexpensive places are more likely to get infected. The area where I live has many foreigners." Surprisingly, Hong Kong Babe does not draw more hostile responses. Instead, the message board evolves into a tug of war between two mainland cities.

Louis Vutton: "Hi, I'm from the mainland. To be specific, I'm from Shanghai. I feel safe living in Shanghai. Once again we've done a better job than Beijing."

Magic Dragon: "Beijing's situation is so bad because so

many sick people from out of town have come to Beijing to get treated in the hospitals. When they need help, the first place they think of is Beijing, not Shanghai. Beijing people have never been as selfish as the Shanghainese!"

Seeing the situation disintegrate, someone named American Passport posts his message: "Guys, stop fighting. It doesn't matter if you are from Hong Kong, Taiwan, Beijing, or Shanghai— you are all deemed the same here in the United States! Nobody is better than anyone else. Do you know that many U.S. Chinatown businesses have dropped severely? So has the business in the Japanese enclave near my house. Some of my American coworkers think everyone with an Asian face might have relatives who live with pigs."

Following American Passport, I post my own message. I give myself the name, China Doll.

China Doll: "A Taiwanese author once said that each Chinese individual is a dragon, but when the Chinese group together, they become a fat worm. Do you know why? The Chinese have never been united. They always try to categorize themselves and others. The city people look down on the country people; the rich look down on the poor. It is so stupid!"

Domestic Love posts a response: "Who are you? Writing slogans here? Where are you from? How dare you refer to the Chinese as 'they'? How dare you call us stupid?" I feel funny, but being attacked online doesn't upset me. Instead, it is entertaining for some reason. I understand why Hong Kong Babe has written those provocative messages. She must be bored and wants attention. Under a new identity, you can do anything you want and say anything you want.

So China Doll writes: "I'm a Chinese American. My family

tree consists of a Taiwanese father, a stepmother from northeast China, and a Beijing mother who married an American. In one word, I'm Chinese."

Louis Vutton: "This 'China Doll' sounds suspicious with such a complicated background. Might be an American spy. We'd better report her to the online police."

77

The (Brief) Return of Ximu

*I*t takes Lulu seven months to finish her first book, *Lover's Socks*. The book originally was called *Love in the Time of SARS.*, but by the time the book is out, SARS is passé. Inspired by Sade's *Lovers Rock,* the publisher has given the book this current name. *Lover's Socks* is based on Lulu's six-year on-and-off relationship with her former boyfriend, Ximu. The male character, Daiwu, goes to France to study fashion with his new-lywed wife after graduating from a top university in China. In France, like many Chinese émigré couples, the wife abandons the husband, marries a Frenchman, and stays in France. Some-how, the wife's decision sets Daiwu free.

He returns to China and soon emerges as a top fashion de-signer. He has no difficulty hooking up with beautiful young women, but his soulmate and confidante is a young fashion magazine editor named Jade, who worships him wholeheartedly.

Smart and understanding, Jade never pushes Daiwu to marry her because he claims to be a free spirit who would not want the fetters of marriage. But Daiwu betrays Jade by secretly getting married to a woman who is half Chinese and half French. This is his way to get even with his ex-wife.

The publisher is keen on promoting Lulu, the young, fashionable, and talented author. They plan to list the book as semi-autobiographical, a method sure to generate more buzz and sales. But Lulu wants to change the location from France to Japan to make the characters less identifiable. Her editor persuades her not to. "Don't be afraid of revealing your private life. You see, even Hillary Clinton has to write about Monica Lewinsky in order to sell her book. Victims like her, and Nicole Kidman, get a lot of sympathy. Your book will be a tear-jerker. You'll get a lot of supporters, especially sympathetic female readers who'll rally behind you against those heartless womanizers. But to get this effect, you have to make us believe it's a real story."

Lulu says, "But I'm not concerned about my own privacy. I'm concerned about Ximu's."

The editor says, "If you worry about us getting involved in lawsuits, don't. We'd be thrilled if he sued us. It's called free publicity! If he were to sue, we'd invite all the journalists and hold press conferences—way more effective than book signings to pump the sales."

"But I just don't think it's fair for Ximu." Lulu mumbles quietly as she looks at her feet.

"Was he fair to you? He lied to you and cheated on you. Why are you still treating this shameless man kindly?"

As they are debating, the telephone rings. Lulu picks it up and gestures to her editor that it is Ximu. The editor puts the speaker on so that she can also hear what he says.

"So I heard you wrote about me," Ximu says to Lulu.

Lulu doesn't deny a thing. "Yes. Do you mind?"

"No. Not at all." Ximu sounds happy. "As a matter of fact, I'd prefer you to use my real name."

"But the character is not an honorable man, as you may know better than anybody else," Lulu mocks.

"It's flattering to be written about by a young, beautiful, and very promising writer. I'd rather be notorious than normal. If you want, I can help you find investors who might be interested in turning the book into a movie. Our story might become a legend!"

Hearing his words, the editor gives Lulu an I-told-you-so expression.

"You're treating my book like free advertising for your fashion designs," says Lulu, displeased. Despite all his flaws, Lulu still can't believe that the artist Ximu would promote himself so shamelessly.

"Why not? Nowadays the most difficult thing is to be taken seriously. Movie actors, fashion designers, and pop singers reinvent their love stories to promote themselves. We have a real one—why not go for it? Lulu, let's make some noise and sell our past together to the public!"

For a moment, Lulu says nothing. The she regains her confidence and replies, "What do you mean, 'we'? You didn't have any trouble going your own way before. You wanted to write some new chapters in your life without me. Now, I'm the one writing it, so I'll be the one selling it. Bye-bye!"

78

Marketing Trauma

*L*ulu's debut novel *Lover's Socks* is published with a first printing of 100,000 copies. Lulu is sent on a ten-city book tour. In every city, with every journalist and interviewer, she repeats the tales of her sad love story with Ximu who cheated on her and only wanted to take her as a lover, not a wife. She's heard on radio, seen on TV, and written about in newspapers.

Although Lulu enjoys the stardom of a rising new author, she cannot help but feel a sense of irony about the whole thing: Her relationship with Ximu almost destroyed her and made her look like a failure in front of her family and friends. But now, she is going to achieve some fame and make a fortune out of this story. She needs to smile at her readers as she signs her name on the flyleaf of the sad book they have purchased.

She calls me: "Niuniu, believe it or not, I'm selling my own pain. I guess everything is commercialized nowadays. The market is what counts."

I recently just finished reporting a story on the Chinese literature scene. I know exactly what she is talking about. I comfort her: "Nothing is wrong about making a living off one's pain. Mo Yan, the author of *The Republic of Wine* always writes about hungry peasants in his stories. Jung Chang, the author of *Wild Swans*, tells the stories of the three generations of women's suffering. Amy Tan is another successful writer who made a bundle by selling sorrowful Chinese stories to the West. Look at Hollywood—movies about the Holocaust always tend to win the awards. Selling pain is a good business model."

Lulu feels more at ease on the other end of the line. "After all, everybody else is doing it. What the heck? It's karma perhaps. I was wronged and now I'm getting paid back."

A few days later, I hook her up with a Hollywood-based Chinese film agent named Doug who is looking for cross-cultural projects.

We meet at Factory 798.

"The story line is great. A Chinese man is dumped in France by his Chinese wife and then he goes back to China and becomes a womanizer who takes revenge on Chinese women. You have done a great job exploring the psyche of Chinese women who abandon their Chinese husbands after moving to the West and the sense of defeat that Chinese men have in the West. But your story is not sad enough!" Doug tells this to Lulu as soon as we sit down, showing his American impatience.

"What do you mean?" Lulu asks.

Doug continues. "From Hollywood's perspective, if a movie is about China and it is not about *kung fu,* it needs to have some cultural flavor. The sad cultural and political situations in other countries often make American audiences feel guilty about their own comfortable lifestyle. As long as you can pull on Americans' heartstrings, it will sell. So I suggest that you add in more about the low status of Chinese women. It's best to include the topics of prostitution and foot binding."

"But my story is a modern-day story. How can I write about foot binding? It's no longer practiced in China?"

Doug laughs. "What about creating an older woman whose feet were bound—the male character's grandmother or great-grandmother, for example. The whole point is to show how backward China was. "

"What about prostitution? Why is it needed?" Lulu asks.

"Nowadays, even a Nobel laureate says that prostitutes inspire him. You see, many Western men come to Asia to get cheap sex. So create an intriguing Chinese prostitute."

Lulu's anger is quite visible as she gets to her feet. "Doug, Richard Mason wrote *The World of Suzie Wong* fifty years ago. You Hollywood dream merchants need to update your collections."

Lulu then gives me a broad wink as she says, "Let's go, girl. We have to meet Beibei at the opium den."

The two of us giggle as we walk off arm in arm.

79

The Ups and Downs
of Female Friendship

People say that making friends becomes more difficult as we grow older. Friendship between women is tricky. Women can be compassionate, sympathetic, and giving, but at the same time, we can be catty, jealous, and moody. At a certain point in our lives, we all crave friendship to some degree. When it comes to friends, there have never been too many.

Beibei, CC, Lulu, and I are four girlfriends who have been confidantes for some time. We talk, listen, and help one another. One reason that we get along so well, according to Beibei, is that we come from similar family, financial, and educational backgrounds.

But lately, I have a burning desire to make friends outside of my own clique—even among people who are opposite to me. I don't know why. Perhaps friendship also has a seven-year-itch cycle.

Twenty-something May May, one of my interviewees who works as a secretary at a foreign enterprise, wants to be my friend.

We start to hang out.

May May likes to talk about herself. Being a journalist, I enjoy being a good listener. May May thinks she is fashionable and likes to criticize me from time to time.

"Your clothes make you look fat," she comments out of nowhere.

"Your hair is wrong. Short hair doesn't go well with your facial structure."

At first, I take it as constructive criticism. After all, I'm tired of the superficial, meaningless compliments of Americans. But I soon find out that every time May May scolds me, she adds, "You should look like me." The latter part annoys me sometimes.

Nevertheless, I want to test my limit. Although I don't think of May May as gorgeous, I never object when May May becomes self-indulgent. But there was one time that I felt very awkward. As we are having dinner, she tells me, "Niuniu, can we switch seats? That weird guy has been staring at me since we walked in. I don't know why this type of thing always happens to me."

I agree. As I sit in May May's seat, I notice a man who is looking this way. But it is so obvious that he is looking at the clock on the wall. No doubt, May May is a narcissist. But, I think, who is not? Every young woman is a bit like that. If I want to make friends with her, I should look at her positive side.

But apparently, May May is not only narcissistic but also competitive. If I wear a Bebe T-shirt to dinner, next time May May wears the same T-shirt in a different color. If I carry a new cell phone, May May will make sure to bring a newer model next time. Once I take May May to the Rose Garden, where she has never been before. A few weeks later, she brings me back to the Rose Garden. "You should thank me for taking you to this in place," she says, as if doing me a favor.

"Wait a minute. I was the one who took *you* here," I think, but I check myself. What's the point? After a cup of English tea, I leave the bar. After I get home, I call my friend Lulu right away, recounting the story.

"May May is typical of the one-child generation," says Lulu. "Their problem is that they want to be number one. They see everyone as rivals, not friends. They've lost their ability to keep friends."

80

The New Chinese Woman

*H*uman beings have their own rules for games. It doesn't matter what culture we are living in, there are certain rules we all observe. For example, we should not sleep with our bosses. We should not sleep with our girlfriends' boyfriends. And we should not sleep with married men, in their bedrooms or anyplace else.

China has been a conformist society for too long. Perhaps that explains why the new generations want to be different. They defy conformity by breaking the rules and testing the limits. But sometimes, they challenge the rules set not only by Chinese standards but by Western standards as well.

May May is such a rule-breaker. She doesn't believe in the existence of limits. She has many hobbies, one of which is sleeping with middle-aged M.B.A.s—men who are married but available.

She tells me about her theory in a hot-pot restaurant called the Imperial Mama. "Young men are like grapes and middle-aged men are like wine. Their bellies may grow bigger, and the number of hairs on their heads may become fewer, but they are more attractive; they make me feel intoxicated."

"Why is that?" I ask. I come from a different school of thought. As a woman who is reaching her thirties, I become more and more interested in younger men, the so-called boy toys.

"Middle-aged men tend to be more generous in bed than younger men, who often don't want to control their desires. Middle-aged men tend to be more successful financially. They can buy you expensive gifts, whereas young boys can only send you flowers or a box of chocolates. Since middle-aged men have been around, and they have more status and more networks, they can help you with your career. They also understand women and know very well how to please us." May May speaks as if she is giving a lecture at a university.

I say, "Well, what you say might explain why you love middle-aged men, but it doesn't explain why you always go out with the married ones."

May May laughs. "Don't you think that middle-aged M.B.A.s are a more desirable group than those who are still single?"

"That can be true in China." I nod.

May May continues with a smile. "Our parents' generation is the generation of obedience. I like to live on the edge. I like to sleep with married men because the thrill of stealing makes the sex even more exciting! It's so cool to do it in their own bedrooms during the day when their wives are at work."

"In the same bed that they share with their wives? Not a motel or something? Don't you think it's an intrusion into the wives' territory?" I ask.

"That's exactly the point. I am like an invader. Society encourages us to be competitive! I hate losing. It feels so good that these smart men are willing to betray their women and come to me. It's called charm."

"Do you think they like you because you're so irresistible?" I ask.

"Well, I'm a modern liberal woman. I can give them the level of passion that their wives can't. In return, I get the uninhibited, carnal sex that I want," May May says proudly.

I can sense that May May believes totally in her unconventional lifestyle and her ability to entice men into bed. She considers herself superior to the wives because she has the fun and none of the work relating to marriage.

"May May," I ask, "do you think that the M.B.A.s' attraction to you comes from the fact that you're a plaything for them and they don't have to be serious with you. That they are merely on the hunt for another good time, a cheap thrill that they can brag about to their buddies?"

May May replies with a sneer. "So what, it beats having a bowl of instant noodles and renting a movie while home alone by myself. If men can brag about their conquests, why can't I?"

Her speech echoes that of Colorful Clouds.

"May May, do you know Colorful Clouds?" I can't help asking.

"Yes. I know of her. Both of us publicize our sexual adventures on a Chinese blog. I've got far more hits than she has. Apparently, she's a bore. Her pictures are ugly too. I have the talent and charisma. Plus, I believe I'm younger."

Just then, a good-looking couple comes into view. May May notices and says to me, "I wonder what she sees in him? When I find out, I'll give you all the details." May May starts to preen and adjust her clothing. She is about to enter another playground.

81

A Good Life Needs to Be Told

*T*here is a regular get-together of some of the nouveaux riches in Beijing. Often, the less rich—the reporters, models, and authors—are invited to party with them as their guests.

Just as Hollywood celebrities sometimes need groupies and paparazzi to create certain scenes, the new Chinese bourgeoisie need those who are not quite as rich to be their listeners. It is simply not good enough to enjoy the good life in private. A rich life has to be told and retold, and then gossiped about.

On a Tuesday evening, just a regular hot summer's day in Beijing, Beibei and I attend a party organized by these parvenus in a house that is located in a discreet and well-manicured sub-urban neighborhood.

When we arrive, some investment bankers have already gath-ered to discuss plans while sipping Jack Daniels. Their long-term goal is to retire at forty-five and their short-term goal is to improve their golf games. Everyone agrees that their approach shots and their putting techniques could be better.

Apparently, this is all standard talk in such gatherings of the newly rich, and part of the game. The thinking is that the good life needs to be told, especially to those who are have-nots. The hangers-on play their part too. Their envy and attentiveness are all part of the same game.

An interesting conversation between two female authors gets the attention of both Beibei and me.

One of them is called Andrea. "My English lover has a ranch in New Zealand. I love to do my writing there."

The other female author named Yani raises one eyebrow. "Really? Then, we're neighbors! I write from my beach house in Australia. If we have an attack of writer's block, we can fly over and meet for coffee."

An attentive female listener who looks a bit unsophisticated and naive like a college student exclaims, "Wow, you guys are real international freemen—no, free women! So cool! It's my first time to meet such people. I'm honored."

The two authors' faces radiate pleasure, the pleasure of being admired and envied. Yani smiles at the listener. "Well, I might be an international woman. But it doesn't matter where I go, I always like China the best."

"I know why she likes China the best: only China can guarantee her an audience when she brags." Beibei says under her breath to me.

As we walk around, we hear more hilarious lines popping up from the newly rich and famous. Some are quite creative and subtle:

"My life has been crazy! Breakfast in Hong Kong, lunch in Singapore, and dinner in Beijing!" "I only eat fresh vegetables from my own garden." "I walk nine holes every day." And so on. Always, there are listeners who show great admiration and envy.

I spot a friend whom I haven't seen for ages. Immediately he comes over to greet me. His name is Kevin Chen. Like many of my childhood friends, Kevin is one of the best and the brightest of the generation born after 1970. His path is also quite typical: he graduated from the People's University with a degree in international finance and then went to Stanford to get his M.B.A. He currently works for AIG.

"How's life?" Kevin greets me.

"Not bad. You?"

"The usual. You know—making friends in Beijing, doing business in New York, living in Shanghai, shopping in Hong Kong, vacationing in southern France and the Greek Islands," says Kevin nonchalantly.

Beibei murmurs to me, "This is the second time I've heard him say that."

"I bet you get a lot of frequent-flyer miles!" I say to Kevin.

Kevin nods. "Yes, but I really do hate flying. Of course, I hate eating lobster more." He punctuates this sentence with a laugh, obviously thrilled to enter the game again.

"Remember when we were young, you said in a class that your biggest dream was to fly someday," I remind Kevin.

"Really?" Kevin seems not to remember.

"Of course that was a long, long time ago, when China was still poor and you were still called Kai Wan," I say with an impish smile.

82

Turnoffs

When CC, Beibei, Lulu, and I get together, we are eager to get an update on CC's first date with the guy we call S. CC has been talking for months on the Internet with S. She thinks S is attractive and intelligent, perhaps the right person for her.

"So what's the news with S?" As usual, the impatient Beibei starts probing.

"Well, we finally met, but it lasted only fifteen minutes," CC says with disappointment.

"Was he the same guy as in his photos? Or was he much older? Did he turn out to be ugly? Was he way shorter than you expected? Did he have as much hair on his head as he did in the photos?" I shower CC with questions.

"Yes, no, no, no, and no." CC shakes her head.

"Did he have yellow teeth that aren't shown in his pictures?" Lulu continues the inquisition.

"No. His teeth are like the model's teeth in a Crest ad."

"Did he say something rude to offend you?" I guess.

"No."

"Was he too aggressive? You know, fast with his hands? Did he try to take advantage of you?" I ask, wondering what could have been wrong with this man.

"Well, what happened? Fill us in," Beibei says eagerly.

"He passed wind ten minutes after we sat down. I know how to do it myself. I don't really need him to demonstrate it in front of me. So I left."

"I can't believe this guy was so rude. He should try at least to hold it in on the first date," I say.

"That's exactly what I thought. Everybody tries to look and act his best on the first date with someone he likes. If S didn't give a thought about passing wind on our first date, he really didn't care about what I thought of him," says CC.

"But I remember you told us that he's very educated and intelligent. I don't understand why he could be so lacking in manners at the same time," I say.

"I've had a similar experience," Beibei jumps in. "Once I had a date. The guy was humorous and funny, but the whole time he was telling the jokes, he had spinach in his teeth. He was making fun of others, but he looked funny himself. The image was so ironic that I had no choice but to leave him."

"What's wrong with you guys? What if some man just leaves you on the first date because you happen to have a lipstick stain on your teeth when you eat," says Lulu, who is apparently sympathetic to S.

"I grew up in England, and I'd never be that sloppy!" CC rebuffs.

"Don't be so arrogant, CC. Everyone makes mistakes. I just

think nowadays people have more choices and less time. We become less tolerant and more impatient! That's why relationships become so shallow. A small thing can kill a person's chances, just like that! A person might have a lot to offer, and we won't get to know it because of one event or mistake." Lulu protests.

"The fact is that small things really annoy us. Things like bad breath, nose picking, body odor, continual belching, and dirty socks can really turn us off," says CC, getting visibly annoyed.

"But you've got to give others a second chance!" Lulu begs.

CC speaks. "I indeed gave S a second chance. The first time he passed gas was right after he told me that he had a Ph.D. from Duke University. I tried to ignore the sound and appeared to be impressed by his education. The second time he did it was when I asked him what brand of cologne he was wearing. He told me that it was Calvin Klein's Obsession. But believe me, I smelled something else. I told him that I had to make a quick phone call. As I left, I passed the waiter bringing the salads to the table. What a shame. The spinach salad looked great."

83

Sampling the Menu

For Beibei and her husband Hua, adultery is not a good word. They call their union an open marriage. Married with extramarital affairs is the most apt description of their lifestyle. Both Beibei and Hua belong to the growing group who claim that they are too lazy to get a divorce.

"What's the point," says Hua.

"Men are all the same," claims Beibei, echoing the familiar mantra of women with unfaithful husbands.

Not surprisingly, Beibei doesn't believe in fidelity within marriage anymore, and she is not alone. A rising population of young white-collar Chinese embrace the idea of the one-nite stand. Traditional Confucian moral values that the Chinese have clung to for thousands of years have simply lost their validity and make little sense in this world of instant gratification. If you see something you like, go for it. This is the new dogma.

According to a recent survey, 37 percent of all one-night stands take place between partners who meet on the Internet. Beibei doesn't like the uncertainty of the information super-highway. She sticks with the traditional way, picking up guys or waiting for guys to pick her up in bars, at dance clubs, or even on the street. This way she won't be surprised or disappointed on the initial meeting.

Beibei tells Lulu and me about her most recent rendezvous with men on the street. "It's so easy. Sometimes I just wear some makeup and revealing clothes. As I walk on the street, men come to me and ask me if I'd be interested in being their girlfriend for a day or two. It's all upfront—there's no need to wonder if he will call you the next day."

Beibei is daring, but she also sets a rule for herself: no repetitions—one time and she's done. For her, the most embarrassing moment is to meet her playmate again in the same bar they first met. Normally, she pretends that she doesn't know the man and looks for new faces to talk to.

One night, Beibei brings Lulu and me to a place called The Bananas. As we order some cocktails, Beibei spots Luyi, her passionate fling from just yesterday. As usual, she ignores his existence. But Luyi walks toward her. Beibei starts to complain, "That guy that is walking toward us was with me last night. It looks like he wants to bother me again. Let's get out."

Before we can make our move, Luyi makes a turn toward the girl who sits alone not far away from us. He moves through the crowded and dimly lit bar as if he was wired into some ultrasensory neural network to locate an available and accommodating miss. But his neurons may have misfired, as the young woman waves him off with hardly a glance.

So he walks toward Beibei. Beibei confronts him first,

"Sorry, I won't have the same item on the menu on consecutive nights."

"I was going to say hello to your lovely friends to see if they have some free time tonight," Luyi says politely.

"Why not that young woman over there?" Beibei points to the woman that has already rejected him. As he turns to see who she is pointing to, Beibei, Lulu, and I vanish from his sight—just like signing off in an Internet chat room, one click and we're gone!

84

Higher Age, Lower Value

*B*aobao, Beibei's sister in Texas, is coming back to Beijing on a business trip. She is on her way to her company's Beijing office on Ritan Road. It was opened a year ago and currently has seventy employees.

In the red cab, the taxi driver talks to her nonstop as if she was his old pal. "In the old days I was driven by a chauffeur. Now I have to be a driver myself to make ends meet. The older I get, the less useful I become. Shame on me! I was laid off a year ago when our work unit was in the process of *youhua zuhe,* optimization. I was a *chuzhang,* a department chief. In other cities, I would be a big deal. But a *chuzhang* is nobody here. I guess you've heard of the popular saying: 'Only in Beijing will you know your rank is low, only in Guangdong will you know your pay is low, and only in Hainan will you know that your energy level is low.'"

"Oh, yeah?" Baobao laughs out loud. It seems that every Beijing cab driver knows how to be Jay Leno. Although the car engine makes weird annoying noises and the air conditioning is broken, Baobao doesn't regret not taking the more expensive Citroën cab: this driver is funny.

"I was laid off 'cause I was over forty, too old to be a *chuzhang*," the driver continues in his slippery Beijing accent. "My replacement is only thirty-two. After staying at home for eight months, I decided to be a cab driver, since I needed bucks to send my kid to college. I tell ya, the adjustment isn't easy. I have to swallow all kinds of shit. Just a while ago, a kid got upset when I honestly told him I was new and didn't know the roads well. He left the car immediately. I heard him calling me an old idiot after he got out. He's younger than my son," the man exclaims, almost in disbelief.

"He was rude!" Baobao shakes her head.

"Nowadays, kids become so bad-mannered—I was better off as a Red Guard," the driver comments as Baobao pays him. Nicholas Tse's "Everybody Is Stupid" plays loudly on the car radio.

Baobao walks toward the building, and Big Chen, the office manager, greets her outside the door. As they walk in, she sees lines of model-type young women sitting and standing along the hallways.

"Why are there so many girls here? It looks like a beauty pageant," Baobao says to Big Chen.

"We're conducting interviews for administrative jobs today," Big Chen replies, giving Baobao a stack of résumés. To her surprise, on each résumé, next to the applicant's name, is her age, and they are all between twenty-one and twenty-five.

"What are their requirements?" asks Baobao.

"Female, twenty-one to twenty-five, pleasant-looking, college graduate, good phone manners, Chinese and English typing skills, college English six plus," Big Chen recites.

"We can't do this. American companies won't tolerate ageism," Baobao warns Big Chen.

"We aren't just an American company. We're an American company with Chinese characteristics," Big Chen corrects Baobao. "China has too many people. We need to find the most qualified people in the shortest amount of time. It's what we call efficiency."

"But what about women over twenty-five?"

Big Chen chuckles, making Baobao feel like he was telling her, "You are over the hill."

"China changes at an incredible rate, much faster than the United States. Five years here is like ten in the States. It's already another generation, with new knowledge that is lost on their elders. There are a lot of limitations to older people. They can't keep up with the Internet age, their English is poor . . ." Big Chen explains.

"You can't make such generalizations. A Chinese man just won the U.S. national book award for writing in English. He's over forty."

"But he is in the States, not in China," Big Chen says, shrugging.

If age and beauty play such an important role in job seeking, what about finding a boyfriend? What are the fates of women who are neither young nor attractive? Looking at those starry-eyed young women, Baobao says good-bye to Big Chen and wishes him good luck.

She strides into the street, thinking, "What on earth are the

Chinese thinking these days?" She enters a bookstore out of curiosity. On the new releases table, she sees several titles: *I Say No to My Parents* by Cold Mountain, age fourteen; *Young and Wild* by Chuchu, age eleven; and *My Problems with Boys* by Nuzi, age seven. Baobao can't help but laugh; there is a market for books by little rebels.

Baobao was a rare rebel in her generation. She abandoned her comfortable life for the United States at a young age. Now, a dutiful wife and mother of three, and an engineer who works nine to five and lives in a San Antonio suburb, she is not edgy or antiestablishment. Suddenly she feels old.

Walking out of the bookshop, she enters an art gallery nearby. In each painting, whether the subject is peonies or horses or monkeys or landscapes, all the painters signed their age along with their name. Yani, eighteen years old; Xixi, fifteen year old. The younger they are, the more expensive the paintings are. Since when has this old civilization become youth-obsessed? she wonders.

"Hey, Baobao. Is that you?" A woman calls her.

"Oh, Mimi!" Baobao greets Mimi, Beibei's lawyer friend, "What are you doing here?"

"I'm searching for paintings to place in my new living room," says Mimi.

"You bought another house?"

"My husband and I are expecting a baby. We bought a second home so our parenets can visit us and the baby and stay there."

"Can I go see the condo with you?" Baobao asks. "I'm thinking of buying property in Beijing as well."

"Sure," Mimi agrees.

In the Soho condominium, they and two other couples are taken on a tour of the luxurious "Manhattan-style" model homes by a young salesman.

"How old are you?" the salesman asks one of the young, fashionable-looking couples.

"Twenty-eight," the couple answer with pride.

"So young! You are from the new new generation. I admire you for having the money to buy a Soho. Are you also from the new new generation?" The salesman asks the other couple, who also look to be in their twenties.

Now Baobao understands how fast the generations change in China. The new generation used to mean the young revolution-aires, the generation that participated in the Cultural Revolution from 1966 to 1976. During this time the "ideological purity" of the party was reestablished and the revolutionary spirit was rekindled. After the Cultural Revolution ended, the new gener-ation meant those who became college students and gained West-ern influence in the late 1970s and early 1980s. They were the ones who could look back at the Cultural Revolution and give it a fair evaluation with their knowledge and new ideas. Nowadays the 'new' new generation means the GenXers and GenYers who were born in the 1970s, who drank Coke at an early age, who don't have any painful memories of the Cultural Revolution, and who are more liberal in their lifestyle.

"Although we were born in the 1970s, we aren't part of that new new generation, we are the 'post-new' new generation, those born after 1976. We started to learn English in grade one. The 'new' new generation didn't start learning English until middle school. There is quite a difference here."

"So you're even younger and more successful!" says the sales-man.

"That's correct!" The woman grabs her husband's arm, looking at the others triumphantly.

Baobao finds the conversation unbearable, so she speaks. "Talking about age and success, you are in no position to be competing with my friend's baby," she touches Mimi's belly. "He's already living in a big house and he's going to live here before he is even born! And Soho is only his second home."

POPULAR PHRASES

CHUZHANG: Department chief.

YOUHUA ZUHE: Optimization.

85

Mimi and Lee

I first met Mimi when she joined the Jeremy Irons Club I started on the Internet. We became acquainted after she came to our events a few times. Like most of my other friends, Mimi is a successful young woman with a strong Western education. Unlike my other friends, she is much more family-oriented and stable, with a loving husband named Lee and a quiet home. She is also a lawyer who pays special attention to social issues and civil injustices—maybe the furthest thing from the world of entertainment and fashion that most of my other friends inhabit. These days, I get to know her very well through working on an article that Hugh has me write about returnees and their experiences in and impact on China. Hugh is very passionate about this for some reason, so I want to do the best job possible. I am always especially proud of myself when I can make Hugh happy with a job I have done. Mimi's husband, Lee, is a well-known IT personality in China, and everybody knows that he worships his wife and has abandoned the United States to follow her around. Many in the media want to interview Mimi, but she is a very private woman. Perhaps because of Jermey Irons, or the fact that we both graduated from Cal Berkeley, she agrees to an interview.

She invites me to her home at the East Lake Villa's Dongzhimen, where I know the rent is $10,000 per month. The house is huge, full of wood carvings and bronzes she and her husband have collected from all over the world, and with a garden full of palms, bamboo, orchids, Japanese red maples, and roses. There is a conservatory, with a Persian carpet on the floor, and some soft-colored cushions. Mimi explains that this is Lee's meditation room, and he often sits in here. This house would be considered extremely expensive even by American standards, so you can imagine the status that it brings them in China.

On the living room walls are photos of the couple in places all over the world, skiing, rafting, camping, climbing, water-skiing, diving, and horseback-riding. There are also some of Lee's still-life photos, photos of broken pottery and wildflowers, and portraits of Mimi. Mimi has an oval-shaped face, olive skin, spirited eyes, and full expressive lips. Wandering around barefoot, she brings me a cup of peppermint tea, and then sits down on a Qing dynasty style bed and begins to chat with me. Celtic music floats through the room.

Standing out among the wooden and metallic art objects and expensive antique furniture is a colorful plastic baby's crib and several stuffed animals in all sorts of colors. Mimi explains that she and Lee are expecting a child, so they have been extra busy preparing the house for the new arrival.

After Mimi graduated from Beijing University in 1994,

with a degree in sociology, she went to the United States to study. There she completed her law degree at UC Berkeley in 1997; she went to work at a law firm in San Francisco and quickly became one of the most successful lawyers in the company. Mimi met Lee through a friend she had in the high-tech industry. Lee was a senior manager at a nearby high-tech firm in Silicon Valley that was hugely successful. In 1998, when they were married, his stock options went through the roof. They used the money they had earned on the Nasdaq to buy a house facing the sea on a hillside in Silicon Valley. They both drove late-model sports cars, and had a holiday home at Lake Tahoe. The young, hard-working Mimi comfortably realized her American dream, and also traveled all around Europe.

Suddenly one day, Mimi was driving her car along the highway to work when she asked herself, Why did all those fairy stories she read when she was a child always end with "And they lived happily ever after"? Why didn't anyone ever write exactly what "happily ever after" meant? She thought and thought, and unconsciously drove to a nearby national park. That day, she didn't go to work but sat alone in the forest for a day, until she thought of the answer.

The next day, she resigned.

The third day, she said to Lee, "I want to go and work in the third world."

Unlike many of the other Chinese returnees, Mimi did not come home looking for new business opportunities, but instead to help better the lives of her countrymen. This was something about her that I admired immensely.

"What does China mean to you?" I ask Mimi, eager to learn why she came back to China.

"That is really very complicated. I don't know where to begin."

"Then try speaking stream-of-consciousness style," I suggest.

Mimi closes her eyes, like she is being hypnotized, and begins to speak her feelings.

"Throbbing with energy, Great Leap Forward, warmth, tears, blood, quintessence, intense, natural, transforming like a demon, unknown, crossroads, anxiety, friendship . . ."

"I like your description, 'transforming like a demon.' It's exactly right."

"It's true. It feels like, having been overseas for nine years and coming back to China, one can see more clearly than those who have always stayed in China. You have a comparison, a contrast, with the West, and with your own impressions of China."

"Culture shock coming back to China!"

"Right."

"Do you like this feeling of looking in from the outside?"

"I really like it. There is an ancient Chinese saying; 'I can't tell the true shape of Lu Mountain, because I myself am in the mountain.' The truth is incomprehensible to one too deeply involved to be objective. So you often have to leave to be able to observe. You should do the same for the United States."

"Then what does the United States mean to you?"

"It is the crystallization of order, the rule of law, rules, credibility, reason, and justice. It is a kind of ideal, created by humankind. This piece of land gives people hope, gives people space, lets people discover their own potential. To me, the most fascinating thing about it is that it gives people a path of struggle. This path of struggle is far more stimulating and enriching than the path of enjoyment."

"You left China in the 1990s. So did I. What do you think the differences are between this generation and the generation who left China in the 1980s?" I ask, and then go on to tell Mimi about my experience with Professor Wang Xiaoyuan, and then add, "He left China in the 1980s."

"In the United States I met many people who had left China in the 1980s, and they were all like Wang Xiaoyuan, not assimilating into the country, especially the culture, and at the same time defending themselves by saying American culture was shallow. They even still sang old Communist songs like, 'The Proletariat Is Powerful.' However, our generation is different. We read books like *The Catcher in the Rye* and *The Old Man and the Sea* growing up. When we were in China, we had tasted Coke and hamburgers, and were already familiar with English songs. So after we left China, there was not such a great contrast, and we didn't have a big problem communicating with Americans. Because of this we didn't feel particularly out of place. When I was studying at UC, our chancellor was Chinese. He said, when you are with Americans, you should be an American. When you are with Chinese, you should be a Chinese. I like that. Furthermore, wherever you are, you should treat things and people with a common heart."

"True. So many people have got it the wrong way around. It reminds me of those old movie stars from the 1980s who married foreigners and went to live overseas, only to find they were lowly housewives over there. So they always felt they had to return to China to show off their superiority as overseas Chinese." I agree with her. "You just mentioned that America is an ideal. In the beginning did you leave your native land and go overseas to pursue this ideal?"

"Yes."

"Then what was it that made you abandon everything in America and return to live in China?"

"I like tension; it makes me feel like I'm alive. In the beginning I had the courage to leave home alone with only one thousand dollars and go to a strange country. Now why shouldn't I have the courage to abandon my car, my house, and other material objects and return to China? China's changes, energy, and dynamism, I think, are just like the United States in the 1960s. I have to join this wave."

"Do you feel nostalgic for the 1960s as well?"

"Do you?"

I nod vigorously.

Mimi laughs. "It seems like we are both people who thrive on chaos. Birds of a feather flock together."

"Precisely because we thrive on chaos, we want to be in the United States one moment and China the next. We leap back and forth," I say.

It is not like a regular interview, but I have found a soulmate. It seems that there is so much we share in common.

It takes only a few hours of talking with Mimi for me to realize more about what I want out of my life and my future as compared to all the time I have spent with my other girlfriends. Spending time with her makes the countless hours we have spent trying to decide where to go out on the weekend or talking about men seem meaningless. Mimi has the power to calm you down and make you feel focused. I would like to lead such a life: a caring husband, a stable family, a child, a rewarding job that actually helps make people's lives easier. I see in Mimi what my own life could be like someday if I am lucky.

86

The Spicy Girl

*T*he Korean movie *My Barbaric Girlfriend* is a hit not only on the mainland but in Hong Kong and Taiwan as well. Young Chinese women identify with the hot-tempered, sometimes rude, yet beautiful female lead in the movie. It seems that the Confucian patriarchal Chinese society has finally come to embrace strong women. Especially among the one-child generation on the mainland, one would have difficulty finding submissive, stereotypical Asian girls nowadays.

Describing herself as the "spicy girl" from Hunan Province, Dolly considers herself a representative of the new generation. Her idol is the barbaric girlfriend who slammed her boyfriend in the face in the movie. She has watched the movie at least five times. Dolly is short-tempered and doesn't want to change in any way for any of her men. She doesn't cook. She prefers that the men cook. She likes to wear miniskirts and doesn't mind talking about orgasms in public with her friends. She even dates her English teacher, Terry, who comes from Texas.

In three months, she convinces shy, meek Terry to quit his job in China, marry her, and take her back to Texas.

Everyone thinks that the free-wheeling American lifestyle will suit Dolly. But one month after she leaves, she calls her friends from a detention center in Austin, Texas.

"I might be thrown in prison. I don't know anybody here to help me," she tells her friends in China.

"What about your husband, Terry? He can help you!" Her friends in China are all surprised that she will ask for help in China when she has an American husband on her side.

"He's the one who is suing me!" The usually tough Dolly now sounds more scared and shocked than anything else.

Hearing her situation, her friends come to me to ask for help. After all, I have been in the States and, at a minimum, can offer some advice. I call Dolly right away.

Over the phone line, Dolly pours out her story, "I tried to send a check of five thousand dollars to my folks in China, but my husband said that he didn't have a job at the moment, and didn't think it was a good idea for me to send so much money. I said, 'I'm your wife, not your appendage. I can make my own decision.'

"He argued that I didn't have a job either and the money was all his. I got angry and said to him, 'We're husband and wife now. There should not be your money or my money.'

"He argued back and I got enraged, so I threw the coffee mug I had in my hand at him. His nose was broken. Can you believe what he did next? He called the police! I didn't expect the police to take the matter so seriously. They arrested me! I was in the detention center for four days. America is a free country—why would the police interfere with my domestic dispute? Also, how could my husband be so cruel to me and call the police?" Dolly's words spill out through the phone.

"You hurt him. You threatened his life," I explain.

Dolly retorts, "But it is common to have verbal, and sometimes physical, fights between husbands and wives in China. My parents often beat each other when I was growing up. I know other kids at school whose parents fought too. How can Terry love me but leave me in the detention center and now threaten to sue me?"

"If you love him, why did you hurt him?" I don't have sympathy for Dolly after hearing the story.

Dolly argues, "But in Chinese, we have the saying, *Dashiqin, mashiai*. Beating is a way of showing love."

"Would you like it if your husband showed his love by beating you every day? You need to change your temperament. Apologize to your husband and make him drop the case."

"He has always liked my wild and spicy side. Men love barbaric girlfriends. If I change, I won't be attractive anymore."

"Do you think you are attractive in a prisoner's uniform?" I ask. I hang up the phone, knowing Dolly's marriage has gone bad, like a pot of soup that has been overspiced.

POPULAR PHRASES

DASHIQIN, MASHIAI: "Beating is a way of showing love."

87

Doing Business with China

China has recently been accepted as a member of the World Trade Organization. International companies are keeping their fingers crossed that China will loosen up on ideology and open their media and publishing markets to Western companies. This willingness works both ways. Many Chinese writers and journalists hope to work for a more free-minded globally focused magazine or a publishing house someday.

I'm one of them. Although I like my job at World News, I'd like to write for Chinese readers. It's more rewarding if my friends can see my byline on a regular basis than having my articles published in countries where nobody recognizes my name. Even Sean once said to me, "Niuniu, you're such a good reporter. Sometimes I think you could contribute more if you were the editor-in-chief of a magazine in China and could write your own column there. I see this happening someday. Also,

China lacks the talent that you have, with your education, experience, connections, and independent mind."

I'm not sure why my own boss would say something like this to me. But Sean is sincere. Some part of me is willing to jump into local international magazines and publishing houses. Knowing this, CC introduces Lulu and me to Robert Payne, editor-in-chief of a New York–based women's magazine, who is in town on a business trip.

Lulu and I meet Mr. Payne in the Beijing Hotel's lobby. Both of us are excited to hear Mr. Payne's newest information and the details of his China trip.

But Mr. Payne doesn't look very eager at all. "This trip is disappointing," he begins with a sigh. "I've talked to some potential Chinese partners. I thought they'd be thrilled to meet a foreign investor with a strong background and interest. But they were not. At one Chinese magazine, their boss didn't show up. Only her assistant came to show me around. I guess my company should have done some prep work to promote our brand awareness before I came to Beijing."

"May I have your business card?" I ask.

After getting Mr. Payne's business card, I say, "I've noticed that you don't have a Chinese translation on the back of your card. On the English side of the business card, you are listed as Editor. In China, even those who understand some English don't know that the editor of a magazine is really the editor-in-chief. So they probably thought you were just an ordinary editor—one of the staff. In China, rank is key. People get different treatment according to their status."

Mr. Payne nods. "I see. That's why their boss didn't bother to come out. Can you explain another thing? At another magazine, instead of asking me about business, their publisher kept asking me about my own life. Why is that?"

"May I know what questions he asked?" Lulu asks Mr. Payne in reply.

"Whether I live in an apartment or a single house, what type of car I drive, even how much money I make. Stuff like that, very personal. Very annoying," Mr. Payne answers.

"May I know your answers?" Lulu and I both excitedly blurt out at the same time.

"I didn't tell him about my salary. But I told him that I live in an apartment in Manhattan but have a country home in upstate New York. Before I came to China, I was told that personal relationships are the key in business deals. So I invited him to visit my country home. I said I'd drive my pickup truck to meet him at the airport. I thought he'd like the idea because George Bush drove his own truck to pick up the former President Jiang Zeming near his ranch in Texas. But the publisher didn't accept my invitation. I don't know why he was so unappreciative." Mr. Payne shrugs with some regret.

Lulu and I look at each other. Lulu says, "Let me help you analyze this. I think this man doesn't know very much about the outside world. He asked you personal questions in order to get a sense of your status in the United States. In China, most people don't have any clue how expensive apartments in Manhattan are. They think if your company is big and you're important, you should live in a single house or a mansion."

"But I do have a big house in the country."

I say, "'Country' might be a good word in the States when used the right way, as country club, or country estate, but in China, it has the connotation of poverty because it's where poor peasants live. Wealthy people live in the cities, not in the countryside."

"Pickup trucks are not fashionable in China," Lulu adds. "They are considered vehicles for cargo, not for passengers."

"No wonder they weren't pleased. I didn't know that the Chinese were so class-conscious. What should I tell them about me and my company to make them want to do business with us?"

"You must stress that your parent company is listed in the Fortune 500," says Lulu.

I add, "Yes. The Fortune 500 is big here." Lulu adds. "You should also say that your annual salary is what an average Chinese would make in one hundred years."

"That sounds so capitalistic!"

"You need to impress your partners with your power and success. We Chinese buy it," Lulu explains and I feel we are like two of his volunteer China consultants.

"Finally, don't forget to say that you disagree with the Falun Gong cultists and the Taiwan separatists!" Lulu adds.

"Are you saying that I also need to make a political statement? I need to be both a big capitalist and a big communist to get a business deal here?" Mr. Payne asks with noticeable contempt.

Without waiting for Lulu and me to reply, he says, "But why should I do business with those stupid guys who have no clue about the United States? They just managed to lose a big deal."

Lulu and I look at each other, then at the same time we say, "Pick us as your China reps!"

88

The Mercedes Matrimony

Getting married is expensive, especially in northern China. Let's look at a couple in a small village in Liaoning Province that I interviewed. The annual income of an average household is less than 4,000 yuan, but a wedding will cost the groom's family at least 20,000 yuan.

The parents of the groom are expected to have a house built for the newlyweds, arrange a banquet with more than ten tables, and buy basic electronic appliances such as a TV and a refrigerator.

When asked why a wedding has to be such a costly affair, a young villager, Little Rock, says to me: "In villages, the boys outnumber the girls. A girl, no matter how ugly she is, can always find herself a husband. The boy faces a different story: if you don't make enough money, you can't get married.

"People from villages are too poor to have an extravagant

wedding, but they go into debt to make the wedding as fine as possible," he adds. "You should go to my cousin's wedding in the township. He started off as a poor peasant too, but now he has a business in Shenzhen and tons of money. Here, you can have my invitation."

I look at the gaudy invitation, which is embossed with gold lettering. "Why did you give this to me? You're his cousin—you should go yourself!"

Little Rock says: "I don't plan to go because I don't have any fancy clothes. You should check it out. Perhaps there is an article for you in it."

He's right. Just the other day, I was invited to attend the opening of Vera Wang's wedding gown store in Beijing. The subject of the sumptuous wedding business could be a good article.

The next day, with the scented invitation in my hand, I hire a car to go to the wedding venue, a restaurant downtown. A traffic policeman flags us down ten streets away from the restaurant. I cannot proceed as all the roads ahead are sealed off. "Why can't we get in? I'm attending a wedding here," I say.

"Attending Mr. Chen's wedding?" asks the policeman.

"Yes," I say.

"Why do you have a Toyota van? Don't you know that only cars like a Mercedes-Benz are allowed to be driving in the procession to the wedding?" says the policeman.

I hear passing sirens wailing. I look around and see a motorcade flying by. A white, Lincoln stretch-limousine is adorned with roses mounted on the hood and silver wedding bells dangle from the back. Following are many Mercedes-Benzes, old and new, in different colors.

It seems all the Benzes in town are there, and likely some

from out of town, just for the occasion. Before coming to this small city, I learned the township had a high population of laid-off workers who live below the poverty line. Now, I am stunned at the sheer size of the Mercedes-Benz motorcade.

"Fifty Mercedes just passed. I counted." My driver says.

I think of director Ang Lee's comment in his movie, *Wedding Banquet,* that noisy weddings result from thousands of years of sexual repression in China. Perhaps a similar analogy is that such an ostentatious display of money and an exaggerated expression of wealth reflect the deep-rooted anger coming from hundreds of years of poverty.

While I am pondering this, a luxurious Bentley approaches and comes to a stop. I watch the policeman deny the Bentley's entrance into the motorcade.

"What type of car is it?" the policeman asks the driver.

"A Bentley," the driver replies with pride.

The policeman waves the driver away in contempt. "This motorcade is only for luxury cars. Don't you see that even a Japanese-made Toyota is not allowed?" He points at my car and me. Apparently, Bentley is too new in the Chinese market to let a small town policeman know about its existence and importance.

I follow the Bentley away from the motorcade, not quite believing what I have just witnessed. Somehow, missing this wedding doesn't seem quite so bad now because my Toyota has just received the same treatment as a new Bentley.

89

Name-Dropping

The ancient art of name-dropping is widely practiced throughout modern China. It is a highly valued skill to know just when to use one's affiliation, however remote, with important people to elevate one's own status. More than one business deal has gone through as a result of impeccable name-dropping. Name-dropping is especially vital today because the more important your connections are, the more likely you will succeed in business. The proper subjects of name-dropping are anyone in a position of political power, rich people, celebrities, and, in fact, any person related to such people. The skill lies not in finding the proper name to drop, or in dropping a name at the most opportune time. For a name-drop to be truly successful, the *right* name must be dropped at *exactly* the right time. I have met a name-dropper at a party organized by my friend Beibei at Factory 798. Qing is a public relations executive from northeastern China.

Handing me a glass of red wine, Qing looks down at his

shoes and asks me, "How do you like my new Armani? I bought them when I was traveling with our governor in Milan. They cost me five hundred dollars—three days' salary. Can you believe that?"

I am turned off right away by Qing's little demonstration of self-worth. I smile at him without saying anything.

Seeing that Armani doesn't impress me, Qing starts sharing anecdotes of playing mahjong with his city's mayor and police chief.

Again, I am not amused. Disappointed with his progress, Qing changes his strategy.

"Niuniu, what is the name of that newspaper you work for?"

"World News Agency."

Qing says instantly, "I know someone who works there. His name is Eric. He's a Harvard grad."

"Yes, he's our big boss," I say.

Qing nods with satisfaction. He has established his superiority to me.

"I'll find an appropriate time to mention you in front of him," says Qing.

"No, please don't."

"Why not? Eric is a good friend of mine."

"He's my boss's boss. I'm just a small potato. I don't really think Eric knows of my existence."

Still trying hard, Qing asks me, "Would you be interested in going to another party? The son of a vice premier is coming to that party and I have been invited. You can come as my guest."

Before I can reply, Beibei comes running up and interrupts. "Oh, the son of a vice premier is not nearly important enough for our Niuniu. Do you know that she went to school with Hu Haifeng?"

"Who's Hu Haifeng?" Qing asks.

"Do you know who Hu Jintao is?" Beibei asks.

"Of course. He's the number-one man!" says Qing.

"Hu Haifeng, Hu Jintao—do you see the relationship here?" Beibei raises her eyebrow.

I can't stand it anymore. I pull Beibei away from Qing and whisper, "Beibei, are you crazy? Hu was my classmate in middle school. We haven't talked to each other for thirteen years. I am sure he doesn't remember me."

"Oh, come on, do you think Qing is really friends with Eric?" Beibei asks me.

"You've been listening to our conversation?"

"Of course! Armani, mayor, police chief, governor, blah, blah, blah. This guy's a serial name-dropper. What a snob."

As we speak, Qing walks up to us. Before he has time to speak to us, his cell phone rings. Beibei and I listen in.

"I'm in a party with my buddy Niuniu. Yes, she is an old friend of Hu Haifeng. Hu Haifeng? You don't know him? Does the name Hu Jintao mean anything to you? Yeah, that's right . . ."

"Look whose name is being dropped now," Beibei says, winking at me.

"The next time you organize a party, don't forget to set a name-drop-free zone," I say to Beibei.

90

Advice for Returnees

*M*any overseas Chinese returnees suffer from reverse culture shock after coming back to China. Often they have difficulty adjusting to their new lives in their homeland. CC is one good example, but her problem mainly comes from social issues, and her coworkers don't cause her trouble. She's a senior manager. Rong is different. He is having trouble getting along with his coworkers and his boss, so he asks me for advice. Surprisingly, I am considered a successful returnee among my peers as well as an expert on returnees issues since I did that big article on returnees that was reprinted several times by the Chinese media and on Chinese Web sites.

"What's happened to me, Niuniu? I feel so isolated at my workplace," says Rong, as we sit in a teahouse. "I see certain problems with the way we do things at the office, so I point out that we do it differently back in the States. But they never take my advice, even though it is obvious that my way is better. It's like nothing I say is valid."

"Well, it is not an easy task to blend back in to your own culture. If you want to be a successful returnee, there are some rules you will have to follow."

Rong listens intently.

"Rule Number One: Never construct a sentence starting with 'When I was in the United States. . . .' People just don't like it. And, frankly, they don't care either. You will only distance yourself with such claims," I say, pretending to be a real expert.

"I see. I didn't realize they didn't like that. I guess I need to keep a low profile."

"Absolutely. Rule Number Two: Never drop English words into your conversation. And never *ever* ask someone, 'How do you say this in Chinese?'"

"Why?" Rong looks puzzled, as this is something that he does often and without a second thought.

"Even if you have honestly forgotten how to say something in Chinese, the locals tend to think you're faking it. They think you're just showing off and they'll resent it. Sure, they respect your education and experience in the West, but they don't like to have their noses rubbed in it. We are talking about proud, sensitive people. If you come across as too westernized, it can backfire."

"Okay! I've got it. What else?"

"Rule Number Three: Under no circumstances should you wear shorts to meet with your coworkers, even after work. Show them some respect."

Rong looks down at his bare knees below his khaki shorts. "It seems to me that I have to make a few changes. But what about me, Niuniu? What if I don't feel that I am being respected?"

"Okay. This is a tough one. You see, some Chinese think those who have returned to China came back only because they were losers in the West. So you have your work cut out for you. You might want to do some things to hint at your success. For example, you could place your UC Berkeley coffee mug on your desk."

"Oh, that is too contrived," says Rong.

"Okay, I've got a better idea," I say. "Next time you go back to California, see if you can attend one of those political fundraisers. If you can get someone to take a picture of you shaking hands with Governor Schwarzenegger, it may cost you a few thousand dollars, but it will be worth it in the long run. Hang the picture on your office wall and I am sure you'll see the difference immediately."

"So, Rule Number Four: Display photos with big shots."

"Exactly," I say, "Yale University has a China Law Center to train Chinese judges from China. In their brochure there is a photo of Bill Clinton with the center's director. You see, you're not alone, Rong. Even Yale needs help from big shots to promote their prestige in China."

91

Dilemmas?
Buddha Has the Answers

*E*verybody has dilemmas. In a fast-changing society like China, life is a drama, filled with events that can only create new dilemmas. According to a recent survey, young Chinese from twenty-five to forty have seven major dilemmas stemming from some basic life choices or decisions.

Highest on the list is actually a question that only applies to married couples: to have children or not? Beibei has been married for over seven years, but having children is a subject that has never entered her mind. Recently, she has taken a trip to the States. Upon returning, she tells everyone that she was surprised that each of the American families she visited had, on average, 2.4 children.

Is it still correct to think that the Chinese are the most

family-oriented people? Probably not. Beibei has her own theory. "My work is number one. I feel respected as a corporate president. To be respected is important. I doubt if my kid would respect me even though I gave all of my time to him. All my friends' kids are spoiled brats and I hate to see them. Another thing is that I need to look beautiful. Chinese women of my generation are so lucky because we can visit department stores, beauty salons, saunas, massage parlors, and gyms to make us look good. As long as I'm beautiful, men like me. I don't need the love of a child."

Beibei might sound a bit selfish to me, who would love to have a few kids someday, but her selfishness is a trait shared by many women. Like their male counterparts, these women learn to love and admire themselves so much that they often find one man's love is not enough, which points them toward another major problem, according to the survey: to take a lover or not? Should the society be more tolerant of married people who take lovers or should they be condemned? In China, arranged marriage was once the practice and true love was once brutally disregarded. Some say that Chinese adulterers are often torn between seeking their true love and remaining true to family obligations. The rising number of adulterous marriages reflects the emotional awakening of the middle class, and thus should be more accepted.

The third dilemma among the young people is whether to work for a boss or be self-employed. Laid-off workers from the northeast tell young people that the iron rice bowl is broken and state-owned factories are no longer reliable. This is nothing new. But overseas returnees from Silicon Valley, whom young people admire so much, also send bad news home from other side of the world: big multinational corporations are not reliable either.

So starting your own business and becoming self-employed grows into a popular goal. Lulu has recently resigned from her job and joined the be-your-own-boss trend. Lulu comforts herself. "Work according to my own schedule means flexibility and freedom." She wants to open a coffee shop but soon learns that getting loans from Chinese banks is very difficult. At the same time, Lulu also learns the hard truth, that being your own boss also means you have to pay for your own pension plan, as well as your own medical coverage and housing benefits.

Lulu feels that only a handful of people, like Beibei, who have both the right connections and access to deep pockets, can benefit from opening their own business.

The fourth dilemma concerns mainly young college graduates or those who have worked for a number of years in China: Should you go abroad for higher education or stay and climb up the corporate ladder within China? The foreign diploma fad has been around for years. Being referred to as "Dr. So-and-So" is considered flattering and trendy, especially when the degree comes from a Western country. But this honor comes at a very high cost. Nowadays, it's not uncommon for students to owe as much as $50,000 in student loans after graduation. Given the ample business opportunities that China provides for talented people, many young people believe it's more worthwhile to stay in China and accumulate wealth.

High Mountain, my former classmate—who hasn't gone abroad—tells me, "In the United States, you can easily become a member of the middle class and earn a fairly decent salary, but it is not likely that you will become one of the superrich. But if you stay in China, this is highly possible." A few years ago, High Mountain's state-owned company was privatized. All of a sudden, High Mountain, as the former party secretary of the company, was the owner of a multimillion-dollar corporation. High Mountain's transformation is an example of a successful deployment of the new market economy in China. But even with his new money, High Mountain still lacks the worldliness, vision, and sophistication of those who have lived in both China and the West.

The fifth dilemma is whether you should buy a house first or a car? Young couples want to own both a car and a house like their peers in developed countries. But when their income is not high enough to own both at the same time, many choose the house over the car. Why? Is it because a house represents a better financial investment? Not really. The stability of the overvalued real estate market is beginning to show signs of strain, especially in big cities such as Shanghai, Beijing, and Shenzhen.

Plus, many work units offer their employees housing prices below market value or provide subsidized housing as part of their employee benefits package. This creates an environment where it is more reasonable to buy a home than to rent. Lulu, for example, bought her flat for only one-tenth of the marketing price. And while cars also serve the practical purpose of providing transportation, their ability to display their owners' social status is even more powerful than that of a house. Public transportation and taxis prove to be much more affordable than owning a car in China, especially if your taxi fares can be reimbursed by your workplace. My friends Beibei and Lulu often collect receipts for reimbursement as a method of supplementing their income. Of course, there is clearly no status in taking buses and taxis. So, both Beibei and Lulu still keep personal cars for the status.

The sixth dilemma is should you join the Communist Party?

It's no longer a question of ideology; it's simply a matter of convenience. More and more young people join the Communist Party these days in order to get a good job or a promotion. High Mountain has his own theory: "The only difference between a party member and a non-party member is that, if you do something wrong, as a party member you are disciplined within the party system first. But if you're not a party member, you are subject to direct legal punishment." For him, joining the Communist Party is like taking out an insurance policy.

Finally, the seventh dilemma is a dilemma that Chinese men have wrestled with since the days of the Yellow Emperor: Should you listen to your wife or to your mother? As a Buddhist, I personally encourage Chinese men to listen to the teachings of Buddha.

POPULAR PHRASES

IRON RICE BOWL: The Iron Rice Bowl refers to guaranteed lifetime employment in state enterprises, which was the central theme in Mao's socialist economy.

92

Gods and Goblins

*I*t is Monday morning. I am at my desk preparing for a new story on successful executives. I reserve Monday morning—the traditional day of dread—for routine tasks such as setting up appointments for interviews and booking hotel and flight reservations. As I thumb through my Rolodex, I come across the names of several of my former high school classmates. One of them, Xia, is vice president at a Swiss investment banking firm. Hoping he might give me some quotes for my story, I dial his number.

When Xia's secretary explains that Xia is not in, I leave a message saying that I would like to get together for lunch. One hour later, his secretary calls back to say that Xia's driver will pick me up at my office at noon.

Promptly at noon, Xia's personal assistant rings my desk to say that a car is waiting for me outside my office. I step outside and am quickly whisked into the open door of the waiting limousine.

"Mr. Xia has had an urgent business emergency," the driver explains. "He will meet up with us at the restaurant. I hope that is okay."

I sit back in the broad leather seat of the limousine, silently gazing through the smoked glass of the passenger window and contemplating what it must be like to have a personal driver. Or an assistant. Or a secretary.

At the restaurant, I sit alone at a table for two. The driver, who escorted me in, stands off to one side, refusing to sit down even when I invite him to do so.

"I'm sorry. I won't be able to join you. Mr. Xia should be with you very soon. I apologize."

About ten minutes later, a woman walks up to the driver, says a few words to dismiss him, and then approaches the table.

"I'm Ms. Yi," she says. "I'm Mr. Xia's executive assistant. I'm so sorry to inform you that Mr. Xia won't be able to come to lunch today. A very important matter has come up. He has requested that I keep you company. If you don't mind, may I take his place?"

Since when did my classmate become so insulated by a personal army of loyal guards? I clearly remember a day when we shared class notes, when I bought him lunch, when I lent him my bicycle. Now, I was being bumped for "important business." And he couldn't even deliver his own message.

This incident reminds me of my class reunion. In as little as seven years since graduation, the difference in levels of success between my classmates has become almost immeasurable. While some were arriving in chauffeured limousines bragging about their designer suits and the quality of their personal chefs, others were busy patting down their hair, so obviously blown askew from the wind as they rode their bicycles to the party. And this in a society that once championed mass conformity over individuality and personal achievement.

For a brief moment, I feel oddly nostalgic for the days when I could leave my apartment without concern for whether my shoes matched my bag. Once, a person's wealth was measured by the size of his bag of watermelon seeds, not the number of servants at his side. Now, simply getting some face time with an old friend requires one to penetrate a strong line of defense. And laborers work for such low wages that China's social elite have even taken to hiring them for no other reason than to impress their neighbors and friends.

I recall the Chinese expression that says, "The god of death is easier dealt with than the goblins." For now, I think, I would have to make do, dining with the goblin sitting across from me.

As I try to make idle conversation with Xia's assistant, my cell phone rings. It is Xia.

"Niuniu, I'm so sorry about this," says Xia. "Did my assistant explain to you what happened?"

"Well, she said that something important came up," I say. "I'm sure you are very busy."

"Yes, my son has come down with a fever and his mother is away on holiday. I had to pick him up from kindergarten myself. Can I make it up to you?"

Then I recognize the sound of children playing in the background—unmistakably the sound of a kindergarten at recess. And I realize that things aren't always as they seem: Xia has his own little goblin to deal with.

"Sure," I say. "Don't think twice about it. Call me when your son is well."

93

Putting the Fat in Fat Choy

I am having dinner with Lisa, who is visiting from the United States and complains to me about the sluggish American economy.

"Times of fortune yield to times of hardship, which later yield to more times of fortune," I say. "Ask any person who has lived through a couple of these cycles and they will tell you that a bear market is nothing to get worked up over."

It is common knowledge that consumption is a key factor in driving economic growth. Consumer demand leads to increases in manufacturing, leads to more jobs, leads to more money to satisfy the demand for more consumer goods. Perhaps not coincidentally, consumption is also the key to an expanding waistline.

By the end of last year, between all the parties I attended and a temporary bout of depression—brought on by the on-screen jilting of one of my favorite prime-time TV drama stars—I added nearly eleven pounds to my slight frame. It took me six weeks of cardio kickboxing and denying myself such comforts as Sichuan noodles and onion pancakes to recover. This year, however, I have vowed to engage in a proactive battle with the yearly trend. I have begun my diet early.

"Do you want dessert?" asks Lisa.

"No, I can't. I'm dieting," I say.

"Dieting?" asks Lisa. "You're crazy! You're so thin! You don't need to diet."

This was a common problem when I lived in the United States. I was always told I was too thin. Any time I complained about my own weight gain, I only offended whomever I was talking to, making them more conscious of their weight problem.

"When I lived in the United States," I say with a frown, "all I wanted was to have sexy curves. I did aerobics. I even ate more ice cream to add something to my figure. I felt so inferior to all the curvaceous women around me. But when I went back home to visit, my family told me I was getting too fat. My grandmother even took me to her acupuncturist. She was afraid I would never find a good husband if I didn't lose the weight."

Weight loss has become big business in Asia, from holistic approaches to weight loss such as massage therapy, acupuncture, and yoga to more traditional methods, including calorie counting and exercise. In recent years, scores of young people have taken up bowling, mountain climbing, tennis, and many other activities, all in the name of staying thin.

"The different standards for beauty in the United States and China make it very frustrating for me," I tell Lisa. "In China, people say I am fat. As soon as I land at San Francisco

International Airport, people say I am thin. But I have an idea for making the best of this situation."

"What's that?" asks Lisa.

"I'm thinking of marketing direct flights to the United States as a new instant weight-loss plan."

94

Chinese Barbies

*A*mid the uncertainty of the recent accusations against Michael Jackson, one thing is clear: plastic surgery is a spooky business.

But consider the case of my cousin Lingling. Lingling felt that she wasn't attractive. Sure, she was attractive. Sure, the real problem was in her mind, not in her looks. But for 300,000 yuan, she was able to buy herself a cosmetic surgery package that included liposuction on her stomach, back, and rear, double eyelids, and a three-centimeter lengthening of her legs. Thinking ahead, Lingling also invited the Chinese media to record the entire process of her surgery. Shortly after her recovery, she debuted her new goods on the public market to rave reviews. Now she is registered with a top modeling agency in Beijing and getting offers from film producers and book publishers. Lingling no longer has to sleep her way to the top. But if she wants to, she's got the package to do it with.

"Niuniu, you really have to try this," Lingling tells me. "It'll do wonders for you. Look at me, I'm not only a beauty, but a celebrity, too."

"Oh, I don't think I could do something so drastic to my body," I say.

It's Friday night at my place. Lulu, Beibei, and CC have come over for a meal.

"Do you know what my local friends said to me?" says CC. "They said I have a fat ass! Do I have a fat ass?"

"No way. They're so rude," I say.

"Well, do you know that girls in China don't care much about being flat-chested? They are more paranoid about gaining weight. I bet if Jennifer Lopez walked on a Beijing street, she'd be laughed at for her butt," says Beibei.

"The sense of beauty is different between East and West," says Lulu.

I add, "Speaking of beauty, my cousin Lingling had plastic surgery recently. She's very happy with the results."

"Look at Korea," says Lulu. "All those young models getting face-lifts, boob jobs, and cosmetic eye surgery. They're becoming a nation of plastic beauties."

"That doesn't seem to bother our men," I say. "Those girls are very popular here."

"But it's too much!" says CC. "What if they start giving birth to plastic babies? And what kind of milk comes out of fake boobs, anyway? Vitasoy?"

As young Chinese women find they have more disposable income, they are choosing to have elective surgical procedures in the hopes of attracting a better mate. The old rule of the Big Three still stands as a standard in pursuing the ideal man: a big house, a big physical stature, and a big income. For women, the math isn't so simple.

"We need to have long legs, but small feet; big breasts, but a small bottom; wide eyes, but a small face," Lulu says. "At the end of the day, we have two choices: genetic mutation or plastic surgery!"

Without giving any thought to how my friends might react, I say, "When I dated a white guy in the United States, he said I had a nice little butt. But when I dated a black guy there, he said my butt was small. His roommates always sat around the living room teasing me, saying 'James, whachoo doin' bringin' that skinny-assed girl to our house?' "

The room falls silent for a moment. Mouths are agape. Not because my friends are impressed with my familiarity with African American dialect, but because they had no idea just how much "game" I had back in the States.

Just in time to change the subject, cousin Lingling arrives. I introduce everyone at the table. There is a brief uncomfortable silence before Lulu speaks up.

"Lingling, Niuniu tells us you have found a good surgeon. Do you have his business card?"

The group bursts into a frenzy of questions and fawning. Lingling is the star of the banquet, telling the ladies the story of her recent successes.

Now, is Lingling more successful because she is prettier or because she thinks she is prettier? Maybe her surgery has given her the confidence to strive for new opportunities that she would not have tried before. I don't know—and neither does Lingling. But the important thing is that Lingling expects a 500 percent return on her investment by the end of the year. Chinese girls are clever about money nowadays.

95

Women in Different Societies

I get together with my high school friends Yan Yan and Han in Beijing. Years ago, when I left China for the United States, Yan Yan went to Japan and Han to Hong Kong. This is our first reunion.

Yan Yan has changed so much that I can hardly believe she is the same woman I went to school with. While Han and I sit cross-legged and laugh loudly, Yan Yan sits upright, speaks in a soft voice, and constantly uses her hand to remove the lipstick print left on her teacup. She even covers her mouth with her hand as she smiles.

Every three minutes, she bows to Han and me.

"Yan Yan, I can't believe you've become so feminine. I remember when we used to climb up walls barefooted!" I say accusingly.

Yan Yan replies almost timidly: "You don't know what it feels like to be a woman in Japan."

I say with interest: "Tell us!"

Yan Yan explains: "Japanese people pay much attention to subtle detail. As a woman, to get things done, you have to look pretty and behave properly. If you cross your legs in a business meeting, you lose the deal. It's as simple as that."

Han exclaims: "Sounds like being a woman is more difficult in Japan than in China."

"Sometimes I feel that being a woman in Japan is like putting on a show," says Yan Yan. "As long as you're a good actress, you get your rewards. Especially if you're a good actress with long legs and speak some English, you'd find yourself very popular."

Yan Yan is a success story among the Chinese students in Japan. She has a Ph.D. in art, has held art exhibitions all over Japan, and published a few art books. As a constant guest of Japanese legislators and corporate chief executives, she has become a member of the country's upper class.

I ask Han, "What about you? What's it like to be a woman in Hong Kong?" Han is a success story among mainland women in Hong Kong. She is a director of an American company's Hong Kong headquarters, earning a seven-digit salary.

She has two secretaries and an office at the top of the Lippo Centre, overlooking the Victoria Harbor. "Your language ability is important in doing business in Hong Kong," says Han. She has mastered English, Cantonese, and Shanghainese.

"I can speak Cantonese like a native. So I can hide my origin as a mainlander and pretend to be a native. By doing that, ironically, I've gained more respect from Hong Kong people."

"That's it?" I ask.

"Another secret is to watch your weight all the time," says Han with a smile. "The thinner you are, the more beautiful you're thought to be."

Yan Yan asks me, "What about being a woman in the United States?"

I laugh. "It's easier than being a Beijing girl. First, don't worry about your weight. Asian girls are normally petite there. Second, you can laugh aloud without covering your mouth, and nobody would think of you as rude. Third, there is no need to pretend to be a native. Speaking English with a foreign accent is often considered cute."

Yan Yan says, "It seems you had it easy being a woman in America."

"Yes, I felt free and at ease," I say. "I guess that's why I don't have friends from the Senate or an office that overlooks the bay. Everything has a price."

96

The Communist Englishman and the Capitalist Chinese

$\mathcal{M}$y colleague Sean, after learning Chinese for four years in London, has come to China as a foreign correspondent. Coming from a working-class neighborhood in Liverpool, Sean calls himself a socialist. He claims that the reason he wants to be a reporter is to speak for the poor. He comes to China because he believes there are more voices from the poor here than in England.

But he is disappointed at the Chinese journalists. He complains to me, "They are capitalists now, always writing about millionaires and celebrities. It's so boring. If China's journalists don't speak for the people, then I will have to speak for them. Look, whenever they talk about disabled people, they always say disabled people should support themselves. Where is the social security system? If parents give birth to a disabled child, does it serve them right? Doesn't society have any responsibility at all? And what about the peasants—the revolution is over fifty years old, but they still don't have medical insurance or pensions, and the local governments still force them to pay all sorts of exorbitant taxes like population taxes, family planning taxes, road construction taxes, textbook taxes, as well as pig taxes. The peasants in the countryside can't earn any money, so they flood into the cities! But look at how the cities treat them—even worse than Americans treat Mexican immigrants!" He is showing me an article of a Henan immigrant worker who was gang-raped in Shenzhen.

The poor woman didn't bring the proper identification card with her so the police put her in the correction center. But for some reason, she was placed in the men's cell and was raped repeatedly by the inmates and guards. After she got out, her parents didn't support her for telling the story to the media because they thought it was scandalous and also they were afraid of retaliation. At first, she listened to them. But her husband insisted that they needed to fight back. With him on her side, she told the local newspaper about the horrifying experience she suffered at the correction center. Soon, it caught the attention of the national media.

"I've been writing an article on this case, but nobody wants to talk to me. I'm sick to death of it. Whenever I go anywhere to report on something, as soon as people hear I am a foreign journalist, they are afraid. The husband of the victim originally agreed to an interview, but then he changed his mind. His lawyer also changed his story. They don't trust me. Why?"

"You are . . ."

"I'm a foreigner? So I can't be trusted? But doesn't everyone welcome international friends now? Especially foreign business-men. Is it only their money that's welcome? Is that right? Chi-nese people are great to me. But why won't they let me interview them?"

"There is a saying: Don't air your dirty linen in public."

"It seems to me that these Chinese people still remember when they were bullied by the English. Niuniu, let's work on a piece about China's underclass together! At least, the Chinese will speak their minds to you."

Sean's words remind me of Mimi, my lawyer friend who al-ways represents the Chinese underclass. Since I interviewed her for my article on returning Chinese, we have become close friends. Unlike Lulu and Beibei, Mimi doesn't talk about men; instead, she loves talking about books, art, and social issues with me. She takes me to a deaf school, to a migrant workers' dwelling in the south of the city, and to a center for abused women, and helps me gather materials.

In the course of my startling research, I learn about the mis-erable world that some women still live in today. It is a world of dog-eat-dog poverty, despair, sixteen-hour workdays, struggle, tears, never seeing the light of day, unfairness, prostitution, rape, discrimination, abduction, and slavery. Making these hardships even more unbearable for me to observe, let alone write about, is that in the midst of all the suffering there are women with firm, indomitable, and loving hearts.

The most unforgettable conversation was with a pedicurist from Yangzhou called Huanzi. Huanzi spends twenty-four hours a day, seven days a week, in a bathhouse—she works, eats, and sleeps there. She earns 1,500 yuan per month and has no medical insurance. She says to me that if she becomes ill, then she would rather die than be a burden to her family. Medical bills are too expensive.

I am unable to keep my usual detachment from my interviewees. Beyond seeing their suffering and writing about their suffering, I have to do something more for these people.

I speak to Mimi urgently. "Maybe besides our Jeremy Irons club and Ricky Martin fan club, we should also set up a Little Women's Club. The mission of this club would be to raise money for the poor, uneducated, and mentally and physically traumatized girls through hosting cultural events."

"Sounds great! We should make the club exclusive and the membership fee expensive," Mimi says.

"Why?" I ask.

"Charity, like golf, is a fashion among the rich. They will only do it when they think it is fashionable," Mimi adds with a bored expression and a wave of her hand.

97

The Little Women's Club

*F*ollowing my experiences on my trip to the countryside, I return to the city and set up the Little Women's Club with CC and Mimi. We are all little women—shorter than five foot four. China is fascinated with models and the Brooke Shields type of tall Western beauty, and many Chinese women are risking their lives with leg operations to gain height, so we decide to celebrate being petite. "I was told Lucy Liu is only five foot three," says CC.

"Zhang Ziyi is only five-foot-three," Mimi says.

"Not to mention Mother Teresa, Liz Taylor, and Aung San Suu Kyi!" I add.

We set the requirements for membership in the Little Women's Club: a woman no more than five foot four in height, with a postgraduate degree or better and a strong CV.

Our shortest member is Dove, a poet, author, singer, and

film star. She has published a collection of essays called *Size Doesn't Matter*. We set up a reading at CD Café, where Dove reads, sings, and screams. That night, we sell seven hundred copies of her book.

Although the membership fees are $1,000 per year, the response to the Little Women's Club advertisements exceeds all expectations. Female entrepreneurs, artists, authors, actresses, engineers, lawyers—all extremely intelligent women—donate money and offer suggestions. Some even voluntarily design the Little Women's Club Web site. Being a member of the Little Women's Club becomes fashionable and something of a status symbol.

Beibei, who has been doing business for so many years, knows clearly that in China, connections means money. She arranges for a concert to be hosted jointly by the Little Women's Club and her Chichi Entertainment Company and invites her protégés, the Young Revolutionaries, to be the only male special guests.

My father's company donates 500,000 yuan and Mimi's husband, Lee, provides 200,000 yuan on behalf of his company. In return, we give their companies exposure everywhere and one hundred VIP tickets.

Advertisements for the Little Women's Club Concert quickly appear at Beijing bus stops, and on radio stations, television stations, and even buses.

Beibei is pleased. Foreign company sponsorship, popular big-shot stars taking part, a public benefit concert, and television coverage—with the Young Revolutionaries as the only male act—it's a perfect chance for her to promote her band and gain publicity. She jokes, "Although I'm excluded from membership because of my height, I'll make the little women work for me! This is a battle between the tall and the short!"

On the day of the concert, Mimi and her husband Lee, Weiwei and his latest girlfriend, CC, Lulu, stepmother Jean, and I all sit in Lee's company minibus. It is like a family picnic.

After all the female artists have performed—the sweet, the crazy, the angry, the weird, the loud, the wild, and the sick— the Young Revolutionaries, surrounded by their entourage, come out onstage. The Young Revolutionaries were born and raised in Manchuria and have drifted down to Beijing, where they burst onto the music scene. Growing up listening to pirated foreign CDs, they are influenced by Western pop and punk music. They enjoy the limelight, being packaged, signing autographs for fans, and putting on cool poses for the cameras.

When the music starts, I see two groups in the audience: There are kids with dyed hair and vacant expressions who dance wildly; these are from China's one-child generation which doesn't believe in limits. And there are older folks who twist their stout beer bellies, trying to shake away their midlife crises.

The Young Revolutionaries rap out their song:

My great grandfather Mao
Who I have never met
You are the coolest rock star
The greatest punk
The heaviest metal
All Chinese rock fans
Rock with you
On the new Long March
Rock and roll
Beat America, beat England
Let's get it together

"These Young Revolutionaries have the dance steps of the Backstreet Boys, John Lennon's hair and political sensibility, Michael Jackson's crotch-grabbing, Ricky Martin's butt-swinging, Nirvana's smashing guitars—the only thing they don't have is themselves!" CC declares.

"China is currently in a stage where it can only imitate. Everything is like that, including entertainment," says Lulu. "Young people will do everything possible to be different, but they end up falling into the same old conventions." Lulu doesn't like the Young Revolutionaries either.

Beibei is unhappy. "What's wrong with imitating? Even Hollywood movies are imitating Chinese martial arts movies!"

"Chinese kids today are really something. They haven't practiced their skills, they haven't trained their voices, but they dare to come out and be idols? Do they think we're all stupid?" Jean shows no respect for the Young Revolutionaries.

As everyone is talking, Weiwei opens his mouth: "I can smell marijuana."

In front of us, a group of students with nose-rings are lighting up, and several girls with fluorescent bands around their arms and necks are violently shaking their heads to the music.

Although it is superficial, vulgar, and drug-fueled, the Little Women's Club Concert has raised 250,000 yuan. Mimi, CC, and I bring the money to a poor village in Xi'an. On the way, I say, "If such a manufactured and unremarkable event can lead to such good, perhaps it should be encouraged after all!" Mimi says, "The event allows big women and men to see what our little women are capable of." CC shakes her head as she replies, "I don't want our club to be associated with brats like the Young Revolutionaries. What I can't bear the most isn't their stupidity. Plus, as men, they are just too short!"

98

Too Far Ahead of Her Time

CC decides to go back to England. As she tells me about the decision, I'm shocked.

CC says, "It's been five years since I returned to China. I did my best to become more Chinese, but it didn't work."

"You don't like China anymore?"

"Sometimes, coming back to China is like living in Hong Kong twenty years ago. It's so hard to find people who are at my level. I'm a misfit here."

One of CC's problems is that she's too far ahead of her time. In China, it's considered cool to carry a credit card, for instance, but CC has five or six. It's considered cool to drive a Buick, but CC was chauffeured in a Bentley as a young girl. It's considered cool to drink Blue Mountain coffee, but she's gone through her coffee-drinking phase and has moved on to green tea. It's considered cool to drop English words into your conversations even if your pronunciation is incorrect, but CC speaks fluent English. It's considered cool to know how to bowl, but she grew up playing golf with her parents. It's considered cool for young educated women to discuss works of the Beat Generation such as Jack Kerouac's *On The Road* and Allen Ginsberg's *Howl,* but she read them when she was a student.

"I can't stand people who show off their brand-name clothes that are at least two years behind New York and London fashions. I have to lower myself again and again in order to stay popular among my Chinese friends. I'm getting tired."

"There are two choices for Western-educated Chinese who return to China," I say. "You either hold on to what you've learned abroad, applying it to your new life in China to become part of its native-born expatriate community, or you try to hide your Western values and pretend to be native all over again."

"Apparently, Niuniu, you have chosen the latter. But for me, that choice is a step backward. I don't really want to go native," CC replies, as her arms flail about in desperation. "For a while, I tried. But I can never forget that, at a beauty salon, some women thought I was the second wife of a Hong Kong man," she adds, as if it was the ultimate insult one could receive.

"What happened?" I ask.

"I told them I was local, but they knew that the clothes I was wearing could only be bought at The Peninsula shopping arcade in Hong Kong. So, they concluded that I could only be a second wife. I guess they must have a lot of experience. From then on, I decided not to hide my Hong Kong roots anymore," CC says with a tone of finality. "I like China, but I don't like to be a Chinese woman living in China. I lost Nick and I don't find Chinese men attractive. We used to make fun of this, but it's not fun anymore. I want to go back to see my online date in London or find a former classmate to get married."

"You feel the urgency to get married?" I ask CC.

"Yes. And you, Niuniu? Don't you want to get married?"

"Yes. Someday, but not now," I say.

"I really would like to have my own family by the time I reach thirty-three."

"So you don't think you can find Mr. Right in China?"

CC sighs. "I don't want a rich guy. All I want is a man I can communicate with. But most men I've met here are so shallow. Those who aren't shallow often become so popular that they don't want to stay faithful. China isn't a paradise for educated women to search for spouses: that's the sad simple truth."

After my failed relationship with Len, I came back to China to return to my Chinese life. I didn't want to fall in love immediately. I have chosen to become a detached observer of other people's lives; my passion has been left in the States. CC's words make me wonder: Do luck and love have anything to do with location? Sometimes it seems as though in certain places, you're luckier than other places. Perhaps, that's why so many Chinese tourist groups take Chinese women to Silicon Valley for matchmaking, Japanese girls spend romantic holidays in Bali, and European tourists escape to Thailand for sexual adventures. But if China is really like CC says, a wasteland for educated women, what about America? Why did I fail there where I had no shortage of admirers and sex partners?

"If you want to go back to England to get married, what about your career here in China?" I ask CC.

"My career in China? Don't you see those job ads? Women over thirty-five are hard put to find jobs here. This is another sad truth. But the saddest fact for me is that my Chinese friends are all becoming CEOs and their companies are going public. Even though many of them are clearly behind the times in terms of fashion and philosophy, they've become part of the superrich, whereas I'm still a PR account manager. I'm not stupid, and I've got a great education, but they have occupied the resources here. If I can only be a member of the middle class, I'd rather be middle-class in Great Britain where my kids don't need to breathe smoggy polluted air every day."

"What about your parents?"

"They'd love to give all of their money to me if I married a Hong Kong man. It's my freedom that they want to buy. I won't sell myself short."

"So you're determined to leave."

CC isn't listening. She's admiring a woman's shoulder bag dangling off the back of a chair a few tables away.

"Niuniu, is that Prada real or fake?"

I say, "You said that it's not a matter of what one wears; it's where one wears it that counts."

"Yes. A real Prada can look fake here in China. But a fake Prada can look real in London. She should be walking in London now."

Listening to CC, I realize that CC really misses England, which is her home. China isn't.

Where is my home? I wonder. Ernest Hemingway says Paris is a movable feast. Can I carry my roots with me? Wherever I go, I make that my home.

99

Changed Yet Unchanged

To celebrate my birthday, my partner in crime, Beibei, has organized a dinner party at her newly purchased restaurant, China Planet. Beibei wants to turn the place into China's Planet Hollywood. Her concept is to sell stardom. Her singers will often dine here, as well as bring along other stars. This will help attract ordinary customers who will come hoping to meet celebrities. Beibei is as smart in money as she is dumb in love.

Her unfaithful husband, Chairman Hua, is the first one to show up at the dinner party. I can tell that he comes straight from his lover's flat. Hua sits on the left side of Beibei. On the right side is Beibei's new young lover, Hai, a singer and the latest sensation and heartthrob among the teenage set. The three don't seem to mind the situation at all.

Lulu enters, trailing the seductive scent of Lancôme's Miracle. With her long straight hair, high heels, grace, and elegant style, she oozes sex. With six years of hysteria, three abortions, endless encounter sessions where she discussed philosophy with Beibei and me, shrinks costing thousands, and one fortune-teller, Lulu has finally left Ximu and is standing on her own feet. She is a best-selling author and a disciple of *feng shui* master Bright Moon.

Other guests include my family friend Weiwei, the knowledgeable slacker who claims to be China's last aristocrat; Lily, the Harvard M.B.A. who doesn't want her Chinese friends to know she had a black lover back in the States; Gigi, my acrobatics coach, whose professor husband left her for a lusty student who needed some "private tutoring"; lawyer Mimi and her model husband, Lee; Yi, the CEO of ChineseSister.com, who cochaired the online forum on Chinese beauty as seen through Western eyes; John, the gay guy from the Jeremy Irons Fan Club; and finally, Master Bright Moon, my colleagues Sean and Hugh, and painter Jia. CC doesn't come. She's back in England now. I miss her.

I arrive with a flourish. With my nails blackened, my lipstick a dark brown shade, and those hideous baggy trousers, I am making a fashion statement. I am the center of attention today.

What a comic life I have been living since coming back to China! My life has been so eventful. I have learned so much, yet so little. I am an insider as well as an outsider. I feel connected, yet isolated. I have changed, yet I remain the same. I have a sense of belonging, but also a sense of alienation.

"When everybody inside China is trying to get out, why do you decide to come back and stay?" Weiwei asks me.

I think for a second. "We Chinese no longer keep our desires hidden; that is what turns me on. I guess it makes bad girls like me feel like a good girl again," I say with a mouthful of chocolate mousse.

100

Discovery

*T*he morning after the birthday party, I oversleep and don't go to work. At my courtyard home, the side where CC used to live is now empty. I walk around in the courtyard, and my thoughts jump constantly like the pieces on a chessboard. Those memories of America that I have suppressed for so long, that I have tried to put behind me, suddenly start exploding like firecrackers in my mind. I walk down the alley, my shadow following me.

"I spend every day working with other people's stories, finding stories, listening to stories, writing stories. Why do I suddenly feel so lonely?" I ask myself.

I feel that the storm in my heart is about to break. I'm anxious—and filled with longing.

I want to talk about myself. To whom? I think of my newly discovered bosom buddy.

I drive to Mimi's office.

I cut straight to the chase as soon as I see Mimi. "Mimi, are you free? Can we have a chat about love and stuff?" I say.

Mimi laughs. "Of course."

"We've known each other for some time. Could I hear your love stories? Not as a reporter, but as a friend," I say.

Mimi nods.

"Mimi, you are a person with stories, right?"

"What about you, Niuniu?"

"My story?"

"Yes."

"Of course I have stories," I say. "Perhaps to other people they don't seem like anything much, but to me, they have had a deep influence. I really want to tell you. But I'm such a bad storyteller when it comes to my own story. I guess I'm more a listener than a storyteller."

The two of us sit by a window looking over the Avenue of Heavenly Peace, and as the traffic flows past outside, Mimi begins to speak:

"My most deep-rooted experience wasn't love, but hurt. I once hurt a man who loved me. I hurt him very deeply. At the time, my family sent my sister Wenwen and me to the United States. I went to graduate school, and she was in high school. We lived together, looked after each other. We were best friends as well as sisters. We had a deep affection for one another. Our family was always very close. Wenwen was extremely clever, always the best female student in her class, better than me. We all thought that she would end up going to Yale Law School. But it all changed, because a man appeared.

"I fell in love with this man. My little sister Wenwen also

loved him. I thought I should look after my younger sister, so I bowed out. But perhaps that man loved me. Because I gave up, he stayed with Wenwen for awhile. He tormented her, then left her, and disappeared. Later, he found me. By then I was already married. He had changed. He was very depressed, heartbroken. Only then did I realize how much I had hurt him when I rejected him.

"Wenwen loved him so much she went a little crazy. She was one of those obsessive girls. After she was dumped, Wenwen quit school, started taking drugs, gave up on herself, and cut off contact with me. My parents were worried sick. Wenwen must have been deep in depression. She bought a gun—she wanted to die with him. When she saw him, she discovered she couldn't do it, but it was too late, because she had threatened him with a gun. She was arrested and went to jail. When she got out, she didn't love men anymore. She only loved women."

"Is she still in the States?"

"Yes."

"Where?"

"In Montana, with her girlfriend. Her girlfriend is an environmentalist. They do environmental work together."

"It sounds just like a movie. What kind of man was he?"

"It's very difficult to use words to describe him. He was the kind of person who could be laughing and chatting at the most desperate times. But he seemed destined to be a tragic character. I can't explain."

"What does he do?"

"He is an ophthalmologist."

"What was his name?"

"Len."

"Len?" As I repeat the familiar name, I nearly lose control.

Tragic character, ophthalmologist, Len, could there be more than one man like this?

"Yes, Len. L-E-N."

"Where is he now?"

"We haven't been in touch for many years. A year ago, after Wenwen got out of jail, he phoned me once. He said he regretted hurting Wenwen, and that he had hurt another girl. But he could never find that other girl. He was extremely unhappy."

"Did he say what that other girl was like?"

"He said she was sweet and innocent, just like Wenwen."

"What else did he say about her?"

"He didn't say anything else."

"Why is he still unhappy? Is his work not successful?"

"He is an outstanding ophthalmologist."

"Then why?"

"Perhaps he's just always been that kind of person."

"Perhaps Len still loved you, Mimi. He's unhappy because he still thinks of you."

"I didn't want it that way."

"But you know it in your heart. Giving way to Wenwen was your crime against him. You destroyed him! You destroyed Len. Never in his life could he attain you. Of course he is unhappy," I say, losing my gentleness.

"I used to think I was right. For the sake of my sister's happiness, I sacrificed my own love. But I was wrong. It was too simple. I wasn't a god, but I insisted on playing the part of a god." A tear trickles down Mimi's cheek. It is the first time I have seen Mimi cry. Mimi, this woman who has inner strength and self-confidence—crying. When she cries, it is so touching. She seems so frail. Such a perfect combination of inner strength and delicateness. What man could not be charmed by a woman like this?

"Tell me, do you still love Len?" I ask.

Mimi raises her head, closes her tearful eyes, and says, "The only man I love is my husband, Lee."

There was something ruthless about her curt finality. In an instant, Lee—elegant, tolerant, and healthy—has made Len's painful and melancholy love appear insignificant.

"If it weren't for Wenwen, if you had the freedom to chose, would you have chosen Len?"

Mimi tilts her head and thinks. "Probably not."

"But why? You loved him."

"Yes. Very deeply."

"But in spite of that, you would not have chosen to be with him?"

"He is a character from a story. But we live in the real world, not in a story."

"I don't understand."

"Some emotions last only for a moment, and some emotions can last forever."

"Do you mean that the feelings between you lasted only for a moment and not forever?"

"I don't know precisely how to explain this kind of emotion."

"You know. Someone as clever as you—of course you know how to explain it. You know the answer." I suddenly become angry with Mimi. Why did Len love this woman, care for this woman, when she didn't care?

"What answer?" Mimi sounds confused.

"I know what you really thought. You and Len had a moment of passion, you were turned on, and then you didn't want him. For you, he wasn't a good choice for a husband. He was too depressed, too crazy. You took advantage of the excuse to leave him to Wenwen. You wanted both an instant of passion and everlasting love. You really are a businesswoman. You will never come off second best. When you dumped Len, did you ever think about how he might feel?" I say, passionately making accusations at her.

Mimi looks at me, then lowers her head. "Niuniu, you can think whatever you want, I'm not going to stop you. But it's not at all the way you think it is."

"But don't you feel bad for Len? You have found happiness, but he is still unhappy. Because of you, he will never be happy for the rest of his life." I think of Len's sighs and heartache. How could I have expected that it was all for this mysterious Mimi.

"People can only destroy themselves, and people can only save themselves. Other people's strength is always limited. I hope Len can find his own happiness."

"Mimi, I have to go. Sorry for being so hysterical all of a sudden. It's probably P.M.S." I decide to leave and get up to hug Mimi. As we embrace, I can feel her pregnant stomach press against me. For a moment my anger and confusion subside and I am filled with a feeling of serenity. She told me before that she was expecting a baby.

"Take care of yourself and the baby!" I say to Mimi.

101

In Search of My Own Story

As I walk down the street, I think of Mimi. I like her so much. Why is it she? Why is she the one true love of Len's life? Everyone has secrets, sweet secrets and deadly secrets. There are reasons why some of them cannot be told. And this secret about Len, it seems, I should never have heard.

What makes me feel saddest is that, with this love and that love swirling around him, what did I mean to Len?

His world is so complicated. Is there a corner in it for me? Len, a man with such soul-stirring love. In his life, I was in-significant. But I have rewritten my life for him.

I remember the first time I went to Len's office to have my eyes tested. He was so gentle and delicate, a doctor who really cared for his patients. I remember his wild look as we made love. I remember him holding my hand as we strolled along the Seine. How could this not be real love?

From Mimi's office at the World Trade Center, I walk west along the Avenue of Heavenly Peace, past the Nikko Hotel, the Jianguo Hotel, and the Silk Market. When I reach the Diplomatic Apartments, I stop a middle-aged man getting off the number 9 bus and ask him for a cigarette.

I don't smoke and didn't feel like it when Len left me, telling me that he didn't need love. But now, I suddenly, desperately, need something bitter in my mouth. At least the bitter flavor of tobacco could give me a kind of comfort. The cheap cigarette makes me start coughing violently. In the midst of a violent cough, I take a kind of delight in my self-abuse.

Jianguomen Wai. Such a familiar place. My office is right ahead, that yellow-brick building, a symbol of China's 1970s modernization. There are so many new glassy buildings towering over it. I awkwardly puff on the cheap cigarette and walk through the crowds waiting for buses, selling newspapers, and begging.

I am a girl who collects stories.

A girl who lives on reminiscences.

The wind begins to blow.

It begins to rain.

One of Beijing's unforgiving thunderstorms.

I stand in the rain thinking about my past in the States, and all of the experiences of love, lust, and hatred that I have seen in this world. After such a long period of mourning for what I lost by loving Len, can I put an end to this? I decide to resign from my job. I don't want to run away from where I failed. I should go back to the United States and face my fears. Some things cannot be avoided, and only through confrontation can they be resolved.

It is time for me to learn to love again, to be intimate again.

When I first came back to China I used to think that real love was hopeless and I would be alone forever. But looking at my life in America through my new Chinese lenses has shown me otherwise. It is time for me to take a chance with my life again. Going back for a visit to the States was one of the best things I could have done for myself. The answers to the rest of my life lie somewhere in America. I still have unfinished business there. Even if I face defeat, I still have to go. Even if I have to search to the ends of the earth, I will never give up.

Every great story should have its share of risk. It is time to find my own story.